Praise for
JOANNE PENCE's
ANGIE AMALFI MYSTERIES

"First-rate mystery."
Romantic Times

"Pence's tongue-in-cheek humor
keeps us grinning."
San Francisco Chronicle

"A rollicking good time . . .
murder, mayhem, food, and fashion . . .
Joanne Pence serves it all up."
Butler County Post

"Joanne Pence just gets
better and better."
Mystery News

"A winner . . . Angie is a character
unlike any other found in the genre."
Santa Rosa Press Democrat

"[A] great series . . . [Pence] titillates the
sense, provides a satisfying read."
Crescent Blues Reviews

"If you love books by Diane Mott Davidson
or Denise Dietz, you will love this series.
It's as refreshing as lemon sherbet and
just as delicious."
Under the Covers

THE
DA VINCI
COOK

AN ANGIE AMALFI MYSTERY

JOANNE
PENCE

AVON BOOKS

An Imprint of HarperCollinsPublishers

This is a work of fiction. Names, characters, places, and incidents are products of the author's imagination or are used fictitiously and are not to be construed as real. Any resemblance to actual events, locales, organizations, or persons, living or dead, is entirely coincidental.

AVON BOOKS
An Imprint of HarperCollins*Publishers*
10 East 53rd Street
New York, New York 10022-5299

Copyright © 2007 by Joanne Pence
Excerpts copyright © 1993, 1994, 1995, 1996, 1998, 1998, 1999, 2000, 2002, 2003, 2003, 2004, 2006 by Joanne Pence
ISBN: 978-0-06-075806-6
ISBN-10: 0-06-075806-6
www.avonmystery.com

First Avon Books paperback printing: March 2007

Avon Trademark Reg. U.S. Pat. Off. and in Other Countries, Marca Registrada, Hecho en U.S.A.
HarperCollins® is a registered trademark of HarperCollins Publishers.

Printed in the U.S.A.

10 9 8 7 6 5 4 3 2 1

Acknowledgments

For their help with some of the details of this story I'd like to give special thanks to my sister, realtor Loretta Barra, and to author and Italian translator, Elizabeth Jennings.

"*The most beautiful thing we can experience is the mysterious. It is the source of all true art and all science. He to whom this emotion is a stranger, who can no longer pause to wonder and stand rapt in awe, is as good as dead: his eyes are closed.*"

—ALBERT EINSTEIN

Chapter 1

Four marble gargoyles glared down from the roof of the stately home in San Francisco's Sea Cliff district. A FOR SALE sign had been stabbed into the small patch of lawn beside the driveway.

No one was home. She'd just called, using her cell phone.

A crisp ocean breeze whipped against her thin summer suit, causing her usually perfectly coiffed pale blond hair to fly askew as she opened the lockbox hanging from the doorknob with a Supra key, a computerized entry device. It would leave a record that she'd been there, but at this point that hardly mattered.

Inside the box was the house key, and she used it to enter.

She knew the house well, with its overabundance of electronics gear, its lack of flowers and houseplants, and its need for colorful luxurious towels and a few candles to soften the bathrooms—all easy-to-remedy problems. The large living room looked untouched. Expensive gold and marble *objets* were exactly where she'd last seen them.

In the bedroom, the safe was located behind a Warhol print. Not very original, but easy to get at. Any good burglar could find a wall safe no matter where it was hidden, anyway. She swung the picture aside and punched in the combination.

The distinctive flat black leather box was gone.

Her heart sank. How could she prove—

An ear-splitting crack, like a gunshot, echoed through the house.

She started, holding her breath.

It was a car backfiring, nothing more.

But even as she thought that, she was struck with an eerie feeling about the house and felt an overwhelming need to get out of there.

On rubbery legs, she headed toward the entry, when she heard a door slam. The sound came from the far side of the house, from the kitchen.

She forced herself to stop, to be rational. The earlier sound couldn't have been a gunshot, not in this neighborhood. Her imagination had run away with her, that's all. The home owner must have just returned. Now, she could confront him, force him to explain everything.

She hurried to the kitchen.

Sprawled out on the floor before her lay the body of a man, facedown. A gaping, bloody hole covered the base of his head, blood oozing all around him.

No one could survive that, she thought. She turned cold, deathly cold, as she crept closer. *Is it . . . ?*

Relief coursed through her. She couldn't see his face, but his black hair was streaked with gray. He was older than the man she'd feared he might be.

Still, the world began to spin at the sight, and she immediately looked away, stumbling backward and gripping a countertop.

Through the kitchen window, she saw the shadowy figure of a man dash from the house. Behind this home and its neighbors was an alleyway for garbage trucks, service deliveries, and the like. There, the man got into an older, black Volvo. She only saw him from behind, and he wore a flat gray cap with a small visor—very European looking.

In his hand was a black box. The color and shape were like that of the container she'd expected to find in the safe.

The one she'd been looking for ...

He was taking it ... getting away!

And at her feet lay a dead man.

Then, completely unlike the normally composed, contained, self-controlled businesswoman that she was, Caterina Amalfi Swenson let out a string of curses.

Angelina Amalfi hung up the phone and cha-cha-cha'ed her way around the living room of her Russian Hill penthouse apartment. Life was good. She was engaged; she'd lost the six pounds she'd gained vacationing in Arizona—well, half; and now ... *now!* ... she could scarcely breathe she was so excited.

Internationally known chef Jacques Poulon-Leliellul was going to be in San Francisco next Monday, and he wanted to meet with her, Angie Amalfi, to talk about assisting him in the writing of his next cookbook. Recipes from his restaurant in the city, which apparently wasn't doing very well, would be featured, and he wanted a local food writer to be involved. He'd heard about her from a friend of a friend, and had his secretary phone to make an appointment if she was interested.

Was she ever! "Mr. Poulon-Leliellul is a creator of food, not sentences," his secretary explained.

"I understand completely," Angie said, bursting with enthusiasm for the project. "I can't wait to meet him."

"You'd be his ghostwriter," the secretary added.

Angie thought a moment—ghostwriters were called "ghosts" because they were unseen; their names weren't given. Could she get around that? She was sure she'd do such a fantastic job that not only could she convince the chef to include her name on the cover, he'd positively demand it. "I understand."

"Just one more thing," the secretary warned. "Be sure you pronounce his name correctly. Americans tend to do really horrible things to French names."

"Of course—Monsieur Leliellul." Angie spoke clearly and distinctly.

The secretary sounded relieved. "You have a lovely accent, but keep in mind that he prefers Poulon-Leliellul."

"I'll remember," Angie promised.

The conversation ended with another word of caution. "Noon on Monday. Be prompt. Chef Poulon-Leliellul demands punctuality."

"No problem," Angie said, before lavishing thanks and a good-bye. As it was only Tuesday, she had an entire week to study his recipes, his culinary philosophy, and anything else she could learn about the man. That was plenty of time since the only other thing she had to do was to finalize her wedding plans. She still had a few decisions to make: what kind of wedding, where to have it, and when. Matter of fact, the only thing she'd nailed down was who.

She was just about to phone that "who"—her tall, handsome, broad-shouldered, blue-eyed fiancé, San Francisco Homicide inspector Paavo Smith—with the exciting news when the phone rang again.

She hoped it wasn't Chef Poulon-Leliellul's secretary calling back to say the whole thing was off.

"Angie, it's Cat. Get Paavo! I need him right now."

The voice belonged to her sister Caterina, who these days preferred to be called Cat, and her asking for Paavo was not a good thing. Cat rarely had anything to do with her, let alone her fiancé. "Where are you?" Angie asked.

"I'm on Nineteenth Avenue, heading south to 280. Write down this license number."

Angie did as told. "What's going on? Did you call 911?"

"Of course, but they don't understand. They think it's road rage! Heaven forbid they deal with two problems at once—a theft and a murder. That's why I need Paavo!"

"A murder? Cat, slow down," Angie insisted.

The words came out in a bulletlike rush. "I was at the house of a client, Marcello Piccoletti. You remember the Piccoletti family, don't you? Anyway, one man's dead, the other is in the black Volvo I'm following. Tell Paavo to get some cops here to take over for me!"

Angie gasped. "You're following the killer?" When had her sister become brave enough to chase down a murderer?

"Of course not! I think it's my client. I suspect he's a witness."

"Don't lose him, Cat!" Angie shouted encouragement. "You're doing great."

But the cell must have hit a dead spot, because the call was suddenly disconnected.

Chapter 2

Homicide Inspector Paavo Smith studied the scene before him.

The kitchen had been remodeled with high-end dark gray granite countertops, cherry-wood cabinets, stainless appliances, and a monstrous Sub-Zero refrigerator. Copper pots hung from a rack over the central island cooktop. The flooring was tile.

Murder victims weren't usually found in kitchens like this.

Paavo squatted down to get a better look at the body. Blue pullover, black trousers, gold chain around his neck, large onyx pinky ring, expensive Italian leather shoes, and graying black hair now matted with blood from the gaping hole at the base of his skull. He lay facedown. As Paavo lifted the victim's shoulder to look at his face, he had a fair idea of what he would see. It was as he'd suspected.

The bullet had entered from behind and exited through the face, destroying the nose and shattering the eye sockets. Death must have been instantaneous or close to it.

Carefully, he lay the man back down.

"Has the neighbor who called, or anyone else, seen this man?" Paavo asked the rookie who had been the first to arrive at the crime scene. Officer Justin Leong looked simultaneously thrilled and terrified to be at what was very likely his first murder. Paavo knew the feeling. He'd had it once himself some years ago.

"No." Leong stood so close he felt like an appendage. "Audrey Moss is elderly, a widow. She didn't enter the house."

"Do you have the name of the home owner?" Paavo asked.

"Mrs. Moss wrote it down for me. It's a really long name. Lots of vowels." He pulled a piece of paper from his pocket. "*Mahr-sel-loh Pee-koh-let-ti.*"

Paavo took the paper and read the name for himself. "It's pronounced Mahr-*chail*-lo," he said. He'd learned something from Angie about pronouncing Italian. A little, anyway.

"Okay, Mar-*chail*-lo"—Leong rolled the *r*; show-off, Paavo thought—"Piccoletti. Forties. Lived here alone after divorcing his wife. Mrs. Moss said he's out of the country. In Italy."

"When did he leave?"

"Yesterday."

"So who's the dead man? Did she have any idea?"

"No. She insisted Piccoletti lives alone."

Paavo began to pat the victim for some ID. In a back pocket he found a wallet and pulled it out. The Florida driver's license showed Marcello Piccoletti, age forty-one. The picture was old, as the license had been automatically renewed by mail. The height, weight, and thick head of hair matched that of the victim.

A couple of credit cards were the only other things in the wallet, along with about two hundred dollars in cash.

"Looks like the neighbor was wrong about Piccoletti being out of the country," Paavo said. "Also, there was another caller, minutes before the neighbor. She didn't identify herself. Has anyone come forward?"

"No, Inspector," Leong replied. "The people who

live around here don't seem to be very forthcoming. I don't think they want to get involved."

True enough, Paavo thought. The number of neighbors showing up to help or watch police dropped geometrically as the income level rose. In this area it was surprising anyone at all was outside watching the proceedings.

The remaining pockets were empty. As Paavo observed the body from a different angle, he noticed some cloth under it.

He reached down and pulled. It was an ivory-colored satin handkerchief with an embroidered monogram—C.A.S.

Where are the cops?

Cat couldn't believe the way her day had gone, or that she was now stuck in traffic trying to follow a thief—who was also stuck in traffic—and waiting for her idiot little sister's idiot cop boyfriend to get off the stick and help her here!

Did she have to do absolutely everything herself?

She wasn't sure which had her more upset, having that know-nothing slime of an office manager, Meredith Woring, dare to attempt to fire her for no good reason, or finding a dead body in her client's kitchen.

No one, ever, fired Cat Amalfi Swenson. That's the sort of thing that happened to Angie, not her.

And maybe it happened because Angie couldn't follow simple instructions like getting the police to help her own sister!

Cat's fingers tightened on the steering wheel. Somehow, she would straighten out this mess, and when she did, Meredith Woring would live to regret it.

Her thoughts reverted back to Marcello's kitchen, to the dead body—whoever he was—to the huge puddle of dark red blood-soaked saltillo tiles . . . and the smell. She'd hardly noticed it at the time, but now she couldn't get it out of her nostrils. Her stomach roiled.

She vaguely remembered getting into her car to drive away. It seemed she'd passed a priest standing near Marcello's house, watching her. No, it couldn't have been. It had to be her imagination conjuring an eerie image because of that body. It was the most grue-some sight....

The traffic lanes painted on the pavement began to quiver and shake, and she gripped the wheel even harder, taking deep breaths and forcing herself to fo-cus.

She wondered if the cops were at the house yet, if they'd found out who the dead man was.

From the lockbox records they'd know she'd been in the house when the gun went off. What if they ques-tioned why she was there?

She was Marcello's realtor, and his house was up for sale. Why shouldn't she be there?

What if they spoke to Meredith Woring? What was that two-faced bitch going to tell them?

What if they investigated further? What if they found out about her and Marcello?

Where in the hell is Paavo?

Directly across the street from the murder scene was an imposing brown-shingled house with white cross beams. Immaculately kept rosebushes circled the home.

A woman with lacquered bluish-white hair opened the front door. Mrs. Audrey Moss was fairly short, a little overweight, and wore a pale green dress with matching medium heels, both clearly of excellent quality. Blue eyes darted from Paavo to Officer Leong. She smiled with familiarity at Leong as she invited them in.

The living room was furnished in gold and white designer perfection. Only a pair of binoculars on the drum table at the front windows was out of place. Leong started to follow Paavo into the room, but Paavo shot him a look that said otherwise. The rookie wisely parked himself by the door.

"What can I do for you?" Mrs. Moss asked as she sat down on a brocade chair.

Paavo took a seat on a many-cushioned gold velvet sofa. "Please tell me what you saw or heard this afternoon."

"Certainly, although I've already told that nice young man everything once." She smiled again at Leong. Paavo cast him a frown. Leong studied the ceiling. "But I expect you need to hear it directly from me."

"That's right," Paavo said with a nod.

She'd been in the kitchen preparing dinner when she heard a loud crack. She tried to dismiss it, but curiosity won and she looked out the window. "At first, all was quiet," she said. "I waited a moment, just to be sure, and then I saw that woman come running out of Mr. Piccoletti's house. She got into her car and drove off quickly. Dangerously quickly."

Paavo took a small notebook from his breast pocket. "Do you know who she was?"

"No, but I've seen her there before. She's visited Marcello a number of times." Her lips pursed with disapproval. "*Quite* a number of times."

Her message about the relationship couldn't have been clearer. "Can you describe her?"

"Most definitely." She sat up tall. "She's about five-two or so. Very thin. She likes Chanel and Armani style suits—although from this distance I can't tell if they're real or reproductions. She's probably in her late thirties, early forties. Her hair is somewhat bouffant and tapers at the neck. She wears it tucked behind her ears to show off gold and sometimes diamond earrings. And her eyes are brown."

Paavo was impressed. The binoculars were obviously used for a lot more than bird watching. "Hair color?"

"How could I forget? It's dyed the color of . . . well, of my guest bathroom. The toilet, sink, and Jacuzzi are in a color I believe is called biscuit. Looks dreadfully fake."

A funny comment, Paavo thought, coming from a woman whose hair was blue. He'd rarely gotten such a precise description. She'd do great in a lineup. "What kind of car was she driving?"

"I couldn't see the license, I'm afraid, but it was one of those foreign SUVs . . . not a Mercedes . . ."

Leong's voice called out, "A BMW, maybe?"

"Yes! That's it." Mrs. Moss smiled at him. "Very good."

Leong grinned like a student who'd just aced an exam.

Paavo ignored him. "Did you phone the police immediately after that?"

"Not quite. I didn't want to come across as some nosy old lady who had nothing better to do with her time. But then I got to thinking about the woman leaving the front door open, and Mr. Piccoletti . . . he's an interesting man." Her voice softened. "Handsome, too. Of course, he doesn't exactly come from one of our better families, from what I could tell. In fact, I'm not even sure how he can afford the house he lives in, and maybe that's why he's selling it. He owns a restaurant in Rome—a small place called Da Vinci's—and a cheap furniture store out in the Mission district."

"When was the last time you saw Mr. Piccoletti?"

"A couple of days ago. He's gone to Italy, as I told

the young officer. He does that a lot. For his restaurant, I suppose."

"How long has he lived in that house?" Paavo asked.

Mrs. Moss thought a moment. "About five years, I'd say."

When Paavo requested a description of Piccoletti, she smiled as if picturing him. "He's in his forties, I think. Not quite six feet tall. Getting a little thick around the middle, but he has a full head of thick black hair—"

"Black?" Paavo stopped her. "Not gray?"

Mrs. Moss thought a moment. "There is a little gray, yes. Very distinguished, now that you mention it. And he has the most devilish brown eyes and a wicked sense of humor. He loves to flirt." Her smile widened, as if she were lost in a memory. Then she primly patted her hair and continued. "His clothes are a bit garish, but suit him. He likes jewelry, too, which I usually don't approve of on a man, but with Marcello, I make an exception."

Paavo's and Leong's eyes met, acknowledging the similarity to the victim, before Paavo turned again to Audrey Moss. "Would you be willing to come across the street to identify the victim? I should warn you, the scene is bloody."

"You think it's Marcello?" Her eyes were wide and she began to wring her hands. "Oh, no! Oh, my, I'm so sorry to hear it! He was such a nice man. So handsome, too. More Al Pacino than Paul Newman, if you know what I mean. I'd really rather not see him dead. I should call my daughter—ask her what she thinks. And my lawyer—"

"Don't worry about it, Mrs. Moss," Paavo said. "We'll find someone else."

"Thank you." She was clearly relieved.

He could get relatives, friends, other neighbors to ID the body. He'd use Mrs. Moss later to help with a different identification—that of the suspect with biscuit-colored hair. If her initials were C.A.S., the case should be a slam dunk.

Chapter 3

Angie fretted. Paavo still hadn't called her back. When investigating a case, he often shut off his personal cell phone and she had to wait for him to check his messages.

That didn't mean she was going to sit by the phone and twiddle her thumbs, however. Not when her sister needed help! Cat had called back a couple of times, but between cell phone problems and crazy drivers, the only part of the story Angie clearly understood was that her sister might be chasing a murderer—alone. Cat refused to consider that her client might have killed anyone, but if he was in the house when a murder occurred . . .

Also, another question plagued Angie. Even if Cat's client wasn't a murderer, why would Cat run after him? There was something going on her sister wasn't telling her. Something, Angie feared, that was potentially dangerous.

She gunned her Mercedes and bounded down the San Francisco hills, heading south.

Her poor sister! She couldn't imagine Caterina, of all people, being involved in anything that required asking her for help. Usually, Cat acted as if she'd rather eat worms than go to anyone for assistance, especially Angie, given the job troubles and the little . . .

foibles . . . that seemed to plague her, which Cat looked down on with total dismay.

But not this time.

Angie was going to help her sister. Nobody messed with the Amalfi women. Not with any of them.

Of the five daughters of Salvatore and Serefina Amalfi, Angie was the youngest. Caterina was second born.

At forty, Cat was exacting, a perfectionist, a what-ever-she-touched-turned-to-gold person. She was the glamorous sister who never had an ounce of fat or a hair out of place. She was constantly being massaged or rolfed, belonged to an exclusive health club, and went to spas for baths, oils, mud, facials, manicures, and pedicures, until Angie had no idea how she had time to enjoy the perfection she worked so hard to achieve.

When they were kids, Caterina had certainly never found time for her squabbling, round-faced, candy-covered little sister. Every so often Cat was delegated to baby-sit, and Angie could still remember the way Cat dug her skinny fingers into Angie's arm when she wanted her to behave.

Quite the opposite was the eldest of the sisters, Bianca, who had mothered Angie shamefully. In fact, Angie still often went to Bianca with her troubles, knowing she'd always find a kind and sympathetic ear. The third sister, Maria, was a devout Catholic, and seemed more interested in Christ's teachings than family—until she met, fell in love with, and married a wild-living jazz trumpeter named Dominic Klee. He gave Maria plenty to pray about.

And finally, Angie's fourth sister, Francesca, was only a couple of years older than her, and had always been the I-don't-give-a-damn tomboy of the family. Angie and Frannie had been close growing up, Angie struggling to keep up when Frannie climbed trees, fished, played baseball with the boys, or clambered over sand and rocks along San Francisco's beaches. Unfortunately, as Frannie's marriage to Seth Levine soured, she became increasing jealous of anyone else's happiness—Angie's included—and the two drifted further and further apart.

A loud horn jarred Angie from her reverie, and she stepped on the brake to see what the problem was. Tires screeched behind her and horns honked, but she saw nothing wrong and drove on.

Families! she thought with a shake of the head.

The Mustang that had been so raucous a moment earlier zipped around her, nearly taking off her fender, while the driver waggled his finger in an obscene gesture.

"Same to you!" she yelled from the safety of her locked car, and continued on.

Still, she admired her sisters, and compared to them, found much about herself to criticize. She was sure she could never be as warm, maternal, or understanding as Bianca, as glamorous and efficient as Caterina, as devout as Maria, or as free-spirited as Frannie.

God, but she felt boring. But maybe not for long. Having her name associated with Chef Poulon-Leliellul's would change all that.

Now, though, she had a job of a very different sort.

From the rearview mirror she saw more drivers tailgating and waving their fists at her. She looked at the speedometer.

No wonder they were upset. She was going the speed limit.

In California, nobody did that if they could help it. With the French manicured fingers of one hand speed-dialing on her cell phone and the other on the steering wheel, she sped up.

* * *

Toshiro Yoshiwara was talking with the CSI team when he saw Paavo, his homicide partner, leave the witness's house and wend his way through the bevy of reporters already gathering, dismissively telling them, "No comment." A murder in the tony Sea Cliff was automatically "big news" in this town.

Yosh followed, wanting to find out what the witness had to say. Instead of going in, Paavo took out his phone. He frowned as he looked at it, then walked around to the side of the house. Officer Leong, who couldn't have been more attached to Paavo if he'd been using Krazy Glue, had the good sense to stay back while Paavo made a call.

Yosh watched. As the conversation continued, he grew concerned at the expression on his partner's face.

While Yosh, a big man, tended toward jolliness and enjoyed laughing and joking at every opportunity, Paavo wasn't one to show his emotions. The Great Stone Face was the moniker Angie had tagged him with when they'd first met, and around Homicide, it had stuck. His expression wasn't stony now, it was worried.

Yosh moved closer.

"Caterina?" Paavo said. "Your sister?"

He was talking to Angie, Yosh thought, and wondered if something had happened to her sister. He listened openly now.

"Angie, where are you?" Paavo asked. And then, to Yosh's amazement, Paavo actually looked stunned as he said, "You're where?"

Chapter 4

 On Highway 101 south, near San Francisco International Airport, the Volvo suddenly exited.

Cat followed it to a private company's long-term parking lot. From there, shuttle buses brought passengers to the various terminals. She trailed behind the next shuttle, and could only hope the Volvo's driver was on it. She still hadn't gotten a clear look at him. For one thing, he drove much too fast—as if he owned the road, as if his other car could be a red Ferrari convertible, which was the only car she knew Marcello Piccoletti owned. And yet, something about the shape of his shoulders as he drove, his posture and form as he ran to the Volvo, made her sure she'd been following her client.

It had been all she could do not to lose him.

When the shuttle stopped at the Alitalia terminal, since there was no open space for her car, she simply double-parked to watch and see who got off. A security guard appeared immediately and rapped hard on her window. He gestured for her to move. She argued it was just for an instant, but he insisted she leave immediately or he'd arrest her and impound her car.

He wore a gun.

Seething, she left, parked in a legitimate space, and hurried back to the terminal. By the time she'd gotten there, though, the area around the Alitalia ticket counter was all but empty. She was pondering her next course of action when a familiar voice had her spinning around and gaping.

"Cat!" Angie ran toward her, a large tote bouncing against her side. "I saw you while I was parking. Where is he?" She looked around the deserted terminal. "Where is everyone?"

"Why are you here? Where's Paavo?" Cat asked, doing her own search for the figure of her sister's fiancé. "Where are the cops?"

Angie chewed her bottom lip a moment, her brown eyes big and round, which Cat knew meant she was hiding something. "He's at the crime scene at your client's house. Things are happening fast."

"I need him here to stop Marcello." Cat studied Angie warily, wondering what she was hiding.

"I've got bad news," Angie said softly, a comforting hand on Cat's arm. "Paavo is all but certain Marcello is the victim. Cat, Marcello is dead."

Cat brushed her off. "Marcello is not dead! I don't know who is, but I would certainly recognize my own client." Irritation mixed with anger as she paced. "The problem is, I can't be positive I was following Marcello. I only saw him from behind, and he was wearing a hat. It looked like him, but when I tried to reach him earlier today, his furniture store assistant manager told me he was in Rome." Cat stopped pacing and shook her head, hands on hips. "I found that hard to believe as well. Marcello wouldn't leave the country without telling me."

Angie's eyebrows rose at that comment. "He wouldn't? Cat, before we do anything more, you've got to slow down and explain all this to me. Why are you following him?

"Because . . . a crime was committed." Cat lifted her

chin. "I was at his house, and he was running. Following him is called being a good citizen. You'd have done
the same thing."

I would, Angie thought, but not Cat. Her sister had
many positive traits, but risking her neck for civic duty
wasn't one of them.

When Angie learned from Paavo about the blond
woman the neighbor had seen, and the handkerchief
with C.A.S.—which could stand for Caterina Amalfi
Swenson, and Cat loved to have her things monogrammed—she realized she needed to take a moment
to carefully think this over, and then to talk to her sister
before telling Paavo where to find her.

In the eyes of the law, Angie feared, Cat wasn't a mere
witness: she was the number one suspect. Of course,
Angie knew Cat hadn't killed anybody, and Paavo
could prove it eventually, but the nagging thought remained that something big had made her sister rush
after a man who'd been at a murder scene. She wanted
to know what that was.

Another problem was that Paavo was in a house in
the Sea Cliff area, all the way on the northwest corner
of the city. The airport was south of the city, on the east
side. Even using sirens, it'd be difficult for him to reach
the airport in time to stop whomever Cat had followed
from boarding a plane. He'd have to call in local police
reinforcements or airport security. And what would
he say to them? How would he identify the man they
needed to stop? He couldn't very well tell them to stop
Marcello Piccoletti from boarding a plane if he thought
Marcello was dead.

And what if Cat was wrong and the man, whoever
he was, wasn't in the Alitalia terminal?

Angie knew she had to find out more about the situation before she acted. What kind of a fool would Paavo
look like if she caused him to send in cops with guns

and all they could find were his fiancée and her sister
sitting in an empty terminal? And if they realized Cat
was a suspect, seeing her at an airport, they'd arrest
her for sure!

The best thing to do would be for her to find out
from Cat exactly what was going on, and then for
the two to drive to the Hall of Justice, meet Paavo,
and talk rationally and calmly, rather than be in the
midst of something that resembled a police raid on the
airport.

After she made that decision, her cell phone had
rung time and again. She was sure it was Paavo, and
it hurt her not to answer his calls, but she had to wait,
to find out more. Finally, unable to take the incessant
ringing anymore, or the guilt from not answering, she
switched the phone off.

"Angie, are you hiding something?" Cat asked crossly. "You're usually not this quiet, and I know you've
talked to Paavo. Where is he?"

"Before pulling him away from the crime scene,
which could mess up his entire case," Angie said, "I
wanted to make sure we were close to finding the man
you followed. He is taking Alitalia, right?"

Cat looked crestfallen. "I'm not positive. An obnoxious security guard wouldn't let me stay and watch,
but after this stop there's only Air India and Qantas."

"In that case, let's find out if Marcello has a ticket."
Angie hooked her arm in Cat's and headed toward the
Alitalia counter.

"Airports don't give out that kind of information,"
Cat informed her snootily.

"We have our ways, " Angie said with a wink.

At the counter, Angie told the ticket agent that Cat's
husband, Marcello Piccoletti, was taking an Alitalia flight to Rome but he'd left his Palm handheld at
home because Cat forgot to pack it, and wouldn't the

agent please, *please,* tell them which flight he'd be on and which gate he'd be at so they could have security or someone run the Palm back to him in the boarding area?

The agent looked surprised by the request, and he was about to refuse when Angie elbowed Cat, hard. Cat pulled out her Palm—she always carried it, as Angie knew—pretended it was her husband's, and calmly and rationally gave Marcello's name, address, and telephone number.

"Let's see what I can find out," the agent murmured, to a chorus of thank-yous from the two women.

"Here he is . . . no, my mistake. This is a Rocco Piccoletti."

Angie hardly missed a beat. "That's him. Rocco Marcello Piccoletti. Go on, please."

The agent looked back at the screen. "Let's see . . . Flight 437, SFO to Paris, four hour layover, then Flight 89, arriving four P.M. tomorrow, Rome time," the agent read. "And the flight he's on . . . just left."

"Left?" Angie gripped the counter. "It's in the air already?"

"That's right. Sorry, ladies."

The two wandered away.

"Would Marcello be using the name Rocco?" Angie asked Cat, confused by the different name the agent used.

"No. Rocco is his younger brother. I haven't seen him for years. Not since I was a little kid. He and Marcello did look a lot alike, come to think of it." Cat's brows scrunched in thought. "I wonder if I was following Rocco, and Marcello really is in Italy like his manager said?"

"Cat, what is this really about?" Angie's voice grew firm. "What were you doing at Marcello's house?"

Cat seemed momentarily surprised by the question.

"Why shouldn't I have been there? He's my client." Her face fell. "Or, was."

"What do you mean?" Angie studied her closely. "Did he change his mind about selling the house?"

"Nothing like that." Angie waited, and finally Cat drew in her breath and said, "Oh, all right, I'll tell you about it. But don't tell anyone else, because it's all a mistake. Understand?"

Angie nodded.

"I went to Moldwell-Ranker this morning, as I always do," Cat began, "and I was calmly working with a couple of clients to get their pea brains to understand that in their minuscule price range homes did not look like those in magazine spreads, when out of the blue Meredith Woring, the office manager, accused me of stealing a relic that Marcello owns."

"You stole something?" Angie was stunned.

"Of course not!" Cat folded her arms. "For one thing, it looks like a piece of junk. I wouldn't want it, no matter how valuable it is."

"What is it?"

"I hate to say. It sounds like a joke or pious claptrap."

"I won't laugh," Angie promised.

"It's a chain that, supposedly, was once used to shackle St. Peter. You know—Peter the Apostle. The Big Fisherman. The keeper of the keys. The guardian of the Pearly Gates."

"Hah!" Angie blurted. "You've got to be kidding me!"

Cat glared at her. "Didn't I tell you? Anyway, it's just an old, rusty iron chain. Marcello thinks it's priceless. It's priceless, all right, as in 'without value.' The man should have 'Sucker' tattooed on his forehead. I asked him where he got it, and he wouldn't say." Cat put her hands on her hips as she swiveled, her back to

Angie, to look over the terminal. "Probably off eBay!"

"And that's what you supposedly took?" Angie moved around her sister, to face her again.

"That's right." Cat seemed ready to kill. "And because that means clients can no longer trust me, Meredith tried to fire me!"

Angie gawked. "I can't believe you got fired."

"I did not get fired!" Cat insisted. The sympathy in her younger sister's eyes had her grinding her perfectly capped teeth. "She tried to fire me. She can't. I'll fight it every inch of the way. I had my own interior design business for years, and only gave it up because, these days, people are making money hand over fist around here in real estate. But something like this could ruin my reputation in both areas. I will not put up with it!"

"So what did you do?" Angie asked.

"I tried calling Marcello, of course, but when I couldn't reach him, I went to his house to see for myself what was going on. I was sure the chain would still be there. Then I found a dead body. And then I saw Marcello—or someone—leaving the house with the chain I supposedly took! I've got to confront him—and get it back to prove my innocence."

"You went after him to prove you didn't steal a fake religious relic?"

"I went after him to preserve my reputation, my good name, my career!"

Angie still thought there was more to it than that, but before she could say so, Cat wailed, "This day couldn't get any worse!"

Actually, Angie thought, it could.

"There's a teensy little problem you need to know about," she said. "One that's somewhat bigger than a missing relic."

"Aha! I knew you were hiding something!" Cat's

eyes bored in on her like spikes. "Out with it. What's the problem? And how teensy?"

"There's a witness," Angie said. "She heard the gunshot, and then went to the window and saw you leaving the house. The way she put it, it sounded as if you were the killer."

Cat's eyes grew rounder as Angie's words sunk in. "Me? Somebody thinks I'm a killer?"

"I'm afraid so," Angie said.

"This is a joke!"

"I wish."

Cat gasped, nearly hyperventilating. "Do you think anyone would believe that?"

"Paavo doesn't," Angie tried to calm her sister, but she had to be truthful. "He said she's quite convincing, though."

"Convincing?" Now Cat actually was hyperventilating. Angie tried to lead her to a bench, but Cat pulled away. "How can she possibly be convincing when she's wrong? Why would anyone believe her?"

Angie tried to off-handedly toss out, "Maybe because of the satin handkerchief monogrammed with your initials found under the dead man's body." She added quickly, "Don't worry. It'll all get straightened out, I'm sure."

Cat's voice rose three octaves. "Handkerchief? I don't know about any handkerchief! What are you talking about?"

Angie waved her hands soothingly as they received a few curious glances from passersby. "Calm down. It's nothing. You'll be fine."

"Stop saying that!" Cat screeched, then took a breath and forced herself to sound calm. "Have the police located anyone who saw Marcello or Rocco or whoever it was leave the house just before I did?"

Angie hesitated. "Not . . . quite . . . yet."

"Oh God! Then it's the word of a witness against me—and I've already been accused of stealing from him! I don't know what to do."

"We'll get this straightened out," Angie insisted.

"With Marcello gone? And Rocco? And the chain? It's not going to be easy. Damn it all! That's why I called you for help! I wanted the police here!" Cat glared at Angie as if every malfeasance of every police force known to man could be laid at her feet. "They could have stopped him, gotten the chain, and he'd have cleared my name. I'd have been back at my job tomorrow. Now, everything is screwed up!"

Angie's brain churned over Cat's words. Something in the hysterical, angry, frustrated tones lit the proverbial lightbulb. She smiled triumphantly, snapping her fingers. "You're right. Marcello and Rocco are the keys to clearing your name. And Rocco is on that Alitalia flight . . ."

Paavo hung up. "I've got the CHP looking for their cars," he said morosely.

Yosh shook his head. "Let me get this straight. Angie's sister, Caterina, was here when the shooting took place. She saw someone leave and took off after him. She called 911, reported the murder, and then started in about following some Volvo, but the dispatcher didn't really understand what she was ranting about, so Caterina got mad and hung up. Then she called Angie, who, for heaven only knows what reason, encouraged her to continue to follow the guy—a possible murderer, no less—out onto the freeway. And then, as if that wasn't bad enough, Angie hopped in her car and she's also heading south to help her sister?"

Paavo looked a little green. "Yep, that about sums it up."

Yosh sighed. "I thought so. What do we do now?"

"Hope the CHP can find them. Angie's cell phone keeps going straight to messaging. I can't imagine she turned it off. She must be talking to her sister."

Yosh tried not to grin, but was losing the battle. "A black Volvo followed by a white BMW SUV followed by a silver Mercedes—and the last two driven by two women who are probably on their cell phones with each other and all over the road. Shouldn't be too tough to spot."

"One is a murder suspect," Paavo reminded him.

"Wrong—two are murder suspects," Yosh clarified. "If Caterina wasn't your sister-in-law to be, she'd be our prime suspect."

Paavo rubbed a temple. "I think I'm getting a headache."

Chapter 5

"I can't believe you carry your passport around with you." Cat looked at Angie as if she'd sprouted two heads.

"Doesn't everyone? It's in my tote with my iPaq, checkbook, extra makeup, and a few other important things. Something told me to grab the tote when I left the house. Anyway, you have yours." Angie took off her shoes and jacket and set them on the conveyer belt along with her tote bag and purse to go through security. Cat did the same.

"I have mine," Cat said, "because I needed it to get tickets and visas for the cruise Charles and I want to take through the Baltic. It's not something I carry around all the time."

The conversation stopped while the agent took away Cat's manicure scissors, letter opener, metal nail file, a Swiss Army pocketknife tool set, and a screwdriver. Her explanation that she was a realtor was greeted with a bored shrug. He didn't care why she had these things. It was his job to confiscate them, which he did.

Tickets in hand, Cat and Angie continued down the long corridor to their gate.

Earlier, Angie had used her iPaq to log onto the Internet, where she discovered a Lufthansa flight to Rome leaving in an hour. Since its layover in Frankfurt was only fifty minutes, she knew she'd actually arrive in

Rome before Rocco did. She could wait in the restrict-ed terminal area and watch as he came off the jetway.

Once she spotted him, she'd follow him to wherever he was staying. Then she'd phone Paavo, he'd contact the Italian police, they'd arrest Rocco, get back the chain of St. Peter (God willing), extradite Rocco to the U.S., and she could quickly come home—after doing a bit of shopping and eating in Rome, of course. It had been a few years since she'd lived there, and she loved the city. She had no problem with visiting it again.

If only Paavo could be with her, life would be perfect. Rome . . . Italy . . . they were made for *amore*. In fact, Italy might make a very nice site for a honeymoon. She could check that out as well.

When she enthusiastically told Cat her plan, leav-ing out the part about finding a honeymoon locale, Cat clearly and emphatically gave her opinion of her sister's mental condition.

"What do you want to do?" Angie asked, warming to her plan. "Go back and try to convince the police that the home owner's brother just happened to be at the scene of the crime and just happened to take the valuable relic you were accused of stealing that very morning? Or let me go to Rome, find Rocco, point out to the police where he is, and let him do the explain-ing? Without finding him and the chain that will back up your story, what proof do you have for any of this? All the police know is that you were there, and your handkerchief was found under the dead man's body."

"Why did he have my handkerchief?" Cat com-plained. "I don't even know who he was!"

"I'll handle everything for you." Angie patted her sister sympathetically. "All you need to do is describe Rocco to me, clothes and all. I'd hate to go all the way to Italy and then follow the wrong person."

Cat jerked her arm away. She hated sympathy. "How

could you pick one man out of a whole planeload of people? What can I tell you? Look for a guy in a sport jacket who looks Italian? I haven't seen Rocco since I was about ten years old. I'm not sure I would recognize him myself." Cat took a few steps, then stopped. When she turned toward Angie, her face was considerably brighter. "If this idea of yours is any good at all, I'll have to be the one to go."

"Not good, Cat." Angie vehemently shook her head. "The police want to question you. They won't like it one bit if you leave the country."

Cat pondered this, then smiled coyly. "I don't know that they want to question me. No one's told *me* that."

"You witnessed a murder!"

"No, I didn't! I saw a dead body. That's completely different."

Angie couldn't believe her ears. "You were seen fleeing the scene of the crime."

"I wasn't fleeing! I was chasing!" Cat tossed her head. "If there's a problem, Charles can hire a good lawyer or two."

"Martha Stewart had a whole team of them," Angie pointed out. "And look what happened to her!"

"Rocco must be going to Italy to meet Marcello, and I need Marcello to straighten this all out," Cat said, thinking out loud.

"Is that the real reason for your sudden interest in flying halfway around the world?" Angie's eyes narrowed with suspicion.

Cat coolly regarded her for a moment. "Of course! I want it done right. Join me, if you'd like."

"Thanks for your confidence," Angie muttered, arms crossed.

Undaunted, Cat went into logical, controlled mode, ticking off items on her To Do list. "I'll have to ask Mamma to take care of Kenny for a couple of days, then tell Charles to bring Kenny to Mamma's house, call Kenny's school, then all my clients to say I'll be out of town a couple of days—"

"If we're going, we've got to go now!" Angie said. "They won't sell tickets much longer."

Cat's mind whirred. "If we can do that, I should be able to keep my name out of the papers. Charles won't have to contact his lawyer friends—they all have such big mouths! And no one will ever know anything at all about this. It's not that big a scandal, after all."

"Not at all," Angie agreed, hoping her sister didn't notice when she rolled her eyes.

Paavo banged his head against the steering wheel. Okay, it was childish, but given the provocation, understandable.

He sat in the airport parking lot. The California Highway Patrol had contacted him when the two cars he'd sent a bulletin on showed up there, then he and Yosh headed that way. It was Angie's car, all right. He could only assume the BMW was her sister's. Yosh was talking to the garage attendant to see if he'd noticed the two women and which way they'd gone.

From the time Paavo had gotten the call from the CHP, he'd tried to reach Angie, to find out which terminal she was in, but he still couldn't get through.

Then, just minutes ago, she'd called him.

"Nobody saw them," Yosh said as he got into the car, and noticing his partner's agitation, asked, "What's wrong?"

Paavo turned his head to look at him, his expression blank. "They're going to Rome. The two of them are in flight, as we speak...."

Disbelief rendered the big guy speechless for nearly a full minute, then he choked out, "Rome ... as in Italy?"

Paavo nodded as the ramifications of what they'd done hit him. Angie had told him they were following Rocco Piccoletti, the home owner's brother, that he'd taken a three P.M. flight to Rome and had the relic Cat had been accused of stealing with him. Angie seemed to think that all she and Cat had to do was to track down this Rocco Piccoletti in Rome, tell Paavo and he'd ring up the Italian police and ask them to send Rocco back to the U.S., where he'd immediately clarify everything, turn over the relic, and leave Caterina free and clear.

But he knew that wasn't going to happen. He'd been about to explain to her that there were rafts of laws involving extradition, and that, to begin with, he'd have to get all the higher-ups in the SFPD involved, not to mention the State Department, Justice Department, and the various embassy staffs. What she wanted—without clear proof that Rocco Piccoletti was the murderer—was practically impossible. But he didn't get any of that out before she had to hang up because their plane was taking off.

"Get off the plane!" he'd shouted into the phone. "Don't go!"

But it was too late. She'd already disconnected.

Now, Yosh faced Paavo. "Is it possible that Caterina doesn't know that she's wanted for questioning in connection with a murder investigation?"

"She knows," Paavo said haltingly.

"Holy shit!" Yosh shook his head with dismay. "That means Caterina's skipped the country! And since Angie helped, she's now an accomplice."

Paavo banged his head one more time.

Chapter 6

Paavo and Yosh returned to the Sea Cliff district and the Piccoletti house. They spent the day canvassing the neighborhood to see if anyone besides Audrey Moss had seen or heard anything, and to find out all they could about Marcello Piccoletti. All they got for their efforts was a ringside seat in a game of see, hear, and touch no evil. None of the neighbors knew anything. Most didn't even know Piccoletti's name, let alone a brother or other relatives he might have. The sad part, Paavo thought, was that he believed them. So much for big-city neighborliness.

The only out-of-the-ordinary information they learned was that several people had noticed a strange black truck a half block from the Piccoletti house. They had no idea what it was doing in that neighborhood.

One neighbor's gardener thought he recognized the man sitting in it as being the person who had installed Piccoletti's security system. He'd waved to say hello, but the man looked at him as if he didn't know him. The gardener described the truck driver as looking like a bear—overweight, not too tall, young, and with curly brown hair.

Two women, both au pairs from down the block, near where the truck was parked, noticed a priest walking in the direction of the Piccoletti house, but lost sight of him shortly.

It wasn't much to go on—a black truck, a priest, and a bearish looking fellow who resembled a former workman on the property—but it was a start. Piccoletti's neighbor had speculated that the reason he was selling his house was because he could no longer afford it. That, too, was an angle worth pursuing.

Cat opened her eyes to a blinding headache. It couldn't possibly be a hangover. She'd never had one in her life.

As she settled into her first-class seat, the flight attendant offered drinks, and she took a scotch and soda. The whiskey was warming and calming. So much so that against her better judgment she ordered a second. This was an extraordinary circumstance. She fell asleep halfway through it.

Even asleep, all that had happened that day plagued her.

She was certain she had no choice but to go to Rome after Rocco. Angie didn't know what he looked like, so how could she follow him to take back the chain of St. Peter or to talk to Marcello? Marcello, Cat was sure, knew exactly what his brother was up to. And she had to find out as soon as possible. Especially now that it involved murder.

That was when her head began to throb, waking her.

She buzzed for a flight attendant, who handed her a couple of Tylenol and coffee. The caffeine coursed through her veins, clearing the cobwebs and fuzziness.

Settling back, she shut her eyes again. The plane was quiet as most people tried to sleep. Whether it was the peacefulness, the coffee, or simply having a moment to think, the heavy cloud of confusion and despair that had swirled around her since her boss accused her of stealing Marcello's relic, worsened by the horrible shock of seeing a dead body, suddenly lifted.

The day flashed before her with clarity, in Technicolor.

Her eyes sprang open, and she didn't think she'd be able to sleep anymore that night. Maybe never again.

As much as she needed to find Rocco and straighten out everything with Marcello, in the eyes of the police she could well be seen as a fugitive from the law.

They wouldn't look at her that way, would they? Anyone could tell she was a good person. But there was that damned witness ...

She'd have to get Charles to talk to his lawyer friends after all. If they got involved, however, they could find out about her and Marcello. She couldn't let that happen.

What in the world was she going to do? She lay her head back, trying to relax, trying not to let this upset her any more than it already had, then bolted upright.

A monogrammed handkerchief? Satin?

Wasn't that what Angie had said?

A strange and horrible thought came to her, and with it a chill, the kind that caused old women to say someone had walked over your grave.

No, she told herself, *it can't be....*

Lieutenant James Philip Eastwood, the new chief of the homicide bureau, was pacing the halls when Paavo and Yosh arrived back at the Hall of Justice.

The wide, marble-covered corridors of the government building usually teemed with employees and those members of the public called there by the city's municipal and superior courts, by the District Attorney and his staff, by the administration and special bureaus of the police department, or by the coroner's office or the city morgue. Now, though, all was quiet Almost everyone had gone home.

But not Paavo and Yosh's new boss.

The old chief, Ray Hollins, a forceful, knowledgeable, yet unpretentious man, had been reassigned to be head of the Traffic Division to make room for a virtual celebrity.

"It's about time," was Eastwood's only greeting. He turned and marched into Homicide. The two inspectors followed.

Jim Eastwood was in his late forties, and had transferred to San Francisco from Los Angeles to take a promotion. He'd made a name for himself working the murder of a movie star's wife—a case that had actually resulted in the star's conviction, to everyone's amazement. From all Paavo could tell, Eastwood was ambitious and planned to use his new job as nothing but a PR opportunity. He liked seeing his picture in the newspaper, and it was obvious that he wanted to be Chief of Police. His first day on the job he gave a rah-rah talk and announced to his team that they'd be the best damn homicide detectives in the city. They didn't bother to remind him that, as opposed to the sprawling metropolis of Los Angeles, which had an immense police force with detectives doing homicide investigations in every large precinct, San Francisco was physically small, and homicides were handled centrally by the Bureau of Inspections in the Hall of Justice. That meant they were the only homicide inspectors—as they were called in the city, rather than detectives—in town.

Eastwood's first job as the new boss was to build himself what he considered to be a proper office. Hollins had used a small area separated from the inspector's desk by floor-to-ceiling partitions. Eastwood wanted one about twice the size—an expansion that resulted in the main homicide room, where all the inspectors sat with their desks, files, and bookcases, becoming even smaller.

The workmen had gone home for the day. Two-by-four studs for the walls had been put into place, and now Sheetrock was being cut and attached. White dust hung in the air, floating like an ominous cloud of fall-out.

When Eastwood pushed the door to his small temporary office open, it banged against the wall.

The room had been Homicide's supply closet. With the renovation, all the supplies were moved into an electrical closet off the women's room. Since there was only one female inspector and one female secretary in the bureau, retrieving the necessary forms and papers was now difficult—if not awkward and embarrassing.

"A murder in the Sea Cliff is the biggest thing to hit this department since I've been here," Eastwood roared as Paavo and Yosh joined him. "And I'm left in the dark." He stood behind his desk, his expression haughty and arch. The room was beyond claustrophobic.

Paavo had nothing to say in response. To explain that he was too busy working the case to rush back to Homicide to give Eastwood a briefing would have sounded like sarcasm. With good reason.

Eastwood sat down. Nodding at a small leatherette guest chair, he said, "Have a seat, one of you." Only one extra chair fit in the closet. Yosh immediately backed up against the wall, leaving Paavo the hot seat.

The two quickly briefed Eastwood.

"I'd like to request that the Italian police be asked to find and hold Rocco Piccoletti," Paavo said in conclusion. The airline had confirmed for him that the suspect was on the flight.

Eastwood leaned back and regarded the detective a long moment. "On what grounds?"

"He left the country after leaving the scene of a murder that took place in his brother's home. I understand the brother is also in Rome. I have a number of questions for them both."

Eastwood steepled his fingers. "The murder, you said, occurred at about one-thirty. Piccoletti's plane left at three. Aside from the fact that you need to arrive at the airport two hours early for international flights just to get through security, it would take him at least forty-five minutes to get from his house to the airport, and then he'd still need time to park. It would have been practically impossible for him to be home at one-thirty and still make the flight unless it was delayed . . . Was it?"

"No. But it is possible, barely." Paavo knew how quickly one could board, as he'd figured out Angie's movements earlier that day. Damn! Who would have thought she'd leave the country with Cat to chase a murderer! It made him all but physically ill to think about it, but he couldn't stop. He needed to be working this case, not sitting in a closet answering asinine questions.

Eastwood was addressing him. " . . . do you know when he bought his ticket?"

"Last week," Paavo admitted. The airline had that information.

Eastwood stroked his chin. "So, a man has a ticket, goes to the airport, leaves for Rome, and in the meantime, someone is murdered back in his brother's house. The victim has the home owner's wallet in his pocket, and meets the owner's physical description. At the same time, a woman is seen leaving the house immediately after the murder—a woman who is the sister of your fiancée, Inspector Smith. Strangely, she's the only person who claims the victim is not the home owner, and the only one who places this Rocco Piccoletti anywhere near the house at the time of the murder. Interesting, isn't it, that no one else saw him?"

Paavo's back stiffened. He couldn't believe what he was hearing. Yosh glanced his way and shook his head. They'd left any mention of Caterina's identity out of the briefing. How did Eastwood know? "That has nothing to do with anything."

"Given the sensitivity of the situation, I'd like to question her myself," Eastwood said. "Bring her in."

"She's . . . on her way to Italy." Paavo's jaw snapped shut.

Eastwood stared at him. "You have insufficient cause to contact the Italian police about Rocco Piccoletti, Inspector Smith. I see no reason to grant your request."

Rage building, Paavo stood to leave. "Yes, sir." He had to get out of there fast. "Thank you."

"However," Eastwood thundered, also standing, "the woman is the one the Italian police have got to hold! I want her questioned and sent back to this country immediately. In fact, given the prominent location of this murder and this 'other' circumstance, I'll handle it myself."

Paavo's teeth clenched. "I believe Caterina Swenson was only at the house because someone called and accused her of stealing a valuable religious relic. She went to express her innocence to the owner—her client—and saw the body."

"Did it ever occur to you that perhaps she did take the relic?" Eastwood was barely able to contain a snarl. "And perhaps killed the home owner when he discovered she was a thief, and then dreamed up this entire nonsensical story because she knew that you, as her future brother-in-law, would believe her?"

"No," Paavo said pointedly. "I would not consider such a scenario credible."

Eastwood's face reddened. "I've been told that you were my best inspector, Smith. I'm sorry to see that you're allowing your personal life to get in the way of this investigation. It makes me think I'm making a mistake in allowing you to continue with this case."

Paavo's gaze never wavered. "I can handle it."

Eastwood's face betrayed his suspicions. "Can you?"

To that, Paavo turned and walked out the door.

Chapter 7

Paavo was with her. Angie rested her head on his shoulder and flung her arm across his chest. He gazed down at her, his face, his sensitive mouth, near hers. She snuggled closer. "I want . . . " she whispered lovingly. "I want . . . "

"Whatever it is, li'l lady," a man with a southern accent said. "I'm sure as hell the one to give it to you."

Angie opened her eyes to find her head on a stranger's shoulder. Abruptly, she scrambled upright. "Excuse me."

The big man grinned. "Anytime."

She faced forward in the narrow airplane seat, her face on fire. She sat near the tail, center section, three seats in from the aisle. Her sister had gotten the last first-class seat and wasn't about to give it up to spend ten hours worth of quality time with Angie.

As a result, some of the most disgusting hours of Angie's life had been spent crammed between two gargantuan men who'd grown increasingly smelly as the hours on the hot and stuffy plane crept by. One had fallen asleep and slumped in his chair so that he flopped halfway onto her seat. No wonder her head ended up on his shoulder. The other stayed awake all night long and played video games on a Game Boy. He kept the sound on, low enough that only he—and she—could hear it. She was sure she'd *pow! whap!* and *oomph!* him before the flight ever touched down.

Earlier, she had used the air phone to call Paavo's house, not his cell, and had to admit to being relieved when he didn't pick up. The more she thought about it, the more worried she became about leaving the country with Cat. They never should have done it. She had visions of the Italian police, wearing highly polished black boots and high-crowned caps with shiny black visors, waiting for them as they stepped off the plane to whisk them away to some dank dungeon for questioning.

Unfortunately, the more she thought about it, the more she suspected Rocco was a murderer. Why else was he seen running from the house almost immediately after the gun had been fired, and carrying the chain of St. Peter? Cat had to realize that as well, only refused to admit it. Angie wondered if her sister was having some obscure denial syndrome so she wouldn't have to face up to the inherent danger of what she was doing.

Angie couldn't help but suspect that the chain wasn't nearly as worthless as Cat thought. Men had killed for a lot less than an artifact believed to be "priceless." Especially since the chain was thought to have been missing, and someone—presumably Rocco—had called Cat's office manager, pretended he was Marcello, and accused her of stealing it.

The logic of that made no sense, however. Why would Rocco complain about someone stealing the chain if he were stealing it himself? And if not Rocco, who had it been?

All she knew was that the situation Cat was heading into was very likely a lot more dangerous than her sister imagined, and she couldn't let Cat face it alone.

She was glad she didn't have to attempt to explain her actions to Paavo. She wasn't sure she could, except

that Cat was her sister, and despite Cat's brave and an-
noyingly obnoxious front, she was scared, hurting, not
thinking clearly, and hiding something. Angie was convinced of it. Nevertheless, she couldn't turn her back
on Cat. She'd simply need to think clearly enough for
the two of them. *Be calm*, she told herself.

The more she tried, however, the more anxious she
became.

Somewhere on the plane, a baby cried all night. It
seemed there was always a baby crying on overseas
flights, almost as if the kid was trying to see how many
passengers he could morph into homicidal maniacs.

The food was plastic and tasteless.

The bathroom line long, and *Fat Albert* wasn't her
idea of entertainment.

Given that start, Angie guessed she shouldn't have
been surprised when the situation deteriorated. Security in Frankfurt pulled her and Caterina aside to ask
in-depth questions about why they'd suddenly bought
one-way tickets to travel to a European Union country
and carried no luggage.

The two lied for all they were worth. Angie told
a story about going to visit a sick aunt, saying that
since they didn't know how long it would be before
she recovered, their tickets were one-way. Cat added
that they were going shopping in Rome to buy the latest fashions for fall, which wouldn't show up in San
Francisco until sometime the following winter, if ever.
Heaven forbid they bring an out-of-date wardrobe to
Italy!

The furrows in the security agent's already lined
brow deepened.

Angie tried to hurry things along, explaining that
they only had fifty minutes between planes, and going through customs was eating up all their time. The
agent slowly flipped through their passports.

"You've got to hurry," she demanded. "My sister can't miss her flight to Rome."

The agent was a thick-boned, hard-faced, blond-haired fellow. He slowly looked from the passports to the ticket. "Why not?" he said with a frown. "The latest fashions will be there whether you arrive today or tomorrow."

"Tomorrow?" Angie shrieked. "You've got no reason to hold us here. We've done everything right. We've told you the truth! Let us go."

"What if I said I don't believe you?" Steel was softer than his gaze.

Angie and Cat glanced at each other.

Cat raised her nose high. "Are you accusing me of lying?"

Angie didn't think that was the best tactic to take. What if he said yes? She jumped in. "We've told you everything and now we've only got ten minutes to board." She spoke rationally, and only sounded halfway instead of completely hysterical. "Please! This is a waste of time. Let us go!"

"Waste of time?" The agent puffed out his chest.

"All right, then! We're just going to Rome to have fun." Cat scowled as if he were less than stupid. "There's no rhyme or reason for our trip. Does that make you happy?"

He looked ready to burst a blood vessel. "I'll tell you what makes me happy—"

"Wait," Angie said. "I'll answer all your questions, but my sister doesn't need to stay with me. You've got to understand. It's imperative my sister be on that plane!"

"Why?" he asked.

"Why?" Angie repeated.

Cat looked at her, equally at a loss for a reason.

"Let's send her on her way, why don't we?" Angie smiled, the epitome of reasonableness.

"Guard!" the agent yelled. "Take this woman to be strip-searched!"

Angie and Cat looked at each other, horrified.

"Me?" Angie asked in a shaky voice.

"No." He pointed a thick finger directly at Cat. "Her!"

"I—" was the only sound that squeaked from Cat's mouth as she was whisked away down a long, long hallway.

Angie stared open-mouthed at the agent who had shoved her passport and ticket back into her hand and already gone on to the next couple.

She went over to the gateway and sat, waiting for Cat to come out of the search area.

Before long everyone else had gone through security. The door to the jetway was locked.

The plane left for Rome.

And still Angie waited.

Paavo sat at his desk in Homicide. It was the middle of the night, and he was alone.

He'd left off the overhead lights, and only a desk lamp illuminated his computer and paperwork. The office seemed emptier than usual.

Earlier that day, being with the rookie officer, Justin Leong, had made Paavo remember that Homicide was considered the top rung in the Bureau of Inspections, and that it used to be a place young ambitious officers worked toward. These days, with budget cuts and a D.A. who believed it was better to coddle criminals than to prosecute them, every division in the police department with the exception of the horse patrol in Golden Gate Park (tourists loved them) had been cut to the bone. They were down to only six homicide inspectors—five, in fact, since one of them, Never-Take-a-Chance Bill Sutter, was near retirement and did all he could to avoid any work and any danger.

Not even Jim Eastwood's posturing could make this department what it once had been.

Darkness and shadows fell over the remainder of a room crammed with desks, file cabinets, computers, and binders making up "homicide books"—files that captured every step taken to find justice for the dead. Ghosts of the detectives who came and went working those cases, and of the victims themselves, seemed to fill the bureau on nights like this, casting a cold and heartless pall.

Usually when he was feeling this way, his thoughts could turn to Angie, safe and secure in her comfortable apartment, and that soon he could be there with her, surrounded by her warmth and her love. The stabbing realization that she wasn't there, that she was on her way to Europe, struck anew. It seemed like a bad joke—or nightmare. Knowing Angie and understanding her desire to help her sister, the best way to get her home quickly and safely was to find out what really happened today in the Sea Cliff house.

Paavo went back to work with renewed vigor. On both Piccolettis, he ran AutoTrack, a private enterprise that pulled together all kinds of public records into an enormous database. Marcello Piccoletti came up completely clean. The AutoTrack records showed he was in Key West, Florida, ten years ago, then at an address in the south of Market area of San Francisco, and five years later at his current address on Scenic Avenue in Sea Cliff. It indicated he'd gotten a California driver's license about five years earlier. Why, then, was he carrying an old one from Florida? Finally, the system also showed he had two cars—a black Volvo and a new red Ferrari.

Marcello's brother, Rocco Piccoletti, had been in the system until about six years ago. His last record, off a car registration, showed him in Florida not far from Marcello's earlier address, but then the information stopped.

Paavo sat back in his chair and rubbed his forehead in weariness and frustration. Along with these searches, he'd also spent a lot of time calling Catholic priests in the city to try to locate the one seen on Scenic Avenue that afternoon. He needed to talk to the potential witness. He'd had no luck there either.

It went without saying that the best chance to catch a murderer happened within the first forty-eight hours after the crime was committed. That's when the trail was hottest, memories were clearest, and everyone had the time, energy, and will to find the perpetrator. After that, despair, desperation, and finally boredom set in. For that reason, Paavo and Yosh usually worked their cases round the clock the first two days.

But this case was different.

With Angie and her sister involved, Paavo was already deep into the despair and desperation stage. Boredom, he thought, would be a welcome change.

Marcello Piccoletti's papers provided the name of his store, Furniture 4 U, on Mission Street. The store manager's statement was consistent with that of Audrey Moss: Piccoletti had left for Italy the day before.

Despite that, Paavo convinced the manager to come to the morgue in an attempt to identify the body.

They had cleaned up the body quite a bit, and in situations like this, victims were shown on a television screen rather than in the flesh. TV shows presented such garish images that the public seemed to find it easier to take that way—it was less real. Still, the store manager turned jelly-legged at the damage done to the face by the bullet's exit. When he could breathe again, he said the dead man was definitely not Marcello Piccoletti, and reiterated that his boss was in Italy, at the Hotel Leonardo.

If the dead man in Piccoletti's house, carrying his wallet, wasn't Marcello, then who was he? And why did he have Marcello's wallet?

Paavo phoned the Hotel that Piccoletti was supposedly staying at in Rome. In textbook perfect English, the receptionist informed him that Marcello Piccoletti had not checked in yet. He was due later that day.

In answer to his next question, she had no information on anyone named Rocco Piccoletti.

Finally, the call-back Paavo had been waiting for all evening came from the Transportation Security Agency, which confirmed that not only were Caterina and Angie on a Lufthansa, from San Francisco to Frankfurt, with the ultimate destination of Rome, but also that Rocco Piccoletti had caught his connecting flight out of Paris to Rome earlier that same day.

Paavo thanked the agent.

It wasn't that he didn't trust Angie or her sister—it was simply that he'd learned that the Amalfis, all of them, had a tendency to exaggerate or tell only as much as they wanted to. But this time, everything they'd told him was true.

Paavo's request for Marcello's telephone records came through and he was poring over the numbers when he got a call from the Medical Examiner, Evelyn Ramirez. She was pulling an all-nighter, and something told her that he was very likely doing the same. "I can do your John Doe's autopsy now," she said, "or he goes into the queue and waits three days. Things are backing up down here pretty badly."

"Three days?" Paavo said. "I'll be right down. And Evelyn—thanks."

"No sweat."

He took the elevator to the basement. It always seemed darker down there, and much colder. He didn't know if it actually was or if it was simply his imagination because of the work being done there.

Ramirez was already gowned and gloved.

He took a deep breath and nodded to indicate that he was ready for the first cut, which for him was always the worst.

It was odd, Paavo thought, how the autopsy was going to literally turn the man's insides out, yet it wouldn't reveal anything so mundane as his identity.

Chapter 8

 The Alitalia flight Rocco had been on was long gone by the time Cat and Angie reached the Leonardo Da Vinci Airport in Rome.

It was nearly 6:00 P.M., Rome time, after a tension-laden wait in Frankfurt. Angie tried to explain that it wasn't her fault they were stopped by customs security—she was a victim here—but Cat just shook her head, pursed her lips, and absolutely refused to talk about the body search.

Angie hated silent treatments.

While other passengers headed for the baggage claim area, Angie noticed a couple of policemen step closer to the passengers who had been on their flight, as if searching for someone. Her nightmares of being stopped by the police came back to her. She grabbed Cat's arm and dragged her into an alcove that was the doorway to the men's room.

"What are you doing?" Cat jumped back when she caught the eye of a startled Italian making his way into the lavatory.

A number of policemen were converging on their area. "Let's get out of here," Angie said.

"You don't think they're looking for us, do you?" Cat cried.

"Who knows?"

"But Paavo is in charge of the case. He wouldn't . . . would he?"

"We don't know how things progressed while we were in flight," Angie said. For all she knew, it only took a couple of phone calls for the San Francisco police to contact the police in Rome and ask them to detain two passengers for questioning. They wanted to avoid that.

"You're scaring me, Angie."

They snuck stealthily along the wall, darting between alcoves and behind free-standing bulletin boards and advertising posters until they spotted an exit.

They scurried from the building.

A policeman was standing near the taxi stands, so they fled in the opposite direction. A sign pointed them toward the nonstop Leonardo train to Termini, the main train station in Rome. They hurried in that direction. They had to take a number of up escalators, which gave them a bird's-eye view of the terminal. It was filled with people, their voices creating a loud din as they bustled about, stopping to hug and kiss or shout and argue with equal enthusiasm. Yes, Angie thought, I'm in Italy again.

On the other hand, more cops than she'd ever remembered being at the airport were circling around, although the police presence in Rome was quite high. A part of her almost hoped they were looking for terrorists, and not her and her sister. Paavo wouldn't send the full weight of the Italian constabulary down on their heads, would he? Surely, she was just being paranoid.

Of course, the last time they spoke he was yelling at her not to leave the country. He'd sounded awfully angry.

She took out her cell phone to call him. It showed that she had many messages, but the phone itself wouldn't connect. She belatedly remembered that European phones used GSM, a different service from most American ones, and dropped the phone back into her tote.

At the Fiumicino train station, they stopped at an ATM for euros, a *tobacconista* for train tickets, and ran down a *binario* to board the train about to depart. Inside, they leaned against the walls of the train's corridor to catch their breaths. All the seats had been taken.

Angie had ridden this train many times in the past. After spending a year in Paris at the Cordon Bleu culinary institute, she had moved to Rome to perfect her knowledge of Italian food. Or, at least, that was her story.

The real problem was that she wasn't sure what she wanted to do with her culinary education. She loved food, and loved its preparation, but the more she had learned about the life of a chef, the less she wanted it. The hours were incredibly long, and the work physically demanding. It was hard enough to serve a large dinner for friends and relatives—trying to cook a variety of foods for strangers, all arriving at different times, many demanding slight changes to suit their own tastes or medical conditions, was nerve-racking.

So, she didn't want to be a chef. Unfortunately, she hadn't yet found the right outlet for her education. But it wasn't for lack of trying. Paavo often told her she tried too hard.

If it wasn't that her parents expected her—the youngest child and the one given the most financial assistance by them—to make something of her life, to do something with her talent, education, and ability, she'd have been perfectly content to simply become Mrs. Paavo Smith.

Or would she?

He worked long hours at an interesting job he valued.

Sometimes, when a case was new, he'd work around the clock and she wouldn't hear from him for a couple of days. She knew she couldn't make him her entire life. That would stifle them both. She needed something stimulating that was hers alone . . . but what?

"Angie, did you hear a word I said?" Cat's glare was frightening.

"Oh, sorry. Guess I dozed off."

"I said," Cat repeated tersely, "where are we going?"

"You're asking me? You're the one who rushed off to find Rocco and Marcello. I'm supposed to be following you, remember?"

"I know, but you lived here. You know Rome better than I do. Besides, I had trouble sleeping. The pillow the stewardess gave me was lumpy, and I wasn't about to use the blanket. Do you know how many germs live in blankets?"

"They wash them, I'm sure." Angie didn't want to hear a single complaint from Cat about first class after the night she'd had.

"I wasn't about to take a chance," Cat declared. "It's my theory that it's the blankets, not the air system, that cause the illnesses on planes."

"In that case, the pillows are probably much germier than the blankets," Angie said, aware that a sadistic streak was not a positive trait, but unable to help herself. "After all, it's harder to wash and dry them."

Cat paled and raised a hand to her forehead as if checking for a fever.

Angie leaned her head back against the wall of the train once more. This wasn't going at all the way she'd expected.

At eight in the morning, Paavo was jarred awake by the ringing of his phone. Normally, he was up long before then, but due to the autopsy and then lying awake trying to figure out what to do about Angie and Caterina, he hadn't gotten to sleep until after four.

"Paavo, this is Serefina." It was Angie's mother. He bolted upright, instinctively pulling the covers up to his waist.

Last evening, when he hadn't heard from Angie except for an apologetic message on his home phone, and couldn't get through to her cell, he'd spoken with Charles Swenson, Caterina's husband. Charles had had no better luck reaching his wife. The two men promised to keep each other posted. Charles didn't ask if Caterina was in any legal trouble, and Paavo thought it best not to break it to him.

Now, though, he feared Serefina might have heard something, and the news might not have been good. Cold fingers clutched at his heart. "Is everything all right?"

"All right? All right? Hah!" Serefina all but shouted into the phone. "My girls, *le mie bambine*, are running around Italy looking for God only knows what. *Madonna mia!* Nothing will be all right until they're home."

"We'll get them back soon," Paavo hurriedly promised. "Have you heard from them yet?"

"*Dio mio, ma che figlie!*" Serefina cried. "I'm only their mother! Why should they call and let me know that they're still alive?"

"Do you know where in Rome they'll be staying?"

"If they don't tell me they're alive, would they tell me where they're staying?"

"You must have relatives or friends they can go to," Paavo said hopefully.

"In Rome itself, I only have a cousin, but they won't go there. We don't talk about him. Tell me, Paavo, why this is happening?" Her tone had changed from cranky to pleading. "No matter how old your children are, you still worry about them. You must know something about all this."

Maybe it was because his own mother disappeared when he was a young boy, or maybe it was simply the force of Serefina's personality, but he could never refuse a request from her without feeling like the lowest form of life. As much as he'd have liked to shelter her, he told her what had happened. He knew that much of it would come out in the newspaper. A murder didn't occur in the Sea Cliff without the newspaper and every TV and radio station in town being there. Reporters were already hounding him.

"Marcello Piccoletti?" Serefina gasped when he'd finished. "Why would she be so crazy as to get mixed up with that family? Even Marcello's mother, *pazzato*. Crazy."

"You know Marcello Piccoletti's mother?" Paavo was astounded.

"Of course—Flora. Flora was okay when she was younger," Serefina went on to say, scarcely taking a breath. "But then—*dio!*—that Marcello. Even when he was a little boy, he was wild. When he got older, it was even worse. Too good looking, for one thing. He had a way with women that wasn't good. Not that his mother would ever say anything bad about him. She spoiled him rotten."

"Do you know Rocco Piccoletti?"

"Rocco? He's Flora's second son. Always in Marcello's shadow. First Marcello, then Rocco, then a daughter, Josie."

He'd never worked a case this way before, but this was too good an opportunity to save time, and time was of the essence to get Angie home. "Do you know where Flora Piccoletti lives?"

"Sure I do. Russian Hill. Not too far from Angie, come to think of it. I'll find the address and get back to you.

But first, listen to me, Paavo. This is important...."

She paused, waiting for his assurance. "I'm listening," he said.

"You will not tell Salvatore about this," she said, referring to her husband. "If he asks, the girls are . . . I don't know . . . in Las Vegas. Angie went to a wedding convention—designers and wedding planners from across the country—and convinced Caterina to go with her. If Salvatore hears the truth, he'll try to do something about it. Maybe go to Italy himself. With his bad heart, that could kill him! This is our secret. All right?"

"That's fine," he replied. The last thing he needed was for Salvatore to get involved. Serefina, he was sure, was going to be quite bad enough.

Chapter 9

Angie and Cat got off the train at Termini, the central station in Rome. It was a cavernous structure, overwhelmingly gray from both its concrete walls and floor to the soot and grime from the cars and taxis that converged there.

As she emerged from the station, Angie's heart skipped a beat just being in Rome again. She immediately took in everything—the masses of people, the noise, the warmth and sunlight of an early evening in June. Where San Francisco was a pastel city, the colors light, the sky often white if not gray from the fog and haze cast by water on three sides, Rome's sky was bright blue, and the buildings colorful. If San Francisco could be likened to silver, Rome was pure gold.

Cat knew Marcello owned a small restaurant in town, Da Vinci's, and routinely stayed at the Hotel Leonardo nearby. Between the two, she was confident they'd find him easily. She'd tell him what had happened, and he should be able to lead them to Rocco.

Cat assured Angie that there was no danger from Marcello. Angie trusted her judgment. Cat couldn't have succeeded for years as an interior designer if she wasn't an excellent judge of character. Also, no way would Caterina Amalfi Swenson do anything that might muss one hair on her head, let alone endanger it.

Angie, whose Italian was better than Cat's, called the Hotel Leonardo and asked to speak to Signore Piccoletti. He'd checked in a short while earlier, but wasn't answering.

"Let's get a hotel and try again later," Cat said, marching toward a taxi. "The St. Regis is lovely."

"Wait a minute." Angie grasped her arm, stopping her. "We've got to think about this."

"What's to think about? I'm tired, achy, and want to soak in a bath for an hour. They have nice dress shops nearby for us to pick up some clothes. I've got it all worked out."

Angie looked over her shoulder at the armed, tough-looking *carabinieri* milling about outside the train station. One noticed her and stared.

She pulled Cat down the crowded street, past rows of magazine and newspaper vendors, in the direction of the metro, Rome's subway. They found it quite warm as they walked, and took off their jackets.

"Have you also worked out what happens when we show our passports in order to get a room?" Angie's voice was low, her head bent toward Cat's. "You know that's the rule here. What if the police are looking for us? They'll have gotten word out, and as soon as anyone sees our passports, they'll grab us."

"You're being overly dramatic, just as you were with security in Frankfurt, and then at the airport in Rome." Cat held her purse close as she tried to avoid being bumped or jostled by the masses of humanity rushing toward the metro. This was the most dangerous spot in Rome for pickpockets, and on top of that, Cat detested public transportation. She was a taxi person. "I'm through listening to your wild ideas, Angie. The police never act that fast."

"How do you know?" Angie jumped onto a down escalator. Cat hesitated, and got knocked from behind.

She hurried to the same step as Angie. "Do you want to take the chance that, instead of a four-star hotel, you end up in an Italian prison? I've heard scary things about Americans getting locked away in foreign prisons. Everybody fights about jurisdiction and what laws were and weren't broken. Then the American embassy comes in and starts throwing their weight around, which pisses off the other country's government, which then digs in its heels, and the poor American pays the price!"

"You know that isn't the sort of thing we're facing. This is Italy! The police don't act that way."

"Which police? Between the *carabinieri*, the *polizia di stato*, the finance police, the antimafia police, and the antiterrorist police, we could get caught up in an internal fight that would be worse than an international one!"

They were off the escalator now and walking down a long underground corridor.

"Stop, already! Let's just get out of this horrible subway." Cat looked for a way up, back to street level, but didn't see anything.

Angie hurried her along. "We simply need to make sure nobody stops us. We need to find Marcello, let the police know, spend some time checking out a few things in Rome, and then go home. I miss Paavo already!"

"That, I can agree to," Cat said.

"Good. Now, we used our ATM cards at the airport, but that was okay. If the police were alerted about us, they knew we landed there anyway. We can't make that mistake again, however."

Cat sucked in her breath. "What are you suggesting?"

Angie stopped at a wall map of the metro system. "You have a lot of cash on you, don't you?"

They huddled together as Cat opened her wallet. "Seventy dollars and a couple dollars in coins. Plus, I always carry emergency money." She slid some folded cash halfway out from under her driver's license. "Two hundred dollars in case ATMs break down."

"Very smart," Angie said as she went through her own wallet. She had a $153. "Four hundred twenty-three dollars, plus the two hundred euros we got from the ATM, minus the cost of the train tickets. That's a fortune. We'll be just fine." She looked at the metro map and pointed to the Ottaviano station. "I think it's time for dinner, don't you?"

"Dinner?" Cat looked with dismay from the map to the turnstiles that led to grimy, graffiti-filled boarding areas.

The doorbell rang. Paavo tightened the sash on his bathrobe and went to answer it. After Serefina's call, he put on coffee, then showered and shaved to get ready to go to Homicide.

Nobody ever came to his house except Angie. Unless—a great possibility entered his mind—Angie had come to her senses and taken a plane home. He flung open the door.

Angie's eldest sister, Bianca, stood on the porch. "Good morning," she said cheerfully. "I brought you some fresh muffins for breakfast." She held up a pastry bag.

Chubby, in her forties, with straight chin-length brown hair cut in the same practical bob that she'd probably worn for the past twenty years, Bianca was the most perennially good-natured person Paavo had ever met. Sometimes, he had to admit, it was really hard to take. Warm, kind, and motherly, she was completely uninterested in politics, religion, world health, or even fashion—her clothes were as plain and practi-

cal as her hairdo. The only thing she seemed to genuinely care about her was family.

At least with the Amalfis she was never bored.

"What a surprise," Paavo said, finding his voice.
"Come in. I guess you're here to ask about your sisters."

"I can't begin to understand what's going on!" She
gave him the muffins, and immediately began fluffing
the pillows on his sofa. Paavo's yellow tabby, Hercules, awoke with a start from his favorite corner. Back
arched, tail fluffed, he marched from the room in a
huff. "Mamma's so worried about the girls she can
hardly talk. They're chasing a potential murderer! My
God! Anyway, Mamma sent me here to take you to
Flora Piccoletti's house."

"She could have just phoned with the address," he
managed, the bag of muffins in hand.

"She wanted to be sure. And she was afraid Papa
might get suspicious if she kept having secret phone
calls. She's already had a bunch of them. We all have
to be sure Papa doesn't hear about this." Bianca
stacked the magazines on his coffee table and began
gathering up the newspapers. "Do you save the cross-
words?"

"Uh, no," he said.

"Good." She lifted the papers. "Where's your news-
print recycle bin?" Everybody in San Francisco had
several recycle bins of varying kinds. It was the only
way to get garbage picked up without going through
the third degree.

He took the papers from her. "You don't have to do
this."

She took the papers back. "It's nothing. I enjoy it. Besides, it helps take my mind off . . . " Her eyes turned
teary. "What in heaven's name were they thinking?
If anything happens to them . . . " She bustled to the

kitchen to find the newspaper stacks on her own. "I can understand Angie, but Cat?"

Paavo followed her, and couldn't help cringing at the truth of her last words. "Coffee?"

"Sounds good. And I bought enough muffins for both of us. You get ready to go. I'll take care of everything here."

Muffins had all the appeal of sawdust to Paavo under the circumstances. He escaped to his bedroom. Once dressed, he called Yosh to fill him in.

"You're taking a civilian with you?" Yosh asked.

"It'll be okay. She's calm and mature." Paavo peeked into the kitchen, where Bianca was at the moment washing down the outside of his refrigerator. He hadn't even known that the outsides of refrigerators were supposed to be washed. He sucked in his breath. "Anyway, their mothers are friends. Having someone Flora Piccoletti knows with me when I question her about her two sons will be a good thing."

"You may be right. Keep me posted."

"Will do." He gently took the Formula 409 out of Bianca's hands as she was about to shoot it at his light switches. In this old house, she'd probably cause a short.

"I see finger marks," she explained.

"They're part of history." He understood all this hubbub was a reaction to being upset. He led her to a kitchen chair. "Coffee and muffins await."

Chapter 10

"*Ecco* Da Vinci." The cab driver pointed to a restaurant as he double-parked.

Angie thanked the driver and paid him, including a generous tip. Unsure which way to go after their metro ride to the northwest part of Rome, near the Vatican, they found a driver who knew the restaurant. It was on the Via Porta Cavalleggeri, facing the high, yellow-beige walls of Vatican City. The street was busy with shops—clothes, handbags, jewelry, appliances, gelato, a *farmacia*, a deli—and the small, unimposing restaurant owned by Marcello Piccoletti: Ristorante Da Vinci.

Inside, the dining room was fairly dark, the walls a dingy off-white, with dark wood-stained trim around the doors and windows. Wooden tables and chairs were situated close together in a way that would barely be tolerated in the U.S.

They were greeted by a short, round man with a bald head and wide, black mustache. "*Buona sera*," he said in greeting, and showed them to a table.

Cat immediately requested a bottle of his best merlot. The menu was long, but Angie saw that it was basically different variations of basic food. For the *primo*, there were a variety of pasta noodles with an equal variety of toppings, a number of risotto dishes, and several kinds of *zuppa*. The *secondo*, or entrée, had far fewer choices of meat or fish. The menu listed several rather simple antipasto dishes which came, as the name implied, before the pasta. Salads, small and with less variety, were generally served after the entrée to clear the palate—except in restaurants that catered to tourists, where they were served early to be eaten in whatever order the customer preferred.

They ordered an antipasto of *caprese*—tomatoes with mozzarella, basil, and spices—a *primo* of porcini mushroom risotto for Cat, and linguine with pancetta for Angie. As their *secondo*, both chose the day's special of veal scaloppine with green olives. For dessert, they decided on one that was typically Italian—sliced melon and walnuts, with a demitasse of espresso.

"We made it," Angie said as they clinked their wineglasses together. They both took long sips. Angie could all but feel the drink helping her relax for the first time in twenty-four hours.

"I can't believe we're here," Cat said. She looked around. "Unfortunately, I don't see Marcello. I was hoping he'd come out to say hello. He'd better be here."

"Let's eat a bit before we ask about him," Angie said. She didn't want disappointment to color their meal or dampen her optimism about this adventure. Who could be anything but optimistic in Rome?

They quietly enjoyed their antipasto and *primo*.

In the restaurant, a family with a couple of children were settling in at one table, and near them an elderly couple were just leaving. Two men who looked like they might be father and son were huddled together having an intense conversation, and sitting alone was a young priest. He was blond and wore glasses with thin gold rims. His long, narrow face was intriguing enough to catch Angie's attention, as it bore a troubled, almost moody, demeanor.

She was speculating on what the problem might be when the waiter, the same rotund man who had seated them, brought out their veal scaloppine.

Angie nodded at Cat, who nodded back.

"The linguine and risotto were excellent," Angie said to the waiter. "I'm Angelina Amalfi and this is my sister, Caterina Swenson."

He stood as if at attention. "I am Bruno Montecatini." He patted his bulbous stomach. "I am the maitre d' of this dining room."

Cat spoke up. "We are friends with Signore Piccoletti. Is he here this evening?"

Montecatini looked surprised. "Signore Piccoletti?" he repeated, confused.

Cat and Angie glanced at each other. "Marcello Piccoletti," Cat said. "The owner."

"Ah!" The maitre d' said. "I believe he's in his summer home in San Francisco."

Cat cocked her head. "That's where we're from." Her voice was completely matter-of-fact. "He just left there for Rome. Please tell him we're looking for him."

"I will do so . . . if I see him," the man said.

"And what about his brother, Rocco?" Angie asked casually.

"Rocco?" Montecatini again seemed uncomfortable with the question. "I have never met his brother. Excuse me, please."

With that, his stubby legs took him away quickly. As Angie watched him go, something made her glance at the other diners. The family paid no attention, but both the priest and the father and son were watching. All three men looked away when her eyes met theirs.

"That was strange," Cat whispered to Angie, drawing back her attention. "Everyone in San Francisco thinks he's here—and here, they think he's there. I don't like it. Why didn't he tell me about this?"

"All right." Angie faced her sister squarely. "Just what is going on between you and Marcello?"

Cat's wide-eyed innocence was completely fake. "When I was a kid, I'd go to his house with Mamma and play with his little sister, Josie. I knew the whole family, but then we lost touch for nearly thirty years."

"You didn't answer my question." Angie's tone was firm.

"I have no idea what you're talking about," Cat filled her mouth with veal and mushroom.

"I think you do," Angie argued. "You said he wouldn't go to Italy without telling you. What's that supposed to mean?"

Cat swallowed. "I don't like what you're implying! Marcello is hardly my type. What about Charles? Damn! I'd better call him soon."

Angie was developing some definite ideas about Cat and Marcello, but a restaurant was hardly the place to confront her sister.

"We've been so hung up on finding Marcello," Angie said after a while, "that we've forgotten what started all this today—or I should say yesterday, since we lost a day traveling."

"It feels like we lost a month," Cat lamented. She'd practically cleaned her plate. Notwithstanding the drab decor, the food was quite good.

"It began with someone, presumably Marcello, accusing you of stealing from his house."

"Yes. Or, I should say, that's what the office manager, Meredith Woring, claimed was said." Cat grimaced. "What a bitch! The whole thing is ridiculous!"

"Of course it is. But why would Marcello, or anyone, have said such a thing? And it couldn't have been Marcello, since he was already in Italy."

"Was he?" Cat wore a thoughtful frown. "The more I think about it, the more convinced I am that it was

Marcello I followed. He might have used Rocco's passport if the two still look alike. And keep in mind, a passport is good for ten years, so the photo could be an old one. But why would Marcello travel using Rocco's identification? That doesn't make sense either!"

Just then the scraping of chairs caught Angie's attention. The father and son got up to leave and were heading for the door when the son abruptly turned toward the kitchen. Bruno Montecatini met him in the doorway and the two men shook hands before the son followed his father out.

Angie thought he must have really liked the meal until she saw the waiter surreptitiously slip something into his pocket. Just what was going on here?

"How does that idea strike you, Angie?" Cat repeated. "That Marcello used Rocco's identification."

"That's as good as anything," Angie admitted, puzzling over the strange interplay she'd witnessed. "Even if it was Marcello you followed, why would he have called Meredith with such an accusation? Why lie and say you stole the chain? Especially if he had it himself."

"It's illogical!" There were few things Cat hated more than lack of logic. "I believe whoever did it wanted me fired. For all I know, Meredith made the whole story up so she could sell Marcello's house herself and get my commission! On a five and a half million dollar sale, it could be big enough to kill over."

"You really think she made it up?"

"I guess . . . not really," Cat said wearily. "One of the owners, Jerome Ranker, was in the office when she fired me, and I went to him. He said Meredith was overreacting, to go home and try not to think about it. He promised to talk to her, and he was sure I'd get back my job and good name soon."

"But you didn't go home," Angie prodded.

Cat flushed. "No."

Angie remained silent as their dessert was served. "Have you ever seen the chain you're supposed to have taken?"

Cat nodded as she speared a melon. "Yes. It's about a foot and a half long, with rusted metal links and large loops at the ends for wrists or ankles. It looks like something you'd find in a junkyard, except that Marcello kept it in a black leather box."

"The box you saw him carry as he ran from the house."

"I think so," Cat admitted.

Angie couldn't believe what she'd just heard. "You think? First you guessed it was Marcello, and now you only guess it was the box? What's going on here?"

"Well, it's a good guess because . . . " Cat put down her fork.

Angie waited. "Because?"

Cat explained that she'd looked in Marcello's bedroom safe and the chains were gone.

"Are you telling me you know the combination to his safe?" Angie could hardly believe it. "Is he aware of that? No wonder he thinks you stole it!"

Cat archly lifted her eyebrows. "No, he doesn't know that I know. In any event, as a realtor, I am thorough."

And as a sister, Angie knew when Cat was lying through her teeth.

With each question, the tension between them increased.

It was time to go. As they paid for the meal, Angie was surprised to see that the tables around them were now empty.

They were the last to leave that night.

Chapter 11

Paavo drove Bianca to Flora Piccoletti's house in his Corvette. Angie had given it to him for Christmas because she was worried about the old car he'd been driving. He'd once mentioned that, years ago, he enjoyed watching the TV show *Miami Vice*, in which Don Johnson played a cop who drove a Corvette—rather ridiculous in hindsight. He guessed those comments stayed with Angie. When he let himself think about the car, it seemed an awful indulgence. Most of the time, though, he simply enjoyed it.

Bianca was still fussing, even as she sat in the car. She took out a Kleenex and used it to shine the knobs on the heater and radio controls. Paavo half expected her to start washing windows—the outside ones. He asked her about Flora Piccoletti, hoping to distract her.

Flora was in her late seventies and in good health. The family was large, but not close, and she had lived very much cut off from the others since her favorite sister became afflicted with dementia. No one knew what Flora's sons were up to, and the daughter, Josie, had been estranged from her mother for years.

"She's a tough old thing," Bianca said. "She and Mamma were friends years back, but then she got more and more sour about the world. Mamma found her tiresome, especially as Papa's money grew. Flora was always bitter that her husband died before he became rich. I think she expected her children to make it up to her."

"Did they?"

Bianca opened his glove compartment and started to stack the papers inside it neatly—maps on the bottom, registration next, gas card receipts on top. "I never heard that they did. In fact, I think they all pretty much took off and left Flora on her own. Mamma hasn't heard from her in years, but then, leopards don't change their spots, do they?"

"No," Paavo said, "I guess not."

"Do you need to keep two-month-old receipts?"

He reached over and shut the glove box. "Leave them."

She folded her hands and stared out the side window. "You're worried about Angie, aren't you?"

"Shouldn't I be?" he asked. "She's following someone who well may be a murderer. It's insane. Sometimes, I don't understand your sister at all."

"Don't worry about her," Bianca said. "She knows what she's doing, and she'd never take an unnecessary chance. Besides, Cat is with her."

"Oh, that makes me feel a whole lot better," Paavo said.

"I'm glad." Bianca smiled, and Paavo wondered if she really didn't understand sarcasm. "Are you eating all right? Getting enough sleep?" She wrapped a fresh Kleenex around her forefinger, dabbed spit on it, and began to rub it along the seam where the dash and windshield met—that little groove where dust and dirt could collect and was impossible to get out short of using a toothbrush. She used a fingernail.

Paavo drove faster.

"Angie said she really likes your little house, by the way," she said, her brow furrowed in concentration as she tried to get out some infinitesimal grit that lodged in the groove.

"Once we're married, we'll have to move," Paavo said. "My place isn't big or modern enough for Angie."

"When she was a little girl, she loved to make cute little cardboard houses for her dolls. For herself, she'd draw chalk marks as her 'house' out on the sidewalk or in our backyard. I guess that's what came of living with four older sisters and always sharing a bedroom. She wanted her own space."

He thought about what Bianca had told him. "Are you saying she might be happy simply moving into my place?"

Bianca came him a sidelong glance. "I wouldn't go that far."

Flora Piccoletti's home was on Vallejo between Polk and Larkin, at the foot of Russian Hill. It consisted of two flats over a garage. They walked up the stairs and looked at the large brass numbers on the doors. Paavo rang the doorbell. Bianca stood smoothing her jacket and picking off minuscule pieces of lint.

When there was no answer, he pounded hard on the door. A lot of older people, some young ones as well, didn't open the door unless they were expecting someone. Between solicitors, Jehovah's Witnesses, and people coming to case the place and rob you, he could understand why they didn't. "Mrs. Piccoletti?" he called. "Are you in there? Open up. Police."

He knocked again.

"Look under the flowerpot near her door," Bianca said.

At the top of the stairs, against the walls of the entryway, were two large cement flowerpots filled with fake nasturtiums, one beside each door. "You're kidding, right?" he said. "That's a cliché. Nobody would leave a key there."

"Flora would."

He tried it, and sure enough, found a key.

He unlocked the door. "The police can't go searching someone's house for no good reason," he said, eyeing Bianca.

"Oh? Okay." She took a step forward, but he grabbed her arm, stopping her.

"You're worried that she didn't answer," he prompted.

Bianca formed her mouth into a big O, then nodded. "Go."

He entered a long hallway. Just past the front door was the living room. He looked inside and saw that cushions from the sofa and an easy chair were on the floor, drawers opened, and a few books and papers strewn on the floor. "Wait here," he said to Bianca.

She inched toward the living room, her eyes wide. "Oh, my God, look at this—" She reached for a pillow on the floor.

"Don't touch it!" Paavo ordered. She snatched back her hand.

He went down the hall to the kitchen, which was also torn up, but empty. A bathroom came next. Empty.

When he reached the bedroom, he found that the room had been torn apart worse than the others. But that wasn't what caused him to freeze in the doorway.

He didn't need to check to see if she was dead. Rigor had already begun. Her lips and skin had a bluish-white tinge, and her opened eyes were unfocused with the strangely sightless lucidity of the dead.

She lay on the carpet, papers strewn around her. Her nightgown was twisted around her body and had ridden high on her thighs. Her legs were skinny, the skin sagging as if she'd started to shrink within her own body. A pale blue terry-cloth strip was around her neck. For a moment Paavo wondered what it was, until he noticed the bathrobe tossed on the foot of the bed. The sash from her robe had been used to strangle her.

That meant that whoever came here might not have planned to kill her. If they had, they would have taken something to do the job, and not relied on what was available.

Her sheets and blankets were half off the bed and on the floor, as if she'd grabbed them as she was being dragged.

"What's wrong, Paavo? Why are you just stand—"

He turned as the sound of Bianca's voice came closer, and as he did, he no longer blocked the view. From the hallway, she could see into the bedroom.

All his life he'd heard the expression "her eyes bugged out of her head," but he'd never seen it so completely as with Bianca. He moved toward her, to turn her around, get her away from the crime scene, when suddenly she let out the most bloodcurdling yell he'd ever heard. Her whole body went stiff, her bulging eyes rolled back in her head, and she began to topple like a statue.

Somehow, he managed to catch her before her head hit the floor.

And, he thought, she's the calm, cool, collected one.

Chapter 12

Via Porta Cavalleggeri had been bustling with cars, taxis, and people when Angie and Cat arrived at the restaurant, but now the shops were closed and the streets practically empty. Still, in the distance they could hear the ever-present sound of Rome's traffic, and the air was filled with the scent of fresh herbs, spices, and citrus. Although night had fallen, the heavy warmth of the Italian sun lingered, a tangible thing that one could almost reach out and touch.

Dinner at Da Vinci's had come to over ninety euros, thanks mainly to Cat's wine. Since their ATM money was evaporating right before their eyes, and the Hotel Leonardo was less than a mile away, they decided to walk.

Angie hugged her jacket close. She had the alarming sense of being watched, but that was silly, she thought. It was just the circumstance. Still, she paid close attention to the surroundings.

The direct route from the restaurant to the hotel led them through a tunnel. It had sidewalks, but at that time of night, no one was using them. Widely distanced yellow lanterns cast an eerie glow onto the black tunnel walls. "No one's in here but us and the muggers," Cat muttered unhappily as she and Angie clutched each other and walked as fast as they could.

Behind them they heard the echo of footsteps.

They paused and listened. The footsteps began to move faster, as if running toward them. Some people say brothers and sisters can often read each other's minds. Cat and Angie could have proven that was so because they didn't waste a nanosecond checking, they both took off at a good clip, running to the mouth of the tunnel. Soon they were out of it, facing the Tiber River.

Nearby, they saw a police car.

Hearts pounding, they hurried toward it in unspoken agreement that it would be preferable to deal with the police than a tunnel-lurking madman.

Whoever was following them—if anyone had been—apparently didn't like seeing the cop car either because when they turned to see who emerged from the tunnel, there was no one.

A bridge led over the Tiber, and in record time they reached the hotel. Angie had heard of running the four-minute mile; she felt they'd just walked one.

As they stepped through the entrance, she glanced back. A dark shadow darted into the doorway of the building next door. It meant nothing, she told herself. Rome was filled with people. It was just a coincidence that someone had reached his destination just as she turned around.

Still, relief filled her as they approached the front desk. Their search was almost over.

Almost, but not quite. Signore Piccoletti still hadn't returned.

"Now what?" Cat asked. "I'm so tired I can hardly see straight."

Angie spotted a phone booth just off the public restrooms. "Why don't we call home and see if things are any better," she suggested.

Cat went first, calling collect to talk to Serefina, Ken-

ny, and Charles. As Cat spoke, Angie saw a familiar
face approach the front desk. She racked her brain as
to where she had seen him, then realized he was the
elder of what had appeared to be the father and son
duo at the restaurant that evening. He asked the clerk
something. The clerk picked up the house telephone,
waited, then shook her head.

He backed away, disappointment on his face. Angie
couldn't help but wonder if he was looking for Marcello, too. He turned and took in the people in the bar
area. As his gaze swept her way, she faced the wall,
pressing herself between it and the phone booth.

When she turned around again, he was gone.

Cat hung up and stepped out. "Mamma told Papa
we're in Las Vegas, so if you call home and he answers,
don't forget. She wants us home, but added she'll send
money if we need it. Also, she thinks we're staying in a
luxury suite at the St. Regis."

Angie nodded. Sometimes it was difficult keeping
all the family's white lies straight, but she also recognized why both sides of the Atlantic were spinning
them.

She attempted to call Paavo, but after his cell phone
rang it went to messaging. Since she was making a collect call, she couldn't even leave a message.

In a corner of the lobby was a small bar with several
tables with a view of the registration desk.

"I suppose we could sit there," Cat said. "We'll have
to order some drinks, though."

Angie agreed. "It's not as if we have anywhere to
go."

They each ordered a limoncello, a liqueur said to
have originated in the Sorrento-Capri area. The bartender brought them to their table with a bill.

When Angie glanced at it, she could hardly believe
what she saw. "Since the euro, the price of everything

has skyrocketed. These drinks alone are costing us about eight dollars each."

"Eight?" Cat looked appalled. "I thought it was made from lemons, not gold."

Angie opened her wallet. Where in the world had all their money gone so quickly? "We might need help. Hasn't Mamma said something about a cousin in Rome?"

"I met him once." From Cat's expression, it hadn't been a pleasant encounter. "We don't talk about him."

"Well, I guess it won't matter. It's late. Marcello should show up soon," Angie said, more as an affirmation than from any knowledge of the man. "We'll get this straightened out right away."

"Right," Cat said with a groan. "But what do we do in the meantime?"

At least she didn't throw up, Paavo thought, but Bianca's reaction to seeing what a violent murder looked like in real life had included just about everything else, from faints to prayers to tears. He could well imagine what her parents and husband would say to him next time they met. Yosh had been right about taking a civilian with him.

Why had Flora been killed? And when? Was it before the murder in the Sea Cliff or after? And if after, did that mean the murderer was still in the city and not in Italy after all? Or were there two murderers?

When the M.E. arrived, he borrowed one of their blankets to bundle up a now stone-faced Bianca into a taxicab. He sent her straight home after calling her husband to tell him what had happened.

A couple of hours later Paavo had concluded his canvass of neighbors, and the CSI team was just finishing up when he heard the slapping sounds of sandals against bare feet coming up the outside steps. He turned, and the sinking, desperate, get-me-the-hell-out-of-here feeling that had struck earlier when he saw Bianca hit again. Twofold.

It was Frannie, Angie's fourth sister, the one closest to her in age.

The one who hated his guts and didn't try to hide it.

"You sure screwed this up," Frannie said as she tried to stick her nose in his face. She would have been closer to the mark if, like Angie, she wore platform shoes with high heels, but she was wearing Birkenstocks, so her nose met the knot of his tie. "Mamma's in tears."

"I'm sorry about your sister," Paavo said.

"That's not why she's in tears." Her face scrunched into a scowl. Frannie was Angie's "tough" sister. Skinny to a fault, her hair was permed until it looked like she'd stuck her finger in a light socket. She could have been attractive, but everything about her shrieked of unhealthy veganism and ecoterror. She supported every radical cause that came down the pike, and he wouldn't have been surprised to hear that she was arrested for taking part in an illegal PETA activity. Or Earth First. Or last. "It's because Caterina and Angie aren't on their way home yet. I need you to come with me."

"Frannie, there was a murder here."

Her neck slowly cranked from far left to far right. "With all these people, you can't spare a lousy fifteen minutes to get your fiancée home? Mamma did all the work for you. She's been on the phone all morning and set up everything. It won't take long. Do you love Angie enough to bring her back here or not?"

He didn't have time for twenty questions with this neurotic harridan, but the investigation was at a point where he could leave for a few minutes. "What do you have in mind?"

* * *

As Angie went off to harass the desk clerk yet again about finding Marcello, Cat's thoughts went around and around about being there. She was one of those perfectly practical people who always did what was logical, sensible, and staid. Until now.

Marcello . . . was he the cause?

She still remembered how, as a girl, Marcello would make her eleven-year-old heart beat faster. He was the first boy she ever had a crush on. He was twelve, and she thought he was the coolest thing on two feet. He never paid any attention to her, and by the time he reached thirteen, he was too old to hang around the house when his mother's friends came to call. Soon after that, Cat stopped going to visit as well. She certainly didn't want to see Rocco, who was two years younger than her and a royal pain in the butt.

She'd been stunned when she ran into Marcello at the Wholesale Furniture Mart about a year and a half ago. He was there buying items for his store, and she was there hoping for a miracle. One of her interior design clients wanted a genuine Eero Saarinen chair in a particular style, and she was having a terrible time finding one.

She didn't even recognize Marcello that day, but to her surprise, he remembered her. And flirted with her shamelessly.

All kinds of thoughts went through her head. That finally, some twenty years later, he had taken notice of her. That he didn't seem half so cool now as he had back then. That as an eleven-year-old, her taste in the opposite sex had been abysmal. In fact, as she took in his flashy clothes and jewelry, she was quite put off, not to mention disappointed. Still, being around someone from her youth who was so obviously impressed by her was a huge boost to her ego.

When he heard about her problem with the Saarinen

chair, to her utter amazement, he offered to help. And that was the beginning—

"Nothing," Angie said.

Cat started. She hadn't even heard her approaching.

"It's late." Angie remained standing. "Time for our next move."

Chapter 13

The San Francisco regional office of the State Department was located on the eleventh floor of the Federal Building at 450 Golden Gate Avenue. Frannie strode from the elevator and approached the receptionist as if she owned the place. "Please tell the Regional Director that Francesca Amalfi Levine is here to meet with him. With me is Inspector Smith from the San Francisco Police Department."

The receptionist lifted a note from her desk and handed it to Frannie. "He isn't available, but he left this for you. Kevin Delaplane, on four, will help you."

Frannie took it, but didn't look happy. "Hmm. Well, I guess that'll work."

She and Paavo rode down to the fourth floor. There, she handed the receptionist the note. "The Regional Director said Mr. Delaplane will help me."

The white-haired woman scanned the note quickly. "I see. Is your 10-5-39 filled out?"

Frannie blinked. "My what?"

The receptionist's mouth turned down. "Didn't they tell you upstairs? Mr. Delaplane can't do a thing without a 10-5-39. It starts the entire process."

"There's no process here." Frannie forced herself to smile. "I simply need to explain the situation to Kevin Delaplane and have him help me."

"I'm sorry." The receptionist's chin rose. "But we need our 10-5-39."

Frannie's nostrils flared ever so slightly, but then she squared her shoulders, her jaw tight as she said, "I see. Well, that's reasonable. Give it to me and I'll fill it out."

"I don't keep forms here. They're on six."

Frannie's right eye began to twitch. "On six?"

"Correct."

Paavo's body tensed. He was ready to physically drag Frannie away from the receptionist if it came to that. The woman didn't know how close she was to meeting her maker. Frannie's nerves were on edge at the best of times. He feared that adding worry about her sisters could drive her right over it.

She surprised him, however. "We'll take that elevator right over there, and we'll be back in two shakes of a lamb's tail." Smiling with her teeth clenched so tightly she looked like someone displaying her bite to a dentist, she waltzed over to the elevator and jabbed the button. Hard.

"You okay?" Paavo asked.

"I'm doing this for my sisters," she said, teeth still gritted. "For them I can go to the sixth floor to get a goddamned form that I don't give a shit about. No problem."

Management on six had had all forms moved to the basement, and in the basement they found out that the 10-5-39 wasn't a single form, but a form packet, requesting information that went back to grammar school.

"I can't fill out all this crap!" Frannie fumed, flipping through the sheets. "It'll take a week."

Paavo looked it over. "If Serefina was thinking of having the government bring her daughters back, was she told we'll also have to deal with the Department of Justice?"

"That's what you think! I'm going to see Delaplane right now!" Frannie stabbed repeatedly at the elevator button until it arrived.

They returned to four. Waving the 10-5-39 packet in the air, she leaned over the startled receptionist's desk. "Where is Delaplane's office?"

The receptionist's eyes were wide. Just then the telephone began to ring. "Excuse me." She reached for it.

Frannie slammed her hand down atop the receiver. "I said, where is Kevin Delaplane's office?" She gave her bared teeth smile again, looking wolfish.

"It's at the end of the hall, but—"

Cursing a blue streak, Frannie took off in a rush, Paavo after her, and the receptionist chasing both of them.

Frannie found his door and pushed it open. The room was empty.

Furious, she spun around. Heads peered over the tops of cubicles, and some people even stood on chairs to see what all the fuss was about. She glared at the receptionist. "Where is he? Is he hiding from me?"

"No! He's at a training program on improving customer relations."

That was when Frannie lost it.

Angie slept like the dead. She remembered getting into bed thinking, *Chef Poulon-Leliellul*, and the next thing she knew, she opened her eyes, and the sun was beginning to rise. The clock read 6:00 A.M. She couldn't believe it. She never woke up this early at home. But then, Rome was nine hours ahead of San Francisco. For Paavo, it was only nine o'clock, *last night*. No wonder she was awake. And confused. And miserable. She missed Paavo badly. Since meeting him, except for a short stint at a Napa Valley winery, this was the longest they'd been apart. She needed to get this situation settled and go home to her honey—and show him exactly how much she missed him!

Cat was snoring loudly.

Last evening, as it grew late, they faced the fact that Marcello most likely wasn't going to return to his hotel. They wondered what might have happened to him, and a litany of dire thoughts came to mind.

Near the Leonardo they found a small hotel that they expected wouldn't check their passports the way the larger ones did. They were right.

Angie showered and dressed, again putting on her Donna Karan pantsuit and knit top. The knit was itchy and the wool already looked limp. At least her shoes were comfortable ankle boots with stacked heels.

She roused Cat. They had things to do—like find Marcello.

"I feel terrible!" Cat moaned. She flopped onto her stomach, one arm over the side, then slowly dragged herself to a sitting position. She groped for thick eyeglasses on the nightstand, put them on, and gasped.

Angie jumped to her feet. "What's wrong?"

"Look!" Cat pointed at the mirror. She was able to see herself from the bed. "My hair, my makeup! And look at my clothes on that chair! They look like I slept in them!" Her peach Chanel skirt and jacket were wrinkled, and her silk blouse looked ready to revert to being a cocoon for worms.

"You did. On the plane." Angie had no sympathy. She knew she looked, and felt, equally rotten.

Cat ran her fingers through her hair, which was jutting out jagged and strawlike. "The first thing we've got to do is go to the shops around the Spanish Steps and Via del Corso to buy something decent to wear, and some makeup. I need a hairdresser. And let's find a better hotel. I'm not crazy about this one."

"How long do you expect to be here?" Angie asked, alarmed. "I've got a wedding to plan and I've got to be back in San Francisco on Monday."

"Hah! You and that wedding. We're all going to be a hundred years old before you get it worked out," Cat scoffed, starting her morning face exercises. Between opening and closing her mouth wide, she asked, "What in the world do you need to do on Monday?"

Angie, who had been irritated at Cat's reaction to her wedding dilemma, suddenly smiled. "I have an interview. I'm being considered to co-author a cookbook with one of the best known chefs in the world—Jacques Poulon-Leliellul."

"Who?" Cat tilted her face to the ceiling. *"Pooh-lone-lay-loo?"* She rolled back her eyes and stuck out her tongue.

"No! *Pooh-lon-leh-lee-ai-luhl.* Do you know how ridiculous you look?"

Cat sneered. "Do you know how ridiculous his name sounds? It's as if you're saying ee-ai-ee-ai-oh, but with *l*'s in front of it. Like 'Old McDonald's Farm' with a weird speech impediment."

"It's not funny!" Angie fumed. Cat was hard to take at any time of the day, but in the morning before coffee, Angie had the urge to strangle her.

Mercifully, room service arrived with the four espressos Angie had ordered. She feared one each wouldn't be enough.

As she drank her first cup, she studied her sister curiously. "We shouldn't do anything but find Marcello," she said.

"Of course, but I detest looking sloppy. I've got it all worked out." Espresso in hand, Cat headed for the shower.

As Angie put down her empty coffee cup, she had to rethink her earlier position. Even *after* coffee, she had the urge to strangle Cat.

It was night.

Charles Arthur Swenson pulled onto his driveway, hit the garage door opener, and drove in. After turning off the ignition, he remained in the car rubbing his aching forehead. He stared, without seeing, at the far wall with its flawless workbench and master set of Snap-on tools untouched in their case.

The day before, after getting Cat's phone call, he'd taken off early from work to drive north of the Golden Gate to Tiburon, pick up their son, and take the boy to his in-laws in the town of Hillsborough, south of San Francisco. Afterward, he'd driven around the city and along the ocean for a couple of hours, trying to understand.

Today, instead of going to work, he'd stayed home waiting for a phone call from Cat asking for his help, saying she needed him. Her call, when it came, was businesslike, cold, and distant. When he hung up, he went for a long drive until he realized he had nowhere to go to . . . only someplace he'd been going from.

As he headed back home, he had to admit that even though he and Cat had been married twelve years, he'd never understood his wife. He was one of the top investment bankers in the San Francisco area, but sometimes he wondered if he had any people skills at all.

If he had, wouldn't his wife have talked it over with him before she rushed off to another country? Maybe asked his advice about the situation? His delicate stomach soured as the legal ramifications of all she was involved in played over and over in his mind.

He reached up and pressed the garage door remote

to close the door behind him and shut out the world.

Why hadn't she taken the time to explain more fully what was going on? He had a dozen questions he'd wanted to ask, but when they talked, she'd hung up quickly.

As much as she worked with people, and spent all day on the phone or meeting them and showing off houses—and before, practically living with them as she helped them redesign and decorate their homes—she rarely said two words to him that weren't completely necessary.

He had told her he'd take care of Kenny while she was gone. He liked being with Kenny on those rare times when the boy wasn't going to soccer or to basketball practice. Or taking swimming or piano lessons. Or having a "play date" or sleepover with one of his school friends. Or doing one of the myriad other things he did rather than being home with his dad so that the two of them could get to know each other better.

He couldn't remember the last time he and Kenny had done something together—father and son—that hadn't been programmed for them by Cat or one of the coaches, teachers, or instructors who seemed to think they knew so much more than he did about his own son.

Maybe they were right. What was it Cat had said to him on the phone right before she hung up?

He finally got out of the car and shuffled across the garage to the interior door to his home. He was only forty-five, but looked a decade older. He was one of those serious, dour-looking men everyone assumed to be much older than his years. His shoulders were stooped, and he wore his forelock long and combed back in a vain but useless attempt to cover the ever-widening bald patch on his crown.

Cat had laughed at the idea that he would take care

of his own son, and said it was impossible.

Impossible, he thought, as he opened the door and stepped into his home. The door led from the garage to a small hallway. A utility room and bathroom were on one side, a large laundry and sewing room on the other. Not that Cat ever sewed, of course. It amazed him when she did laundry. He guessed even she couldn't justify sending Kenny's T-shirts and jeans out to be washed.

From the hallway, he entered the family room. A sixty-inch plasma TV was mounted high on the far wall, surrounded by an entertainment system with theater level sound. Recliners faced the TV. Cat had wanted movie theater seating, but he pointed out that they never had guests over to watch movies, so why should he sit alone surrounded by empty chairs?

It was one of the few arguments that he had ever won with her. Probably because she didn't care all that much.

The house felt so very empty.

He was used to coming home to an empty house. He'd done it many nights. Why, then, did it feel so strange?

Was it because Cat and Kenny wouldn't be joining him here in a few hours, or because he'd be alone for days and didn't really understand why?

He turned on the light in the kitchen.

To his surprise, the doorbell rang. Nobody ever came to a house in Tiburon without phoning first.

Unless it was one of Kenny's little friends. That must be it, he thought, and felt almost happy to have someone to talk to, if only for a moment or two, as he went to answer the door.

Chapter 14

If the Italian police were, in fact, looking for them, they already knew they were in Rome, which meant that if she and Cat went to an area far from where they were staying, used their credit cards to buy a few necessities, and then left, they wouldn't be giving anything away.

They could do it, Angie thought. They were good. They'd do "drive-by shopping" to pick up underwear, cosmetics, and a simple change of clothes.

Outside the hotel, the sun was bright as they looked for a cab. On the corner, she noticed a slightly built man with a goatee leaning against the building, and taking an interest in her and her sister. Why shouldn't he? she told herself. They were attractive women, and he was an Italian male. There was nothing to be nervous about.

Memories of running through that dark, creepy tunnel last night caused her to shiver.

A taxi came by and they caught it. Angie happened to notice, as they drove off, that the goateed man put his arm out as a second cab approached. That explained why he'd been standing there. Or did it?

The shopping area both women knew well was around the Spanish Steps and Via del Corso. That was also the area with all the big designer boutiques—Prada, Armani, Valentino—but they had neither time nor reason to shop there, which was in itself a sacrifice.

Get in. Get out. Get Marcello.

That was their motto.

The first thing they bought were international calling cards. No identification required. Angie had to talk to Paavo. Eventually, they found a pay phone in the lobby of an office building. In this age of cell phones, pay phones were scarce in Rome.

Cat went first. Since it was very late at night back home, she didn't call Serefina. That would have aroused Salvatore's suspicions. She phoned her husband. To her surprise, Charles didn't answer.

"That's strange," Cat said as she turned the phone over to Angie. "Charles must be staying out all night. That man! 'When Cat's away, the mice will play,' they always say."

"Charles is no player," Angie chuckled at the idea. Charles was about as exciting as a bowl of cream of wheat. She began to press in the multitude of numbers required with her prepaid phone card.

"I wonder if he's gone off with some buddies," Cat said, her irritation increasing at the thought. "Maybe to Reno. He does have a taste for poker. Damn! I'm completely miserable and he goes off to have fun. Wait until I get my hands on him!"

Angie stopped listening to Cat's rants as her call connected.

"Angie! It's about time! Do you know how worried—" Paavo stopped himself. "I'm sorry. Are you all right? Where are you?"

Angie assured him they were fine. She gave him the name of their hotel, as well as Da Vinci's and the Hotel Leonardo, which he'd already discovered from Piccoletti's store manager. With every other breath she assured him that she and Cat were quite safe, that she loved him, missed him, and he needn't worry. They hadn't caught up with Marcello yet, but would soon.

"Angie, it's not Marcello you're following. It's Rocco. And their mother, Flora Piccoletti, was murdered the night after the murder in the Sea Cliff." Paavo sounded simultaneously upset, worried, tense, and angry. "I don't know what's going on, but it's nothing you two can deal with. Come home!"

"Oh, my God!" Angie clutched the phone tighter. "I can't believe it. His mother?"

"What?" Cat tugged on her arm.

Angie turned her back to continue talking to Paavo a moment longer, then handed Cat the phone. "Paavo needs to talk to you."

As Cat answered Paavo's questions about all she'd seen and done in the Sea Cliff house on the day of the murder, Angie walked around the lobby. One wall was covered with granite slabs, the wall opposite it mirrored. From a particular angle, the mirrors showed the street. As she watched the passersby, she noticed the goateed man among them, the same man who'd been outside their hotel. Not only did she recognize his face, even though he now was wearing sunglasses, but she definitely recognized his ugly blue jacket, black shirt, and clashing brown slacks. He stood across the street, smoking a cigarette and watching the office building.

It couldn't be a coincidence. He was following them. Who could he be? He didn't look like anyone who would be working for the police.

Alarmed, she wanted out of there. She studied the wall directory of the building. As soon as it sounded as if Cat had finished answering questions, Angie hit an elevator button, then pulled the phone from her. "Paavo, we've got to go"—her mind raced for an excuse that wouldn't worry him—"my phone card is almost out of minutes. But we'll be home soon. I promise."

A bong told her the elevator had arrived. "I love you! 'Bye!"

She grabbed Cat and shoved her in the compartment, then hit B, for basement. "What are you doing?" Cat screeched.

"We were followed!"

The basement parking garage exit took them onto a side street. She hoped that by the time the goateed man realized they were no longer in the lobby, they'd be long gone.

"Wait! Where are we going? We haven't done our shopping yet," Cat said, since Angie was heading away from the shops.

"We don't need to. We're going home. Didn't Paavo tell you that Flora Piccoletti was murdered?"

Cat grasped her arm, stopping her. "Exactly." Her voice was low and determined. "If you would take a moment to think, to be logical, you'd realize that means the murderer is still in San Francisco! It's not Marcello, or Rocco. We're perfectly safe here, and I need to talk to them about the St. Peter chain." Her face fell. "And other things."

"What other things?" Angie asked suspiciously.

"That's none of your concern."

That kind of answer had Angie seeing red. "I told Paavo we'd come home soon."

"Go." Cat turned back toward the Via del Corso. "I'm going to buy some things I need, and remain here until I see Marcello."

Arms folded, Angie trudged along beside her. "Who's following us, then?"

"I think it's all in your head. You know what a wild imagination you've got." Cat looked completely disgusted. "Between Da Vinci's and his hotel, I'll find Marcello today and get this all straightened out."

"Then we'll go home together?" Angie asked.

"Of course."

As they retraced their steps, Angie suddenly shoved Cat into a doorway. "Look!"

At the street corner was a thin, poorly dressed goateed man, clearly searching for someone or something. "That's him!" Angie whispered.

Cat watched a moment and in a hushed voice said, "You know, it's getting close to lunchtime. Since Marcello wasn't at his restaurant last night, he might be there during the day. We should go back."

Angie eyed her. "The metro's just past the Piazza del Popolo."

Cat nodded. "What are you waiting for?"

To reach Da Vinci's restaurant from the metro's Ottaviano station, it was necessary to walk across St. Peter's Square. As impressive and imposing as St. Peter's Basilica was—the largest Christian church in the world—Angie enjoyed being in the piazza even more, enclosed by the curved "arms" of Bernini's colonnade. A hundred thousand people could fit in it.

From there she could look up at the large rectangular building just beyond St. Peter's, which housed the Pope's living quarters, top floor, far right. She had once stood in the piazza as John Paul II came to his window and blessed the crowd.

To the left of it she could see the top of the Sistine Chapel.

Being here, she remembered her Catholic upbringing, the parochial schools she attended, some of the good-hearted nuns like Sister Mary Margaret and Sister Rachel, whom she'd come to truly love, and a few, like Sister Mary Francis, who intimidated her as only a nun could do.

Near her, a group of nuns of the Missionaries of Charity, Mother Teresa's order, in their distinctive blue and white habits, strolled by. Not far from them, a priest in a full-length black cassock hurried as if late for an appointment.

Angie loved seeing the traditional clothes of nuns and priests. She loved this aspect of the Church, the part with the mystery and miracles, the pageantry, formality, and rules. Much of that had been lost in many dioceses as they tried to become more "modern." An inkling of the old, stricter religion seemed to be in the wind these days, struggling to come back, along with the old mass, the saints and their visions, the rules, and even the guilt when those rules were broken.

Something about the serious, almost haunted look of the priest caught her eye, and she quickly realized why. He was the one who'd been dining alone at Da Vinci's last night. He crossed the piazza without hesitation, heading surely and directly toward the Swiss Guards who protected the entrance to the private sections of Vatican City. They allowed him to pass with a simple nod.

"We've still got some time before Da Vinci's opens for lunch," Angie said. "Let's go inside St. Peter's. I'd like to see it again."

They had to go through metal detectors to enter the church, but everything that could set one off had long before been taken from them, so they proceeded with no trouble.

From the moment Angie crossed the portico to enter St. Peter's, she was awed, as always, by the sheer size of the structure. The marble-and-gold-filled church was so massive that the people standing under its dome looked about a foot tall. The tomb of St. Peter was directly under the dome, but many other Popes and saints had been laid to rest in the basilica, both on the main floor and in grottoes below it. The body of Pope John XXIII was in a glass case for all to see. Many chapels lined the side walls, and statues were every-where. Those placed on the walls were actually larger than the ones at ground level, to lessen the perspective of the height of the building. At the top of the walls, circling the entire church, were the words Jesus spoke to Peter, beginning *Tu es Petrus* . . . Each letter was six feet tall.

Angie didn't walk toward the main altar, but imme-diately turned to the right. Before her, surrounded by a crowd and safely behind bulletproof glass ever since some madman attacked it with a knife, was Michelan-gelo's *Pieta*.

Although she had seen it many times, she was trans-fixed for a long moment by the beauty of the Virgin Mary, her face that of a young woman, her clothes heav-ily draped, holding the body of her dead son across her lap. Angie had heard all the criticisms—Mary was depicted as too young, her body too large—but she un-derstood what Michelangelo was doing in creating a face of serenity, acceptance, strength, and innocence.

Yet, even as Angie stood mesmerized by the beauty before her, something felt wrong. She turned her head slightly, half expecting to see the goateed man lurking near once again. He wasn't there, but the feeling con-tinued.

She drew in a deep breath, and turned all the way around.

The priest jumped back into the private staircase to the basement. He was still panting from his dash through the lower chambers and up to the public church area as he watched the two women. Earlier, the expression on the younger one's face confirmed that she'd recog-nized him from Da Vinci's.

Was it an accident, or had they tracked him here? In the restaurant last night he'd heard bits and pieces of their conversation as other diners left and the two finished the bottle of wine and got a little louder. Also, they probably hadn't realized that another American was nearby and could understand their rapid-fire speech.

He'd been shocked by their conversation. From now on he had to be more careful.

Piccoletti stepped back into the shadows when the younger woman turned. She and her sister whispered together, their big brown eyes scanning the crowd and the massive church. He didn't move, quite sure they wouldn't spot him behind this pillar. When Bruno called last night to tell him about the Americans asking about him, he didn't want to believe it.

Something elemental filled him as he watched Caterina Amalfi Swenson make her way from the church. His breathing quickened and he almost followed, but then stopped to cautiously eye the people around him. He had to be careful. He'd worked too hard for this, and far too long.

His mind raged against all that was happening. Against all that had gone wrong. He had to fix it. He would fix it, and no one was going to stand in his way.

His hands clenched in fury. "Why the hell are you here, Cat?"

Chapter 15

"Who'd kill an old lady like that?" Inspector Toshiro Yoshiwara put his morning coffee on his desk, hung his suit jacket over the back of his chair, and rolled up his sleeves. "Who'd they think she was going to hurt? They could have threatened her, sent her off somewhere, even knocked her into a coma. They didn't have to kill her, for cryin' out loud."

Paavo had arrived at Homicide before dawn, unable to sleep well after his conversations with Angie and Cat. Angie said she'd return home soon, and he only hoped she didn't change her mind—or Cat didn't change it for her. He'd used the quiet time to search online databases for information about Marcello Piccoletti, believing he was the key to both murders. "Whoever did it didn't even try to make it look like a robbery. It was murder, plain and simple."

The two had spent the previous day and night on Flora Piccoletti's murder, checking the premises, talking to neighbors working with CSI, and trying to find any clues as to the perpetrators. Nothing of substance had turned up. Paavo found lots of names and addresses. It looked like Flora had kept every card she'd ever received. Some were from Rocco, Marcello, and Josie. None led anywhere.

The only time Paavo took away from the case was

his bizarre foray into government with Frannie. After she'd ripped up the form packet and tried to set fire to a forms cabinet, all the while muttering, "Out, out, damned bureaucracy," he practically carried her from the building, announcing that he was a cop so no one needed to call one. The lone security guard took one look at the raving Frannie and backed far, far away.

Paavo only hoped he'd seen the last of her for a long time.

He again tried to reach Marcello in Italy. If nothing else, he needed to tell the man about his mother's death. Marcello wasn't in his room at the hotel, and the person he spoke with at Da Vinci's suddenly lost his ability to speak or understand English when Paavo identified himself as a policeman. He left messages for Marcello to phone him as soon as possible, emphasizing the urgency.

Paavo's gut reaction told him that the easiest way to solve Flora's murder was to find out what had happened at the Sea Cliff house. Using Marcello Piccoletti's bank, credit, and telephone records, Paavo attempted to trace Marcello's movements on the weekend and Monday, the day he supposedly left the Bay Area for Italy—the day before the murder. Marcello apparently worked at his furniture store all day Saturday, then had a first-time date with a woman who barely knew him on Saturday night. The date didn't go well, and ended soon after dinner. The woman complained that Marcello seemed distracted and scarcely paid any attention to her.

Paavo could find nothing for Sunday or Monday. He called Transportation Security and asked them to find out exactly when Marcello traveled to Rome.

He obtained records from the furniture store to see if he could tell what was going on there financially. Most of the sales were for stock items at low prices and high discounts. A few items, however, jumped out. Several lamps, occasional tables, chests, and porcelain objects sold for what appeared to be bizarrely expensive prices.

And all of it had been purchased by Caterina Swenson.

His thoughts turned to Marcello Piccoletti's relationship with Cat. Client and realtor? Childhood friends? Could there have been more? He didn't like where his thoughts were leading. He made two mental notes: one to question Charles Swenson, and the next to talk to Angie, two people who could shed some light on the state of the Swenson marriage.

He turned his attention back to Marcello.

Eventually, the picture that emerged was of a man who was overextended as far as cash flow. Piccoletti wasn't poor by any means, but most of his net worth was tied up in property—his home, his business, and his inventory, rather than in cash. Da Vinci's restaurant and the furniture store both paid for themselves, but barely. Piccoletti's problem was lifestyle: it was beyond his means.

In fact, he'd sold nearly all of his stocks and bonds over the past five years, when his standard of living took a big jump upward.

Paavo's attempts to come up with any information about Rocco met with even less results than with Marcello. He found no address, no phone number, no one who even knew the man. Only people who lived on the edge took care that there was no way to trace them or their movements. To find nothing about Rocco Piccoletti made Paavo more suspicious, not less.

He stood up to work the kinks out of his back and shoulders from the morning's paperwork. "I finally talked to Angie and Caterina," he told Yosh, and relayed the conversation he'd had. "I can't help but think there's a connection between the priest a couple of neighbors saw near Piccoletti's house and the St. Peter's chain that was stolen."

"That makes sense." Yosh powered up his computer. "I've had no luck finding out anything special about Marcello Piccoletti. The man kept his life quite a secret."

"I agree." Paavo rubbed the back of his neck. "There's not much online either. His furniture store does a steady business, but it's low-grade furniture. The margin is small, the competition tough."

"I want to know where Piccoletti's money came from." Yosh tapped a key. His computer didn't seem to be cooperating.

"Good question. Furniture crates are quite large. They can carry a multitude of sins," Paavo suggested.

"You think what? Smuggled goods? Drugs? I see no evidence so far."

"True, but we'll find out." Paavo's voice carried cold determination.

Giving up on the computer, Yosh went and got his mail. Snail mail, at least, was always available. "Any word back on the vic's ID?"

"No fingerprints yet. It's gone to IAFIS. Backed up, as usual." The Integrated Automated Fingerprint Identification System was supposed to help speed things up in getting fingerprint results, but since all requests were funneled through it, it created its own bottleneck. "Something should turn up," Paavo added. "A high profile case like this, we should have people calling with all kinds of information."

Unfortunately, the phone remained silent.

"Damnation." Yosh was about to drop back into his chair when he froze midway. Officer Justin Leong approached, looking as if he'd just won the lottery. He held a plastic bag high in his hand.

* * *

"This is definitely not a good idea, Angie," Cat complained as her sister practically carried her around the block to a back alley that led to the rear entrances of the restaurants and shops along the Via Porta Cavalleggeri. It was about fifteen minutes before Da Vinci's opened.

"It's a great idea. Trust me," Angie said. The words were no sooner out of her mouth than she remembered how people who knew her best—Connie, her closest friend; Stan, her neighbor, and others—often called them "words of doom."

"Hah!" was Cat's only remark. Angie could almost hear Connie warning Cat about the noose around her neck, the steel trap at her feet, or the band striking up a funeral dirge.

"You said you wanted to talk to Marcello," Angie pointed out, trying not to think of how even good friends misunderstood her. "This is a whole lot better than sitting in the dining room stuffing our faces and hoping he shows up. That could take days. And maybe he'd never let us see him. Once we're inside, we'll find a way to look through papers, check phone records, do whatever it takes to lead us to Marcello."

Cat balked at the alleyway. "You may have a point, but there's got to be a better way to go about it."

"Name one," Angie challenged.

Cat paused. "Something will come to me soon."

"Look at it this way," Angie said, hurrying her sister into the soot-filled and littered alley, "you want to go home. I want to go home. Enough said?"

At the back door to Da Vinci's, Cat squared her shoulders. "I'll try it, but if things get dicey, I am out of there."

Angie was already knocking on the door. A skinny fellow with a black toupee opened it. She'd seen him bussing dishes the night before. "I'd like to see the manager," she said.

"*Sì, sì.*" The man bobbed his head nervously before he turned and ran back inside. Angie and Cat exchanged glances and waited.

Before long the short, round, bald-headed man who had waited on them came to the door. "You wish to see me, Bruno Montecatini?" he asked, resting his hands against a bulbous belly. "I remember you both from last evening. What can I do for you?"

"To tell the truth," Angie said, "we're looking for work. That's why we were asking about Mr. Piccoletti last evening. Marcello told us that if we were ever in desperate straits and needed a job, to come to his restaurant. We're desperate now."

"Desperate?" Bruno looked from one to the other, taking in their clothes, shoes, and handbags. Their outfits might be wrinkled, but they still screamed money.

Angie saw the doubt in his eyes. "Something terrible has happened. Back in the States, someone in the family emptied out all our bank accounts and ran off. The banks found out and closed our credit cards. Until it gets straightened out, for a few days we have no money and no credit."

"What? They can do that?" Bruno looked appalled.

"Yes. We know you've heard how uncivilized and lawless the U.S. is. This proves it. Marcello will understand. We'd explain it to him, if we could find him, but we haven't been able to. And we haven't even eaten today." At the thought of food, her stomach growled.

"Marcello's a dear friend of mine," Cat added in a sweet, guileless tone. "Very dear. We've worked together in San Francisco. He would never turn us away. Please, *signore*."

"What will I do with two people who don't speak

Italian?" Bruno asked, his arms extended, palms up. "Most of our customers are not tourists."

"*Parliamo un po 'd'italiano*," Angie said.

"You speak a little Italian?" Bruno looked skeptical. "I'll have to check with Marcello first . . . in San Francisco. You come back later."

With that, he shut the door in their faces.

Officer Justin Leong had overheard witnesses saying they'd seen a priest near Marcello Piccoletti's house about the time of the murder, so when he found a priest's black shirt and Roman collar in some bushes nearby, he brought it to Paavo. One thing about it was especially interesting: it was a fake. It came from a costume shop called Mandell's.

Paavo drove straight there.

The shop was small and dark, with costumes and masks of every kind filling the walls, shelves, and racks. The manager was a short, stocky fellow with a long brown moustache that looked like a costume accessory. When he spoke, saliva collected at the corners, giving him a watery lisp. A fake moustache never would have stayed on. Paavo showed his badge and asked to see the records of everyone who'd recently rented a priest's costume.

The manager went to his records. "I sold one last week, but I can't help you. It was a purchase, not a rental, and the man paid cash."

The manager's answer made more sense than someone having to answer all the questions a rental required. "Do you remember the customer?"

"Not especially." He grinned. "I can only say he probably looked nothing like a priest."

Chapter 16

"I read about the murder in the morning paper and immediately checked our records. Marcello Piccoletti is a client," Peggy Staggs said as she led Paavo into her office. A petite, green-eyed blonde, she owned the Assurance Security Company. Standing up to greet them as they entered was a hundred-pound brown and white dog with long floppy ears and the widest, most gargantuan nose Paavo had ever seen.

"What kind of dog is this?" he asked, stroking the dog's soft brow.

"An Italian *spinone*," Staggs said with a smile. "He's not much of a watchdog, but he's fun. His name's Guido."

"Italian? Is he from Italy?"

Staggs's jaw tightened ever so slightly. "As a matter of fact, he is. The breed is very special to me." She sat behind a large oak desk and faced her computer. "As for Mr. Piccoletti, he signed on as a client only two weeks ago. I'm calling up his records."

Paavo sat facing her, and she swiveled the computer monitor so he could see it. "It shows that his alarm system hadn't been activated. Either the owner was home or he forgot to turn it on. If it's not activated, there's nothing we can do. Especially when there's movement in the house."

"Movement? What do you mean?" Paavo scanned the information, but it was all in code.

She handed him a company brochure. "We have a service where, say, a person lives alone, we can listen in to make sure they aren't hurt or sick. It's sort of like OnStar's car service. You can call OnStar, but also they can listen to you whenever they want to. That's how, for example, if you're in an accident and the air bag is deployed, they'll try to talk to you. If you don't answer, they'll call the nearest 911 to see what's going on. We do the same thing for people living alone."

"Are your installers able to listen to what's going on inside the homes?" Flipping through the brochure, Paavo thought it looked like a good system except for the major loss of privacy that resulted from using it. Did Piccoletti realize that was part of the package?

"Only while they're doing the installation—to be sure everything works properly. Why do you ask?"

"Just curious." The dog came over and laid his head on Paavo's knee, his golden eyes questioning. Paavo petted him. "If a home has a safe in it, do you do any special monitoring of the safe?"

"We usually put a silent alarm on it, and sensors on a safe to alert us whenever it's opened."

"If it is opened, then what?" He tried to hand back the literature, but Staggs indicated it was his to keep.

"If the home owner hasn't punched in a code to tell us the opening is legitimate, we phone the home to make sure the opening was authorized. If not, we contact the police to investigate."

"Can you tell when Piccoletti's safe was last opened?"

She examined the record. "For some reason, Piccoletti didn't want us to monitor the safe—he had no alarm system connected to it. However, that doesn't stop the sensor from recording when the safe was opened." She tapped the screen.

"Really?" Paavo leaned closer.

Staggs gave a shrewd smile. "Absolutely. People often make requests in the heat of the moment, and later they wish we had information they'd asked us not to keep. We find it easier to keep information we don't use than to resurrect something from nothing. The last time the safe was opened was Tuesday, 1:26 P.M."

That was around the time of the murder. Since someone had called Cat's boss that morning about the chains having been stolen, the safe should have also been opened earlier that day. "What about earlier Tuesday or Monday night?"

Staggs scrolled through the data. "Interesting. It was also opened less than a half hour earlier at 1:03. Before Tuesday afternoon, let's see . . . the prior Thursday, five P.M."

That couldn't be right. "You're sure?"

"Our system never lies."

No, he thought, but someone does. "How did you get the Piccoletti job? Do you know why he chose your company?"

"Yes. He said his realtor referred him. She had an odd name. I can't remember exactly what it was, but it reminded me of one of my favorite singers from my younger days, before he got a little—what should I say?—weird." She smiled. "I'm talking about Cat Stevens."

Paavo swallowed hard. "Do you have the name of the installer at the Sea Cliff house?"

"Len Ferguson. He's been with us about two years."

"Can you describe him?"

"Late twenties, about five-eight, blue eyes, curly sandy-colored hair, a bit overweight."

The description was somewhat similar to the "teddy

bear" a witness saw near the Piccoletti home. "Does he drive a black truck?"

"Ferguson? No, not that I've ever noticed. He usually comes to work in an older Honda sedan—green and fairly banged up."

"Do any of your employees have a black truck?"

"Yes. You can see it from the window." They went to the window, which looked down on the firm's parking lot. Staggs pointed out a black Ford F-250, ten years old. "The installers leave their cars and trucks here and take the company vans when they work."

Paavo excused himself and went outside to the truck. As he used his cell phone to take pictures and send them to Yosh's phone, he felt like a college kid. They were the ones who used features like cellular photographs the most. He wouldn't even own such a high-tech phone if it weren't for Angie, who enjoyed giving him the latest gadgets. Whenever he got a new electronic toy, Yosh, a complete technophile, got one for himself.

But even Paavo had to admit that the phone was useful in this line of work.

Within ten minutes, Paavo got a call back from Yosh. The truck looked exactly like the one that had been parked near Piccoletti's at the time of the murder.

Paavo returned to Staggs's office and asked to speak with both Ferguson and the truck's owner.

Ferguson had called in sick that day, but Ray Jones was on a job. Paavo took down Ferguson's home address and phone number, then tracked Jones down at a St. Francis Woods home undergoing a complete remodeling.

Jones had gotten a page from his boss and was told to sit tight and cooperate. He did.

He was twenty-four years old, clean-cut, and pleasant. He said that he'd loaned his truck to Len Ferguson on Tuesday to get himself some lunch because his car was acting up.

"What time did he take the truck?" Paavo asked.

"About twelve-thirty."

"What time did he return?"

"That's the thing." Jones looked hesitant for a moment, and then explained. "I thought he was just going down to Quiznos, so he should have been back in twenty, thirty minutes. But at one o'clock, when I had to go out on my next install, he still hadn't returned. We use Assurance vans on our installs, so I left. But I was kind of worried about my truck, so at two I called back to the office. Helen, the secretary, said Len was back—but that he'd just arrived, maybe five minutes before. He should have been docked an hour's pay, except that the boss wasn't around and Helen felt sorry for the guy. He'd already used up all his sick time."

All of which meant that Len Ferguson was unaccounted for during the time of the murder . . . and was driving a black truck. Paavo could hardly wait to pay Ferguson a visit.

Chapter 17

"I donna care if you are friends with Marcello!" The fat man yelled, his arms rotating like windmills. "You donna touch Luigi's food! This is my kitchen! You put one bay leaf, one pepperoncini, one grain of salt in anything, and I chop off your hand!"

Angie stepped back. His knife set looked very sharp. "But I know how to cook," she said meekly.

"You no cook! I have no spies here. What you wanna do, find out Luigi's recipes and give them to that *fannullone*, that *sfaticato*, that *poltrone* at the Taverna Rosa? He canno cook his way out of a paper bag. He's *cretino*, no sense of taste. And all he wanna do is steal recipes from Luigi! I donna care if you're friends with *il Papa* himself! I donna want you to touch my food!"

Luigi Pugliese picked up his cleaver and whacked it down hard onto a chopping board, separating a slab of spare ribs into individual pieces with fast, precise chops.

"Maybe we should go?" Cat whispered nervously, tugging at Angie's elbow.

Ignoring her sister, Angie faced Luigi. "We were hired to help you. We won't do anything you don't want us to. So, what do you need done?"

Luigi looked at her slyly. "Anything?" he asked.

"Anything," she replied.

"*Venite qui*," he said, and they followed him to a

nook just off the kitchen, which was a lot cooler than the area near the stove. He pointed at a small, hand-cranked pasta machine.

"You use that little thing?" Angie was appalled. "In a restaurant?"

"It make the best pasta." Luigi regarded her as if she had to have lied about her cooking abilities. "Everything we do is *il migliore*—the best. So you use, eh?"

Angie knew there was an art to making pasta. Most was made in factories with semolina flour and water, usually formed into long round strands ranging from the thinnest cappellini to increasingly larger sizes such as vermicelli, spaghetti, and macaroni, as well as shaped pasta such as penne, ziti, rigatoni, shells, and bow ties.

The type most often handmade used soft wheat flour and eggs. These were the flat delicate noodles that ranged in size from the relatively thin tonnarelli to linguine, fettuccine, tagliatelle, pappardelle, and lasagne, as well as stuffed pastas such as ravioli, tortellini, tortelloni, and manicotti.

Angie remembered her mother agonizing that a cousin's noodles were always lighter than hers. It seemed no matter what she did, Serefina was never satisfied with her own product. A cook had to find the right mix of ingredients as well as the right "feel" to the uncooked pasta dough. From that point, shape alone determined the different taste and texture sensations.

Luigi pointed out the attachments for the pasta machine to form differing shapes for the egg noodles. "One of you can work here," he said, "and the other do the tomatoes."

"Do what?" Cat whispered to Angie, who had no answer.

"Now," Luigi announced, "I show you how I want the pasta."

In the traditional way, he dumped three cups of flour directly onto a large wooden board, hollowed out the center, and broke three eggs into it.

"Why doesn't he use a bowl?" Cat's stage whisper caused Luigi to glare.

Taking a fork, he slowly worked the flour into the eggs until the eggs were no longer runny. Then, using his hands, little by little he mixed more flour into the egg. He kept doing this until he was able to poke his thumb into the dough and have it come out dry. At that point he added no more flour.

Some cooks added olive oil, some added salt, some water, to the egg-flour mixture, but using only egg and flour—if done right—resulted in the softest, fluffiest noodles. Angie was impressed.

"Now," he said, "you clean the board. Then you knead the dough. Eight *minuti*. Donna do it no longer. After, you roll it through the machine. Nice and thin, eh? Fold, then roll it out again. *Due*, two times. That make it better. You use the attachment, *questo*, for fettuccine, but you must cut for tagliatelle. *Capite?*"

"Yes," Angie said. At Cat's bewildered expression, she added softly, "I'll explain."

"*Bene*. I want five kilo fettuccine, and five tagliatelle."

"That's a lot of pasta," Angie exclaimed. "Are you planning to feed a small army here tonight?"

"It's no just for tonight." He tapped his temple. "Luigi alla time think ahead, and I donna believe none of the things you told Bruno. He is a businessmen, not a sensitive artist like Luigi. He is—*come si dice?*—gullible. But I, Luigi, can see through you. So, today, you work. If you come back tomorrow, *allora*, I will be the most surprise of all."

Angie rubbed her hands together. She'd show him a thing or two.

* * *

Angie had Cat mix up another batch of dough while she kneaded the one Luigi had prepared. Cat was not amused at trying to mix anything with her long acrylic fingernails. She kept using the fork, and where Luigi mixed the two elements quickly, Cat took forever.

"I'll show you how to use the pasta machine," Angie said, "then I'll go and see what he wants done with the tomatoes."

"It would make a lot more sense," Cat said, picking globs of sticky flour and egg off her fingers, "if I worked on the decor of the place. It completely lacks character."

"Don't be silly. You can handle a simple pasta machine," Angie said.

Cat slanted her gaze at the contraption. "I'm sure I can handle it, but ask me if I want to."

"Cooperate, Cat." Angie struggled to remain patient. "Marcello will soon learn we're here, and he'll come and talk to us." She then took the ball of dough she'd just finished kneading. "I've been taught that the best way to get an idea of how much dough to put into a machine at one time is to multiply the number of eggs used by three, then separate the dough into that many parts. Since Luigi used three eggs, that means nine parts of dough."

"Nine! It'll take forever!"

"It is time-consuming." Angie's jaw was clenched as she divided the dough into three equal parts, then each part into three additional groups, and wrapped each with plastic so it wouldn't dry out. She took one part, patted it flat, and ran it through the pasta machine with one hand, while cranking the machine with the other. A long, thin sheet came out. She then folded the sheet and ran it through the machine a second time. The sheet came out perfectly flat, and she placed it on a towel off to one side to dry a bit and lose its stickiness before being cut.

"Want to give it a try?"

"No need," Cat said. "It's child's play."

Angie ran two more portions of dough through the pasta machine, then added the fettuccine cutter attachment and ran a sheet through it, showing Cat how to hold the cut pasta as it came out of the machine so it didn't clump.

"Nothing to it," Cat said. "What about the tagliatelle?"

Since tagliatelle was wider than the widest cutting attachment on the machine, the strips had to be cut by hand. Angie took a sheet of the flat dough she'd made earlier, made sure it had lost its tackiness, then folded it into a single roll and cut the roll into ribbons about a quarter-inch wide. "That's all there is to it. Want to try while I watch?"

"No." Hands on hips, Cat tossed a look of disgust at the little appliance. "Go take care of the tomatoes. What a ridiculous way for me to spend my evening."

Just wait, Angie thought, and couldn't suppress the smile that spread over her face as she left Cat with the seemingly innocuous device.

The only good thing so far that day, Paavo thought, was that no Amalfi was waiting for him when he returned to Homicide. He left his cell phone on, and kept checking his messages on his home and work phones for Angie's call. She'd said she was going to come home soon, and he was expecting her to phone from the airport.

Trying to concentrate on the case while worrying about Angie was maddening. There was much more here than met the eye, but what it was, he couldn't tell yet. The danger would come as he got closer, and it was very likely that danger would lead to Rome.

If only he could be certain Angie was on her way home, he could concentrate on the case. He'd tried calling the number she'd phoned him from, only to learn it was some calling card. He left messages, one after the other, at her hotel. She wasn't in the room. The bad news was that she still hadn't checked out.

Lieutenant Eastwood called him into his office and proudly showed a map of San Francisco that he'd taped to the wall of the onetime supply closet. He used large red thumbtacks to show the two homes where the homicides occurred, as well as Marcello's Furniture 4 U store and the San Francisco airport.

"These are the key spots we need to concentrate on." Eastwood beamed at his achievement.

"Right," Paavo replied, clearly bored. He brought Eastwood up to date on the investigation, and was happy to escape the office.

Until he saw the person sitting at his desk.

Chapter 18

Cat was disgusted about wasting her time making pasta. Who did these people think she was? It was all she could do not to grab Bruno Montecatini by his fat neck and demand he tell her Marcello's location. She had to find Marcello and talk to him.

Not only about the two of them. Also about her husband.

She put the pasta dough into the machine and began to crank the handle. It came out in a thin sheet. How easy!

She couldn't help but wonder . . . had her secret not been such a secret after all? Did Charles meet with Marcello? Was he somehow involved?

She let the sheet of dough fall onto her hand as Angie had done. The sheet rapidly grew long, and she moved her hand. This caused the sheet to buckle and one part of it to touch another. Then, to Cat's horror, much like Saran Wrap that folded back on itself, the dough stuck together. The more Cat tried to separate it, the more it stuck. She pulled and tugged. One part stretched until it made a hole. She jerked her hand back to stop the break, and more stuck. The sheet turned into one big blob.

She threw it away and tried again. On the third try she got it right.

Slowly and carefully, she turned the remaining balls of dough into sheets of pasta.

She had mentioned the St. Peter's chain to Charles, but he seemed to hardly listen. Had he paid more attention that she'd thought? Had he followed her to meetings with Marcello? He did ask a few more questions than usual about Marcello, but she had put it down to small talk. At the time.

No, she was worrying about nothing. Charles wasn't the type to actually do anything, no matter what she was involved in. He had to be the world's most passive man. Sometimes she wanted to kick him just to get some reaction.

Oh, well, she had other things to occupy her time and energy.

But still . . .

Shaking off the worry, she took the first sheet and ran it through the fettuccine cutter. It took one hand to feed the sheet of pasta into the machine, another to crank . . . and somehow she was supposed to keep the strands of cut pasta from touching each other and clumping together. Or from breaking into short pieces. How had Angie done it?

She threw the messed-up strands away and tried again.

It wasn't working.

Visions of Charles kept distracting her. How much did he know?

Shoving the pasta machine to one side, she took a sheet of pasta and folded it into a roll the way Angie had, then began to slice it. Rather than the neat, perfect rows Angie created, some of her pieces ended up as wide as lasagna noodles. Others started out the right width at the top of her cut and ended up either too skinny or too fat at the other end.

She threw them all away. Damn!

She eyeballed the dough. It would not defeat her. Caterina Amalfi Swenson was not going to be bested by a bunch of noodles.

Just then, the middle-aged busboy, Cosimo, peered around the corner at her.

Smiling like a shark smelling blood, she crooked her finger at him.

Angie stood in the main kitchen area, looking with dismay at the boxes of fresh tomatoes stacked in a corner. She felt like she'd been parboiling and peeling them for hours, and the stack hardly went down.

It was Luigi's job to cook and plate the meals; Bruno took orders, brought the food into the dining room, and settled the bills; and Cosimo cleared dirty dishes and cleaned the tables for the next customers.

"Cosimo isn't keeping up!" Bruno yelled as he headed for the dining room, four dinner plates balanced in his arms. "I need more tables! Angelina, you do it."

"Me? Bus dirty dishes?" Angie squawked.

But Bruno had already gone.

She hurried out to the dining room, a large round tray and thick washrag in hand.

As soon as she stepped out there, she noticed the father and son pair. Studying him, she realized it definitely was the father who'd gone to Marcello's hotel the night before. She needed to meet them. No table near them needed bussing, but they hadn't been served yet.

She went to the only table that needed cleaning and quickly sponged it off. As she was rushing back to the kitchen, she noticed the young blond-haired priest seated once again among the diners. He seemed quite lost in thought, as usual. She wondered vaguely what weighed on him so heavily. An empty antipasto plate was in front of him. She picked it up as she zipped by.

He started. "Thanks, I mean, *grazie.*"

She skidded to a stop, and with a big smile replied in English, "You're welcome. Sorry, I didn't mean to scare you."

He seemed uneasy for a moment, then relaxed and pleasantly smiled back. "It's okay." His accent was pure American.

She went to Bruno to find out what the two men's meals were, and offered to help serve—strozzapretti with sausage and a red sauce for the younger, and spaghetti with olive oil, garlic, and pepper for the older. She brought them out, approaching slowly as she eavesdropped on their conversation.

It set off all kinds of alarm bells. They were discussing some sort of archeological dig. Her mind raced: Archeology. Ancient Christian relic. It fit.

She needed to hear more.

The younger man caught her eye as she placed his dish in front of him. He gave her an appreciative assessment, and she did the same to him. When need be, she could flirt with the best of them.

A short while later she returned with some bottled water, once again hovering near as long as she dared. Her Italian wasn't great, but it sounded as if they were talking about some pottery and mosaics from the time of Augustus Caesar. She opened the bottle and served the water with more ogling interest from the young man.

"*Molto grazie*," he said, and asked if she was a new employee.

Angie answered that she'd just started that day, and immediately he proclaimed, "*Americana!*"

She guessed her pronunciation wasn't as authentic as she thought. "My name's Angelina," she said. "Angelina Amalfi."

"We are Stefano," the younger man touched his heart, then gestured toward the elder, "and Umberto Falcone."

At her inquiry as to whether they were tourists or worked in the area, Stefano explained that they were archeologists, father and son. As she oohed and aahed with interest, he preened like a peacock. Umberto cast daggers at both of them as he shoveled down his dinner. Stefano ignored the looks, explaining that they worked for the Vatican and were involved in excavations at the Forum, right near the Mamertine Prison.

"Oh, that is sooo interesting!" Angie gushed. "What fascinating work it must be."

"Well . . . it's a job," he said with obviously false modesty.

"No, you have to know a whole lot to do that kind of work!" She held her hands up and clenched together like she'd seen teenage fans of boy pop singers do. She hoped she looked sufficiently awe-stricken. "Is there still much left to find? I would have thought it had been all dug up by now."

"We go very deep," Stefano boasted. "We're finding things from the time of Christ."

"How incredible." Angie batted her lashes. "Tell me, do you ever find religious relics?"

Just then two policemen walked into the restaurant. They stood near the doorway and perused the diners.

"Excuse me," she mumbled. Head down, she pretended she was inspecting the floor for stray crumbs and scurried into the kitchen. She had no idea if the cops were there to eat or for more work-related reasons—like arresting her and Cat—but she wasn't about to hang around to find out. Paavo had warned her that Lieutenant Eastwood wanted to send the police after them. While Paavo didn't believe Eastwood could pull it off, if he did, he'd know that a good place to try to look for them would be Marcello's restaurant.

Hiding behind the door, she watched them.

"Go take care of the customers!" Bruno ordered.

"I feel sick," she said. "You go."

Mouth wrinkled, he eyed the police a moment before deciding, "The customers are fine."

Fortunately for those customers, the cops were there less than five minutes.

Not long after that, the dinner crowd began to dwindle, and the archeologists had gone without ever answering her question. Angie sank into a chair, exhausted from peeling tomatoes, busing dishes for Cosimo, and waiting on tables with Bruno.

When she caught her breath enough to look around, she was surprised that Cat hadn't appeared. She must have still been working with the pasta machine. Angie knew it could be difficult, but she'd thought Cat would have mastered the thing by now.

She stepped into the back nook to see what was going on.

Cat sat on a stool, legs crossed, a goblet of red wine at her side. Short bits of fettuccine that had failed were sprinkled on the table and the floor.

Cosimo was literally jumping from one end of the pasta machine to the other as fettuccine oozed out. He was covered head to toe with flour, sweating profusely, and his toupee had slipped to one side. Little tufts of powder billowed up from the floor whenever he stepped on a good-sized spill.

On the table, sheets of pasta looked as dry as ancient parchment, and several balls of dough were all but mummified.

Only a few minuscule mounds of perfectly shaped fettuccine lay on a towel.

"Cat! What's going on?"

She took a sip of her wine and heaved a sigh before answering. "Cosimo isn't very good at this, I'm afraid."

Chapter 19

"No one knows exactly when Peter first came to Rome, but it was probably around 42 A.D.," Maria Amalfi Klee said to the homicide inspectors who had gathered close to listen to her story. "When Paul wrote his letter to the Romans in 57 A.D., he was addressing a large community. It can only have grown that way because Peter was there teaching." Her eyes were large and shining as she relayed this information. She faced Paavo. "Don't you agree?"

"Sure." He wasn't about to argue. He should have known he couldn't spend the entire afternoon without another Amalfi trying to help him do his job. Maria was Angie's third sister—the one so religious she once wanted to become a nun.

The other detectives curiously studied Maria as she sat at his desk and addressed them all. She may have been the most purely beautiful of all the sisters. Her jet black hair reached her waist. She often wore it in a single braid, but today it hung loose and straight. Her eyes were almost black, her skin a flawless olive shade, and she used no makeup except for lipstick and a little blush. While Angie's sister Frannie looked anorexic, Angie and Cat worked to keep their weight down, and Bianca had surrendered the battle altogether, to a man's eye Maria's build was perfect. Lush and cur-

vaceous, she played up her exotic looks in her clothes
and jewelry, which usually had an East Indian motif.
She favored beaded tunics, lots of bangles, and intricate, ethnic-looking necklaces.

The only problem was that she usually wore an expression she probably considered a combination of
piety and otherworldliness, but reminded Paavo of
someone sucking on a sour ball. She wore it now as she
responded to Paavo's questions about the chain with a
discourse on the life of St. Peter.

"The basilica called St. Peter in Chains stands at the
summit of one of the Esquiline Hill's three peaks," she
continued. "The palace of justice, the Praefecura Urbis,
was on that spot, and nearby stood the Templum Tel-
luris where Christians were imprisoned and sentenced
to death." She made a quick sign of the cross. "It is
very likely Peter was among the prisoners there."

"And that's where the chain was from?" Paavo
asked, a little impatient with the sermon.

"You're getting ahead of my story." Maria cast him
a reproachful look. "There's also a legend that has to
do with the Mamertine Prison in the Forum. It was a
damp, dark prison, and water soaked up through the
floor. It is said that when Peter was in that prison, he
used the water to baptize two guards. The guards freed
Peter and told him to run. Since the Church venerates
the guards as the martyrs Processus and Martinianus,
you can imagine what happened after it was discovered that Peter was gone."

A chill rippled down Paavo's back. "Yes, I can," he
said quietly.

Maria continued, nodding. "As Peter was hurrying
to leave the city, via the Appian Way, he managed to
somehow remove his chains. A woman gathered them
up and hid them in her house, and that's how they
came to be saved. Peter, however, didn't leave Rome

that day. As he reached the Via Ardeatina, he saw Christ walking toward him. He said, *'Domine, quo vadis?'*—'Lord, where are you going?' Jesus told him he was going to Rome to be crucified again. Peter said he would follow him there, but then Jesus disappeared." Maria's voice turned very soft. "At that moment, Peter knew he had to return to Rome, and that he would be the one who was crucified."

Paavo knew this part of the story. "Peter returned and was captured again and martyred on Vatican Hill."

Maria nodded. "The Roman historian Tacitus writes how Nero mingled with the people disguised as a chariot driver and raced in his private stadium, which was opened to the Roman public for the occasion. The audience mocked and scorned those who died. Some of them were covered with animal skins and were torn apart by dogs, or were hanged on crosses, or when the sun set they were burned alive to light up the night sky."

Yosh visibly winced at the image.

Paavo felt disgust, and wondered what terrible thing it said about mankind that two millennia later people were still being killed and persecuted for their beliefs.

"The Roman chain that the woman saved was revered," Maria said. "It was housed in an early church on the spot where Peter was held prisoner. Later, on that spot, the present basilica was erected, and the chains that had bound Peter in Jerusalem when the angel visited and set him free—it's in the 'Acts of the Apostles'— were also brought to Rome. That's why the chain displayed at the altar today has two parts to it. The first has twenty-three rectangular links attached to a larger link for the neck; the second has eleven links, plus larger links for the wrists."

"Is it possible," Paavo inquired, "that more chains exist?"

Maria studied him closely. "Certainly it is. Peter was imprisoned several times. He came to Rome for a reason, suffered and died there. Relics or artifacts of the event are sacred. And in Rome"—her eyes seemed to darken—"they must remain."

"What do you mean?"

"You're getting into the heart of the Roman Catholic faith—my faith—with these chains, Paavo," Maria said. "I hope you realize and respect that." She looked at her audience. "All of you. We see Peter as the first Pope, and all Popes who followed as successors to him. That's why Peter is so important to us, and why chains that touched him would be looked on with absolute reverence. Their value would be incalculable."

Paavo and Yosh exchanged glances.

"Now, it's time to go," she announced to Paavo.

"To go?" That was news to him.

"We need to finish this investigation so that my sisters can come home."

Looking at Maria at that moment, Paavo could well imagine her in a wimple and robes. And ready to smack his knuckles with a ruler if he were so presumptuous as to not obey.

Angie and Cat were shooed from the restaurant as Bruno locked up. He insisted they leave, even though they offered to stay and make more pasta, scrub the floors, inventory the supplies—whatever he wanted. He was clearly suspicious of the offer, and wouldn't agree to it.

The two women ended up out on the dark street.

This part of Rome was quiet at night. Many of the people here were visiting clerics who came to be near or to study at the Vatican. They were people who also tended to go to sleep at an early hour.

"Well, that sure worked well." Cat's voice dripped

sarcasm. "They got a lot of work out of us, and we got exactly nothing. Good job, Angie."

"As if you should complain! You sat and watched Cosimo work while I did his job!" Angie sniped. "But I did overhear two archeologists talking."

"Archeologists in Rome," Cat said with fake awe. "Whatever will they think of next?"

Both perturbed, they marched in silence toward their hotel when a car pulled up against the curb. Angie froze. Was it just someone who lived in the area, parking, or was it something more ominous? The streetlights were few and far between on this side street, and she couldn't see inside the car to tell who was in it.

Her eyes met Cat's. Both were unsure whether they should run or not—and if so, toward their hotel or back toward the restaurant?

Two car doors opened. A man got out of one side, a woman on the other. She lit into him, and he argued back. She headed down the street, and he ran after her. Before long they reached the corner, turned, and were out of sight.

"Whew!" Angie said. "I guess our nerves are a little shot."

"Don't say shot around me." A chill came over Cat and she hugged her jacket tight against her. "Let's hurry."

The two sisters chortled in relief over their nervousness, and kept going.

Suddenly, from the shadows, a tall, broad-shouldered man stepped in front of them, the streetlight behind him. Angie gasped and started backpedaling. "Run, Cat!" she cried, reaching for her sister.

To her shock, Cat stood her ground. Hands on hips, she scowled. "Marcello! It's about time!"

Angie blinked, and sidled next to her.

"What are you doing, Trina?" Marcello's voice, a deep rumble, sounded both cross and worried, yet he looked at Cat as if he were starving and she was a feast. "Why are you here? Why are you and others asking for me at my hotel and restaurant?"

As he spoke, he moved closer, and Angie was finally able to get a good look at the man. He might have been handsome, but he was too flashy for her taste. His hair and sideburns were too long, his clothes too fitted, Italian shoes too pointy, and pinky ring too big.

"Others?" Angie asked, baffled. "What others?"

Instead of answering her, he thrust a broad chin in Angie's direction and addressed Cat. "Why did you bring your sister?"

Cat put her arms around Angie's shoulders and pulled her close in what could pass for a hug from anyone but Cat. "Because I didn't know what you were up to! Angie, say hello to Marcello."

Angie said a quick "Hi."

"Yeah, hi," Marcello said, his steady gaze never leaving Cat's face. "You didn't answer my question."

She dropped her arm from around Angie. "Why did you accuse me of stealing your chain of St. Peter?" she asked.

Chain of St. Peter? Angie couldn't believe the question. *What about the dead man in his kitchen? Hello?*

"What are you talking about?" Marcello looked truly shocked. Angie didn't think the man could be that good an actor. "I never said such a thing."

"Where is the chain, then?" Cat demanded.

He hesitated. "Where should it be? It's in the wall safe. I showed you!"

"It's not there," Cat snapped.

"How do you know?

"Marcello, when you use the last four digits of your phone number, and you open it when I'm standing right there watching, how could I not remember?" She looked at him as if he were a child.

Forget about the chain, Angie wanted to shout. *What about the dead man?*

"Why are you in Rome, Trina?" Marcello asked, ignoring Cat's question. "What do you care if my chain was stolen?"

Angie's head bounced from one to the other. The way he called her sister "Trina," the nickname she'd use while she was growing up until she decided it was too ethnic and unsophisticated, and the words Cat almost said . . . the two sounded close, with a history. Could they have been having an affair? She found it hard to imagine her sophisticated sister with someone like Marcello, but what else could it be? Was that why Cat had no fear when she thought she was following him to the airport even though the man could be a murderer?

Cat explained to him about being fired, going to his house, finding the dead body, and then following Rocco. He was shocked to learn a man had been murdered in his home. He swore he had no idea who it might be.

"Whoever was in your house looked like you, Marcello. I thought it was you. But when we got to the airport, we were told he was your brother, Rocco."

Marcello's face went through a panoply of reactions.

"When did you come to Rome?" Cat pressed.

"Monday." His answer was almost defiant. "Something came up real quick. Some people wanted to buy land from my uncle's estate—the uncle who gave me the restaurant when he got too old to run it. I decided to handle it myself, make sure they weren't trying to cheat me, you know?"

"You didn't tell me!"

Surprisingly, he looked hurt. "Would you have cared?"

Cat glanced at Angie, but Angie had no reaction. His words sounded genuine, but she didn't know how good a liar he might be. Cat would know, and she seemed confused.

Angie decided it was time to speak up. "The police are looking for us. They want to question Cat, and some people in the force consider her a suspect."

Marcello's glower was harsh. "If the chain is gone, and a man has died"—he glanced over his shoulder as if he'd heard something—"you could be in serious danger, Cat. Someone might think you know more than you do. Where are you staying?"

Even in the dark, Angie could see her sister turn pale. Could that be why they seemed to be watched everywhere they went?

Cat gave him the name of the hotel.

"No good. It's a cracker box. Go back to the restaurant. There's a room above it. I used it when I was young, broke, and first took over the place when my uncle got too old and sick." He took a key off his key chain and handed it to Cat. "This will unlock the door in the alley. No one will find you there."

"We should go back home," Angie said to Cat.

"Back there?" Marcello regarded her as if she was very foolish. "Back to where this all started? That might be the worst place for you."

Cat's eyes rounded. "He might be right, Angie."

"But . . . " Angie stopped. She couldn't ask right then why they should trust Marcello, not when he was standing there. Cat trusted him, but she didn't.

"You'll be safe," Marcello gripped Cat's shoulders. "I'll tell Bruno and we'll all keep an eye on you." Again his gaze traveled over the dark street a moment before he let her go. "I knew something strange was going on, but nothing like this."

Angie caught Cat's eye and mouthed, *His mother.*

Cat looked stricken as she realized what she was going to have to tell him. From Marcello's demeanor, it was obvious he didn't yet know.

"Marcello—whatever's going on, you might not be safe either."

"I know," he said stepping back, away from them. "Go to the room. I'll find you. I've got to go now."

"Wait!" Cat said, "I have something to tell you."

But he was already running down the street.

Chapter 20

"I'm praying for them, Paavo. Praying very hard," Maria said as they rode to the Valencia district. Serefina knew a woman who was close friends with Flora Piccoletti, and had instructed Maria to bring Paavo to the woman's house.

"So am I, Maria," Paavo admitted.

"It's funny," Maria's voice was soft, "how easy it is to take one's sisters for granted. They aren't like parents, who are older and you know you're going to have to face losing someday, or your children, who are beyond precious and remain in your heart and thoughts every moment they're out of sight. Sisters—and brothers, too, I suppose—are just there. They're part of your foundation, your support. You don't pay much attention or even notice them until something goes wrong, then like a table that's lost a leg, you go all wobbly. It's hard to describe."

Paavo saw the sorrow and worry on her face. "I understand what you're saying."

"Thank you. I don't know what I'd do if—"

"We'll get them back."

Maria drew in her breath then let it out in a rush. "Caterina was always the one I looked up to. She could have done anything. Bianca was always there to support whatever I wanted, but Trina would challenge me. Nothing was ever good enough the first time. I'd have to work hard before she'd say 'job well done.' She's the sister I learned the most from."

"Angie has always admired Cat as well."

Blinking back tears, Maria found a tissue and loudly blew her nose. "I still tend to think of Angie as a kid. Sometimes she'd give the nuns a merry chase. Watching their patience with her and her little classmates is what caused me to wonder where they found so much inner strength and inner peace. It brought me closer to God."

"I guess Angie could be a challenge at times," Paavo said with a smile as he thought about her as a rambunctious young girl. The image struck with a pang, reminding him how much he missed her. He wanted her home, safe in his arms.

"I'll never forget the time she was playing with a squirt gun," Maria said with a wan smile. "It went dry near our parochial school, and she ran into church to refill it from a font of holy water. Sister Mary Faustina caught her and marched her straight to the priest. Angie was crying buckets, as you can imagine. The priest told her she might not have known it, but squirting things around her with holy water meant she'd blessed and purified them. Then he had her say three Our Fathers, three Hail Marys, and promise she'd never do it again. Mamma sent me to find Angie and bring her home, and I found her in Sister Mary Faustina's office, having a long talk. Angie went home that day feeling better about herself and the love and forgiveness of the Lord. She looked about ten feet tall, and I don't think she ever forgot it."

Paavo could imagine his Angie, in her headstrong way, doing something without clearly thinking it through, and then having to deal with a major, "Uh-oh, I'm in trouble now," at the consequences.

Unfortunately, she still did that sort of thing.

"Come on!" Angie took off down the street after Marcello.

Cat took a few steps then yelled, "Stop! The restaurant is back there."

"We can't let Marcello get away. Not after waiting all this time to find him!" Angie called back.

Marcello turned the corner, and so did Angie. She wanted some answers.

Why had he followed them? Why wait until after they had left the restaurant to talk to them instead of doing so earlier? And why did he want them to stay in the restaurant itself?

She followed him for three long, winding blocks, going farther and farther from the part of the city that she knew. She turned a corner, and he was gone. Vanished into thin air.

She had suddenly come upon a neighborhood of apartment buildings, most four or more stories high, that bore signs of the constant soot and exhaust that filled the air. Most were rather heavy, squarish structures in stone, brick, or stucco, painted in earth tones—ocher, terra cotta, burnt sienna, as well as simple tans and beiges, with plain windows but often large, stylish doors and doorways.

Cars weren't simply parked on the street, but were double- and even triple-parked. The tiny vehicles, many so small they'd probably be seen as kiddie cars on U.S. streets, were somehow wedged into spaces so minuscule it didn't seem possible without the aid of a crowbar. Only a narrow one-way lane down the center of the street remained open.

Pity the person who was parked on the inside. How

could he ever retrieve his car? It was madness. Angie decided she would never again disparage San Francisco's parking situation.

Skirting around cars and up and down the hilly, narrow streets was exhausting, and she stopped on a corner, holding a lamppost and trying to catch her breath as she scanned the area. Lights were still on in a number of buildings, but she saw no movement of any kind. Slowly, she walked down the block, half expecting him to jump out and yell at her for following him.

Or whoever he'd been running from—clearly he'd seen or heard something that had spooked him—might jump out at her as well.

"Do you see him anywhere?" she asked Cat. "Maybe we don't want to be here. I don't know anything about this neighborhood."

Cat made no comment, which was unlike her.

Angie turned around.

"Cat?" she whispered. Cat wasn't there.

Angie hurried back toward the corner. She looked down the street she'd been on before turning the corner and losing Marcello.

"Cat!" Her call was loud this time, but it echoed in the dark night.

Looking in every direction, she spun around. Where was her sister?

She retraced her steps as best she could remember, but the night was dark, the streets weren't well lit and tended to curve rather than line up in square city blocks the way she was used to in San Francisco. What's more, the streets all looked the same to her, and she wasn't sure which she'd run down. None of them were familiar.

She saw some movement from the corner of her eyes. It wasn't Marcello. He was far from her. She ran in the opposite direction, and after a while stopped.

She was lost.

And she couldn't find Cat.

Benedetta Rosangeli was in her seventies and dressed all in black. She loudly lamented Flora's untimely, frightening death, tore at her handkerchief, kissed her rosary beads, and then poured coffee, put out cookies, and sat down to gossip with Maria and Paavo.

"Tell us," Maria said after she and Paavo each had an obligatory cookie, "What do you think is going on with the Piccolettis?"

"Well . . . " Benedetta's elbows were on the table, and she leaned forward as if about to share major secrets. "Flora told me that the Vatican was interested in buying a sacred relic Marcello had obtained while in Italy."

"The Vatican?" Maria was surprised.

"That's right." Benedetta's head pumped up and down. Paavo's mind turned toward the fake priest people had seen near Piccoletti's house. "Flora had no idea how Marcello got the relic or what it was. But she believed Marcello when he told her it was both wonderful and priceless. Marcello was going to sell it, and with the money, buy Flora a castle in Italy. Flora was quite excited. But then, his story apparently changed. Flora tried to hide that she was upset, but it was clear to me that she was disappointed in him. Again."

"Disappointed?" To Paavo, it seemed a strange word to use. Benedetta pushed the plate of cookies toward him, but he shook his head.

"All her children were disappointments. Marcello, her firstborn, was the last one she most held out hope for, but he was a failure, too." Benedetta gave a shrug over the perversity of life.

"What about Rocco?" Paavo wanted to know. "What did Mrs. Piccoletti say about him?"

Benedetta waved her hand dismissively. "He's lived in Florida for years. Flora banished him from her house. Same with her daughter, Josie. She was so angry with them both she couldn't see straight."

"Why?"

"They made nothing of themselves. She worked all her life to give them the best. After her husband died, her children were everything. Did they pay her back? Never! At least Marcello tried."

Paavo watched her expression carefully. "Do you know of anyone who might have wanted to kill Flora?"

Benedetta gave it careful thought. "She wasn't a warm person, but dead? No, I don't think so."

After what felt like an eternity of walking in circles, Angie managed to locate the main street, Via Porta Cavalleggeri, and from there, Da Vinci's.

She hurried down the back alley to Da Vinci's rear entrance hoping Cat would be there waiting.

She wasn't.

Angie knocked on the door. Maybe Cat had used the key and gone inside.

No one answered.

Despair settled over her, and she sat on the cement steps, heartsick, her head in her hands. Now what was she going to do? How was she going to tell Mamma that she'd lost Caterina? Or tell Charles, for that matter. One thing after the other had gone wrong, but nothing as bad as this, now—

"I can't believe you're just sitting there taking it easy!" It was Cat's irritating voice, and Angie thought she had never heard anything so sweet.

"Where did you go?" Angie asked, jumping to her feet.

"I didn't go anywhere. How could I run after Marcello in these Ferragamos? Look at how high the heel is, how pointy the toe? Don't you know how much my feet hurt already? I've got blisters on my blisters. So, I sat down and waited by the Vatican wall, figuring it was safer there than in this alley. I expected you'd show up eventually. What took you so long? "

"I couldn't find my way back," she admitted.

"It looks like you didn't find Marcello either."

"No, but I think I know the block he's living on—if I can find it again."

"There may be an easier way," Cat said, holding up the key he'd given her. "Let's see what we can turn up inside."

Angie watched as Cat tried to get the key to work. "Why didn't you ask him why Rocco was at his house?" Angie asked. "Or if he had any guesses as to who the dead man might be? Or if Rocco could be a killer? Or where Rocco is now?"

"Because it was clear he knew nothing about it." Cat jiggled the key. The latch clicked, and she pushed the door open.

"I wonder if there's a security alarm?" Angie looked around the walls for a control panel.

"I think Marcello would have mentioned it," Cat said, sliding the dead bolt back into place. "But he's not much into security. He put a system in his house only to sell it."

"Good. I'd hate for the police to find us here," Angie said with a shudder. "Let's see what we can find."

Careful to leave everything in place, they searched Bruno's office. It had a locked safe. Other than that, they found Marcello's name on some official documents and bills, but nowhere else. Leafing through an old Rolodex near the telephone, Angie found a number with a *P* beside it. "I wonder if this is his cell phone?"

Cat looked at it. "If it is, I doubt he'd like to hear from

us anymore tonight. Tomorrow, however, his curiosity might be high again. I'll give the number a try then." She rolled her stiff shoulders. "I'm too tired to think, anyway. Let's find the bedroom and get some sleep."

One half of the attic had been partitioned off to form a sleeping area with a double bed, dresser, mirror, nightstand, lamp, and alarm clock. There was no bathroom upstairs. The only one was located off the restaurant's dining room, and it had no tub or shower. As Angie switched on the bedroom lamp, Cat shut the downstairs lights. A soft glow illuminated the small space.

"I guess that's the only bed," Cat said with dismay at the small size of it. She pulled the top blanket off, creating a cloud of dust in the room. Angie sneezed.

"What are you doing?" she asked as Cat lifted off the next blanket and a sheet.

"Checking the sheets," Cat said. "I want no surprises when I get under them." She even took off the bottom sheet to inspect the mattress. Seeing its many stains, she wished she hadn't.

Angie, meanwhile, had been opening bureau drawers. "Clean sheets," she announced, lifting out some folded ones. She shook them out.

They remade the bed. Then as Cat used the old sheets to dust off the furniture and the mirror, Angie went downstairs, and soon came back up with a broom and dustpan.

She began to sweep the dust from the floor and under the bed. So much kicked up, they were in a haze. Cat opened the window. It looked out onto the main street. She stuck her head out, then quickly pulled it back inside. She huddled next to the wall and whispered to Angie, "Give me the dustpan."

"I've got to dump it out first."

"No. Now!"

Cat held out her hand, and Angie passed it to her.

Cat dumped the dirt and dust out the window.

They heard a loud *"Kachoo!"* followed by running footsteps.

"Who was that?" Angie asked.

"A policeman," Cat said with almost eerie calm. She clapped her hands to get rid of the dust. "I think they really are looking for us!"

She quickly shut and locked the window.

"A couple of cops came into the restaurant earlier," Angie said, remembering Bruno's odd reaction to the visit. "We might not be the only ones they're after."

Cat's eyes widened. "Marcello said someone was after him. And if Paavo's boss is talking to Rome about me, surely he'd also ask them to look for Marcello and Rocco. What better place than here?"

"If it was a cop outside just now," Angie said, "he'd be investigating why the lights are on. I think it was someone else."

"Whoever it was, they're gone. Screw them!" Cat sounded too tired to care about anything more as she trotted downstairs to wash up in the restaurant's bathroom.

Bemused, Angie stared at the closed window for a second. If nothing else, Cat was decisive. She soon followed her sister.

When she returned, Cat was sitting up in bed. She wore faded men's pajamas, once blue and white striped, but now shades of dingy gray. "There are some old pj's in the drawer below the one with the sheets," she said.

Angie found one pair left in the drawer, but the elastic around the waist had been stretched out, the seat worn thin. She decided not to think about it, and with a shudder put them on. Only one of three buttons was still on the top piece. Cat's pajamas had all of its buttons, and she bet the elastic worked as well. She wouldn't put it past her sister to have checked out both pairs, and then refolded the ones she didn't want.

"I wonder who they belonged to?" Angie said with a slight "ickiness" to her tone.

"I'd rather not know." Cat yawned.

Holding the pants up and the top closed, Angie headed for the bed.

"You sleep over there." Cat pointed at the side nearest the window. "This is the dividing line." Using her hand like a hatchet, she marked the division between the two sides. "You stay on your own side. Don't let your feet get near me. Keep your arms to yourself, and if you sleep on your side, face the window. I hate anyone breathing in my direction."

"Do you give Charles all these rules as well?" Angie asked, pulling the covers up to her chin as she lay down.

Cat's response was to glower. Angie took it as a yes.

The mattress was lumpy.

"Poor Charles," Angie said, bounding around, trying to get comfortable.

"Poor Charles?" Cat repeated. "Why do you say that?"

"You and Marcello are having an affair."

"What?" Cat sputtered. "I could never make love to a man who uses more hair product and wears more jewelry than I do!"

"The truth, Cat!"

Cat reached over and turned off the lamp on the nightstand. "Maybe there was a spark of something between us. But I've never . . . I take my wedding vows seriously, Angie."

"You never talk about Charles," Angie pointed out.

"Why should I? He's just my husband."

The words were only half joking. Angie waited for Cat to say more.

"I know everyone thinks my life is about as perfect as it can get," Cat said. A streetlight near the window cast the room in a pale glow. "I mean, look at me. I look like a happy person, don't I? These clothes, this hair, this face, this body."

This modesty, Angie thought, but kept her mouth shut.

"How could I be anything but happy?" Cat said into the shadows. "Have you ever wondered why I have a job? Charles and I have money, more than we could ever dream of spending even if it weren't for the trust Papa gave all of us girls. Charles makes a fortune with his investment banking. But Angie, the man can be so dull. Sometimes I want to put a mirror under his nose to see if he's still alive. He lives in his own little world. I've created another for myself. I'm good—no, great—at what I do, but sometimes . . . sometimes it gets a little lonely."

Cat's words jarred Angie. She'd never admitted anything like that to her before. "So you were looking for excitement?"

"Probably. It wasn't Marcello. He didn't interest me for himself. It was just feeling alive again. Do you understand what I mean? To think that someone could be interested in me, to flirt, was fun. Nothing more."

"And when you saw him rushing away from a crime scene, carrying the object you went to the house to look for, your adrenaline began pumping and you went after him. You felt alive."

"It was stupid. I should have just gone home," Cat said softly.

Angie conjured up a picture of the stooped, slightly balding man Cat was married to, the sort who looked fifty-five even when he was in his twenties. "Do you still love Charles?"

Angie expected to be told it was none of her damn

business, but Cat was silent a long while. "He's stalwart," she said. "Loyal. Trustworthy."

"So's a German shepherd."

"He's . . . nice. A good provider."

"That doesn't answer the question. Or does it?"

"You ask too many questions, Angie." Cat rolled to her side. "Now go to sleep."

Angie suddenly felt bad for her sister. She no longer doubted there was an ulterior motive for Cat rushing off to Italy on this peculiar adventure, but the reason her sister had done it was quite different from what Angie had expected.

Chapter 21

Daly City, just south of San Francisco, was one of the original "ticky-tacky little houses" communities where every house looked like every other one on the block. Since the homes were once cheap, a number of older San Francisco cops still lived there. As the prices of homes went higher, though, fewer young police could afford the area. Fewer still could afford much of anything in the Bay Area unless their wives also worked full-time.

Sometimes Paavo, who'd grown up knowing what it was like to be poor, felt almost guilty about having a fiancée as wealthy as Angie. With her, if he wanted, he'd never have to work again.

She often worried about the dangers of his job. He knew she'd be perfectly happy if he quit the police force and did something safe, like helping her father with the operation of the many shoe stores he had opened up in malls throughout Northern California. Salvatore was considering setting up franchises. The man was at the age when he should have been thinking about retiring, and his heart condition definitely meant he should slow down.

Sal, however, would probably be so bored if he retired that it might end his life sooner than his heart condition would. The idea of being stuck behind a desk looking at financial reports and purchase orders on shoes gave Paavo nightmares.

He chose to ignore Angie's wealth. He'd continue to live as he always had once they were married. Except for the fancy home he knew she'd want to live in and the clothes she'd buy him and probably expect him to wear. He'd already received enough ribbing from guys on the force about the Corvette she'd bought him as a belated Christmas gift. And that was from men who actually envied him his car.

Paavo turned off Highway 280 and drove to the far western edge of Daly City. He quickly located the nondescript rancher. It needed fresh paint, the lawn was half dead, and along the house's side yard, not in the driveway, was a van with lettering on the side: ASSURANCE SECURITY COMPANY.

He rang the doorbell.

"Yes?" The woman answering appeared to be in her mid-twenties. Her face was free of makeup, her shoulder-length highlighted blond hair uncombed. Her gaze drifted approvingly over Paavo as she ran her hand through her hair, lifting and causing the top portion to flop to one side. A short T-shirt over ample, braless breasts showed four inches of a narrow waist. She wore drawstring sweatpants, riding low, and was barefoot.

Paavo presented his badge. "Is Mr. Len Ferguson home?"

Her mouth tightened. "Yes. What's this about?"

Paavo studied her closely a moment. "I'd like a word with him."

She looked ready to ask her question again, but then grimaced and said, "I'll get him."

Before long, a barrel-chested, sandy-haired, overweight man in need of a shave stood before him. "You looking for me?"

"I have a few questions," Paavo said.

"I'm trying to eat dinner."

Paavo's voice chilled. He could care less, and he let Ferguson know it. "You didn't respond to my earlier calls."

"I couldn't take off work to call you, Inspector," Ferguson said grudgingly, assessing Paavo with hard calculation. "I might have had my pay docked. Wife and kid, they cost a fortune." Ferguson forced a smile as he faced Paavo square on. He wasn't tall, but his shoulders and arms were powerfully muscled. His short hair was curly, and his nose upturned.

"Interesting, since your boss said you'd called in sick today."

When Paavo returned stare for stare, Ferguson looked over his shoulder into the house. "Don't tell the wife, okay?" he whispered, then pulled open the door. "Come on in." He sounded as if he was talking to his best friend.

They stepped directly into a living room/dining room combination. The television was on. Ferguson sat down in an easy chair. On the armrest was a TV tray with a plate of cheeseburgers. He gestured toward a ratty gray sofa. Plastic miniblinds, angled shut, kept the room dim.

"I got in late from a job, and I'm starving," he said loudly, then winked at Paavo. As he took an enormous bite from a burger, catsup dribbled from the bun onto his chin. "What's this about?"

"Someone was found dead in a house where you installed the security system," Paavo said as he took a seat on the sofa. He didn't care about Ferguson's lies to his wife as long as he got answers.

"Really?" Ferguson's surprised gaze met Paavo's. It

was smooth, almost believable. "Which house?"

"Marcello Piccoletti's."

Ferguson nodded. "The Sea Cliff. Nice place."

"What did Piccoletti want done?"

"Top of the line. He said he was putting the place up for sale. Lots of owners do things up big when they're going to sell. They limp along, living like shit as long as they're in a place, then fix it all up for some stranger. Makes you wonder, doesn't it?" He licked the hamburger juice and catsup from his fingers.

"Did you ever notice anything unusual about the house or the owner?" Paavo asked.

Ferguson didn't answer right away. "No."

"Was the owner's brother ever there—a man named Rocco Piccoletti?"

"The place was always empty when I was working."

Paavo placed a photo of a 1995 Ford F-250 truck on the TV tray. "Do you recognize that truck?"

"No," Ferguson answered. His voice was moderate, his expression neutral.

"It belongs to your coworker, Ray Jones. Mr. Jones said you borrowed the truck on Tuesday to go to lunch."

Ferguson peered at the photo once more. "I guess it is his. It looks different in the picture. Better." He chuckled at that.

"Where did you go for lunch on Tuesday?" Paavo asked.

"Hell." He hit the TV remote and stopped at a rerun of *Married With Children*. "Quiznos, I suppose."

"The people at the Quiznos near your job said you didn't show up there Tuesday," Paavo said. "Double jalapeños and raw onions on every order. They all remember you."

Ferguson's brows rose. He finished one burger and picked up the second. "They remember that? Shit, I don't know. Maybe I went to Subway. Or McDonald's. That's right, I did a drive-through for a Big Mac. So, shoot me."

"When did you return to work?"

Ferguson studied Ray Bundy, as if the TV character could help him. He shifted nervously in his seat, slowly realizing that Paavo already had answers to a lot of the questions he was asking. "Wait a minute. Tuesday—I remember now. That was the day my car was giving me trouble. It was the fan belt. It broke. I had to get a new one. I went to Napa Auto out on Geary. Borrowed my friend's truck to get there, and ate lunch out that way. Why?"

"Did you drive over to the Sea Cliff area? Specifically, Scenic Avenue?"

"Hell, I was buying auto parts. I have a receipt around here somewhere, I suspect."

"As I said, a man was killed in the Piccoletti house . . . at approximately one-thirty, Tuesday. This truck"— Paavo's forefinger stabbed at the photo—"was seen a half block away at that time."

"There are a lot of trucks like that one." Ferguson put down his half-eaten sandwich. "I didn't go to that area. Anyone who said they saw me there is a damned liar!"

At his raised voice, Ferguson's wife came to the doorway, her arms folded.

"Let's talk about Flora Piccoletti, Mr. Ferguson," Paavo said.

"Who?"

He gave her address.

"Never heard of her," Ferguson said, then looked as if a lightbulb went off in his head. "Wait—Piccoletti, you said? Okay, that's the mother of the Scenic Avenue guy. He asked me to check out her flat. He was worried about her being there alone."

"Did you do it?" Paavo noticed Ferguson's sudden nervousness.

Ferguson's eyes darted. "We aren't supposed to go talking to potential customers on our own. We could get fired for that."

"Why are you answering his questions, Len?" Nell Ferguson entered the living room. "You know you can't trust a cop. He'll get you in trouble, and you'll lose your job! Don't talk to him without a lawyer."

"Shit, Nell. We can't afford an attorney," Len said.

"You can't afford not to have one." Nell looked at her husband with complete disgust.

"Fine," Paavo said, standing. "I request that you not leave the Bay Area, Mr. Ferguson. I'm sure I'll have more questions. You can have an attorney with you before we talk again."

With that, he left the house.

"Aha!"

Was that a man's voice she'd heard? Angie felt movement on the bed, then heard Cat's gasp. Bleary eyes opened to a sun-filled room, and she bolted upright, wide-awake and holding the pajama top closed.

Bruno Montecatini was standing in the room, staring at them. "So, this is why I found women's underwear hanging in the bathroom!"

"Are they dry yet?" Angie asked. She and Cat had hand-washed their things before going to bed.

"What are you doing here?" he roared.

"Marcello gave us the key," Cat said in unhurried, unruffled tones. "He, at least, was a gentleman about our situation."

"Marcello?" Bruno looked confused.

"That's right!" Cat got out of bed looking almost regal, shoulders square, head high, even as she kept a tight grip on the pajama bottoms. The elastic must

have been worn out on hers as well. "Marcello will talk
to you about it later. Now, I ask that you leave our bedroom so we may get dressed."

Bruno eyed them both a long moment, as if deciding
the best course of action, then held out his hand, palm
up. "If you're going to be staying here, I'll hold your
passports so you don't run off with anything when
you're here alone."

Cat gaped at him. "What's to run off with? A leg of
lamb?"

He raised his chin and jutted out his bottom lip as
if he were the resurrection of *il Duce*. "It is our way.
Marcello knows it, and you should as well." Bruno
wriggled his fingers. "You turn over your passports or
you go. If I trust you alone in the restaurant, you trust
me with your papers."

"I have heard of this practice," Angie said to Cat, "although I don't like it." She faced Bruno. "You'll keep
them here?"

"In the safe."

They handed them over.

"There's work to be done," Bruno said. Tucking the
passports in his breast pocket, he eyed them. "You
should get dressed before the others arrive."

Chapter 22

The long awaited fingerprint report finally reached Homicide.

Paavo tore the envelope open, eager to learn the identity of the John Doe found in Marcello Piccoletti's house.

Nothing. There was no match.

John Doe had never been booked as a result of a run-in with the law, had never been in the military, had never had a federal, state, or local government job, and had never requested a security clearance. As yet, there was no law about being fingerprinted when applying for a passport or social security number. At times like this, Paavo wished that those requirements would change.

He called Transportation Security to see if they had determined when Marcello Piccoletti left the country for Italy. They hadn't.

He kept checking in with Missing Persons. So far, no one fitting John Doe's description had been reported missing.

Paavo's suspicion as to who the dead man might be grew stronger. If he was right, it could be especially dangerous for Angie and Cat. He still hadn't heard back from Angie, and could only conclude that Cat had talked her into staying in Italy. He refused to consider any other possible reason for her silence, even as his mind conjured every gory scenario imaginable from his years as a cop.

Damn it! No one seemed to know why Cat was doing this. None of the Amalfis, at least. He tried to reach Cat's husband, but Charles never returned his calls. That, in itself, was suspicious.

For the umpteenth time he reviewed the information he'd collected on Marcello Piccoletti. A picture had slowly emerged.

Piccoletti called his mother every Sunday, his store manager on occasion, his bookie almost daily, several places in Italy, and lots of women. Paavo had talked with every one of them. By the third, he'd found a definite pattern. Marcello was an attentive lover when they first met, and would see them devotedly for about three weeks, after which, all the calls and attention would abruptly stop.

When the women would try to find out what had happened, they'd be rebuffed or ignored. Most were resigned and took an "it was fun while it lasted" approach. A couple remained bitter, and one was out and out furious.

There was no connection with his brother Rocco, his sister Josie, or any close male friend. Paavo was trying to figure out what it all meant when Angie phoned. "Where are you?" was the first thing out of his mouth.

"Still in Rome," she replied.

Relief at hearing her voice warred with anger that she was still in Italy. "Why? Are you all right?"

She assured him she was fine. "Cat's getting everything worked out. We're safe. We found Marcello."

"You can't trust him, Angie!" Paavo gripped the phone tight. "There's too much about him and Rocco that doesn't make sense. Stay away from him!"

"It's all right. He says he was in Italy at the time of the murder. He knew nothing about it."

Frustration filled him. "Angie, all murderers have alibis. All say they know nothing about it!"

"I know. And we're being careful. But, Paavo, have you spoken with Charles?" she asked abruptly.

"Charles?" *Why is she changing the subject?* "No, I haven't."

"Cat's worried about him. She's tried to reach him several times, but he doesn't answer. He hasn't even phoned to check on their son, and Charles dotes on Kenny."

"I'll see what I can find out," Paavo said.

"She'll appreciate it." Her voice was soft, hesitant. Clearly, she knew how angry and upset he was.

God, but he loved her.

He couldn't stay irritated. All he wanted was to have her home and safe. "Angie, I miss you."

"I miss you, too, so much, Paavo!" It was like opening a flood. "I want to be with you, and to plan our wedding, our whole life together. Not stuck here!"

Even over the distance, he could hear the tears in her voice. His heart twisted. This was only the third day she'd been gone, and he felt empty. "You don't have to be stuck."

"I know . . . but . . . Oh! I never told you about my new career!" Abruptly, she brightened. "I'm going to have an interview with Chef Poulon-Leliellul—that is, as long as we can get this mess all wrapped up so I can be home by Monday. That's only a few days away!"

"Chef who?" he asked.

"Poulon-Leliellul."

It sounded like baby-talk. "Pooh-long-lay . . . ?"

"Don't bother," she said, morose again. "Maybe working with a man who has a name nobody can pronounce won't be such a boost to my career after all. And don't you dare say, 'What career?' You know I'm working hard to make a name for myself in the culinary world."

"I know, Angie."

"I just haven't gotten the big break yet, that's all. But it's not for lack of trying!"

"I love you, Angie," he said softly.

Suddenly the familiar lilt, the warmth, the humor that was second nature to her came through. "You do? Even though I haven't listened to your warnings and I'm still in Italy?"

He had to smile, and missed her more than ever. "Despite that, yes. As long as you, now, get on a plane for home. I'll do my best to clear Cat's name in time for your interview on Monday."

"Of course, Paavo. Anything you say."

He hung up not liking the sound of that one little bit.

Before looking for Charles at the Swenson house in Tiburon, Paavo tried reach him by phone at home and his office, then contacted Serefina to be sure she didn't know his whereabouts.

Serefina hadn't spoken to him for well over twenty-four hours.

Paavo made the long detour on his way home.

He could almost feel sorry for Charles. He was the embodiment of Caspar Milquetoast. A man straight out of a cartoon or TV sitcom—the husband and father who gets ruled by both wife and kids.

Maybe, knowing he was out of Cat's reach, Charles had gone wild. A part of Paavo almost hoped he had, but he didn't think so.

As he crossed the Golden Gate Bridge, he glanced back at the city. House lights lined Russian Hill. Angie's apartment was up there, in view.

It made his heart hurt that she wasn't there waiting

for him to stop by, to greet him with her bright eyes and warm smile. She was impulsive. She could be maddening. But she was good-hearted and loving, and his life had never been so rich or his days so happy and worth living as they were with her. Missing her was a physical ache to him.

The sooner he settled this case, the sooner she'd be back home. He vowed to never let her go off like this without him again.

He pulled up in front of the Swenson house. No lights. No newspapers on the driveway. The mail collected. It appeared Charles had been home that day. So why hadn't he talked to Cat or Serefina or returned his calls?

Paavo rang the bell. When no one answered, he knocked. Still no response. He went to the side yard and began to count stepping-stones. Under the third one, as Angie had promised, he found a metal hide-a-key. The house key was inside. Angie's parents had used that technique and taught it to all the girls. As a result, they all knew how to break into one another's homes—except for Angie's, since she still lived in an apartment.

Key in hand, Paavo opened the door.

The house was immaculate except for the unread newspaper and unopened mail on the kitchen counter. His instincts set off a faint alarm.

Nothing else appeared to have been touched. If Charles had been staying here, he should have at least left a coffee cup out of place.

With each room he checked, Paavo braced himself against finding Charles's body, but the house was empty. In the family room, next to the garage door and directly under the security alarm keypad, there was a small lamp table. On it was a key fob with both house and car keys.

Cautiously, Paavo went into the garage.

Charles's year-old Lexus was there. But Charles wasn't.

When two policemen showed up at the door to Da Vinci's and carefully scrutinized the customers while lunch was being served, Angie avoided going into the dining room, as did Bruno. Only Cosimo ventured out. She wondered why that was.

Angie used the time to cook up an Alfredo sauce and make some fresh fettuccine noodles. As soon as the doors closed after lunch, she served them.

She'd found, when working in a restaurant in the past, the staff sometimes got so tired of cooking, serving, dishing out, and cleaning up the food the customers ate that by the time they sat down to eat, they were sick of looking at and smelling it as well. Bruno's food was quite good, but her fettuccine Alfredo, especially when served atop the freshest possible noodles, was a gift from the gods.

Bruno looked at her with renewed respect.

Luigi looked ready to cry over it—though whether it was because the food was so good or he was so jealous, she had no idea.

Cosimo stuffed his mouth until his cheeks were so full Angie wondered how he could breathe. He jumped up, and to everyone's amazement, ran from the restaurant.

In five minutes he was back and handed Angie and Cat each a clean T-shirt, one white, the other yellow. *"Mia moglie."*

"They're his wife's," Angie translated for Cat. "We told Bruno about our problem with having no money, remember? He must have told Cosimo."

"This is a joke, right?" Cat whispered, horrified.

"They are clean," Angie pointed out.

Cat gulped. "That's more than I can say about what we're wearing." She took the white one, and with a stiff smile at Cosimo, squeaked out, "*Grazie.*"

When Angie said she'd tidy up the kitchen after her fettuccine, everyone else fled. The doors to the restaurant were locked.

Even Cat, who had spent the morning cutting up vegetables and peeling onions for Luigi, which made her mascara run and her eyes red and miserable, left the restaurant to get away for a while. Angie almost went with her, but decided they could both use a little time apart.

As she washed the cookware she'd used and put everything away, she found she enjoyed the time alone, especially being in a restaurant.

Strangely, Marcello had been right about this place being a safe haven—good food and a place to rest her head. If she didn't ache to go home to Paavo, she might even enjoy the admittedly strange camaraderie of Bruno, Luigi, and Cosimo. Beneath a brusque exterior, Bruno was a good-natured man; Cosimo more than a little dense, but helpful; and Luigi was . . . a cook. Temperamental, with an overblown sense of self-worth, he fit the stereotype perfectly.

Angie decided they could all use a treat, and made up a batch of her favorite orange-cinnamon biscotti. As the last cookies were about to come out of the oven, she brewed herself a thick, steamy cappuccino.

Rich coffee and warm cookies. The only thing that could make it better would be if she was home with Paavo and knew she had the job with Chef Poulon-Leliellul.

As she dragged a chair from the dining room to the kitchen, thoughts of her upcoming interview in San Francisco put her nerves on edge. Not only did she have to somehow get home in time for it, but she'd barely had a moment to think about what she was going to say. She could talk about herself and her knowledge of good food and its preparation easily, but she'd have to impress Poulon-Leliellul with her knowledge of his restaurants and his cuisines as well. Even more than good food, these chefs adored flattery. She was going to have to try to remember everything she'd ever heard about the man.

No sooner had she sat down to ponder this when she heard a rattling at the back door.

Heart pounding, she jumped to her feet. Was it whoever was following her and Cat? Or someone after Marcello? Whatever made her think a place like this could be safe?

From the knife rack, she grabbed a cleaver, and was about to turn and run out through the dining room when the door swung open. Marcello stood before her.

"I'll be damned!" He sounded as surprised to see her as she was to see him. He looked at the weapon in her hand and gave a loud laugh. "You planning to hack me up like a fryer chicken?"

Warily, she didn't move.

"Put it down!" he said, sounding tired. He tossed a light jacket on the counter. His black shirt was crisp, the cuffs rolled back far enough to display his thick gold watch. "I'm not going to hurt you. In fact"—he glanced at her cappuccino—"I came here to do the same thing, after I eat lunch. Man, those biscotti smell delicious!" His back to her, he found leftover tagliatelle in the refrigerator. "Luigi often leaves a plate for me."

He put it in the microwave and whistled "Arrivederci Roma" as he poured himself a glass of Chianti. "You mind if I join you? Or do you still want to chop me into little pieces?" His voice boomed over the microwave. "I'm surprised to find you here. Usually, the restaurant is empty this time of day, and I can come in and be alone for a while."

She placed the meat cleaver beside her cappuccino and sat back down. Commandeering a chair from the dining room, he sat beside her.

"Tell me," he said as he began to eat, "how'd you like the food here?" His eyes were so dark they were almost black. They peered at her, not missing a thing.

His query about the food was unexpected, but perhaps he was trying to calm her jangled nerves. "It was quite good," she said honestly. "Basic Italian food, fresh, properly seasoned. It doesn't get much better than that." Her breathing still came a bit too fast.

"Hey! All right! That's what I want to hear." He waved his fork as he spoke. "Did you try the scampi?"

"I took a couple of bites. Excellent."

"It was my sauce," Marcello said, gloating so outrageously she couldn't help but crack a small smile. "I gave Luigi the recipe. I knew he was going to make it today, and I wanted to come by earlier to be sure he got the seasoning right. Of course, when I'm in San Francisco, he does it alone every day, but . . . " He stopped talking. His eyes took on a momentary glumness as they drifted away from her and over the kitchen, at the shiny, clean professional appliances, the shelves of cookware, the food storage, and refrigerator.

What a curious man, she thought. "With all this strangeness going on, you wanted to check some seasonings?"

He had the sense to appear sheepish. "What's a little strangeness between friends—or family?" He twisted a great amount of pasta around his fork and crammed it into his mouth, chewing and swallowing. She'd rarely seen anyone eat so fast. "It doesn't mean I should stop living, and cooking is, to me, a metaphor for life." Between mouthfuls he gulped his wine. "You choose the ingredients, cut them to size, season to taste, mix them together, right?" Before long, he put the now empty dish and glass in the dishwasher. "You let it blend and marry a bit, and hope it all comes out right in the end. And the spicier you make it, the better it becomes—unless, of course, you add too much spice and heat"—he gave a wicked grin—"and then the whole thing is ruined."

Angie chuckled despite herself. As he spoke about something he so clearly loved, his face reflected every nuance of his emotions. He was loud and bigger than life, but she understood exactly what he was saying. "That sums it up, all right." She regarded him seriously for a moment. "How on earth did you come to own a restaurant in Rome?"

Marcello walked over to the refrigerator and opened the door. Looking inside, he murmured, "Somebody had to die."

Chapter 23

It was morning, and Paavo was in Homicide after a sleepless night. He'd made a number of phone calls to the hotel Angie was supposed to be staying at, but she was never there to receive them, and never answered his messages. On top of that, he couldn't track down Charles Swenson.

A heavy foreboding filled him. Where was Charles? And Angie? And why did nothing in this case make sense? He heard footsteps and looked up.

His skin crawled at the sight before him. *Let this be a dream*, Paavo prayed.

Suddenly, the room became a beehive of activity among the other homicide inspectors. Yosh grabbed his coffee and headed out the door. Luis Calderon left, hot on his heels. Bo Benson picked up about a hundred sheets of paper to photocopy, and Rebecca Mayfield announced she was going to the women's room for supplies. Many supplies. Only Bill Sutter, soon to retire, remained impervious at his desk, reading the morning *Chronicle*.

Bearing down on Paavo, wending their way past the familiar chaos of file cabinets, desks, and papers that made up his place of work, came all three of Angie's sisters—Bianca, the eldest; Maria, the devout; and Frannie, the cranky one with the troubled marriage. One at a time was bad enough, but all three . . .

Unless it was bad news. He studied their faces. They were curious, worried, and upset, but not stricken. It was a minor relief.

He stood, adjusted his tie and buttoned his sport jacket. "Good morning," he said.

All greeted him, then it was Bianca who spoke as she heavily plopped herself into the chair beside Paavo's desk. She drew in her breath, shoulders stiff and her brow wrinkled with anxiety. "We've come here to find out about Charles."

"Mamma said he's missing." Maria swiveled Calderon's chair around to face Paavo, her mouth pursed in the sour-ball-sucking way she did so well.

"So sit back down, Paavo," Frannie ordered, her expression more strained and her hair more frizzled than usual, "and tell us what the hell's going on." She eased back, half sitting, fingers drumming on a small bookcase.

"We've turned up nothing yet," Paavo said, taking his seat. "He hasn't contacted anyone at work for two days. No one has been able to give us any leads—"

"Mamma's very upset," Bianca intoned, her expression troubled.

"Are you trying to kill our parents?" Frannie blurted, leaping up. "You phoned our mother last night! Don't you know how much old people worry about these things?"

Her sisters shushed her and pulled her back.

Paavo stared at her. Coldness welled in the pit of his stomach. He wasn't too surprised by her accusation. He knew very well the stress being placed on Angie's mother, and could imagine her worry. It was bad enough that she had to deal with her wayward daughters, but she had to keep the situation from her husband as well. That was another reason why he had to find the killer soon, but to hear his concerns put into words was like a blow to the gut.

"If Mamma knew where Charles was, she would have told Cat," Maria said, shaking her head, as if any idiot would realize that. "It's obvious something's happened to him. First Cat, now Charles. Why is so much being done to hurt our family? We haven't done anything."

Her question echoed his own. "We're doing everything we can."

"How could you let this happen, Paavo?" Bianca said crossly. She sounded like a mother completely dismayed by a wayward child, and Paavo hoped she didn't say—

"I'm so very disappointed in you," she added.

He cringed. "You need to all go home, and when there's word, I'll call you."

"Hell no, we won't go!" Frannie shouted. She was loud, and pumped her fist in the air as if holding a placard. "Not even if you call in the SWAT team!"

The urge to swat her right out of his office nearly won out over good sense.

"He'd never do anything like that to us," Bianca said. Paavo was afraid she was going to reach over and pat him on the head.

Frannie wasn't appeased. "We want action, and we want it now! You've got to tell Mamma that everything is fine. That you've found Charles, he's safe, and that you've cleared Caterina."

"I won't lie to her," Paavo said.

"It's not a lie," Bianca urged, "when it's done to ease her mind. She's frantic over Cat and Angie. We can't have her fretting about Charles, too. Papa already suspects something's going on."

"And if he finds out, he'll be on the next plane to Rome," Frannie said, grimacing as if she couldn't imagine anything much worse.

"Actually, it is a lie," Maria chimed in, harkening back to Bianca's earlier statement. "A sin, I'm afraid, but since it's being done for a good reason, it's venial, not mortal. I believe God would forgive you for it."

Paavo held his hands up to stop them. "I'll admit that Charles has me worried. The good news is that there was no sign of a struggle. The house was untouched, so we have to assume he wasn't harmed."

"Cat's house always looks like that." Frannie brushed off the comment. "Her cleaning lady shows up four times a week."

That explained the newspapers and mail. Paavo had hoped Charles was the one who brought them indoors, but now ...

Maria crossed herself. "Does Cat realize the seriousness of this? I thought she'd come home."

Paavo shook his head. "I haven't told her or Angie yet. The Tiburon police are on it and might track him down soon."

"Give me a break." Frannie's lips curled derisively. "You bureaucrats . . . "

Bianca scooted to the edge of her chair, nearer Paavo, her voice firm yet solicitous. "We want you to come to Caterina's house with us. On the way over, we discussed it, and we want to go inside, but we hesitated to do it ourselves since it might be a crime scene. However, there could well be something that you missed but we would notice since we know Cat and Charles a lot better."

"If I know Charles," Frannie huffed, "he saw what happened, got scared, and he's still running. But I can't be sure until I go to Cat's house and check it out myself. And I intend to do that." She scowled at Paavo as if daring him to stop her.

"Frannie," Paavo said. "Charles's car is in the garage." The implication of that wasn't lost on them.

Tiburon had almost no public transportation.

"That doesn't change my wanting to see his house," Frannie said as she rose to her feet.

Bianca and Maria looked at each other and nodded. "We'll go with you, Frannie," Bianca said, also standing.

Maria jumped up beside her. Three pairs of brown eyes, so much like Angie's, yet so different, peered expectantly at Paavo.

He knew when he was defeated. He wanted to do more digging into Len Ferguson's background that morning, and ask his contact at the TSA if Marcello's flight to Rome had turned up yet. All that would have to wait a while.

Right now, he was going to Tiburon.

"What?" Angie paled, her heart nearly stopping at Marcello's murderous confession.

"I didn't kill him! My God, you should see your face!" He roared with laughter. Angie didn't find it humorous in the least.

"The truth is," he said, taking a carton of half-and-half and heading for the espresso machine, "I got this restaurant after my uncle died. A natural death." He poured some liquid into a stainless steel pitcher. "My uncle started out as the cook here, and ended up owning the place. He enjoyed being in the kitchen, and worked in it until he grew too old and had to give it up. He showed me his recipes and taught me how to cook."

Something in his tone spoke to the cook in Angie. "Sounds like you enjoyed it," she said.

He gave a very Italian "a little yes, and a little no" shrug. "It ate up all my time," he said. "I didn't have a life. My marriage broke up because my wife wouldn't come to Italy with me. She stayed in San Francisco, near her family. She'd come here every so often, but she'd complain that Rome was too crowded and too dirty. Hell, I don't know what she was looking at. Rome looks fine to me, and these days, San Francisco's no model for spic-and-span."

He flipped the switch, and the machine sounded loud in the quiet of the kitchen as he waited for the espresso to brew. He began to whistle the slow, plaintive "Ritorna Me." The familiar Dean Martin song reminded Angie forcibly of her own parents. She blocked the pang of homesickness.

"You enjoy it here." She called over the noise of the brewing machine.

"It's that obvious?" The coffee made, he shut the brewer. Silence echoed.

"Of course. Especially since you kept the restaurant instead of the wife. You loved what you were doing here too much."

"It might have been that," he countered. "Or that I realized she loved me too little."

Angie found his words surprisingly sad. Her confusion about him grew.

He steamed some half-and-half. Like Angie, he made quite the opposite of the "skinny" drinks so popular in the U.S.

"I'll admit," he added as he ladled froth over his espresso, "that there is something special about creating a meal with my own two hands. You're a chef, so you understand."

She inclined her head in agreement, but didn't speak, letting him continue.

"I'm the one who puts the ingredients together, who stirs and blends and tastes and adds until it comes out in a way that makes my customers sit up and say '*Bellissimo!*' He sat down with his cappuccino, took a taste, and rewarded himself with a loud "Aaah."

"You know, Angie," he continued, reaching for a biscotti, "being a chef here is the only time I've ever made anything. I'd worked, sure. I was a salesman, or did 'customer service.' But you know what they are? One is selling something somebody else made, and the other is pretending to help someone with a problem somebody else created—when both of you know you can't help, and that the one who caused the mess doesn't give a damn anyway! Yeah, I was happy here. Maybe the happiest I'd ever been in my whole life."

"Why did you leave?" Angie asked, for the first time feeling a spark of genuine interest and liking for Marcello.

He dunked half the cookie, waited a few seconds, then put the soggy end in his mouth. "Mmm, *squisito!*" He dunked, ate, and reached for another before answering her with, "Shit happens."

"What do you mean?" She drank down her now cold cappuccino as she watched the reply churn in his mind.

After a second and third biscotti, he explained himself, his exuberance fading with each word. "My mother kept saying I was wasting my life in a tiny restaurant on the wrong side of Vatican City, where I couldn't even overcharge the tourist trade. I was always the ambitious one, the one who said he was going to make big money. My mother was sure I'd had a nervous breakdown or something. She said I needed to concentrate on my furniture store in San Francisco—that it would be the thing that'd make me rich. I was a salesman, Mamma insisted, not a cook. I listened to her, hired Bruno to run Da Vinci's, and left. I never told anybody this, Angie, especially not my mother, but leaving here damn near broke my heart."

"I can understand that," Angie said sincerely. With a shiver of regret, his casual mention of his mother made

her remember something else—the man still didn't
know about her death. Did he have no contact at all
with people in San Francisco?

This wasn't the time, and she wasn't the person, to
tell him.

Marcello's face tightened. He downed his coffee and
put their cups in the dishwasher. "I have to admit, I
thought my mother was right—that I was wasting my
life. The thing I didn't realize when I was young is that
it really isn't a waste to be doing something you love,
even if that something will never make you rich or famous. Now I know better. Now that it's too late."

His words tore at her. With genuine sympathy, she
said, "It's not too late, Marcello. This is your restaurant. You just need to find out what happened in San
Francisco. Find your brother, the chain of St. Peter, and
who was killed in your home. Get that behind you and
you'll be fine."

He said nothing and shook his head, a faraway look
in his eyes.

"We can solve this thing together," she pressed.
"You've got to trust us—Cat and I. Tell us everything,
starting with where Rocco is."

He stood so abruptly the chair he'd sat on fell onto
its back, hitting the floor with a loud thwack. Angie
jumped to her feet. He picked up the chair and slid both
of their chairs back into the dining room. "Look, I'm
sorry Cat's involved," he said as he walked to the back
door and opened it. "I know you both want to help,
but you can't. Stay here, and wait until it's over."

His glance lingered over the kitchen before he
walked out the door.

Chapter 24

With Frannie in the passenger seat beside him, and Maria and Bianca in back, Paavo zipped almost silently through the narrow, hilly streets of San Francisco behind the wheel of Frannie's hybrid Prius. It was the strangest car he'd ever driven.

The "key" slid into a slot in the dashboard, and you pushed a power button to make it go, sort of like powering up a computer. When he stepped on the gas— no, the accelerator—the car began to move in electric mode, which meant it was all but completely silent. A stealth car. It was eerie. And, in keeping with its environmentally friendly reason for being, it had a large Energy Monitor console that he kept looking at to see if he was wasting gas as he drove.

As he crossed the Golden Gate Bridge, and then north on 101 to Tiburon, the sisters plied him with questions about the missing chain, Cat being fired from Moldwell-Ranker, and the dead man in Marcello Piccoletti's kitchen.

"Watch out for the bottle!" Bianca cried, but too late.

Paavo drove over it and heard the crunch of glass. "I'm sorry, Frannie. I was looking at the display that tells me how much gas I'm using. If the tire's punctured, I'll replace it for you."

"No problem," she groused. "The car's already got

dings and scratches from me running into things looking at that damned console. There should be a law
against it. Seth was right when he said I was too anal
about wasting natural resources to get this car." Her
voice reeked with bitterness. "After him being wrong
about everything else, who knew?"

No one commented.

They reached Cat's house. Frannie picked up the
morning newspaper, Bianca checked the mailbox, and
Maria prayed. As Paavo unlocked the door, Bianca
asked, "How do you turn off the alarm?"

"It's not on," he said. "It wasn't last night either."

Her eyebrows lifted in surprise.

Paavo pushed the door open and let the women in
with an admonition not to touch anything.

As soon as he moved aside, however, they dashed
inside like kids at the opening of an amusement park.
Maria headed upstairs, Bianca turned into the living
room, and Frannie raced off toward the kitchen.

"Paavo, you'd better come here!" Frannie called. "I
thought you said the house hadn't been broken into?"

"It hadn't." He headed her way. Hearing Frannie's
call, Maria joined him. Bianca, in pure "once bitten,
twice shy" mode, hung back. Way back.

A paned-glass door led from the kitchen to the side
utility yard, a fenced-off area with garbage cans and
gardening supplies. One square of glass had been
knocked out. From the opening, a person could reach
in and unlock the door. Paavo had specifically checked
all locks the night before. The door had been fine.

"Someone broke in," Frannie said, stating the obvious, then frowned at Paavo. "I thought you said the
Tiburon police were watching the house?"

Paavo stepped out to the yard. The door was well
hidden from the street and neighbors. The sisters
looked the situation over.

"Who would have broken in?" Bianca asked. Not having heard screams of anguish, she had joined them.

"This makes no sense," Maria said. "If whoever did it is the same person that took Charles hostage, why not just use his key?"

"We have no proof Charles is a hostage," Frannie argued. "I still think he's scared and hiding somewhere."

Paavo pivoted and headed for the family room. The three sisters, goggle-eyed and frightened, followed like ducklings behind their mother. The lamp table that had held keys was now empty.

The four headed out to the garage. Charles's Lexus looked untouched. Paavo checked inside. There had been a cell phone attached to a recharger cord inside. It was gone as well.

All of them searched the house in case the Tiburon police had moved the keys and cell phone for some reason. Neither were found. Although it was impossible for him to know for sure, as far as Paavo could remember, nothing else seemed to be missing. The sisters affirmed it.

"Why the hell would someone have broken into the house just to get keys and a cell phone?" Frannie demanded. "That's stupid!"

"I don't understand it either," Bianca agreed.

"I can think of a reason," Maria said. "What if whoever took Charles wants to talk to Cat, to find out something from her? I suspect it's about the chain of St. Peter. They can't reach her in Italy and expect Cat will phone Charles on his cell phone. When she does, they'll answer her call. I think it proves Charles is a hostage."

Paavo stared a moment at Maria. Her explanation was bizarre and convoluted—and possible. She was more like Angie than he'd thought.

"What is Charles's cell phone number?" he asked.

No one knew.

While Angie's sisters waited like sentries for the Tiburon police to arrive, Paavo did more investigating on his own. The first place he checked was a his and hers home office.

It did look as if Charles had been kidnapped. But why? Did someone think Cat knew something about all this and had made Charles privy? And did she?

He booted up the two computers. Neither of the Swensons bothered with password security.

He logged on to Cat's e-mail files first, and scanned through the sent and received messages. Almost all were about buying and selling real estate, although some referred to her old interior design business. There was hardly a personal message, joke, or even spam in the bunch. The woman was all work.

After increasingly quick scans of incredibly boring home sale information, Paavo shut down Cat's computer and went to Charles's.

There was nothing on it except some spam e-mail and a couple of get-togethers for golf. His history file showed that he spent all his time on financial centers—Quicken, Smith-Barney, UBS, Wells Fargo Bank—as well as an erotic literature download site. He'd never heard of Ellora's Cave before this.

He soon left Charles's computer and began to rummage through his desk drawers. A notebook neatly listed all of Charles's computer passwords along with the sites involved. Very helpful. Since they had a fax-photocopier, Paavo made himself a copy and stuck it in his pocket, along with a list of Charles's and Cat's cell phone, home, and business telephone numbers.

In the bedroom, he did another search, not for anything in particular, but for something they didn't want anyone else to see. If people like these two had a "secret something," they invariably hid it in the bedroom. Maybe it was some innate nesting instinct, but he never found anything important in a living room, for example, or even a den. It was always in a bedroom.

He was about to conclude they didn't have anything to hide when he opened a small top drawer. Inside, among other things, were monogrammed handkerchiefs—including a perfect match for the one found under the dead man's body.

He stared, but his attention was drawn away by a Tiburon police car pulling into the driveway. Before he went down to meet them, he picked up the telephone in the bedroom. Holding the sheet with the Swensons' various phone numbers on it, he called Charles's cell phone.

"Hello?" a man answered.

"Charles?" Paavo said.

"Who's this?" the man asked.

"Is this Charles?" Paavo repeated, although it didn't sound like him at all.

Abruptly, the phone went dead.

Someone had Charles's cell phone, and presumably Charles as well. His attention snapped back to the drawer where he'd found the matching sets of satin handkerchiefs, all with the C.A.S. initials embroidered in the corner. A drawer filled with men's socks, linens, and boxes of cuff links. Men's accessories.

The drawer belonged to Charles Arthur Swenson.

The handkerchief at the Piccoletti house had belonged to Charles, not to his wife.

Chapter 25

 Angie was in the bedroom above Da Vinci's, replaying in her mind her conversation with Marcello. Something about it bothered her.

Then Cat burst into the room. Her face was pale and haggard, her eyes frightened. "While I was out, I spotted a pay phone at a *farmacia* and decided to call Mamma." She was gulping air, trying to remain calm and scarcely succeeding. "Charles is missing!"

"Charles?" Angie stood, frightened.

"Paavo, Bianca, Maria, and Francesca went to check on him. Our house was broken into." Tears threatened. "What am I going to do? Why would anyone go after Charles?" She dropped onto the bed, elbows on knees, hands covering her face.

Angie found the news scary for two reasons: Charles being gone, and Paavo going anywhere with her three sisters. She sat down on the bed and put her arm over Cat's shoulders. "Paavo will find him."

"Charles couldn't have gotten into trouble on his own," Cat wailed. "It has to be because of me. I need to talk to Marcello."

"Let's call Paavo," Angie soothed. "We'll find out what he knows. Maybe Mamma got something wrong."

"Nobody gets things that wrong. Not even Mamma."

They hurried downstairs to Bruno's office to use

the restaurant's phone. Paavo was still at Cat's house and gave Angie the details not only of Charles's disappearance, but also told her that someone had broken in to pick up Charles's cell phone. He asked to speak to Cat.

Without prompting, Cat recited a list of her husband's friends and associates, and information about Charles's daily routine. She was trying hard to keep her composure. Angie felt helpless and angry.

When Angie took back the phone, Paavo asked if she'd been getting the messages he'd left at her hotel. She explained that she and Cat were staying in a "beautiful room"—sometimes it was necessary to lie—above Da Vinci's restaurant.

"You're staying *where*?" Paavo shouted.

Angie admitted that she rather liked Piccoletti.

She could practically hear Paavo's teeth grind at that. "My contact at TSA can't locate Marcello's flight to Rome," he told her, his voice stern. "I've got some suspicion about that, but no proof yet. Stay away from Marcello. Come home."

"Marcello isn't a worry," Angie insisted. "It's Rocco, and so far, no one can tell us where he is. Cat trusts Marcello."

"I don't," Paavo retorted firmly. "You don't know where Rocco is, Marcello popped up in Rome out of thin air, and now Charles is gone. What more do you need to tell you you're in over your head?"

"It's no safer in San Francisco," she said, using her own form of logic.

"You don't know that." He spoke with the icy, deadly tone Angie detested. There was no talking to him when he got that way.

"Inspector Smith, you don't know it either!" She hung up.

"Ouch!" Cat winced. "That didn't go well, did it?"

Dejected, Angie gazed at the phone. "I don't know what to do, Cat. What if he's right?"

"You can go running back home if you want, but I'm not going anywhere before I talk to Marcello and see if he has any idea what's going on with Charles." Cat flipped through Bruno's Rolodex. "Where is that cell phone number we think is his?"

"Speaking of cell phones . . . " Angie thought back to her conversation with Paavo. "Why didn't you call Charles on his?"

"Why bother? Charles only carries it around in his car in case of emergency. He never turns it on. Why?"

"Paavo said a stranger answered it."

Cat thought a moment, then picked up the office phone. "I'll call his cell phone right now and see what's going on."

"Wait!" Angie grabbed it from her.

A telephone tug of war resulted.

"Let's think about this." Angie yanked so hard that Cat, afraid of breaking a nail, let go. Angie put the receiver back on the hook. "What if Charles was taken hostage because someone wants to talk to you?"

Cat paled. "You're thinking that if I call, whoever took him gets to make threats—to give me a timeline that I have to meet."

"You can't let them do that to you," Angie insisted.

"Of course not." Cat rubbed her aching forehead. "If that's what's going on, any call could put Charles in even more danger."

Angie gripped her sister's arm. "As long as they can't threaten you with hurting him, they'll keep him alive until they can!"

A strangled sound came from deep in Cat's throat. "There's another possibility." She spun away from Angie. Her hand formed a fist that she pressed hard to her lips.

"What?" Angie asked, alarmed.

She could all but see the wheels in Cat's brain spinning. Cat dropped her hand and squared her shoulders. "Nothing," she said. "Forget it. What you said makes sense."

"But?" Angie urged, even as she realized that Cat was hiding something. She remembered her earlier suspicions, before they ever reached Rome. Just what was her sister hiding?

Cat turned her back to Angie. "If someone has taken Charles, what could they want other than the St. Peter's chain? Someone thinks I stole it. Charles's captors must be expecting that I can give it to them for his release."

Angie felt a little sick. "But since you don't have it . . . "

Cat faced her. Her lips quivered and tears filled her eyes. "Charles could be killed! I've got to get that chain back, Angie. Where the hell is it?" She choked back a sob.

Angie could feel Cat's pain and fear. "We need to find out more about the chain, and I know just the place to begin."

Paavo snapped his cell phone shut and stuffed it in his pocket. After his conversation with Angie, his tongue had teeth marks from biting it.

How involved in all this was Charles? His handkerchief was found in the house with a dead body and missing relic. That relic again . . . the fake priest . . . all coming together.

Cat ended up at Marcello's house only because her manager, Meredith Woring, said Marcello had phoned in a complaint about her stealing it. Yet, Marcello was supposedly in Italy at the time.

He needed to talk to Meredith Woring. He'd wanted

to earlier, but the Amalfi sisters kept getting in the way. Just like now.

He drove the sisters in Frannie's Prius back to the Hall of Justice parking lot. He left them and got into his Corvette with a "Don't call me, I'll call you."

Praying they wouldn't follow, he drove to the Moldwell-Ranker office. One look told him the real estate market was every bit as lucrative as he'd been led to believe. The good news was that even his tiny bungalow out in the Richmond district was now worth a small fortune. The bad news was that to buy "up," as they called it, he'd have to spend an even bigger fortune—one not supported by his salary. So he'd remained where he was. When he and Angie married, he expected to sell his place. That way he'd have some money to add to the down payment on whatever mansion she picked out, and wouldn't feel he was living completely off her father's money.

At the receptionist's desk, he asked to see Ms. Woring. She wasn't in the office, but he was asked to wait a moment, then the receptionist disappeared into an office.

An Ichabod Crane look-alike with thinning gray hair approached, the receptionist trailing behind him. "You're looking for Ms. Woring, I understand," he said, holding out a slim hand. "I'm Jerome Ranker, the head man here." Then he chuckled. "At least when Ms. Woring isn't around. Perhaps I can help you? Are you interested in buying or selling a home?"

Ignoring the question, Paavo asked, "Will Ms. Woring be back soon?"

"Not today, I'm afraid." Ranker raised his chin. "But I'm all yours. Do you have a particular neighborhood in mind?"

"I'd like to talk about Caterina Swenson." Paavo showed Ranker his badge.

Ranker's smile vanished and he cast a cold eye toward the receptionist, who scurried back to her desk. "Why don't you come into my office?"

The office was luxurious, a peaceful oasis with rose mahogany furnishings. Ranker invited Paavo to sit on a brown leather sofa next to a coffee table. He took the opposite end. Within minutes the receptionist appeared with a tray of coffee, tea, and dainty cookies. She served both men before leaving.

Upon Paavo's query about Cat's last day at work, Ranker sat back in his chair, steepled his fingers, and searched his memory. "Marcello Piccoletti apparently called Ms. Woring and accused Mrs. Swenson of stealing from him. After taking the call, Ms. Woring came to me, quite concerned. She told me that as he spoke, she'd pulled out his file and asked personal information—SSN, date of birth, and such—to verify his identity since she didn't know him personally. Unless Mrs. Swenson has a very clever enemy who phoned and pretended to be her client just to get her fired—and has personal information about that client—it was Mr. Piccoletti who made the complaint."

Paavo nodded. "Just to be absolutely sure," he said, "I'd like to check the office's phone records for the morning in question."

"That's easy enough." Ranker went to his desk and sat down behind it. "You don't have to bother contacting the telephone company. We have our own PBX. It'll only take a minute to pull off those records." He phoned in the request. Soon the receptionist returned with a three-page printout.

Jerome Ranker moved back to the sofa and spread the printout on the coffee table.

"This is strange," he said, running his finger down a column of incoming calls. "I had the impression from Meredith that the call came in from Mr. Piccoletti's home, but he must have been using someone else's phone. Nothing shows up on caller ID, although we do have a number of calls where the caller ID has been blocked or isn't available."

Paavo studied the printout a moment. "May I take it?"

Ranker gave his consent.

Paavo folded it. "Where is Meredith Woring?"

"She had to go out of town suddenly. To Los Angeles. I understand her mother is very ill, but I expect her back tomorrow."

Paavo thanked the man and found his own way out.

Chapter 26

San Pietro in Vincoli, or St. Peter in Chains, was a few blocks uphill from the Colosseum. From the street, a staircase led to a level, patio-like area in front of the church. As was common in Rome, quite a few people milled about on the stairs and near the entrance. Equally common was the Gypsy beggar sitting on the church's doorsill.

Angie often found that the easiest way to locate an unlocked entrance to a church was to look for the Gypsy sitting at it.

The woman was dressed in a loose robelike tunic of dark materials, bound at the waist, with a long dark scarf covering her head and shoulders. Wide, billowing sleeves dropped low from her wrists.

"Bella donna," she cried as Angie attempted to step past her to enter the church. A thin, clawlike hand reached out in seeming desperation. The woman then went into a lamentation in Italian of how poor and miserable she was and how God would bless the "beautiful woman" if she'd give her some money.

Cat marched past without a second glance.

Angie knew she should learn to ignore the Gypsies the way her sister did. But this woman looked truly old, frail, and hungry. Angie took out her wallet and gave a euro to the woman, keeping the wallet in her hand. She'd been warned that often, while one hand might be outstretched in a pitiful request for money, if you stood close enough to hand some over, the full sleeves blocked your view of the Gypsy's other hand, which was reaching into your purse to pluck out your money. The worst she'd ever heard was in Florence—the "flying baby" scam, in which a Gypsy woman would toss a lifelike baby doll at a tourist. When the tourist reached out to catch what she feared was a live child, another Gypsy would grab a purse, wallet, or camera, and run. At least Angie never had flying babies to contend with.

The basilica was somewhat modest in size for a church in Rome, although it would appear humongous by the standards of most other cities. Against the wall to the right of the altar was a statue of Moses by Michelangelo. A crowd was there, dropping coins in a box so that lights would come on to illuminate the masterpiece, and "oohs" and "aahs" echoed through the building.

No one paid much attention to the rectangular gold urn with a clear glass face that rested in front of the altar.

Angie headed for it. Cat was already there.

Draped inside were lengths of metal chains with large, rectangular links and several larger loops. Angie didn't know anything about the history of the chains. She assumed they were from the time Peter was imprisoned by the Emperor Nero. The contrast between the plainness and cruel symbolism of the chains Peter wore and the richness of this church and others that now bore his name was stark.

"Do they look anything like the chain you saw in Marcello's house?" Angie moved in for a closer look.

"They look exactly like it." Cat sounded awe-stricken. "What if he did have the real thing? He called it priceless. Other than the Church wanting it for display, why would anyone want such a thing?"

"Sometimes Satanists like to take religious items and defile them," Angie said, a worried expression on her face.

"Do you think that's what we're dealing with?" Cat asked, aghast.

"Not really." Angie placed her forearms on the railing surrounding the chains and leaned forward. "I can't help but think that Rocco planned to sell them to someone rich and religious. It could be that he and an accomplice broke into Marcello's home and stole the chain. Then Rocco decided not to share and killed the accomplice. He then flew to Italy to sell the chain and to escape the law."

"I've been thinking along those same lines," Cat mused. "I didn't want to admit it. To steal from his own brother! Although that would fit with the Rocco I knew as a kid. Marcello was the charmer, and Rocco was always jealous, and a bully. His mother used to lament, right in front of him, that she didn't know what to do with such an obnoxious child."

"That wasn't nice!" Angie said, horrified.

"True, though."

"Speaking of the mother," Angie said, "I think someone went to her to find out where Rocco went with the chain, and when she didn't know or refused to tell, that person killed her."

"You've hung around Paavo too long." Cat shuddered. "Still, it makes sense. This is no conversation for a church. I'm going to find a pay phone and see if I can reach Marcello on that phone number we found. No one answered when I called earlier. And I'll check in with Mamma about Charles again."

Cat left, but Angie remained, studying the chains. Looking at them, a sadness descended on her as she contemplated Peter's suffering for his faith.

"This is yours, I believe." A hand was outstretched, holding her iPaq.

She turned to face the young priest from Da Vinci's the night before. She straightened and took a step back. Why was he here? Had he followed her?

Her gaze jumped from the iPaq to the door. The Gypsy was no longer there. "Thank you," she said, taking her handheld. "I thought I was being so careful."

"It happens to the best of us." He grinned a pleasant, albeit somewhat sorrowful smile. He was a slender man, about five-foot-ten. Gray eyes regarded her with frank curiosity through gold-rimmed glasses, yet he seemed almost anxious as he spoke. "I noticed her helping herself to it from your tote bag. I was going to give it right back, but you seemed to be in a very serious conversation with that blond woman."

"My sister, yes. Is this your church?" Angie sought some legitimate reason for his turning up this way.

"Oh, no." He shook his head. His manner was plain and soft-spoken. He seemed to weigh each word before speaking. "I'm in Rome on sabbatical. Here to study and deepen my knowledge of the faith. I'm from Ohio. Father Daniel Tolliver. Where's your home?"

She introduced herself. To be a priest, he had to be at least in his late twenties, yet he looked quite boyish. His loneliness was evident, and more than a little homesickness as well. As they spoke, they walked outside the church so as not to disturb others.

Standing on the patio, she told him about being from San Francisco, about Paavo and her engagement. He seemed genuinely interested. He told her about his own family—his parents and his three married sisters. He was the only one who was very religious in his family, and his parents didn't understand him at all.

Angie could see why. Looking at him, she thought he should be an all-American college student inter-

ested in girls, beer, and pickup baseball games with
his friends. When he spoke of God, however, he did
so with a burning intensity, a fire lighting his face, yet
with a melancholy she didn't understand. "I wanted to
share my faith, to do my part to bring the whole world
the gift of God's love." Somewhere in Rome, church
bells rang. He listened, his gray eyes lifted toward
the skyline, his lips thin yet sensitive. When the bells
stopped, he faced her again.

"Have you?" she asked.

He was clearly surprised by the question. At first he
seemed about to brush it off. How easy it would be to
say, "Of course," and move on. But he hesitated, and
then his shoulders sagged. "For some reason, that isn't
the way it turned out. Sometimes I'm not sure what
I'm all about, as a matter of fact. That probably sounds
strange to you."

"No," Angie said, with more sincerity than he could
know. The stories she could tell him! But even she had
to admit there was a substantial difference between
a problem with a vocation in the priesthood and one
with finding work as a culinary aficionado. "It's not
strange at all, but I'm sorry to hear it."

A tortured sadness marred his features. He seemed
about to say more, then changed his mind. Angie felt
oddly drawn to him, and troubled that so much hope
and promise was being destroyed.

"Tell me, what brings you to Rome?" he asked with
forced lightness.

"I'm here to help my sister," was her evasive answer.

"Working in a restaurant?" His head cocked and she
could see him struggle against a slight uplift at the corners of his mouth.

She relieved him by laughing at herself. "We both
are. It's a long story," she said. "The restaurant is
owned by a friend."

He waited for an explanation—one she wasn't about to give a stranger. She was ready to change the subject when Cat approached.

"Here you are!" Irritation dripped from Cat's voice. "I wish you'd told me you were leaving. I circled around inside three times looking for you!"

"I may be to blame," Father Daniel said, introducing himself, then turned back to Angie. "I'm sorry, I shouldn't keep you any longer. I enjoyed our conversation immensely." He stepped back. "I'll probably see you both again soon at Da Vinci's. I eat there a lot. I'm staying at the rooming house right next door." With that, he bid them good-bye and went back inside the church.

Cat watched him go. "That was strange. What was he doing here? Why was he talking to you so seriously?"

Angie had no answer, but she had the very same questions.

Paavo was at his desk when Serefina called. A strange man had phoned her and demanded to speak to Cat. When she claimed to have no way to contact her daughter, he asked more questions. She kept saying "*No capishe,*" which was terrible Italian, but most Americans understood it.

The caller grew angry, and his ensuing words were chilling. The next time Cat phoned, he said, if she ever wanted to see Charles again, she should leave a phone number where she could be reached.

"I've convinced Salvatore to take our grandson to Disneyland for two nights," Serefina explained. "I'm afraid for the boy. Salvatore still thinks Caterina is in Las Vegas with Angie, but he's getting suspicious, especially because Charles doesn't phone. He wants to know what's wrong with the man. What kind of a father is he? I just keep my mouth shut."

"I'll let the Hillsborough police know," Paavo said. He didn't let on how serious he was taking the call, but Serefina wasn't fooled.

"As soon as Salvatore is out of the house, I'm calling Joey and Rico," she said. "You might remember them. Angie hired them as bodyguards when you two first met. This has to be taken care of before Salvatore comes back home, or I'm going to have to tell him everything. I'm doing all I can, sending people around to find out exactly what's going on, but they're having some trouble. Still, I know the Piccolettis. I know what they could be up to."

The last thing he needed was to have Angie's mother get in the middle of this investigation. "Serefina, leave it up to the cops."

"Umm-hmm." Serefina's inflection told him she'd do anything but. "I'm getting close to something, I think. When I'm sure, I'll let you know."

"Getting close?" That worried him. "Close to what? Tell me."

"You work on getting Angie back. I'll work on the Piccolettis. *Ciao*."

Chapter 27

One scenario after the other played itself out in Cat's mind as she reached the Via dei Fori Imperiali. The sun beat down relentlessly on the wide, car-clogged, nearly treeless street. This had been the heart of ancient Rome. To the south, the Colosseum, a model for modern day sports arenas, once sat 50,000 spectators to witness the victorious and the vanquished. Now it was a surreal mix of muscular men dressed up like gladiators for picture takers, cars zipping by at great speed, and the ruined structure itself filled with visitors sensing the presence of those who had lived and died there centuries ago.

Directly across the street was the Roman Forum, where Caesar and Mark Anthony once walked, the edifice now nothing but ruins.

Cat headed northward, toward the monument to Victor Emanuele, the first king of a united Italy— which Romans mockingly say looks like a wedding cake. Past the monument, Rome became a city filled with shops and businesses. It had a no-nonsense ambience as grim-faced, rather irritated-looking Italians rushed about on foot or in cars that honked incessantly and zigzagged around befuddled tourists, many of whom seemed petrified by the crisscrossing streets, the traffic, and the noise. They often stood on street corners, maps open, trying to make some sense out of where they were and which way they should be going.

Cat didn't need a map. She simply followed Angie. That had been her first mistake, she thought. Disgust filled her.

Logic had always been her strong point, and she'd been relying far too much on her impetuous sister. Angie had experience in criminal matters, and she had assumed that might help. She'd been wrong. Also, if she were making excuses for herself—which she was—it was unnerving to be fired, to find a body in a kitchen, and then to learn you were suspected not only of theft but also murder!

Enough with the excuses. She was in charge now. She would handle this herself, and leave Angie out of it.

She'd reached Marcello earlier by phone and arranged a meeting. She and Angie were heading there now. Her plan was to send Angie off and talk to him alone.

Angie kept giving her questioning glances as they wended their way through the ancient city, but she stayed silent. Thank God for small favors, Cat thought. Some of the time—no, most of the time—her sister's constant flow of ideas and chatter made her want to shove Angie into the nearest fountain.

Speaking of fountains, after a turn down the Via delle Muratte, they reached the Trevi of "Three Coins in the . . ." fame. In a city filled with fountains, this one, with its large marble sculpture of Neptune riding a shell and pulled by sea horses, was the largest. People tossed coins in it hoping that doing so would ensure a return to Rome one day—or hoping to coldcock obnoxious tourists singing the theme song from the old movie. The fountain, nevertheless, was beautiful by day, and spectacular when lit up at night.

"Is this the place?" Angie asked, interrupting Cat's thoughts.

"Yes. It's a good spot to meet. There are a lot of people around. He felt it's safe here for both of us."

Considering that Angie had a long talk with Marcello at Da Vinci's, his sudden desire for many people around made no sense to her. "I don't know about this," she murmured, then took hold of Cat's elbow. "Don't look now, but isn't that the guy with the goatee who was following us once before?"

Cat turned in the direction Angie had been looking. "I don't see anyone."

"I said . . . " It was too late. Angie searched the area. If it had been him, he was gone now. Maybe goatees were suddenly very popular in Italy and it wasn't actually the same guy popping up like a jack-in-the-box all over Rome. "This crowd makes me nervous," she said, and inched closer to her sister.

Cat ignored her concerns. "Marcello's here somewhere. He agreed to meet, and I'm not leaving until I find him."

"Maybe something happened that scared him away," Angie said.

"Maybe he just doesn't want to talk to me while you're nearby. I didn't tell him you'd be coming."

Angie looked offended. "Why shouldn't I be here?"

"Perhaps we have some personal things to discuss," Cat said indignantly.

"Like?"

"Like none of your business! Now, go throw coins in the fountain. I'm going to look for Marcello on my own."

"Just stay away from goateed men!" Angie warned as she went one way and Cat the other.

Not three minutes later, Cat felt a tug on her arm. Instead of Marcello, it was Angie again. "What's wrong with you? I said, go away!"

Angie sidled up close and whispered, "Someone's watching us."

"Are you seeing goateed men again?" Cat was beside herself. "Do you have a beard fixation?"

"I'm not seeing things! And this guy doesn't have a goatee. He has a green cap, and he keeps watching us."

"Great. Now you're seeing leprechauns! This is Italy, not Ireland. Leave me alone."

"He's standing in front of the Tazza D'Oro coffee shop." She held Cat's arm and slowly the two turned as if they were on a merry-go-round. "See him yet?"

"I don't . . . oh! Yes. He's there." Stricken, Cat averted her eyes and looked at Angie. "He *is* watching us!"

"Told you! Let's get out of here."

"But Marcello . . . " Cat scanned the crowd.

"Consider that he just stood you up." Angie took Cat's hand and plunged down a narrow, cobbled side street. A few umbrella-covered tables stood outside shops with panini, pizza, and cappuccino.

They hid in a doorway. The man with the green cap appeared at the end of the street, slinking along the sides of buildings, his eyes searching.

"He'll find us if we stay here," Angie whispered. "Run."

She and Cat ran down the block and turned a corner into a warren of ancient streets. They looked back, and saw him running after them.

A young man walked toward them. "Help!" Angie grabbed his arm. "Someone is chasing us."

"You're crazy," he said, pulling free. "Crazy American!"

The streets were narrow. Only one small car at a time

could fit in them. The buildings were nearly black with centuries of soot, and so tall that Cat felt as if she were running through a maze. "I don't see him anymore," she said, clutching Angie's jacket. "Do you know where we are?"

Angie nervously looked around. Little sunlight reached them. This was not a good place to be, the sisters realized, night or day. "Just keep going straight," Angie tried to sound confident. "We'll find our way out eventually."

They did as she'd suggested, but when they turned a corner, the green-capped man was there. "*Mamma mia!*" he cried.

Angie screamed.

Without giving him a chance to say or do anything, Cat whacked him in the face with her oversized handbag. He tried to grab the bag. Cat kept swinging, and Angie joined her.

A crowd quickly formed around them, cheering the women on.

The man's cap fell off. Crouching, he covered his bald head with his hands. "Stop!" he yelled. Finally, he managed to escape.

The crowd roared its approval.

Surprised and smug, the sisters watched him run.

They were high-fiving themselves when he stopped farther up the narrow street and turned to face them. "Your mother hired me to watch you," he called, patting his cut lip. "She was worried about you two in Rome all by yourselves. I'll tell her she doesn't have to worry! I quit!"

Stunned, Angie and Cat watched him limp away.

Paavo was rereading the Sea Cliff homicide reports in hopes that an overlooked clue would jump out at him when he felt someone's eyes.

He lifted his head, and could barely stifle a groan.

"Frannie," he said. "I thought you'd gone home long ago."

"Mamma called me on my cell phone." Her face wore an ugly scowl as she plunked herself in Yosh's chair. Yosh was out reinterviewing Flora Piccoletti's neighbors.

"Now that Papa and Kenny are out of the house, Mamma's wearing her fingers to the bone on the telephone to get Angie and Cat home. If she doesn't succeed soon, she's going after them herself."

"God help us," Paavo murmured.

"You can say that again. She'd do anything for those two." She held up a scrap of paper. "She gave me some information for you. The phone number of Marcello's sister—Flora Piccoletti's only daughter."

Paavo reached for it, but Frannie pulled back her hand and put the paper in the pocket of her jeans.

"I've already called her. She's waiting for us at a bar in Cow Hollow. I'll introduce you two." Frannie's mouth wrinkled in disgust. "Of course, the way it's going for everyone else in her family, by the time we get there, she might be dead."

"I hate this!" Cat yelled, and stabbed a paring knife into the chicken breast Luigi wanted boned.

Luigi jumped back. "What'sa matter you? You make a hole in the meat! You think you're some Gypsy knife thrower now?" From his fearful expression and gaping mouth, he must have expected her to plunge it into him next.

She'd been tempted. Her husband was missing, her sister was badgering her, and after midnight, alone, she planned to meet a man she wasn't positive she could trust. On top of that, Luigi expected her to bone chicken?

That's what butchers were for. If one wanted chicken fillets, one bought them that way.

The only one around here she wanted to bone . . . no, that didn't come out right. The only one she wanted to debone was Luigi, with all his arrogance and bossiness.

Or Bruno, who was a dictatorial maniac.

Or Angie, who couldn't leave her alone for two seconds.

She yanked out the knife and waved it in front of Luigi's nose. "I'm thinking of making sausage next."

He placed two fingers against the knife blade and gently eased it away from his face. "You wanna break? You got it."

Cat glanced at Cosimo, and suddenly an idea sprang to mind, a way to get herself permanently out of the kitchen and into the dining room, where she could watch and listen to the customers, and just possibly one of them might divulge some connection to Marcello, or the chain, or something that would lead to resolving this mess.

She smacked the knife onto the chopping block, tossed her apron atop it, then took Cosimo by the shoulder of his jacket and dragged him out of the restaurant. As his feet skirted the ground, he looked scared to death.

Angie and the others watched, slack-jawed and silent, as Cat headed onto the Via Porta Cavalleggeri. Angie could only hope Cat would be safe out there, but she, too, knew better than to cross her sister.

Frannie sat back in the Corvette, luxuriating in the leather seats, the growl of the engine. "I thought you were too stuffy for a car like this," she said to Paavo.

He grimaced. "And I thought you were too PETA to sit on leather seats."

"I don't approve, but if the animal must be killed for food, then no part of it should go to waste. That's what the American Indians believed. And so do I."

"A useful philosophy," he said.

She gave him a sidelong glance to discern if he was mocking her. Her eyes narrowed. "I take my work seriously. Mankind has the capacity to destroy the world. It's important to restrict him. It's our duty to save species close to extinction. There's a lot of work to be done. Most of the great animals of Africa are dying out—gorillas, elephants, lions. Also whales. And in this country, wolves, grizzlies, condors, eagles—more species than you can name. It's quite tragic. Most people don't know, or don't care. Not even my own sisters."

"I've heard Angie say that she agrees with most of your causes," Paavo said. "Just not necessarily the tactics used."

"At least Angie listens to me. Cat never would. She always said I was embarrassing. Can you imagine? She said I'd better not get Angie involved in my causes or I'd have her to answer to."

"Cat tried to protect Angie?" That didn't fit Paavo's image of Caterina at all.

"She didn't care so much about Angie as she did the family name. I guess it was bad enough if one Amalfi daughter was arrested for a good cause. Heaven forbid two got their names in the papers."

"That sounds like Cat," Paavo admitted.

"Things worked out the way Cat wanted, since Angie only went on a protest with me once. It turned out badly, I'm sorry to say."

"Angie protested something?" She'd never told him about that.

"That's right. She was going to protest the razing of an old windmill in a park in Berkeley. It's not only animals I care about, it's things as well. Mankind is the problem, you see."

"I see," Paavo said, willing to agree so he could hear the rest of the story.

"Come to think of it, Angie was always enthusiastic about doing things together. Very sisterly and all. I'd kind of forgotten that about her. She was always willing to tag along when we were growing up."

Frannie seemed lost in thought for a moment, then continued with her story. "About the Berkeley protest, we hand-painted some T-shirts and headed off to the sit-in where we expected to be arrested. Unfortunately, it started to rain, and the protest disbanded. I mean, jail is one thing, but not when you're already cold and wet. Anyway, Angie had drawn a big brown windmill on her T-shirt, but in the rain, the ink she'd used started to fade. It turned sort of flesh-colored."

Frannie started to giggle. "She had to walk through Berkeley and ride BART all the way back to the city wearing on her chest what looked like a giant phallus with a propeller on top. You should have heard the comments from men on the street." Frannie's snickers turned to full laughter. "Angie was so mortified, she couldn't even hear the word 'windmill' for a couple of years without turning beet red. Mamma couldn't understand why I kept bringing home library books about Holland."

Paavo just shook his head. If he allowed himself to smile, if even the corners of his mouth turned up slightly, that would be the first thing Frannie would tell Angie when she saw her again. To his surprise, Frannie wiped away a tear. "I never thought I'd admit it, but Angie wasn't half bad for an annoying little sister," she said, her throat thick. "I actually miss the little brat."

This time he did laugh.

Flanagan's Pub was just off of Union Street. The drone of voices, smell of beer and whiskey, and the sound of a television and a jukebox playing at the same time assaulted their senses the instant they put one foot past the door.

A loud whoop came from deep in the bar, and Frannie let out an answering call. She and a tall, heavyset woman met in the center with a big hug. Both talked rapid-fire at the same time about how long it had been, how good the other looked, how sorry Frannie was to hear about Josie's mother's death, and how sorry Josie was to hear that Frannie's sisters were in trouble because of Marcello.

Paavo listened hard, hoping to pick up some bit of news, but everything they said, he already knew. Josie had an attractive face, with short, curly black hair and brown eyes.

"So this is Angie's fiancé?" Josie asked Frannie, as if Paavo wasn't standing three feet away.

"Yes, he's the detective," Frannie replied.

"Angie's doing all right. He's good looking," Josie said with a bold wink.

"If you like cops," Frannie said, then turning to Paavo, added, "Meet Josie Nakagawa. Josie, Paavo Smith."

They went to a table. A cocktail waitress followed, and they all ordered microbrewery beers.

"I'm sorry about your mother," Paavo began. "I'm the lead on investigating her murder, but so far we're hitting a stone wall. No one can think of a reason anyone would want to harm her."

"Nobody but her kids," Josie said, then sadly shook her head. "I shouldn't say that. Mom wasn't easy on any of us. She hated my husband. Nice Italian girls don't marry Japanese men under Mom's rules of the universe. She cut me off. For Rocco, it was the same.

He tried hard, but nothing he did made her happy. But when I got married and settled down, Rocco simply went away. I heard he changed his name, skirted the edge of the law. He grew more and more tough. Tough and bitter."

"Changed his name?" That could explain why he hadn't been able to find any information on him. "Do you know to what?"

"Rocky Pick." She chuckled. "Ugly, isn't it? Only Marcello stuck around Mom, and look at him." At Paavo's inquiring look, she explained, "He's not a happy man. When I look into his eyes, I only see sadness."

"Excuse me," Frannie said, "but all this touchy-feely family stuff is making my stomach turn. I'm going to play some pool in the back."

After she'd gone, Josie continued. "My mother kept pushing. She was never satisfied with her life, her husband—my dad died at a young age—or her kids. She told Marcello he was the only one who hadn't deserted her, that he was the one she could depend on. Whatever he did, though, was never enough. He should be smarter, richer, more famous. Marcello kept doing crazy things, always trying to make her happy until . . . "

"Until?" Paavo asked.

"I'm not sure. Something happened about five or six years ago. I never saw Marcello after that, even though he was right here in the city and I live only about fifty miles away."

Paavo frowned. That wasn't what he'd expected to hear.

"Would you tell me what's going on with Marcello?" Josie asked. "I don't understand any of this. Do you think the murder at his house is somehow connected with my mother's death?"

Paavo told what he could.

"A chain of St. Peter?" Josie shook her head in disgust. "That sounds like the sort of wild-ass thing Marcello would decide to use to make his fortune. Or Rocco. Neither wanted to recognize that the only way to get ahead was through hard work."

"I was wondering," Paavo said cautiously, "if you'd be willing to take a look at the body found in Marcello's house. He might be a friend, someone from Marcello's past or some associate."

Josie studied him uneasily, as if something in his eyes or expression might have given his thoughts away. "I'll do so, if you wish," she said finally. "But I can't imagine I'd recognize him."

Paavo drew in his breath as he gave voice to the suspicion that had been lurking in his subconscious. "I have the feeling you just might."

Chapter 28

In two hours, Cat returned with a bedraggled Cosimo in tow, his legs bowed under the weight of several shopping bags.

"Bruno," she announced with a smile, "you owe Cosimo only a hundred ninety euros for all this. I am the best shopper you'll ever meet."

"What?" he yelled, red-faced. "A hundred ninety euros? For what?"

"You shopped?" Angie was aghast . . . and envious. She was also glad to see Cosimo, since she'd been stuck bussing dishes in his absence.

"I had to do it," Cat said, a smile on her face for the first time since they'd arrived in Rome. "I couldn't help myself. This place needs freshening up."

"You shopped?" Angie repeated, as if it was the most wonderful word in the language.

From her bags, Cat pulled gold Florentine and glass candle holders; matching salt and pepper shakers; white linen napkins; gold brocade curtains; matching round tablecloths; and smaller, square white cloth to go over them.

For the walls, she'd bought a series of framed sketches of Da Vinci's ideas for inventions, from helicopters to crossbows.

"I'm going to redecorate this place and make it look the way it should!" Cat announced to Bruno. Then she smiled at Luigi and said. "I told you you're wasting my talent. I'm a shopper, not a chopper!"

Angie gawked, mouth open. Shopping certainly had put Cat in a good mood.

"The restaurant doesn't need all these new things," Bruno fumed, looking over Cat's purchases. "I won't pay!"

"My customers come here because they like my food!" Luigi bellowed.

Cosimo nodded. "*Sì*, and they like—"

Bruno elbowed Cosimo so hard he nearly toppled over.

"Of course they like the food," Cat said, "but give them good food in a great atmosphere, and they'll come even more often. I'm going to set things up."

"No!" Bruno bellowed. "You cannot disturb my customers while they eat!"

"As each table is cleared and the old dirty linens removed," Cat announced, "I'll put the new linens on it. You'll see how pleased customers will be. I know Marcello will love this."

Cosimo sat in a corner, peering inconsolably at his now empty wallet.

Bruno shook his head and walked away, muttering something about bossy American women.

"Angie, I'm hearing two men say something about digging, but I can't understand well enough to know what it is," Cat whispered to her sister, returning to the kitchen after setting out new linens and candles on an empty table. "Their Italian is way too fast, but I think that's what they said. They look like people who work outdoors."

"The archeologists!" Angie cried. She peeked out the door. It was them.

As she watched, the older archeologist left his seat and headed for the restroom.

Angie took a full bread basket from the kitchen, waltzed over to the young man, and placed it on the table. "Enjoying your dinner, Stefano?" she asked, catching his eye.

"Very much," he said, sitting back in his chair to fully enjoy her company. "Now."

She rested her hand on the back of his father's empty chair. "How is your project coming along? Are you finding much?"

"A lot. We report to the Curator of Antiquities at the Vatican—we work for him. That's why we're here so often."

"I see," she said. "You must know Marcello Piccoletti, then. Or his brother, Rocco."

"I don't know Rocco, but Marcello and my father are good friends."

Noticing the father heading their way, Angie moved to the next table and began rearranging Cat's new place settings on it.

"Time to go," the father said. He glanced suspiciously at Angie as he threw some bills on the table.

The younger man also stood, but couldn't take his eyes from her. "*Ciao*," he called.

"*Ciao!*" she said.

Still smiling at her, he put on a cap and headed out the door after his father.

Angie went to the window and watched them. The father looked like he had quite a bit to say to his son as they walked down the street. To her surprise, the young priest, Father Daniel, stepped from his rooming house and followed them. Why would that be?

She had to find out for herself.

Angie yanked off her apron, handed it to Bruno, and ran out the front door. The poor man probably thought she'd also decided to do some impromptu shopping.

She stayed close to the buildings as she watched the two archeologists and the priest, curious as to what was going on and if they knew each other.

The archeologists turned onto a side street.

Father Daniel crept along behind them in a way that quickly made it clear he didn't want to be seen either.

Angie followed just as stealthily.

When the archeologists stopped and Father Daniel disappeared into a doorway, she ducked behind a Peugeot.

From down the street, a large gray car approached. The older archeologist stepped up to it, while the younger stayed on the sidewalk.

A hand reached out from the driver's side with an envelope. The archeologist took it, nodded, and hurried back to his son.

The two got into a yellow car parked nearby.

The gray car rolled toward her. Angie curled up as much as she could, practically getting under the Peugeot. The car passed by, and from the streetlights, she saw the driver.

It was Marcello.

Paavo accompanied Josie to the morgue, which was every bit as cold and depressing in the day as it was at night. Maybe more so. He asked a technician to let her view the body on a screen.

When the tech motioned to Paavo that all was ready, Josie drew in a breath and watched the monitor. It flickered and came on.

"Oh, my God!" she gasped. She stared, then moved

closer, as if she couldn't believe what she was seeing. Color leached from her face.

Paavo took hold of her arm. "You recognize him?"

"Of course I do." It took her a moment to find her voice enough to say, "It's my brother."

Chapter 29

When the restaurant closed, Cat and Angie went up to their bedroom. As soon as they were alone, Angie breathlessly described the strange meeting between Marcello and the archeologists. It appeared some money had changed hands.

"That explains everything," Angie said. "They've got to be the source of the St. Peter's chain. They must have felt it was too valuable to turn over to the Vatican, and sold it to Marcello. I wonder if he's still paying them off."

"It all fits," Cat said.

Angie chattered on, but Cat ignored her, hoping she'd fall asleep soon. Cat had even more to talk to Marcello about now.

Although exhausted, instead of getting ready for bed, Cat lay atop the covers, closed her eyes, and announced that she wanted to think. Angie said she was going to relax a bit and then call Paavo. When Cat opened her eyes, it was to a dark room, quiet except for Angie's light snores.

The meeting had been set for midnight. The fluorescent hands of the small alarm clock showed one-thirty. After lining up the pillows along her side of the bed and covering them with a blanket so that when Angie awoke in the middle of the night to use the bathroom, which she inevitably would do, she wouldn't grow suspicious, Cat snuck out of the restaurant.

She hesitated about going without Angie, but she had things to say to Marcello best said away from little sister's big ears. There was no reason to be frightened of Marcello, and she had to stop filling her mind with doubts. Even their mothers were once good friends. Her heart lurched at the thought of Marcello's mother.

A short taxi ride brought her to a house to the west of Vatican city, a residential area near the Valle Aurelia metro station.

"*Aspetti, per piacere,*" she said to the taxicab driver, wanting to be sure she got inside before she sent him off.

She knocked twice on the door before she heard the dead bolt being released.

The door opened a crack, then wider. Marcello stood before her in light blue pajamas. The top was unbuttoned and hung open, exposing every follicle on his white, hairy chest. Even his toes were hairy.

"Uh . . . " she said, then shut her gaping mouth.

He glanced down. "Sorry." He started to button the top. "I'd given up on you." His voice was husky with sleep. Something about the way he stared made her uneasy—sort of like being the last piece of chocolate on a tray when a chocoholic had just walked into the room. "Come on in."

"It's this late only because I had to wait until my sister was asleep." She waved off the cab driver.

Marcello took her wrist, pulled her inside, and shut the door. "Go over to the sofa," he ordered.

"The sofa?" Confused, she did as told.

He turned off the lamp and looked through the peephole in the door. It took a moment before her eyes adjusted. Between moonlight and the streetlights of the city, she could see well enough in the room. "Why are the lights off?"

"I'm being watched." He sat beside her on the sofa. "This way, it's easier for us to see them than for them to see us."

She scooted away from him. "Marcello, you've got to tell me what's happening. My husband has disappeared. We think he's been taken hostage, and ..." She stopped. She'd almost told him about his mother's murder. But first she needed some answers.

"I wish I knew what was going on, Cat, but I don't. All I can figure is that someone wants the chain of St. Peter, but I don't know who it is, or why. Or who was killed in my own kitchen!"

"Where is Rocco?" Cat asked. "He's got to have the answers. If he's here in Rome, he must have contacted you. Don't lie to me, Marcello. Not after what we've done."

"I'm not lying, Trina." He squeezed her hands in his. "Believe me, I'd never lie to you. I don't know who's after the chain. And Rocco hasn't approached me. I swear it, Trina." His hands went to her elbow.

She pulled her arms free and looked around the dark space. "Whose home is this? It's a far cry from your place in San Francisco."

"It belongs to a friend. I left my hotel. Too many people knew I stayed there. Who told you where I was? My mother?"

At the casual mention of his mother, Cat's heart twisted. She couldn't keep the truth from him any longer. All her other reasons for needing to talk to him, all her questions, were going to have to wait. Compassion for him, for the horrible news she bore, filled her, and she took his hand. "I want to assure you that I'm here for you."

"And I am for you." He slid closer, his arms snaking around her as he leaned forward to loom above her. "I've always cared about you. You're the most beautiful, the smartest woman I've ever met. Surely, you know that."

"Marcello, please!" She crawled out from under him and stood, then smoothed her jacket. How had she gotten into such a situation? "You've got this all wrong! I'm here because I care—"

"You care? Trina, *cara*, I've always wanted to hear that." His voice was a deep rumble, and she felt it in the pit of her stomach as he, too, stood. His arms circled her again, like an octopus with Velcro tentacles.

She backed away, but he stayed right with her. In the dark, she backed into a table. The lamp nearly toppled over. She kept going. "Marcello!"

"Trina." The way he said her name was heartfelt and passionate.

She wasn't the type of woman who caused men to act this way. They were usually too intimidated, for one thing. Or too put off. If this were a normal situation, she'd give him a tongue-lashing and be done. But this wasn't normal.

First, she was stunned by his reaction to her.

Second, she thought about Flora ...

Get a grip! Hands to his shoulders, she dug in her heels. "Stop."

He lightly stroked her upper arm with his knuckles. "What's wrong, Trina? Cold feet? Although . . . you've got the place right."

Over her shoulder she saw she'd backed up into his bedroom. Her mouth went dry. "I came here to tell you something. Something awful."

"Awful?"

"It's about your mother."

He froze at that. She had him sit beside her on the bed, and as gently as she could, told him what had happened.

For a moment she feared he'd strike her, shouting

that she was lying, that she had to be a lying, heartless bitch. He bolted up, paced, swore, cursed heaven and hell. But even as he ranted and stormed, she could see that he was slowly accepting the truth of her words. Then he sat down again and began to weep, saying it was all his fault.

She sat beside him, cradling him, telling him it wasn't, that he had nothing to do with it. It could have been a robber, some crazed serial killer, anyone.

"No," he said, wiping his tears. "She died because of me. They wanted to know where the chain was. She didn't know. She didn't know any of it."

"Didn't know what?" Cat asked.

Suddenly, there was a loud thud against the front door, followed immediately by another.

"Damn! They must have followed you!" Marcello shouted, jumping up, stepping into slacks and loafers, pulling the pants over his pajamas. He grabbed a gun from his nightstand and tucked it into his waistband at the back. They heard the thud again.

Cat, on her feet now, stared hard at the gun, then from Marcello to the door, unable to move, as if frozen to that spot with fear. Her voice a mere whisper, she croaked, "Who's out there?"

"If you ask me, marriage sucks," Frannie said to Luis Calderon. She was sitting on the edge of his desk, her back to Bo Benson, when Paavo returned to Homicide alone.

"Here comes a man who's happy to be getting married, the poor fool." Calderon waved his hand in Paavo's direction. Luis Calderon was in his late forties. His job had caused the destruction of his marriage to his childhood sweetheart, and he was trying the dating scene again, with fairly disastrous results. He was grumpy, argumentative, and at times seemed to border on depression about the state of his life and his job. It didn't help that he was partnered with Bo Benson, a young handsome African-American who dressed like a *GQ* model and had women practically falling at his feet.

"More the fool," Frannie said, then turned to Paavo and called out, "I hope you and Angie will be happy. I really do. Of course, I have my doubts, but who the hell knows? You two might make it work. Miracles do happen sometimes. Rarely." She chuckled, but her laughter faded at the grim look on his face and the cold hardness in his eyes. He ignored her, went to his desk and picked up the phone.

"Frannie's right," Calderon said with a nod at her. "Marriage would be just fine if you could trust women. But since you can't . . . " He let his words drift, as if, What more was there to say?

"And what the hell do you mean by that?" Frannie demanded. "Everyone knows it's men who are the shits."

He barked a harsh laugh and shook his head. "You're young. You don't know yet."

"You wouldn't believe how much I do know!" she countered, leaning close.

The two eyed each other.

"Okay, I'll agree that men aren't so hot either," he said benevolently. "Life sucks."

"Hey, you two!" Bo Benson interjected. He was ignored.

"Life sucks?" Frannie peered hard at Calderon. "Is that a news bulletin? Jean-Paul Sartre told us that fifty years ago. *No Exit*. 'Hell is other people.'"

Calderon tipped his chair back, hands behind his head. "You read that stuff?"

"Sure." She regarded him a long moment. "I'll bring you a book of his plays. And Camus. Do you know

Camus? *The Stranger*? 'Mother died today; or maybe it was yesterday,'" she quoted.

He stared at her. "I like it."

She was surprised. "You do? The Existentialists are out of favor, but they speak to me. I love talking about them."

Calderon glanced at Paavo, then back at Frannie. "Could you use some more coffee? Or are you going out to do more investigating?"

Frannie didn't hesitate. "I'm finished here for the moment. Let's go find a coffee shop. I find it exciting to be able to talk to someone who understands." She glanced at Paavo, who was still on the phone.

Calderon's gaze never left her as he nodded. "Me, too."

They headed out the door.

Bo looked from the now empty doorway to Paavo, who was setting the receiver down with extra care. Bo was all too familiar with the icy, narrowed eyes. He was quite sure that Paavo wasn't even aware of the drama that had just played out in the room. "What's wrong?"

Paavo stared at the phone coldly. "No one's answering the phone in the Da Vinci restaurant in Rome. Angie should be in bed now, sleeping." A savage look of anger mixed with fear flitted across his pale blue eyes.

"Didn't you say the phone's downstairs in the restaurant—"

Paavo cut him off. "It's Marcello."

"What?" Benson blinked at the non sequitur before he recalled where Paavo had been earlier. "Shit!"

Paavo smiled mirthlessly. "That's right. The body in the morgue is Marcello Piccoletti. The *real* Marcello Piccoletti."

Chapter 30

Angie was in tears. She and Father Daniel had walked around the empty streets near Da Vinci's and over to St. Peter's Square, but Cat was nowhere to be seen.

When Angie woke up at 2:00 A.M. to find her sister gone, she told herself it was nothing to worry about, that Cat was downstairs using the bathroom or making a middle-of-the-night raid on the refrigerator. But she wasn't. As time passed, Angie grew scared.

She didn't know where to go, what to do. The police were the last people she could go to. She didn't know how to find Luigi, Bruno, or Cosimo, and she was afraid to wander the streets alone. She told herself she should just sit and wait.

She tried it, she really did, until, frantic, she found herself ringing the bell to Father Daniel's rooming house. The manager looked askance, but when she explained that her sister was missing, he woke up the priest. Daniel quickly dressed and met her.

As they searched, she told Father Daniel the whole story of why she and Cat were in Italy.

"Let's go back to the restaurant," he said when she finished. They were near the Tiber at the Castel Sant'Angelo, built by the Emperor Hadrian and sometimes used as a refuge by Popes in the Middle Ages.

"I'll make you some coffee or tea. Your sister will be all right. I suspect she contacted Marcello. There may be a lot more going on between them than you know about."

Angie was appalled by the idea. "My sister wouldn't run off to be with Marcello! Or . . . I don't think she would."

Daniel gazed at her with compassion. "Let's wait a while. You're probably working yourself up for nothing."

"Now that I've talked it over, you might be right," Angie said, a little sheepish, and also annoyed, as they turned toward the restaurant. She was going to give Cat a piece of her mind for scaring her this way. "I never should have awoken you. I'm sorry. I should let you go back to bed."

"It's all right," he said. "I'll wait. I haven't had anything so interesting happen since I came to Rome. All I've done is study and pray. It should be enough, but it just isn't. The longer I'm here, the more I think I'm not very good at this profession I've chosen."

The tremor in his voice told her how much this admission cost him. "All I can say, Father Daniel, is that you've made me feel better."

"Thanks," he said, and gave her a wan smile.

Once again, someone or something landed hard against the door to Marcello's house.

Cat watched, stunned, as Marcello pulled the familiar black leather box from under his mattress, thrust it into her arms, and flung open the window.

"But—But—" she sputtered, her gaze jumping incredulously from the box to Marcello.

"Go! Hurry!" he ordered. "Take it with you and hide it. I'll find you when I can. Now, go!"

The front door opened with a crash.

He scooped her up, tossed her feet first out of the window, and slammed it shut.

It was only a short drop to the cement-covered side yard. Cat landed on her butt, and sat there shocked. Until she heard a gunshot.

Scrambling to her feet, the box clutched in both hands, she ran.

Neighbors ran out of their homes and shouted. Dogs barked.

Her legs shook and wobbled as she forced them forward, the old joke playing in her mind: "Why'd you run away from the gunman?"

"Because I couldn't fly."

If she could, she would, especially when she reached a chain-link fence in the backyard. It was about five feet high, covered with flowers and vines. She heaved the box over first, then hiked up her skirt and somehow managed to hoist herself up onto the top metal bar. Her plans to gently lower herself fell apart when she lost her balance and toppled into a thick patch of prickly shrubs. She crawled to the box, picked it up, and stumbled away with every muscle, joint, and bone in her pampered forty-year-old body aching. Her Bowflex machine would feel like child's play after this. Fear that whoever was trying to get at Marcello would spot her with the box and come after her spurred her on.

Someone yelled at her as she ran, and she hollered back, "*Dov'é la polizia?*"—Where are the police?—which she hoped would tell them that she was law-abiding.

At the sound of police sirens, though, she kept going.

When Angie and Father Daniel returned to the restaurant, she made them both a double-shot latte. "Like back in the States," Father Daniel said with a laugh.

"Exactly."

They talked companionably. Angie was a good listener, and soon Father Daniel opened up to her. He talked a bit about himself, his calling to the Church, his life there, and what it was that bothered him. He had a hard time articulating it—but something was missing. He didn't know what it was. He had expected his calling to provide the answer, but it only brought more questions. He sought, but hadn't yet found, and the lack troubled him profoundly.

They were in such deep discussion, it took them a moment to notice when Cat walked in. She stared in shock at the two of them.

"My God! Cat! Are you all right?" Angie jumped to her feet, alarmed. Cat's clothes and hair had dirt, leaves, and twigs stuck to them, and her face and hands looked like she'd rolled in mud. Angie had never seen her pristine sister so grubby. "What happened to you?"

"Father Daniel," Cat said in greeting, ignoring Angie's questions. She placed the box on the table, eyeing the two of them. "What are you doing up, Angie? Did something happen?"

"What am I doing up?" Angie shrieked. "I was sitting here worrying about you, that's what! Pillows on the bed? What do you think I am? Three years old? For one thing, if you were ever as thick and lumpy as those pillows made you look, you'd have entered a fat farm or had your stomach stapled! I was so upset I dragged poor Father Dan out of bed to help me search. Look at you! You owe us an explanation."

"I'm all right." Cat looked down at herself. Her eyes turned glassy and dazed as if everything she'd been through had just then hit her.

Father Daniel eased her onto the chair he'd been sitting on.

Seeing Cat's pale, troubled expression, Angie was

sorry for yelling, but at the same time she wanted to shake her sister. "You were with Marcello, weren't you?"

"Yes." Cat kicked off her shoes and rubbed her feet.

Angie gawked at her shredded nylons. "That animal!"

"As if!" Cat looked appalled and disgusted. "I did this to myself."

"Is there anything I can do?" Father Daniel asked, sliding another chair in place for himself.

Cat shook her head, then gave them both a quick rundown of her harrowing escape and the gun battle she ran from. "They're probably all in jail. Or dead!" Her voice choked as she finished her story. And Angie's latte. "It might have been the police who were breaking in—I have no idea."

Cat's face filled with sorrow and something more. "I told him about his mother."

"Oh dear," was Angie's only comment.

"He didn't take it well, to put it mildly. He swore revenge, but he wouldn't say against who. And, as he was helping me get out of the house, he gave me this." She placed her hand on the leather box.

"That can't be what I think it is," Angie said, but one look at Cat's face confirmed her suspicion. "Did he have it all along? Marcello, I mean, not the elusive Rocco. Sometimes I wonder if Rocco played any part in this at all."

Cat shook her head. "I wish I knew what was real and what was a lie."

Daniel stood, his gaze never leaving the box. "That isn't . . ."

Cat turned the clasp and lifted the lid. Inside was a rusty iron chain, twisted round and round like the coils on a snail's shell. Two large loops were on the ends.

"It's just a plain old chain." Father Daniel sounded

disappointed as he dropped back into his chair.

The metal wasn't smooth, but was pitted and scored by time. Or perhaps when it was made, no one bothered to smooth the iron used on prisoners. As Angie looked at the large, rectangular links so similar in size and shape to the chains she'd seen displayed in San Pietro in Vincoli, her heart began to beat heavily.

"It's the chain I saw in Marcello's house," Caterina said.

"Isn't it what you expected, Father?" Angie asked, seeing his still crossed brows.

"Not at all," he murmured.

She touched the chain with just a couple of fingers. "I find it remarkable." A small symbol was chiseled into an end link. "What's this?"

Father Daniel studied the link. "It . . . it's Aramaic." His voice slightly quivered. "It's a symbol used by the earliest Christians for Peter. It stands for 'Cephas,' which St. Paul and the early Christians in Rome called Peter. They got it from the Aramaic word *kephas* or *kipha*, for 'rock.' Christ said Peter would be the rock upon which his Church was built. The name Peter comes from 'Petros,' which is the Latin equivalent."

Angie slipped her hand under a few of the links and lifted. It was heavy, deceptively so. She imagined what an effort it would be to move while bound with these chains.

"That means it must have touched St. Peter."

"Not necessarily," Father Daniel said. "It could also simply mean it was forged by someone whose name started with a *K*. The Aramaic equivalent of Kevin the Ironworker."

Angie was shocked. "Don't you feel anything special in its presence?"

"No," he replied glumly.

"That's strange." She touched the chain again. "Because I do. Think about it! This chain, something I can touch, reminds me that Simon Peter was here in Rome. He walked over the same land as we walk today. He was just a simple man, a fisherman. He felt pain and fear when he was captured. Felt the weight of a chain binding him—even if not this one. I'm reminded that Peter was no different from you and me, and I can't help but think of how horribly he suffered."

He stared at her with envy. "I wish I could find even a smidgen of that feeling."

"Could it be that you're searching too hard?"

His eyes widened, almost stricken, as he contemplated her words.

"You've been talking to Maria way too much," Cat said to Angie, referring to their third sister. "I don't feel anything either, but then, I've never been one for woo-woo of any kind. What I want to know is where Marcello got this. I've been thinking about the archeologists who eat at Da Vinci's. The father is supposed to be friends with Marcello. What if they found the chain and worked out a deal together?"

"You know them, too, don't you, Father?" Angie prodded.

"No. I don't think so."

"You followed them," she said.

"Me? No." He shook his head.

"I saw you. Last night," she insisted.

"I take a walk every night," he said, looking at her strangely. "I didn't follow anybody." He lightly ran his fingertips over the chain, then shook his head with dejection before facing Cat. "Marcello gave it to you for safekeeping. What does he intend to do with it? I can take it—"

"No!" Cat put the chain back in the box and shut it. "I'll handle it." She headed upstairs, clutching the box tight.

"Cat, wait!" Angie called, but her sister didn't listen.

She walked with Daniel to the door. "I'm sorry, Father."

Daniel's face darkened. "She's upset. Go to her. We'll come up with something tomorrow. But whatever else you do—just in case—keep the chain safe. It's in your hands now." He stared glumly at the stairs Cat had climbed. "God truly does work in mysterious ways."

Angie found Cat sitting up on the bed, pillows against her back, the leather box on her lap. "We've got the chain now," Cat said. "We can go back home."

"That's what I was hoping to hear!" Angie said, crossing to the window. "Good-bye, Rome!"

Did something just move on the far side of the street? She blinked and stared. It might have been a passerby who'd stopped. Or someone watching …

She backed away from the window. "Didn't Marcello think you'd been followed to his house?"

"Yes." Angie's stark expression made Cat suddenly wary.

"What if someone followed you back here?" Angie whispered.

Cat scrambled to her feet. "My God, you're right. We've got to get out. Maybe the American embassy?"

"It's probably locked up for the night. Security guards won't let us in."

"A hotel?"

"Remember how hard it was to find a vacant one last time?"

"The airport?"

"We don't have our passports."

Exasperated, Cat said, "What then?"

Angie smiled. "A place no one will talk about."

Chapter 31

"What do you mean, you want to hide here? You're crazy!" Cousin Giulio's arms were upraised and gyrating like an Italian stereotype as he yelled at them. He was in his sixties, with grizzled gray hair and a hawklike nose. The house, on the outskirts of Rome near the catacombs, was large and quite nice. They stood in the front courtyard under a lemon tree, and hadn't been invited in.

Cat had tried to visit him a couple of years earlier, when she and Charles were in Rome. It hadn't worked.

The fact that Giulio was awakened at five in the morning and had to pay the taxi driver because Cat and Angie didn't have enough money wasn't making this visit any more propitious than the last.

Not even his medium-sized brown and white dog liked them. It barked incessantly, despite Angie's best attempts at making friends. When it bared its teeth at her, she stopped trying.

"How can you turn us away?" Cat shrieked right back, making her voice easily heard even over the dog's continuous *woof*s. "We're your cousins! Family!"

He clasped his hands in prayer and looked toward the still-dark sky. "My grandmother is spinning in her grave!" He flung his arms wide and bellowed, "Why does she keep pestering me, this American cousin? Why doesn't she leave me in peace?"

"Believe me," Cat said with disgust, "it's not by choice!"

He glared at her. "You aren't welcome here!" He glanced down at the dog. "Be quiet, Luciano! They're leaving."

The dog wouldn't stop barking. It now ran in circles.

"Fine!" Cat's voice boomed as she turned toward the gate. "But if we get killed, you'll have to explain it to our parents. You think family relations are bad now, just wait!"

"What's wrong with you two?" Angie took hold of Cat's jacket, stopping her. Much as she didn't like what was going on, she liked the idea of being out in the street even less. "How can things be bad between our families when no one ever talks about Cousin Giulio?"

The dog barked even more hysterically.

"There!" he yelled back. "What did I tell you! You only want to use me. No wonder our families don't speak."

"Why don't they?" Angie found herself shouting to be heard.

"Your grandmother was a hateful woman," Giulio proclaimed loudly. "She insulted her sister, my grandmother. She was never forgiven. We swore a blood oath on my grandmother's dying day that we would never forget or forgive."

"Why?" Angie curved her hands around her ears, trying to hear.

"It had to do with your grandfather," Giulio hollered. "He courted both sisters. Your grandmother married him."

Angie cringed. Sisters. It all made sense now.

The dog had barked so much it was losing its voice.

Its deep *woof* became a squeaky *weef*. Thank God, Angie thought. Her ears were ringing.

"Isn't it time we got over it?" Angie was beside herself now. "It happened ages ago. "

Giulio proudly lifted his chin. "For an American, yes. For an Italian, it was only yesterday."

"But they're all dead!" Angie screeched.

Giulio rolled his eyes at that, then turned to Cat. "Who are these people after you?"

"We don't know," Cat answered. "All we know is we don't want them to catch up with us."

"What do they want?" he asked.

Cat and Angie glanced at each other. "We don't know that either," Angie said. "That's what makes it all so scary."

His brows crossed skeptically. "Sure, you don't. You think I believe you? My grandmother was right about your family!"

"Who cares?" Disgust dripped from Cat's voice.

Weeeeef! The dog sounded as if he was in pain.

So was Angie—in pain from all this family nonsense. She regarded Giulio with great unhappiness. "Do you know anywhere we could hide? Could you lend us some money for a room? We're running low."

"Do you know how expensive rooms are in Rome?" he asked. "Nobody but tourists can afford them! When we had lira I was a rich man. Now that we have the euro, I'm poor. That euro is the ruin of us all! It's probably an American plot!"

"Do you have a friend, or anyone, to help us?" Angie pleaded.

"*Mamma mia!* I can't take it!" He threw up his hands. "I have a room over the garage that I rent. It's vacant until Monday, when my new tenant moves in. I must paint and clean it up. You can stay there one night. One night! You hear me?"

"That's fine," Angie said, "because tomorrow, as soon as we can get our passports back, we're going home."

Although bone-tired after what felt like the longest day ever, Angie couldn't sleep, unable to convince herself that she had nothing to worry about.

A rattling sound caught her attention. She sat up. The dog, Luciano, began to bark even though he hadn't regained his voice. He sounded as if he was gargling.

The rattles seemed to be coming from the front door to the above-garage studio.

Angie reached over to Cat's side of the bed and shook her. "Stay quiet! Someone's outside!" she whispered. "Get dressed, Cat! Fast. We've got to get out of here."

"Maybe it's Giulio," Cat said hopefully, immediately awake.

"Maybe it's someone who followed us here!"

"My nerves can't take much more of this," Cat whispered. She quickly pulled on her T-shirt, skirt, pumps, and put on her thick glasses. "If anyone takes a picture of me this way, they could blackmail me with it for the rest of my life!"

"Stop whining and grab your things," Angie said. "Maybe we can sneak back to Giulio's house and he'll protect us."

"Fat chance." Cat took the tote and ran into the bathroom.

"What are you doing?"

"I'm getting my contact lenses. I can't go around with glasses! Where's the wetting solution?"

"Will you hurry! You can put your lenses in later!" Angie yanked Cat away from the toiletries. She'd put on her clothes and was ready to run.

They crept to the door, listened, and when they heard nothing, snuck out. Cat pushed her glasses higher on her nose. The two tiptoed away from the garage and were heading for the main house when two men appeared in front of them, blocking their way. One was huge, the other short.

The men froze, gaping in almost as much surprise as the women.

"*Stooopah!*" the smaller man cried in fractured English. The big one raised a crowbar high and started toward them.

Angie and Cat screamed, turned and ran toward the backyard, hoping to find someplace to hide. The men charged after them.

Almost immediately they reached the fence. They screeched to a halt, trapped.

"Throw it!" Angie whispered to Cat.

"Are you crazy?" Cat whispered back.

Angie didn't have time to explain. She reached into Cat's tote and took out the black box. She shook it so the two goons could hear it rattle. "Is this what you want?"

"Don't let them have it!" Cat shrieked, grasping wildly for the box.

Angie flung it as hard as she could out over the fence.

The flat box spun like a Frisbee, then plummeted down, landing in a neighbor's clump of blackberry bushes.

As Cat gaped in horror at her sister, the men looked from the women to the box, trying to decide which to go after.

Richie Amalfi showed up at Paavo's door that evening. Why not? Paavo thought. Just about everyone else in the Amalfi family had. Paavo was starting to feel as if he lived at Grand Central Station.

Angie's cousin Richie was the Amalfis' "go-to guy"

—the one who could always be counted on to find out the who, what, when, where, and why of anything happening on the wrong side of the law. As far as Paavo could tell, Richie walked a narrow line between what was legal and what was not, and somehow managed to stay out of jail. Most of the time, he was up on a balance beam, but sometimes the beam seemed to shrink to a tightrope. A very thin, bouncing tightrope.

"Serefina sent me over," Richie said. He was in his forties, about five-ten, husky, with wavy black hair that was worrisomely thin at the crown. "There's someplace I gotta take you."

"Now?" Paavo asked.

"Serefina says." His dark eyes had a hang-dog look. "I guess Angie's at it again."

Paavo tucked his gun into his shoulder holster and put on a jacket. "She tries to say it was Cat's idea."

Richie snickered. "I can't see Cat putting herself in danger. That idea has Angie's fingerprints all over it."

Paavo just shook his head as he got into Richie's Cadillac.

"She's always been that way," Richie added, as if that might be some consolation.

"I hate that she's out of reach." Paavo shuddered.

Richie started the car, and then, hands on the wheel, he faced Paavo, his dark eyes sympathetic. "You want to stop somewhere for a beer or something first?"

"I'm okay." Paavo's mouth was a thin, tense line. "I want to see what Serefina's set up this time."

Richie headed down Geary Boulevard. "Serefina came up with this latest after learning that Marcello's dead. With the chain of St. Peter gone, she put two and two together, and wants us to meet a good friend of hers. He'll help us."

"Who is it?"

"Alfonse Lorentino. You might know him as Alfonse Cement."

Paavo's head snapped toward Richie. "Serefina is friends with Al Cement?"

"Sounds like you know him. Or know of him." Richie gave a toothy grin. "He controls all the cement in the Bay Area. If you want anything built, you gotta go to Alfonse Cement, 'cause if you don't, you might not get good quality cement in your foundation and then you know what happens."

Paavo's jaw tightened. "The building comes down." He'd heard more than that about Alfonse Cement's exploits, but he kept his mouth shut.

Richie smiled. "Exactly. It's a sad, sad thing when people don't go through Alfonse Cement. Serefina phoned him and told him what's going on. He thinks Angie's great. She's his favorite of all Serefina's girls. He'll help us."

Richie led Paavo to a nice home in the Marina district. An elderly woman opened the door, greeted Richie with a kiss and a squeeze of his cheeks, and frowned at Paavo. Instead of leading them up into the house, she took them to a room off the garage. It had a plush sofa, easy chair, big screen TV, Bose radio, and small wet bar.

A white-haired man, his dark olive skin crisscrossed with wrinkles, sat on the sofa and peered at them through eyes like thin slits as they entered.

Richie made introductions.

"I can tell you some stuff, if you want," Alfonse said. Under the slits of eyes were three layers of bags. "But it's all just hearsay."

"That's fine," Paavo said.

He lifted a gnarled forefinger. "I'm telling you what I heard and nothing more. Don't plan on me coming down to court and testifying. That ain't gonna happen

in this lifetime or any other. Anyway, not even you cop-
pers use hearsay these days, do you? That law hasn't
changed with all this Piracy Act shit, has it?"

Paavo thought a moment. "You mean Patriot Act?"

"Yeah. Whatever. You guys can get a lot more info
now. Like with RICO—not Rocco."

Paavo wanted to get on with it. He still hadn't been
able to reach Angie at Da Vinci's and was feeling more
than desperate. If this kept up, he was going to Rome
himself. "I won't expect you to testify about hearsay."

"Good. And these guys are ones I heard of, not ones
I actually know," Alfonse clarified.

Paavo nodded.

"Okay, here's the deal," Alfonse began. "There's
some guys. They got a lotta money, but they done
some bad things in their lives. When they heard that
there was this holy relic, they wanted it."

"How did they hear about it?" Paavo asked.

"This kid, he owes them money. A lot. But he can't
pay it. Wife wants to buy a lot of stuff. New baby. Meth
habit. The guy's broke. Busted. But he's on the job one
day, and he hears about this holy chain, and it's supposed to be real valuable. He's thinking: the guys he
owes money to, they're religious. He goes to them, and
they want it. They want him to steal it, but he convinc-
es them that they ain't gonna save their souls if they
steal something, right? So they make an offer to Rocco.
But Rocco, he's a greedy son of a bitch. He wanted top
dollar—five million. They wouldn't go no higher than
two."

"Wait." Paavo stopped him. "You said Rocco. They
went to Rocco, not Marcello?"

"You think these guys don't know who's who? Of
course they know who's Rocco and who's Marcello."

"How?"

Alfonse Cement rolled his eyes and looked at Richie as if to ask what the hell kind of idiot cop did he bring him? Richie just shrugged.

"Here's the story," Alfonse said. "Marcello got himself in trouble with . . . I'll call them the Boys. They didn't want him dead, they just didn't want to see his face around here no more. He went to Belize or someplace like that. Some place cheap, you know? But he's got a couple businesses. His brother, Rocco, has nothing, so the mother, she tells Rocco to run the businesses so Marcello won't lose it all until this problem with the Boys gets straightened out. Rocco does as told. More than that. He buys a house with Marcello's money, lives high on the hog, and if anybody questions him, he leans on them. Or Flora does. If you know the Piccolettis, you don't question them if they say Rocco is King of England, *capishe*?"

"I understand," Paavo said. "These men who wanted the chain of St. Peter were negotiating with Rocco but getting nowhere."

"That's right. So they find Marcello and say if he wants all to be forgiven, he'll help them out. He agrees, comes back to the U.S. and goes to see Rocco." Al Cement stopped talking to make himself another whiskey and water. So much talking was drying his throat.

"Then what?" Paavo shook his head in response to Alfonse's silent offer of a drink.

"Then? I don't know." Alfonse poured himself three fingers. "Next thing we know, Marcello's dead, and Rocco and the chain are gone."

"What about Flora Piccoletti?" Paavo asked. "Any idea what happened to her?"

"No. That's bad. I mean, what kind of jerk kills someone's mother? It wasn't the Boys. They wouldn't do that. Nobody knows."

Instinctively, Paavo felt he was telling the truth.

"What about Caterina's husband, Charles Swenson? Is he involved?"

For the first time, Alfonse smiled. It looked like his face might crack from the strain of it. "Involved? Charles? You're shitting me. He's no more involved than a puck is in a hockey game—just something everybody else knocks around."

"Do you know where he is?"

"I don't know. I got my suspicions, but I can't really say." Alfonse started to cough. "I gotta take my medicine and lay down. Things aren't always what they seem. Remember that, and I think you'll find him."

Chapter 32

 The men chose to go after the leather box and chain. They climbed over Cousin Giulio's high fence into his neighbor's yard.

Cat and Angie ran shrieking like banshees to the house.

Giulio opened the door immediately. "What's all the noise? You woke up my dog."

The dog looked miserable. His voice was completely gone now.

Cat and Angie rushed inside. "Call the *carabinieri!*" Cat screamed. "Some men want to kill us."

"What men?" Giulio cupped his hands to the window and peered out. "I see a couple of men running from my neighbor's yard."

"Are they carrying a black box?" Cat asked.

"They have something. What the hell's going on?"

"Damnation!" Cat sat down, fanning herself with her hand. "At least we're safe, Angie. We can hide here until it's all straightened out. I give up."

"Hide here?" Giulio yelled. "You *are* crazy!"

"I don't think we should," Angie said, her voice quavering.

Cat looked at her crossly. "Why not? Those goons won't want anything more to do with us. They have the chain now, thanks to you!"

"Uh . . . Cat," Angie began, "there's something I need to tell you."

Cousin Giulio insisted that they leave his house immediately, which wasn't such a bad idea since the goons would probably be furious and come looking for them as soon as they discovered Angie had put a dog's choke chain in the leather case.

Giulio gave them money for a taxi and asked that they never darken his doorstep again.

They took a cab to Marcello's house, Angie protesting the entire way and Cat swearing they could trust him.

He wasn't there.

The front door lock had been ripped from the jamb, so they walked in with no trouble.

They found few clothes and even less food. Luckily, no blood. It looked as if Marcello had taken off, presumably in one piece. The house had no phone.

They put a chair under the front doorknob to keep it shut and sat down to consider what to do next.

Before long Cat stretched out on Marcello's bed to think better, and Angie did the same on the sofa.

Soon they were sleeping like the dead.

Paavo's home phone was ringing as he unlocked the door. He'd left Richie, and was going to pick up his car then drive to Homicide to check up on Alfonse Cement and his cohorts, and see what ties he could find to the Piccolettis.

He hurried to the phone, hoping against hope that it was Angie. His hope died with Bianca's greeting.

"Paavo, you've got to help me! I'm in North Beach, at The Leaning Tower bar. I'm with Maria and Frannie. Frannie was here with some cop, but he left after we showed up."

She sounded strange. "Are you all right?" he asked.

"Yes." She sniffled loudly. "But what if something happens to Trina and Angie? We're all worried, and we feel so helpless." Her sniffling turned to blubbering. "I just don't know what to do."

Paavo pressed the phone closer to his ear. The slurring, weepy voice hardly sounded like the-world-is-wonderful, always controlled, motherly Bianca. She said they were at a bar. "How much have you had to drink?"

"Me? Nothing! Not much, anyway. It's the others. You've got to help us! I just can't do it! I give up, Paavo, I really do!" She started crying harder.

"Bianca, what's wrong?"

"The drinks made us feel better for a little while. Forget how upset we were and all—"

"I'm sure," Paavo interrupted impatiently. "What do you want me to do?"

"Could you come and get us? I can't call our husbands. They'll have conniptions. I need you! Maria was ready to duke it out with every man in sight before—God have mercy—she passed out under the table, and Frannie's flirting with the bartender."

He couldn't handle this. "All right," he said through gritted teeth. "I'll be right there. Just sit tight."

"Ohmigod!" Bianca murmured.

"What is it?"

"Frannie. She just climbed up on a tabletop. And my concerned-and-caring sister is now shouting that she doesn't give a damn about saving any goddamned whales!"

It's not really an Assurance van.

The realization hit Paavo like a tsunami.

He wasn't asleep and he wasn't in bed, but sitting in his dark living room after taking care of Angie's sis-

ters. The stress on them of worrying about Cat and Angie at the same time as trying to placate their mother
and simultaneously not doing anything to give away
how they felt to their father had caused them to all but
collapse.

It made him appreciate even more the strength Angie always showed in the face of challenges. She might
concoct wild schemes, but she wasn't one to give up or
act completely out of character. She was just Angie—
sweet, tough, brave, and optimistic. The sisters seemed
one way, but underneath . . . underneath . . .

And that was when it all came together for him.

The van! He'd stood right next to it.

He could have kicked himself. He phoned the owner
of Assurance Security, waking her from sleep. With a
start he realized it was 3:30 A.M.

The company had four vans to be used by their
installers, and all four were accounted for. They all
looked like the one Paavo had seen when he went to
talk to the employee, Ray Jones.

The van he'd seen parked next to Ferguson's house,
however, was different—much older, the lettering
far less professional. At the time, had he given it any
thought, he would have probably assumed it was one
of the company's earliest vans.

But he knew better than to assume anything in this
job.

He drove to Ferguson's. The van was gone, the house
empty.

He put out an APB.

Five hours later the call came in.

The van was going east on Bay Street when he and
Yosh caught up with it. The patrol officer who'd called
in the number and had been trailing the vehicle put
on his siren as they converged. Suddenly the van took
off through a red light, zipping between other cars. It

turned onto Hyde Street, one of the longest, steepest streets in the city. It was a stupid move on Ferguson's part because the police car and Paavo's Corvette were both able to go up the hill a lot faster than the old van. Reaching the hill was the hard part, however. Bay Street was filled with traffic as usual, and the van running a red light had caused a major tie-up. Cars attempted to get out of the way, but it took a while.

As Paavo drove up Hyde, a cable car was in front of him. He was forced to swing into oncoming traffic to go around it.

When he finally reached the top of the hill, he couldn't see the van. He continued along Hyde. As he crossed Lombard, he looked at the lineup of cars going down the so-called "crookedest street in the world." It was one-way with no room to pass, and cars could go no faster than the slowest car ahead of them. Halfway down was the van.

Paavo sped around the block, careening from Hyde to Leavenworth and back to Lombard. Ferguson must have had a slow, scared driver in front of him because he'd gotten to the intersection only seconds before Paavo. Ferguson hurtled across Leavenworth and continued down Lombard to North Beach.

It was an area filled day and night with people and traffic. Between high, steep hills, often slippery from cable car tracks, not to mention the cable cars themselves, double-parked cars and delivery trucks, tourists who had no idea how to drive in San Francisco, and Muni bus drivers who were probably the scariest of all, it wasn't a good area for a car chase.

Ferguson was probably hoping Paavo would back off.

He didn't. At stake were Angie's and her sister's life and safety.

He went down Columbus Avenue, past Angie's favorite little restaurant, The Wings of An Angel, and past Angie's church, St. Peter and Paul's. Ferguson turned onto Stockton Street and drove past Angie's favorite pastry shop, Victoria's. Paavo wondered if everything in the city was going to remind him of Angie before long. And if so, that was okay.

They zigzagged their way through North Beach without incident. Things got worse when Ferguson neared Chinatown, which was always filled with a crush of people. Someone opened a car door without looking and Ferguson knocked it off. He kept going.

The car owner started to get out as Paavo approached, but smartly nosedived right back into his car.

In Chinatown things went from bad to worse. Two tiny, elderly Chinese women in long black dresses, each carrying two shopping bags filled with groceries, were slowly crossing an intersection when the light changed. Ferguson had to stomp on the brakes, hand on the horn, trying to get them to hurry. The women began to beat his car with bok choy, and yelled at him for being so inconsiderate of his elders.

Somehow, he got past them. As Paavo raced by, the old women were still standing in the street, shaking their fists. Now they added Corvette drivers to their harangue.

Paavo had a sudden macabre image of Angie and her sisters as little old ladies, doing much the same thing. The thought was at once humorous and a little scary, but also made his insides twist with worry and love for her. He shook it away to concentrate.

Ferguson must have realized his mistake by then because he had nowhere to go. To the east was Grant Avenue, which was impossible to cross in less than two lights. To the south was the downtown, a traffic nightmare of one-way streets, blocked streets, buses and trolley cars with center islands to load and unload passengers. Paavo approached from the north. The remaining direction was westward, to Nob Hill.

Ferguson's van strained to go up Sacramento Street, another brutally steep street for any heavy vehicle to climb. Halfway up the block was a narrow side street, and he turned into it, hoping to pick up speed.

Paavo was right on his tail by this time, and pulled into the side street behind him. At the same time, the police car had gone up the parallel street and stopped at the mouth of the side street, blocking it.

Ferguson went up on the sidewalk and jumped out of the driver's side. His wife sprang from the passenger side. Both began to run.

The wife was picked up immediately by one of the officers as she attempted, unsuccessfully, to go over the cyclone fence that surrounded a small neighborhood playground.

Ferguson ran in Paavo's direction, then broke toward Yosh, perhaps thinking that a fairly large, rather rotund Japanese-American was no match for him. He was wrong. Yosh easily caught him and flattened him against the sidewalk.

Paavo pulled the car keys from the ignition. Ferguson had leaped out so fast, he'd left the car running. Paavo unlocked the door to the storage area.

Inside, bound and trussed, was a very scared-looking Charles Arthur Swenson.

Angie and Cat didn't wake up until it was dark out. They scraped together their last few euros and went to a deli for dinner. Foccaccia came in large sheets with a variety of toppings, much like American style pizzas. They selected a sausage-mushroom mixture. The shop owner cut them each a long rectangular piece, warmed it, folded it in half, and wrapped one end in a paper holder. They ate it like a sandwich. It was delicious.

For water, they drank from a public fountain, as did many Romans. Clean, cold water from mountain springs was found all over Rome in fountains called *il nasone* because the outlet pipe was shaped like a nose.

Next they found a public telephone.

"Angie!" The relief in Paavo's voice pulsated across the wires. "God, but you worried me! Where are you?"

"Worried? How did you find out about the men?"

"What men?" he asked, tension building.

"The ones who broke into Cousin Giulio's. I didn't even tell you about Cousin Giulio, did I? Anyway, I gave them a dog chain and they took it and ran. We're fine. Although they may be back, once they discover what they've got."

"You're kidding me," Paavo said, seemingly following her rambling explanation.

"Actually, Paavo, when a person's been through all I have the past few days, it sort of takes away one's sense of humor."

Paavo apologized, and then let her know that Charles had just been rescued. A medic was checking him over at that moment.

Angie broke off to quickly tell Cat.

"Angie, listen carefully," Paavo said, and she knew a pronouncement was coming. "The dead man is Marcello."

"No. We've been through that," Angie said dismissively. "Marcello is here. We've spoken with him."

"Wrong. You've been talking to Rocco! He's pretended to be Marcello for some years. When the real Marcello came back, it appears Rocco may be the one who killed him. The man you've been talking to—the one you say you like—is very likely a murderer." He let the words sink in before adding, "Come home!"

"Wait until I tell Cat," Angie said, horrified. "We'll

be home soon." Relief coursed through her at the thought.

"You're telling the truth this time?" he asked.

"Absolutely! We're leaving for the airport right away."

She could hear the smile in his voice as he said, "I'll be right here waiting."

Chapter 33

Angie and Cat couldn't leave the country without their passports, and Bruno had locked their passports in a safe at Da Vinci's.

It was a shock to Cat to learn that Marcello was dead, and that all this time Rocco had convinced her he was his brother. They wondered how much Bruno knew about the brothers, and how much he was in on. They didn't want to alert Bruno to their plans if they could help it, since he might tell Rocco.

"I always thought there was something fishy about Marcello," Cat said. "Now I know why."

"Now you tell me!" Angie didn't want to discuss it.

They waited until the restaurant was closed for the night. Using their key, they snuck inside, locked the doors, and put boxes in front of them. They searched high and low for the combination to the safe, hoping Bruno had written it down and hidden it somewhere in the office.

Angie found numbers, all right. Lots of them in a special slide-out compartment under Bruno's desk. She now had a good idea why so many customers showed up even if they weren't having dinner, why so many wanted to shake Bruno's hand, and why he never let anyone else compute tabs or handle meal payments.

None of those numbers, however, opened the safe.

Finally, they gave up and phoned Cosimo, waking him.

He didn't know the combination or where to find it. They asked him not to tell Bruno or Luigi about their call and to go back to sleep. He sounded asleep before he ever hung up.

They knew if they phoned Bruno, he might contact Rocco, so they decided to wait until Bruno arrived at work the next day. Then they would get their passports and immediately make a run for the airport, hoping that with all the security in place, Rocco couldn't try anything.

Assuming that the people after the chain would think they were long gone from Da Vinci's, they decided to remain right where they were.

The restaurant was large, dark, and eerie late at night. Angie found a rolling pin and Cat an iron frying pan, and they went up to the bedroom to wait out the hours.

The bed was inviting, and even the old pajamas were more comfortable than the grubby clothes they were wearing. Morning would come more quickly if they could at least doze a bit.

They got into bed, lights out.

"I'll be so glad to get home," Cat said into the darkness.

"Me, too," Angie said. Only a sliver of light from a street lamp reached the window. "Are you as shocked as I am that Marcello is really Rocco?"

"You know why I should have picked up on it?" Cat put her hands beneath her head, elbows out. "Because I just never cared for him. The old 'zing' I felt as a kid around Marcello was never there. You'd have thought some spark would have continued, wouldn't you?"

Angie's thoughts turned to Charles, along with relief

that he was safe. "Do you think Charles might be involved in any way?"

"Poor Charles." Cat shut her eyes a moment. "I feel so bad about him. I'm sure he's completely innocent."

"Let's think about this," Angie said. "You were set up when Rocco called Meredith Woring to accuse you of theft. A handkerchief with your initials is left at the crime scene to further implicate you. Then Rocco takes the chain and runs off with it."

Cat thought about it. "The timing is all off. Rocco—I should call him 'the phony Marcello'—told people he was leaving San Francisco on Monday, but then he stayed there until Tuesday, when the real Marcello showed up and Rocco killed him. Why would he do that?"

"I have no idea. It makes no sense." Angie rolled onto her back and held her head.

Cat yawned. "As long as I'm not implicated, I don't care. I just want to go home. Stay on your side, Angie. I'm going to sleep." She rolled over, her back to her sister.

"One good thing, at least, has come out of this visit to Rome," Angie said. "It's brought home to me the importance of tradition, of my roots. I've actually figured out where I want my wedding."

"Miracles do happen!" Cat looked over her shoulder at her. "Where?"

Angie sat up. "I know you're going to laugh after all my fussing about something special, but I want to have it in the church where Mamma and Papa got married—St. Peter and Paul's in North Beach. It's a beautiful church, and I can't think of a better place to begin my own married life."

"And it can hold an enormous number of people," Cat said in approval, "so that won't be a problem. My my, after all this, you decide on a traditional wedding!

Frankly, I think you'll be happiest with that. If you
went with trendy, a lot of trendy things simply end up
old and dated before long, whereas traditional always
looks good."

Angie was thrilled to hear Cat affirm what she'd suspected. "Great! Now I've just got to figure out where I
want my reception."

Cat sat up as well, plumping a pillow behind her
back. "It'll be so huge, too bad the *Queen Mary* isn't
for rent."

"A ship!" Angie clapped with delight. "We could
rent a ship and sail from Fisherman's Wharf down to
Monterey or Carmel. Paavo and I could get off there
to get on a plane and go on our honeymoon—maybe
somewhere here in Italy. The guests can sail back to the
city without us. What fun!"

"Don't you think that's a little extravagant, even for
you?"

"You think?"

"Yes!"

"As I recall, your wedding was extravagant," Angie
pointed out. "And anything but traditional."

"Teal and purple were the big colors that year. Being
in design, I wanted to go with whatever was chi-chi.
Big mistake. And no one needs a convention center
for a reception. I steer my clients away from doing the
same thing. Back when I had interior design clients,
that is."

Angie noticed her poignant tone. "Do you miss it?"

"I do. Selling houses is hard work, takes a lot of
knowledge, creativity, time, and energy, but most of the
time I feel more like a lawyer or a kindergarten teacher
than anything. I try to suggest things for people to do
to make their homes more attractive to buyers, but the
bottom line is money. Is it worth the expense, time, and
trouble? If not, forget it. It's not like sitting down with

clients who love their homes and want to make them as beautiful and livable as possible. I guess I've gone from one extreme of home owner to the other. It's a bit of a shock."

"What would Charles say if you went back to design?"

A long time passed before Cat answered. "What does he ever say? Whatever I want, he goes along with. Sometimes, Angie . . . " She paused. "Sometimes, I don't think he cares about me anymore."

"That's not true!" Angie said. "He sits quietly in corners, true, but I've seen how he looks at you. And he's always been quiet."

Cat pursed her lips. "All I know is, I see no reason to ask his opinion when I know he's going to tell me to do whatever I want."

"So you don't ask because you know what he'll answer?" Angie regarded her sister incredulously. "Have you ever considered that if you don't ask, he might take that to mean you don't care? And if you don't care, how could he give a thoughtful reply? You two are in a rut."

"It's not my fault!" Cat began, but suddenly stopped, eyes wide, listening.

She and Angie stared at each other. Had they heard something?

The steps to the second floor were wooden, and some squeaked.

They heard the sound again.

"How could anyone get in here?" Cat whispered. "I barricaded the doors."

"And the windows, right?"

"Me?" Cat said. "No. You checked the windows. Besides, you said lightning doesn't strike twice in the same place—that we'd be safe here."

"And you agreed."

"It did seem logical," Cat intoned.

Barely moving so the bedsprings didn't squeal, they eased themselves to the floor. Angie clutched her rolling pin and went to one side of the doorway. Cat took the frying pan in both hands, lifted it like a baseball bat, and flattened herself against the opposite side.

All was quiet. Suddenly, without warning, a dark figure entered the room.

Angie whacked him hard across the back with her rolling pin. He grunted, and as he arched in reflex, she hit him in the stomach. He doubled over and Cat clobbered him neatly on the head with the frying pan.

The man fell to the ground, out cold.

They were about to congratulate themselves when a second man ran into the bedroom with a shout, his arms swinging. This one was about twice the size of the first. The women had the advantage of darkness and a room unfamiliar to the stranger. Angie smashed the solid wood cylinder across the man's face. He howled and covered his nose, hunched over.

Cat hit him on the back of his head. The frying pan vibrated so badly she almost dropped it.

While the first man was out cold after that, the second one staggered, but that was it. With one hand on his nose, he lifted his other hand to his head to protect it. Cat came down hard on his fingers with the frying pan, and got a satisfying shriek of pain and anger.

Still, he didn't fall.

Cursing, he grasped the pan and pulled it away from her.

Angie whacked him with the rolling pin, hitting his neck, ear, and shoulders, but he wouldn't go down. Each blow only seemed to make him angrier and more ready to fight back. He smacked the rolling pin with the frying pan, and it flew from Angie's hands as if it were a toothpick. She was defenseless, backed against the wall. In the shadows, the assailant looked beyond enormous. King Kong's double.

Suddenly there was the clinking of chains, and then a loud *thwack* as heavy iron chains smacked the man across the nose and eyes. This time he clutched his face, and as he staggered, Angie kicked the back of his knee, hard. His leg buckled, and it was like felling a redwood as he went over backward onto the floor.

Angie and Cat fled the restaurant as fast as their legs could carry them.

They could think of nowhere to go but to Father Daniel's.

The rooming house manager's eyes spun when he opened the door to them. He hurried them up the stairs to the priest, his face a combination of concern, shock, and abject disapproval.

Father Daniel was equally stunned at the sight of two frightened, barefoot women in loose, half-buttoned pajamas standing in his doorway. He put on his glasses as if hoping his near-sightedness had caused his vision to go wildly haywire. It hadn't.

In Cat's hand, clutched like a weapon, was the chain of St. Peter. Daniel swallowed hard, trying to ignore the manager's severe frown as he opened the door to his room wide and bade them enter.

Chapter 34

Charles refused to go to a hospital. Once they determined he wasn't physically hurt or in pain, Paavo drove him to his Tiburon home, where he could shower, change clothes, and eat before the inevitable trip to the Hall of Justice to answer questions.

On the way there, Paavo stopped at a McDonald's and ordered burgers and coffee with extra sugars and half-and-half. The burgers could wait until they got to the Swenson home, but Charles, shaking from cold and shock, needed the warmth and sugar. He wore no jacket or sweater, and Paavo had given him his jacket and turned the Corvette heater to high.

Once in the house, Charles scarcely looked the place over, but headed off to take a hot shower. Minutes later he returned to the kitchen wrapped in a heavy robe with thick socks and slippers. His face, once again, had some color to it.

Paavo watched him practically inhale the two double cheeseburgers and a large fries. Charles was starting on his second coffee and third burger when he gave a loud sigh. Hands trembling, he put the food down and sat back looking dazed.

Paavo poured him a straight shot of brandy. "Are you ready to talk about it?"

Charles gulped down the brandy. He choked and

gasped, but pushed the empty glass out for another shot. He rubbed his forehead, his expression crumbling. Awareness and delayed shock were overwhelming him once more, and he made a visible effort to compose himself. "I wondered if I'd ever see my home or family again." He tried to force a smile or even a laugh, but soon gave up the ruse as his eyes filled with tears.

"Start at the beginning," Paavo said.

Charles seemed to take strength from Paavo's calm. "I had just arrived home when the doorbell rang. I opened it and two people with stockings over their faces pushed their way in. They asked where Cat was—a man and a woman, from the sound of their voices—and I said she wasn't here, that she'd gone to Italy. They didn't believe me at first, and threatened me. I swore it was true."

"You knew about the chain?" Paavo asked.

"Very little. Cat had mentioned that if I knew a potential buyer, to let her know." With a shaking hand, Charles downed another brandy.

Paavo waited patiently.

"They tied me up, blindfolded me. I could tell that they searched the house. I was terrified. All I could think about was Cat and our son. They tried calling Cat's cell phone—they found the number in the house—but it was turned off. The two argued. I overheard some of it. They thought she'd stolen the chain. It made no sense. Cat would never steal anything. They figured Cat would call me, and they'd force her to turn over the chain or they'd kill me." He shuddered, his voice plaintive. "We waited all night. She never phoned!"

"What happened next?" Paavo asked as gently as he could.

"The two started to get nervous. It was nearly dawn, and people in the area would be getting up soon for work and school. They decided to leave and take me with them.

"I was shut up in the back of a van, told to lie down and not move. I didn't dare do anything but obey. We ended up somewhere in San Francisco—I knew that because we stopped to pay the bridge toll—and then I could feel the van going up and down the hills, and stopping for traffic lights. The guy complained incessantly about hitting every red light. The woman told him to shut up. Finally, they stopped. I don't know where. They only untied me a couple of times to use a chamber pot. Said if I soiled the van they'd kill me for sure."

He grimaced. Of all the terror and indignities of the past few days, nothing galled him as much as the lack of privacy and the ensuing humiliation. Coupled with his wife's seeming lack of consideration, he was beginning to get angry now that he was out of danger. Anger was good, Paavo thought, as he observed the glint behind the eyeglasses. It was a step in recovering from the trauma of being helpless and frightened.

Charles stared morosely at his cold coffee before beginning again. "At some point, they realized I didn't have my cell phone on me, and the reason their calls didn't get answered was because Cat's cell phone didn't work in Italy. Since they couldn't call her, they had no choice but to wait for her to call me. They went back to Tiburon and got my cell phone." He mangled a french fry. "She never called. She never even cared enough to try to find me."

"She did make phone calls," Paavo said. "She phoned a few times. When you didn't answer, she got worried. She asked me to see what I could do to find you."

"At least she did that much." Charles poured himself more brandy. "But it wasn't quite enough, was it?" He stared at Paavo. "If the situation was reversed and

Cat was the one missing, I'd do everything I could to find her. I'd fly home under my own power if need be. I wouldn't care if she didn't normally turn on her cell phone, I'd have tried it, and would have kept trying every number I knew until somebody answered. I thought . . . I thought she was becoming a little bored with"—he cleared his throat, trying to hide the crack in his voice—"with our lives, but I hadn't realized it had gone this far. That she cared so very little. When did it all go so wrong?"

Paavo had no answer.

"When we first married, I was so crazy about her," Charles said into his whiskey glass. "She was all the beautiful Italian actresses of my youth rolled into one, like Sophia Loren, or Gina Lollobrigida. Turns out she was more Anna Magnani than either of them."

"Who?" Paavo asked.

Charles just smiled. "It's not important. I was intrigued by her Italian heritage. I found it more interesting than she did, in fact. I even learned Italian. Cat laughs at my pronunciation, so I don't speak it around her, but whenever I found myself alone in Italy, I was able to make myself understood. Italians aren't like the French. They appreciate you trying to speak their language."

"Charles, Cat had no idea things would go this far," Paavo said. "No one did. We need to go to the Hall of Justice now."

As Charles went off to get dressed, Paavo checked for messages. Angie should have called from the airport to tell him which flight she'd be taking home.

There were no new messages.

He phoned Da Vinci's one more time to see if Angie and Cat were there.

Once again there was no answer.

* * *

"You know nothing about women's clothes, Father." Angie tried to be kind. He wanted to be helpful, after all. Still, she couldn't hide how ludicrous she felt in her outfit.

"Fashion is my least concern. I wanted to be able to get you both out of here without being reported to my superiors for indecent behavior. It's going to be hard enough explaining to the manager why you came here."

"We told him we needed help," Angie said.

"I know," he said. "Still . . . " The priest had to suppress a chuckle as he looked at them.

When the women arrived, they immediately decided several things. Daniel needed to get them clothes and a place to hide as soon as possible. When the restaurant opened for lunch, he'd get their passports from Bruno and immediately help them get to the airport.

In the middle of the night, he left them to go to a church-run homeless shelter, concocting a story about two women who had lost everything in a fire. The female night attendant was cajoled into picking out clothes, including shoes and undergarments.

When he was asked to describe the women's size and height, he froze. If he described what the two really looked like, he could find himself in big trouble. They were two of the most attractive women he'd seen in his life. Just thinking about their somewhat revealing state of dress when they arrived at his place, he knew he was going to spend a lot of time on his knees in the confessional.

He only took comfort remembering the words of a much loved older priest who was once asked how long it took for a man to become used to being celibate. "About three days after he's dead," was the honest reply.

Daniel drew in a deep breath. The church never said the life he chose was easy.

He described the women as elderly, not too fat, and a little over five feet tall. He hoped that sounded innocent enough.

The clothes he was given proved how good an actor he was.

Angie wore metallic blue polyester slacks and a top with thick yellow and white horizontal stripes. The clothes were baggy, with the slacks not quite reaching her ankles. Cat's outfit was brown slacks and a top with little orangey blossoms on a yellow background. Both women wore white sneakers and thick white socks. He didn't want to think about the unmentionables he also bought for them.

"I've never been so humiliated in my life," Cat said, looking down at herself.

Angie pointed and laughed. "You look so short and stubby."

Daniel had to agree. For some reason, Cat reminded him of the way children drew mushrooms with dotted tops and boxy brown stems.

"Anyone who looks like a bumblebee on steroids has no right to point fingers," Cat retorted. The two sisters beamed death stares at each other.

"Ladies," Father Daniel said, holding up his hands, "we've got to get out of here before more people start milling around. You should put on the rest of your things so we can get going."

He had also bought wool overcoats and head scarves. Cat studiously inspected the coat for lice, moths, or other bugs before putting it on. They covered their hair with the scarves, knotting them under their chins.

Daniel put the St. Peter chain in a paper bag for Cat, and handed Angie a heavy wooden rosary. "Pull the scarves forward onto your foreheads a little and keep your heads down. I think we can do it."

He nodded and opened the door. The women stepped

out to the hallway and headed for the stairs. Angie's sneakers were so large, they slapped and squeaked with each step she took.

Daniel followed behind them. They met three residents as they passed, all of whom stopped and gawked at the strange procession. Angie and Cat said nothing, knowing even a *"Buon giorno"* would give away their American accents. Daniel nodded, trying to act as if nothing the least out of the ordinary was going on.

He'd been able to borrow a car at the Vatican. Fortunately, neither Angie nor Cat asked how.

When they reached the street, he saw a huge, scowling man with a bandage across his nose, standing in a doorway, watching the passersby.

Angie shivered, and Daniel quickened his steps to pull alongside her, hiding her from view. Did she recognize the huge man? Was he one of the assailants?

Perspiration beaded on Daniel's brow as he contemplated his next steps.

The car wasn't far, and he quickly hustled them into the small black Mercedes Smart Car. Back in the States, he had no idea Mercedes made anything so tiny. But then, most of the cars in Rome were minuscule by U.S. standards.

As he drove nervously away from the Vatican, he looked into his rearview mirror. The man with the bandaged nose was no longer in the doorway.

Chapter 35

"I know a small church that's been all but abandoned," Father Daniel said as he drove. He was a slow, careful driver who sat up rigidly in the seat, eyes straight ahead, and tended to make the Italians around him have fits. Angie could see that many wanted to honk their horns at him or do worse for his slowness, but when they saw his collar, they refrained.

"It's the Church of St. Monica," Daniel continued, "named for the mother of St. Augustine. She prayed for twenty years that her world-loving pagan son would become a Christian, and when he did, he developed into one of the intellectual fathers of the Church. St. Monica's is on the outskirts of Rome, on the road to Ostia, where Monica died. As the number of people in parishes has declined, many of the smaller churches with no history, nothing special to keep them open, are being closed. There are fewer and fewer priests as well."

"I hadn't realized that," Angie said.

"It's true. It's a strange time for Europe and the Church. A dark time."

Angie felt a chill as she stared at the gray industrial buildings off the highway. She couldn't help but reflect on Monica and the kind of mother she was to Augustine, as opposed to the way Rocco had spoken of his own—how she'd talked him into leaving the restaurant he loved to concentrate on a furniture store. Had he been left alone, Angie wondered if so much tragedy might have been averted.

Daniel parked the car at the bottom of a steep hill and they walked up. The church sat at the top. Halfway up the hill, along a narrow path off to the left, was a small house. He unlocked the door and they entered. "This is the caretaker's cottage. It's empty now, so you can stay here. The caretaker from St. Boniface comes by occasionally to check on things." He led them into a two-room house. It was sparse, but comfortably furnished. It had no telephone, Angie noted. She would have to find one and tell Paavo soon everything that was happening. *Soon*, she told herself, *soon she'd be with him again*. That one word, soon, had become her mantra.

"The rectory is closed up as well, and the church is locked. A key to it is on the ring I'll leave you. You can go in if you'd like. It might be a comfort," he said as he rubbed his hands together from the cold, then lit a fire in a woodstove. It seemed to be the only source of heat in the house.

"In the meantime," he continued, "I'll talk with some people to find out all I can about getting you two out of Italy and back to the U.S. without being arrested. Your instincts were right about not wanting to get tied up in the Italian legal system. It's something to avoid at all costs."

"Good," Angie said, "especially since I need to get back to San Francisco in time for my meeting with Chef Poulon-Leliellul."

"Who?" Daniel asked.

"Don't start, Angie," Cat warned.

Angie shrugged. "It's nothing."

* * *

Once they were alone, they watched the sunrise until Cat announced she was going to lie down for a while and headed for the bedroom.

Angie stretched out on the sofa and stared at the ceiling. She didn't like the idea of being so cut off in this strange place, and wondered if it was wise to trust Father Daniel.

She told herself she had no reason not to, and her instincts said he was a good man. It was odd, however, that he just happened to talk to her in English at the restaurant that first night, and then he just happened to be at St. Peter in Chains, and he just happened to be staying right next door to Da Vinci's.

Also, why did he deny following the archeologists?

They were now completely dependent on him. Everything they owned—their few euros, credit cards, passports, even their makeup—was all back at Da Vinci's, and they had no way to get there.

While Cat snored, Angie decided to look over their surroundings. She took the key to the church. There were times in life she prayed for divine intervention. This was one of them.

She took the back route to the church from the caretaker's cottage. It was winding and overgrown with shrubbery. A turn in the footpath gave her a glimpse of the small church. Signs of neglect were evident even from a distance, and yet, against the gray, overcast sky, there was an aura about the place that was mystical, even spiritual. Her step lightened as she neared it.

Around the far side of the church stepped an elderly priest. He stopped and stared, as shocked to see her as she was to see him. He had close-cropped white hair, a white beard, and a gray moustache, while his eyebrows were thick and dark. In the gloom, his eyes appeared black. He wore a brown friar's robe with a cowl.

"Why are you here?" His voice was harsh, his gaze severe.

In nervous, clumsy Italian, Angie apologized for disturbing him. She had to admit that older nuns and priests still had the whammy on her, and in their presence she often reverted to feeling like an awkward schoolgirl. "I'm staying at the caretaker's cottage with my sister. Father Daniel, who is studying at the Vatican, let us in."

The priest's gaze narrowed as if trying to determine if she was lying. In nearly accentless English he said, "Our bishop must have approved, then."

Angie hadn't thought about that, but it made sense. Father Daniel didn't seem to be a person who would do anything without permission.

"Is this your church?" she asked.

"No, but I check on it from time to time. None of the local people come here anymore, and there's nothing inside to draw pilgrims to it. It's simply a lovely old church that has stood for nearly three hundred years. That is neither old nor special in Rome."

He invited her to see the church if she wished. She agreed and told him her name and where she was from. He said she could call him Father Pio, and that he, too, was only a visitor in the area. His manner was gruff, but oddly comforting, and she followed with no hesitation.

They entered through a side door, and Father Pio turned on lights, which only illuminated a small part of the nave, near the altar. The heat had been turned on and a few candles burned. The rest of the church was shrouded in darkness, but she could see the gold and marble surrounding the altar, statuary, and artwork. "This is lovely," she said.

The old priest placed his hand caringly on the rail. "It saddens me to see it going to ruin."

Angie realized she was with a person who could probably explain some Church history to her.

They sat down in a pew, and Father Pio answered her questions about Peter in chains in Jerusalem and Rome and his imprisonment and death. As the padre spoke, his words echoed through the empty church. The lights flickered, and the outside wind, which had been a gentle breeze, suddenly howled. Rain fell and made a patter on the roof. Yet inside, the church felt warmer, and the candles brighter.

"*Grazie*, padre," Angie said when he finished.

"Why do you ask about such things?" Father Pio inquired.

"I wonder if it's possible that . . . that there's another chain that held St. Peter, one the Church doesn't yet know about."

Together they left. The rain had diminished and was now only a gentle mist. Dark, piercing eyes studied her. "If such a thing existed, it would be a great find. Something that the people should be allowed to see. Something that might help them remember. I will pray that you are given guidance."

With that, he made the sign of the cross over her, then turned and walked back into the church.

Angie was halfway down the hill to the cottage when she paused. What had Father Pio meant by "remember"?

Although it was night, Yosh, Calderon, and Benson were still at work in Homicide when Paavo entered with Charles.

Calderon was sitting at his desk, reading through some paperwork and whistling an old show tune that Paavo recognized as a favorite of Angie's. He remembered some of the words. "Two lost souls on the highway of life . . . "

Calderon must have felt Paavo's eyes on him because he looked up, then all around the office. Benson and Yosh were grinning broadly. "What," he said, "you guys don't like music all of a sudden?"

Paavo remembered the song ended with something like, "Ain't it just great, and ain't it just grand . . . we got each other."

He hadn't seen Calderon since Luis went for coffee with Frannie, after she had quoted something about mothers.

Mothers. He couldn't help but reflect on Flora Piccoletti and Serefina Amalfi, and the very different, albeit strong, influences both had on their children's lives.

As he glanced back at Calderon, he wondered if the time Luis Calderon had spent with Frannie was the reason he seemed so happy now. No. Impossible.

He introduced Charles to Calderon and Benson, then led him to the interview room. Before taking his statement, Paavo went to his desk to check for messages from Angie.

Yosh stopped him. "We've got a match! Len Ferguson. His fingerprints were found on Flora Piccoletti's back door. We don't know when, we don't know why, but I'd say it's pretty suspicious."

"Especially since Ferguson denied being in the house." Paavo quickly scanned the report Yosh had drawn up when he'd booked the Fergusons. "We've got him and his wife for kidnapping Charles, but if they killed Flora Piccoletti, we're looking at murder one."

"I thought you must be hungry," Father Daniel said with a big smile as he walked into the cottage. He put plastic grocery sacks with bread, milk, eggs, pancetta, cheese, butter, coffee, and tea on the table. "We can have bacon and eggs, American style." He opened a cupboard in search of a pan. "I'll even cook."

"No need," Angie said, taking the pan from him. "Cooking is my forte."

"It's the one thing she does better than me," Cat offered.

As she made brunch, Angie told Daniel about her strange conversation with the elderly priest. "He said the church will be destroyed if there isn't some reason for local people or pilgrims to visit it. He sounded very unhappy about that."

Daniel listened to her story with a perplexed look. "There's no priest connected with this church, Angie," he said, shaking his head. "Only a caretaker from St. Boniface, once a week or so."

"But the electricity was on, as was the heat. Candles were lit." Angie was equally puzzled.

"The electricity is off," Daniel insisted. "The church is locked up."

"It's open. I was inside," Angie countered.

"Maybe you dreamed it, Angie," Cat said. "You were lying down when I got up."

"How could I have dreamed the story of the life of St. Peter? Besides, look at my shoes." She held up her feet. "They've still got some dried mud on them. Or are you suggesting I was sleepwalking? After we eat, we'll go back. I'll show you."

"You've been under a great deal of stress." Daniel's words were soft and troubled. "The scene you described was comforting. That might be the reason for it." The concerned way he looked at her made a chill run down her back.

Angie cooked brunch in silence. Everyone felt better after eating, and she was almost ready to concede that she had dreamed the conversation—the whole thing did seem rather otherworldly—but she hadn't. She was determined to show Father Daniel what she'd seen.

Cat refused to waste her time or energy.

When Angie reached the church, the main doors were shut with a large chain and a padlock. She hadn't noticed them earlier. They walked all the way around the church and found the side door she'd entered with the priest. Strangely, there was only one set of footprints going up to and leaving the church. And the door she supposedly used was locked as tight as the one with the padlock.

Daniel unlocked the door and they entered. The church was icy cold and dark. Other than that, everything was exactly as she remembered it.

"How can this be?" She looked around, dazed and confused.

He held her arm. "I'm sure there's a rational explanation."

Angie couldn't believe what she was seeing. She was sure it hadn't been a dream. She'd never been inside the church before, yet knew exactly what it looked like. That was impossible. She shuddered from more than cold.

Father Daniel led her outside again.

"I don't understand." She clasped her hands. "I know what I saw!"

He frowned. "You must have visited years ago when you lived in Italy. You forgot, but subconsciously you remembered all of it."

"No! I'm sure I was there today. I don't get it."

Her eyes searched his clear gray ones, but he had no answer for her. He put his arm around her back and turned her toward the cottage.

"Getting a little familiar, aren't you, Father?"

Angie and Daniel froze at the gruff voice. Cautiously, they turned, and the two "goons," as Cat had called them, who'd broken into both Cousin Giulio's place and their bedroom at Da Vinci's, stood before them.

For the first time, Angie could see them clearly. The slim one had a goatee. He was the goateed man who'd followed them when they first arrived in Rome. The hulking one was ugly with a bandaged nose. He was so huge it was no wonder they couldn't knock him out last night.

"Where's the chain?" Goatee demanded brusquely.

"We don't have any chain," Angie said.

"Don't get smart!" The Hulk stepped forward, raising his hand to smack her.

"No!" Daniel jumped in front of Angie. The Hulk changed his open hand to a fist and punched the priest in the face. Daniel went down hard. His head hit a tree trunk, his glasses flew off, and he was out cold.

"Father!" Angie started toward him, but Goatee grabbed her and dragged her toward the cottage.

"We can't just leave him!" she cried.

"You're going to get that chain for us right now," Goatee said.

They opened the door to the cottage. Cat wasn't there. They searched, but she and the chain were nowhere to be found.

"Where'd she go?"

Confused and miserable, Angie shook her head. She couldn't believe Cat was gone.

Chapter 36

"You made us look like idiots!" the Hulk yelled as he stuffed Angie into the backseat of a tiny two-door Fiat Panda—all three inches of it—and got in front. "A dog chain! Goddamn it!"

She was curled up like a pretzel. "I did no such thing! I don't know what you're talking about, and I demand you let me go. You don't know the trouble you're going to be in."

"Do we look worried?" Goatee asked with an evil chuckle. He got into the driver's seat.

"Where's the chain of St. Peter?" the Hulk demanded.

"You took the only chain I've ever had," Angie said. "If it's not what you want, go find Marcello, or should I say Rocco Piccoletti?"

"We've watched Piccoletti. He doesn't have the chain. We know he thinks you and your sister have it. We want it. Where is it?"

"I don't know!"

"Then your sister does!" Goatee started the car and peeled from the church grounds. "If she ever wants to see you alive again, she'll give it to us."

"What do we care about some old chain?" Angie watched the roads. Entering the highway, he turned toward Rome. "You saw how fast we gave it up once already. We'd give it to you in a heartbeat if it meant we were safe."

"It's worth a lot of money," the Hulk said.

"So am I," Angie told him. "Let me go, and I'll pay you."

"You'll pay all right! Believe me."

"Please." Angie clutched the back of the driver's seat. Goatee drove so fast and the car was so small, she wondered if they'd survive to ever get to Rome. "Let me talk to Piccoletti. Listen in as I do. You'll see that my sister and I don't have the chain. He's got it! You've got to believe me. Would I lie to you?"

"Sure you would." Goatee spat the words at her, then said to his partner, "I think we should start to send little pieces of her to her sister. That'd get us the chain real fast." He glanced over his shoulder at her and grinned. "Maybe first an ear, then a little finger."

"The wife, Nell Ferguson, is ready to deal on the Flora Piccoletti murder," Paavo reported to Lieutenant Eastwood. It was early morning. "She and her husband were paid to make Flora talk—to tell them where to find her son. Flora refused. The wife said Leonard kept getting rougher as his frustration grew with the old girl. Finally, he wrapped her bathrobe sash around her neck, threatening to pull it tight if she didn't talk. She spit at him, and he yanked. Nell tried to pull him off, but couldn't get him to stop until it was too late."

"The loving wife," Eastwood said. "I had one of those once. Did she say who paid them?'

"She swears she doesn't know. Len Ferguson made the contact. She also claims no knowledge of Marcello Piccoletti's murder, and added that if her husband did it, he should fry."

Eastwood grimaced. "At least we agree on that."

* * *

"Your wife gave you up," Paavo said to Len Ferguson. "She fingered you for Flora Piccoletti's murder. She said she tried to stop you, but she couldn't."

They were in an interview room at City Jail, Ferguson's attorney by his side.

"That bitch!" Ferguson added a few more choice words. "None of it's true! She's the one who killed the old lady. She was just supposed to hold the tie around her neck to scare her, not pull it tight, but she was mad because it was taking too long. I can't believe she'd blame me! All I was doing was asking the woman some questions." He did all he could to look wide-eyed and innocent. This time his act didn't work.

"Tell me about Marcello Piccoletti."

"I know nothing about Piccoletti," Ferguson said, "except that him and his brother had pulled some kind of switch. One pretended to be the other or some damned thing. That's all I know, except that he was supposed to have gone to Italy on Monday. The house was supposed to be empty."

Paavo's stare was icy. "But it wasn't."

"No. Both brothers were there."

"Why were you there, Leonard? You'd already set up a deal for some men to buy the chain from Piccoletti. What were you trying to do?"

Ferguson shrugged. His attorney shook his head. "No comment," Ferguson said.

Paavo leaned toward him. "When the men you worked with sent Marcello to buy the chain from Rocco, they cut you out of the deal, didn't they? Suddenly, you were useless to them."

"No comment."

"There was nothing in it for you except to get a few debts forgiven." Paavo watched every nuance of Ferguson's expression. "By this time, you'd learned exactly how valuable the chain was. You wanted more."

The attorney placed a hand on Ferguson's shoulder. "My client doesn't wish to comment on that line of questioning at this time, Inspector."

"You were wearing a priest's costume." Paavo never took his gaze from Ferguson. "Why?"

"No way!" Ferguson replied.

"We showed your photo to the owner of the costume shop. He identified you."

Ferguson sucked in his bottom lip. "I was . . . I was curious about what was going on. That's not illegal. I wanted to watch. Most people don't really see priest's faces, you know. They just see the collar."

Paavo didn't know that Ferguson's assertion was true at all. Just the opposite in his experience. He moved on. "As you headed for Piccoletti's house, what happened?"

"I heard a gunshot," Ferguson said. "I hid and waited. Soon I saw the realtor. She followed one of the Piccolettis. I figured she was there all along, working with them."

Suddenly the attorney put up his hand to stop Ferguson from saying anything more. "Inspector Smith," he began, "my client might have a statement to make. Before he does, I'd like you to discuss with the D.A. what good it would do for Mr. Ferguson to be so cooperative. Until we get a reply to that, my client will answer no further questions."

Paavo stood. Ferguson was at the point where he'd explain who sent him after Flora Piccoletti and Charles. He wasn't smart enough to do anything on his own.

Frustrated, Paavo ended the interview.

Goatee drove around the block while the Hulk looked for Cat inside Da Vinci's. It was lunchtime, but she wasn't there, and no one had seen her.

Angie listened with horror as the goons each tried

to one-up the other with the dreadful things they were going to do to her eventually. They didn't, however, seem to know what to do with her or where to take her right then.

How had she gotten herself into this? Why hadn't she simply stayed in her beautiful apartment in San Francisco, gone to her interview with Chef Poulon-Leliellul, and planned the perfect wedding for her and Paavo? No, she had to get involved. When would she ever learn?

She wondered if Father Daniel had woken up or if he was lying there with a concussion and no help. Had Cat found him or even knew that Angie was gone? Were Cat and Father Daniel trying to find her?

No one knew who these men were who had her, why they were here, or who they were working for.

Given all that, how would anyone rescue her . . . ever?

Paavo hated law-enforcement politics and game playing. They wasted time, and he had no time to waste. He also hated making deals with criminals. And he particularly hated that where his old boss, Lieutenant Hollins, had been a good cop who'd worked his way up in the ranks and whose main goal was to see that bad guys were put away, Lieutenant Jim Eastwood brought whole new elements of politics and complexity to the bureau.

Paavo had to go to him before approaching the D.A. for a deal for Ferguson. Ferguson not only could provide evidence to charge someone with Marcello Piccoletti's murder, but also the person who hired him to go after Flora and Charles.

Paavo needed that name.

Ferguson was a pawn—a murderous one, but a pawn nonetheless. Paavo wanted the king.

Eastwood insisted on talking to the D.A. alone and personally, and Paavo got the definite impression that this arrest was suddenly going to be presented as Eastwood's own. That Eastwood wanted the chief of police job was clear to everyone from the moment they met him. To do so, he needed the D.A.'s support to break into the "old boy and girl network" that was a huge part of San Francisco's political scene, both locally and nationally. Even in Washington, D.C., California's most powerful politicians were a female triumvirate from San Francisco. Those women all frequented the same San Francisco social set. So did the D.A. and the current police chief. Eastwood was going to find getting ahead in this small, close-knit town a lot more difficult than he ever imagined.

Which might be a good thing. Eastwood just might slink back under the Southern California rock he came from sooner rather than later.

The only problem was that Paavo's case was being delayed in the meantime. And any delay could be making things worse for Angie. He'd never been so frustrated, so completely in the dark for hours and days about what was happening to her. Once he got her home—and he had to believe he would—he never wanted to let her out of his sight again!

As Paavo waited, word came that Marcello Piccoletti's Volvo had finally been located. He contacted the CSI team that would impound the car and do full forensics work on it.

He also checked the airlines in hopes that Angie was on a flight home and simply couldn't phone for some reason. She wasn't.

Paavo seethed as he waited for Eastwood to return. As he watched his boss's office, Office Justin Leong knocked on Eastwood's door, then opened it and stuck his head in as if he was expected. Finally Paavo knew where Eastwood had gotten so much information about him and the case early on.

As Leong backed away from the empty office and shut the door, he must have felt Paavo's eyes boring a hole in him because he suddenly glanced toward Homicide's main room.

When he saw Paavo, his face paled. He bowed and bobbed a couple of times before he turned and fled.

Paavo sighed, checked his watch, and went back to his desk.

When Eastwood finally returned, he glanced at Paavo, declared, "No deal," and turned toward his office.

Checking the expletive burning on his tongue, Paavo stood. "I'd like an explanation!"

Eastwood stopped, head down. When he heard Paavo's footsteps behind him, he lifted his chin. "The D.A. says our case is a slam-dunk against Ferguson for Flora Piccoletti's murder, along with kidnapping your soon-to-be brother-in-law, and he wants that prosecution. The public is getting antsy about his record, and next year he faces reelection. He's decided to change his image. The killer of an old lady in her home is important. The mastermind behind a plot that ended up with some shady character dead is not. In fact, according to him, whoever did that should get a civic award."

"Did you tell him—"

"I told him as much as I could. Don't harass me about this!" Eastwood went into the supply closet/office and slammed the door.

Obviously the meeting hadn't gone as he'd hoped.

But Paavo was left with the problem.

Chapter 37

"There's no deal because your wife already made one." Paavo had hurriedly put together another meeting with Len Ferguson and his attorney. "The D.A. is through dealing."

"No good, Inspector." Ferguson's attorney began stuffing papers back into his briefcase to leave. "You're wasting our time."

"The only way I can do anything for you," Paavo said, addressing the prisoner directly, "is if I can show that all of this wasn't your idea, but that you were only working for someone else. Cooperate with me on this, and everything will go easier on you."

"My client has nothing more to say at this time." The attorney stood. "Come back to me when you can deal. It'll be worthwhile, believe me."

"Mr. Ferguson?" Paavo didn't avert his gaze.

Ferguson looked ready to speak when the attorney stopped him. "I . . . I'll have to think about it," Ferguson mumbled.

Paavo knew he had to get out of the interview room fast before he reached across the table and throttled Ferguson or his pigheaded attorney to force cooperation. For now, his hands were tied, and the interview was over.

He met Yosh and Charles back in Homicide. Paavo again checked his phones for messages, and again

Angie hadn't called. He nervously ran his fingers through his hair. The sickening fear that something was wrong filled him.

"We've got to figure this out logically," he said, forcing his attention back to what he could do. He wondered how much Charles really knew. "Did Cat ever mention Marcello to you before he became her client?"

"No, not that I remember."

Paavo pulled out the financial records he'd gotten from Piccoletti's store. "She shows up as a purchaser of some items."

Charles looked it over. "That's when she was doing her interior decorating. It looks like she bought some things from him."

"Cat had high-end clients, and Furniture 4 U sells cheap merchandise. Does that make sense?"

Charles shook his head. "No, but now, I remember something strange. A while back, when she asked me if one of my clients might want to buy a Christian relic Piccoletti wanted to sell, she said this one was 'real.'"

"'This one'?" Paavo repeated, puzzling over the words.

"Let's go back to the handkerchief," Yosh said, still eyeing Charles with suspicion. "It belongs to you, Mr. Swenson. How did it get to Piccoletti's house?"

"I had nothing to do with it!" Charles picked up on Yosh's look. "I can't imagine Cat would have either, unless you're suggesting Piccoletti was at my house at some point . . . in my bedroom, and helped himself." He clamped his mouth shut. "That's impossible!"

"Who put in your security system?" Paavo suddenly asked.

"I'm not sure. Cat handles the household bills. I think she said something about going with a new company that impressed her." Paavo had Charles use his computer to access the Svenson family's online bank information. "She learned about it through someone at Moldwell-Ranker," Charles said. "They deal with a lot of household professionals.... Oh, my. Our company is Assurance! That's the name on the van I was in!"

"Ferguson knew how to override the system." Yosh looked over Charles's shoulder at the computer screen. "He could have gone in, taken the handkerchief. But why? And why steal something of Charles's?"

"It was white, satin, and had Caterina's initials," Paavo said. "He might have thought it was a woman's."

"I hardly think so!" Charles exclaimed indignantly.

Since both Yosh and Paavo had thought it was Cat's, neither responded.

"Someone had to send Ferguson to get the handkerchief, right?" Yosh said after a moment. "And most likely to frame Cat." He looked at Paavo and Charles for agreement. "I think Cat showing up at the crime scene was a fluke. No one could expect that she'd go to Piccoletti's house at that time."

Paavo recreated the crime in his mind. "That was where the problem came in," he said. "If Cat hadn't gone to the house, we'd have found the handkerchief, learned she was the realtor, learned she'd been accused of stealing something of value that was also missing, and we would have wasted all kinds of valuable time proving her innocent while the murderer took off with the chain! Cat and everyone else would have had no idea what really happened."

He began to pace as the original plan grew clearer. "We wouldn't have found out that Rocco Piccoletti was in Italy because we wouldn't have even had a reason to look for Rocco. We'd have found the body. Flora would have identified it as her son, Marcello. Once he was identified, there'd be no reason for anyone else to look for him. Besides, he was shot in the head. Closed casket. No one would have told the police that Rocco had been pretending to be Marcello for several years."

Yosh's and Charles's eyes widened as they recognized the truth of what Paavo was saying. Paavo continued. "I want to think we would have easily gotten Cat off—the evidence against her is small and circumstantial. But we'd be stumped as to where to look for the real killer. Only because she was there and followed Piccoletti to the airport did the entire plan fall apart."

Charles gaped. "You have to admit, it was a clever idea."

Paavo nodded. "Not Ferguson's."

"Never," Yosh said. "We've just got to find out from him whose it was."

"We don't have time to pussyfoot with him and his attorney!" Paavo said, his anxiety about Angie reaching the breaking point. "Whoever came up with this is a lot cleverer than we thought. And a lot more dangerous."

"Cat and Angie still haven't called," Charles's desperation matched Paavo's.

Yosh put out his hands to calm both men. "Let's back up, guys. The answer is here. We're just not seeing it yet. Start at the beginning. What was the first thing that happened?"

"Marcello wanted to sell the relic," Charles said, "and he put his house up for sale. I guess he was going to cash out."

"Especially since he wasn't Marcello," Paavo pointed out.

"But the relic didn't sell, and neither did the house," Charles said. "Cat was lamenting that. I do remember."

"And then?" Yosh asked.

"Then all this." Charles threw his arms up in frustration.

"Wait," Paavo said. "Then out of the blue, Meredith Woring said Marcello called to accuse Cat of stealing the St. Peter chain. That's the piece that never made sense. Why would he do it? I never did contact Woring. You neither, right, Yosh?"

"Whenever I called, I was told she was still with her mother somewhere in Los Angeles and would return 'the next day.' I left messages on her cell phone, but she never answered."

Paavo glanced at Charles. "We know there were two groups after the chain—Ferguson all but admitted to it."

"He did?" Charles said.

"The first group ditched him to deal directly with Rocco and Marcello. They cut Ferguson out of that deal. He wanted more, so he had to go somewhere with his complaint. And the place he went had to have a connection to Cat because she was the red herring. Which means"—Paavo and Yosh looked at each other and said at the same time— "Meredith Woring."

Angie sat docile and in tears in the backseat as the goons drove through the streets of Rome. She had no idea where they were taking her, but she'd determined that to get out of this, she'd have to do it alone.

Her chance came when Goatee turned a corner and she saw a double-parked police car up ahead. A policeman stood beside it, looking up at a building. The Hulk took his eyes from Angie to watch the officer.

As quickly as she could, she glommed on to Goatee's head and stuck her fingers in his eyes. As he yelled and reached up to grab her hands, she managed to evade him just long enough to jerk the steering wheel toward the police car before the Hulk got hold of her and flung her hard against the backseat.

Goatee was too slow to free himself from Angie,

adjust the wheel, and put on the brakes—or his brain wasn't big enough to think of three things at once—because the little Fiat headed straight for the cop's car.

Angie ducked and covered her head.

The cars collided with a shrieking, clanging crunch of metal.

For a moment the goons sat stunned, then they leaped from the Panda and ran. A little dizzy, Angie heard shouts and more running. She popped her head up behind the backseat.

First she saw the cop chasing the goons.

Then she saw the car keys still in the ignition.

"I'd like to speak to Meredith Woring," Paavo said to the receptionist after introducing himself and showing his badge. Yosh and Charles were beside him. "Is she in the office yet?"

The young woman blanched. "I'm sorry, but Miss Woring is out of the office? We don't expect her back today?"

Paavo was initially taken aback by her questions, then realized the woman had one of those irritating styles of speech where every sentence ended with her voice lilting upward.

"Exactly what does that mean?" he asked.

"It means her mother's sick? Or she is?"

"Is she?" Her questioning tone was confusing.

"I guess?"

"When will she be back?"

"I'm not sure she said?"

"Is she home?"

"Probably?"

The receptionist was beyond irritating. "Miss, uh—"

"Ashley?"

"That's as good a guess as any," he muttered.

"Pardon?"

He was gritting his teeth. "Ashley, I need to talk to Miss Woring immediately. I want her home phone number and address right now."

Her mouth moved open and shut like a fish, then she brightened. "I can call her for you and she can tell you?"

"Fine," he said.

Ashley studied the telephone, then hit a button on speed dial. The bored look she wore quickly changed as the phone went directly to messaging. "I don't get it? She never turns off her cell phone?"

"What's her address?" Paavo demanded.

The receptionist was probably trained not to give out such information, but seeing the look on his face, she did.

Paavo, Yosh, and Charles went to the small but exclusive house Meredith Woring lived in. A Mercedes was in the driveway and the lights were on, but no one answered the doorbell or when they knocked.

The front door had a slot for the mail, and Paavo peeked inside.

Several days worth of mail was strewn on the floor.

He and Yosh went around to the back of the house, followed by Charles. The back door was much thinner than the one in the front. With a couple of hard whacks from Yosh's shoulder, it sprang open.

"Ms. Woring?" Paavo called. "Are you here?"

They followed the muted sounds, Paavo and Yosh covering each other while Charles cowered anxiously by the door.

The television in the den was on.

Guns drawn, they slowly headed toward it.

Meredith Woring sat in front of the television set,

but she wasn't watching. She'd never watch anything again.

A bullet had drilled through the creamy smooth skin of her forehead.

Chapter 38

Angie crawled over the seat of the Panda. It was the tiniest car she'd ever been in, and that included bumper cars at amusement parks.

After several tries she managed to shove the stick shift into reverse. She slowly lifted her left foot off the clutch as her right gave it some gas. The car lurched and died. She had learned how to drive a manual transmission on Paavo's ancient Austin Healey, the car he'd struggled with until she bought him a Corvette. She should have practiced more.

If she couldn't get away from the police car fast, she might be arrested.

Again she tried to get the tiny auto to move in reverse. Once more the car died.

At this rate, leaving on foot would be faster.

The front bumper of the Panda had somehow gotten wedged under that of the police car. That required strength and power.

She gave a lot more gas and raised the clutch slowly. The engine revved louder and louder. Suddenly, the bumper sprang loose, falling to the ground with a clatter. The clutch engaged and the car, free now, shot backward at Mach 5 speed, throwing her hard against the steering wheel. It zipped away from the police car, raced right across the narrow roadway, bounded up onto the sidewalk on the opposite side of the street, knocked over a trash barrel, and died.

Then the back bumper fell off.

Oncoming cars honked and slammed on brakes.

Angie stripped the gears as she hunted for first. Eventually the little Fiat began to jerk and shimmy in a forward direction. Somehow she got it off the sidewalk and onto the middle of the street, where it died again.

People opened windows and shouted, disturbed by the sound of car horns and flying garbage. With cars blocked on both sides of the street, drivers gesticulated furiously and obscenely. The traditional American "one-fingered salute" was mild compared to the whole arm gestures Angie witnessed. Finally, head high, she engaged the gear and putt-putted away.

She thought driving in San Francisco was difficult with the hills, cable cars, tourists, and crazed Muni bus drivers, but it was child's play compared to the terrors of Rome's traffic.

Travel lanes were ignored, speed limits considered foolish suggestions. Cars cut in and out in front of her with only a hair's breadth separating them. The only bit of traffic control anyone paid attention to were lights, but sitting at a red light reminded Angie of Nascar: "Drivers, start your engines." Engines revved and Angie knew that if she didn't burst from the gate at the first flicker of green, she'd be rear-ended, run over, and possibly the featherweight Fiat would be picked up and tossed into the nearest junk heap.

She was sure her hair would be completely white before she ever saw her sister again.

She had to find the road to Ostia and then the church. Fortunately, she was familiar with Rome's geography, more or less.

When she saw the church, she drove as close as she could to it, then parked. She took deep, quivering breaths before nearly crawling to the caretaker's cottage.

Father Daniel was lying on the sofa, his head on the armrest on one side, his feet up on the other. An ice pack sat atop his head. "Angie," he said hoarsely.

"Are you all right?" she asked.

He nodded, then winced.

"You're back." Cat was making a pot of tea. "I was wondering how we were ever going to find you."

Angie stared at her sister. What kind of a welcome was that? "Do you have any idea what I've been through?" she ground out.

"Of course. Earlier, I decided to follow you and Father Dan up to the church after all. I took the chain with me and happened to see the whole thing. Once you drove off with those men, I helped Daniel. He came up with a hiding place for the chain that's perfect. We were going to go looking for you as soon as he could drive. Right now, his vision is double. But here you are! You've saved us a lot of trouble."

Angie had the urge to kill. "Big of me, wasn't it?"

I've got to be the unluckiest person in the whole goddamned world, Rocco thought, staring morosely at the telephone.

Seven o'clock, he'd been told. At seven o'clock he could call one of the biggest collectors of religious antiquities in the world right here in Rome. The only bit of luck he'd had all week was getting his hands on a phone number for the guy.

Now he had to wait. He didn't see why he was letting himself get all jacked up about this. In his heart he already knew it wasn't going to work out. He'd just be disappointed again. Ever since he'd gotten the chain, things had gone wrong for him. It was as if it was cursed. He should have ignored it—ignored everything. He never should have left Rome in the first place. He'd been happy here, as he'd told Cat's little sister that day at Da Vinci's.

Marcello had never appreciated Da Vinci's the way Rocco did. It was just a tired little restaurant when his brother owned it. When Rocco took over, he fired the old staff, then hired loyal people, all the while continuing his pretense of being Marcello.

He'd done the same with the furniture store staff. It, too, was now operating well. He bought a house that tripled in value in five years, and even Caterina Amalfi finally looked at him as if he was almost human. When they were teenagers, he was so crazy about her, it hurt. And she never noticed him, not at all. That hurt worst of all.

In short, he was much more successful as Marcello than he'd ever been in his own life.

Then Marcello turned up and wanted it all back. He'd expected Rocco to walk away with nothing.

Rocco had wanted to trust his own brother, but he couldn't. And now Marcello was dead, and everything had gone to hell.

All he had left was the chain—once he got it back from Caterina.

He had to sell the chain. With the money, he'd buy himself a new identity. He could do it. It wouldn't be the first time. He'd lived as Rocky Pick for years in Florida until his mother convinced him to help out Marcello.

He'd only done it because his mother asked him to. All he'd ever wanted was for her to look at him and say, just once, "You're a good son."

It never happened.

Now, even she was dead.

His eyes filled with tears.

If he couldn't sell the chain, that'd be it. He needed to get away and make a new life for himself.

The timer on his cell phone beeped. Seven o'clock. Pessimistically, he made the phone call.

"I've got an extremely valuable relic," Rocco said into the phone. "It's something that every Catholic, maybe every Christian, would give anything to own. The Catholic Church is the owner of something very similar, and they've built an entire basilica around it."

"Every knuckle joint of every saint to ever walk through Italy has a basilica built around it," the collector said scornfully. "Tell me more!"

Rocco told as much as he could without giving away too much, such as his location. How was he supposed to know that Italy had a special law against selling or removing artwork and archeological treasures from the country? The prison time, the fine, both skyrocketed. Hell, if he were to get arrested for owning this lousy chain, he'd be better off back in the States. At least there, in a jury trial, he'd probably be able to convince jurors that he didn't even think he was stealing. You can't steal junk, can you? And the old rusty chain sure as hell looked like junk to him. Cat herself said that. He could have smacked her at the time, and might have, except that she scared the shit out of him. But she did have a point.

"As long as the age can be authenticated by my own appraisers, I want it," the voice on the other end said.

Rocco was so busy with his own thoughts, with the misery of believing he was never, ever going to be able to get rid of the god-awful chain and what a mess his life had become because of it, that he hardly heard what the man said.

"You want it?" he repeated, too late to realize how foolish that sounded.

"That's what I said. Why? Something wrong? Of course, three million is a little steep. I'll pay two million euros. Not a penny more."

Euros? The man was willing to pay in euros! Right now, the dollar was down, the euro up, making each euro worth about a buck thirty. "I understand," Rocco said, trying to hide his glee. "But I can't go a *centesimo* — less than two and a half."

"Two-point-three and that's my final offer."

Rocco smiled. "Sold!"

Chapter 39

 The Woring house was packed with crime scene technicians. Yosh was inside waiting for the M.E.

Paavo stood outside by his car with Charles. He had just gotten word from the two police officers he'd sent to Moldwell-Ranker that the real estate agent was gone. Other police dispatched to Ranker's house reported he wasn't home either. Neither was he answering his cell phone.

Paavo had a good idea what was happening here in San Francisco. He wished he knew what was going on in Rome. The longer he didn't hear from Angie, the stronger his foreboding grew.

Angie still hadn't called. The only people who might know where she was were at Da Vinci's. He knew someone should still be there for the dinner crowd. He took out his cell phone and called the Da Vinci number.

A male voice answered. *"Pronto?"*

"Hello?" Paavo said. "Is Angelina Amalfi there?"

"Che cosa? Chi é che parla?"

"Who is this?"

"Chi sono? Sono Cosimo Mandolini."

Paavo scowled, and to Charles said, "I have no idea what he's saying."

"Let me." Charles took the phone. As he spoke, he

grew increasingly distressed. Yosh came out and waited beside Paavo for the conversation to end.

When Charles hung up, he took a deep breath before speaking. "The fellow was a waiter. He said the
women are gone, but they left everything there—their
passports, even their clothes. It looked as if a fight had
taken place in their room. There was blood on the floor.
He said no one at the restaurant has any idea where
they are—" His voice broke.

Paavo was more composed. Just barely. In past situations when Angie was in danger, she was always
nearby, and he was in familiar territory. He knew that
if he just searched long enough and hard enough, he
could find her. He always had faith that he'd get to her
in time.

This time, though, was different. The thought of her
being held against her will somewhere in Rome terrified him. He didn't know the city, the language, or the
laws. To save her, he was dependent on the Italian police. He knew they'd try, but to them, she was probably
a nutty American tourist who was on an even crazier
mission. "Did they call the police?"

"No. It was clear that someone at the restaurant
didn't want the police involved at all," Charles answered bleakly. He closed his eyes for a second, hard
in thought, then gazed steadily at Paavo. With a new-
found conviction and confidence, he said with ferocity,
"Enough is enough!"

After Angie's near death experience, she wanted nothing more than to go home. Cat agreed it was time. Father Daniel, although still rocky, was ready to help.

"You have the chain, right?" she asked Cat.

"You can't take it!" Father Daniel protested. "For one
thing, you'll never get it out of the country!"

"It's safe where it is," Cat interrupted. "No one will

ever notice it. We can leave it there, and then come back and get it when it's safe. Only you know, Father Daniel. Can we trust you to keep our secret?"

"Me?" He seemed torn and didn't answer right away.

"Where is it?" Angie asked. Daniel's reaction set off alarms in her head.

Cat smiled slyly. "It's being used to hold a pair of St. Monica's doors shut. We attached a padlock to it. It's old and different, but unless a person knows what they're looking for, they'll assume it's a chain like any other."

"Clever." Angie eyed Daniel closely as she said, "Don't you agree, Father?"

He looked at her a long time before nodding. "I agree."

Serefina was standing at his front door as Paavo pulled into a parking space. Barely over five feet tall, nearly as wide, with long black hair pulled tightly into a stylish bun, her black eyes looked ready to take on the world. At her sides were Bianca, Maria, and Frannie. Salvatore and Kenny were still in Disneyland.

"Serefina, what are you doing here?" Paavo hurried to her, Charles right behind him.

"I came to help—" Serefina's voice broke and she lowered her eyes.

Paavo ached to see the usually strong, cheerful woman so desperate. He put his arms around her, hugging her tight. "It'll work out, Serefina."

At his warmth, she cried harder, and seeing their mother in tears, the three sisters began to cry as well. Even Charles looked weepy. Paavo held Serefina until she regained control of herself again. Then she straightened.

"Charles called me," she explained, and gave him a quick hug.

"He did?" As Paavo unlocked the door, he glanced quizzically at Charles.

"He's very brave," Bianca added as they all entered the living room.

Brave? Paavo wondered what he was missing.

"We know what you need to do, Paavo," Serefina said. "Don't mind us."

Paavo didn't like what he was hearing. Serefina handed Charles a case. He tucked it under his arm.

"Salvatore has had it many years, but it works perfectly," Serefina said.

"What's going on?" The sudden coldness in Paavo's voice caused them all to jump. A chill descended on the room.

"The man's finally discovered he's got balls! Let him use them," Frannie said, bottom lip thrust out defiantly.

"Force for a righteous cause is just," Maria chimed in. "Read the Old Testament."

"He needs it." Serefina opened her purse and put a box of .38 caliber shells on the table.

Paavo didn't like what he suspected was going on. The temperature in the room dropped even further.

Charles put the case on the coffee table. Paavo gave him a look that unmistakably told him what he had to do.

Inhaling deeply, Charles opened the case. Inside was a Luger revolver.

"I'll be so glad to get out of here!" Angie said as she, Cat, and Father Daniel piled into the Vatican's Smart Car. Angie was forced to drive since Daniel's vision was still shaky and Cat had no idea how to handle a stick shift.

Once at the airport, security would be so tight that even if the goons were following them, they could scream and the security guards would come running. She could then safely call Paavo and tell him they were on their way home. Finally!

They had to go by the restaurant to pick up their passports. It would be dangerous—the goons might be watching it—but they had no choice.

Hopefully, the goons had either been caught by the police or were still running.

Wearing heavy overcoats with the scarves pulled low on their foreheads, Angie and Cat reached Da Vinci's along with a still woozy Father Daniel. Angie and Daniel kept a lookout for dumb, scary men, while Cat entered the back door and convinced Bruno to turn over their passports. He was full of questions, but she had no time for them. While there, she also took their belongings.

With Cat back in the car, Angie sped off for Fiumicino and the airport.

Angie kept peering out the back window, half expecting to see the two goons bearing down on them at any moment.

The traffic in Rome was even worse than earlier, but eventually they made it out of the city. They relaxed as they reached the highway heading southwest to the airport. It was about a thirty minute ride.

Cat eased against the seat, lolling her head back. "Thank God!" she breathed in a sigh of relief.

"I know," Angie said, feeling as if she'd been holding her breath until then. "We should have done this a long time ago."

"I knew everything would work out," Cat said smugly.

"And we'll be home soon." Angie cheered, pumping a fist in the air.

"It'll be so great to be free." Cat took off the scarf and fluffed her hair.

Angie took off hers as well, and started to sing "Free-dom, freedom." Laughing, Cat high-fived her. Daniel remained quiet and thoughtful.

Angie's jubilation was short-lived as she noticed car lights bearing down on them at great speed.

"Who's that?" she asked, wary.

Cat and Daniel turned around. In the evening darkness, they could only see the outline of the large car heading right for them. Angie changed into the slow lane. The behemoth did as well.

She sped up and pulled in front of another car, putting it between her and the pursuer. The little Smart Car had power, but not nearly enough.

The large car pulled alongside her. It was a gray BMW. The window was rolled down, and a gun pointed at her. Holding the gun was the young archeologist, Stefano.

Angie screamed as the BMW inched closer, near her fender. She had nowhere to go, and moved toward the shoulder. The archeologist pointed to a highway exit, and the BMW swerved toward her again.

She took the exit, not knowing what else to do.

The BMW followed.

She kept going, driving fast, trying to get away, but it was hopeless. The BMW suddenly sped around and in front of her, cutting her off and forcing her from the road and onto a steep, soft embankment.

As the Smart Car jostled to a standstill, the BMW driver opened the door, his gun aimed their way the entire time. "Going someplace?" he asked with a malicious smirk. "Get out!"

"Rocco!" Cat's voice was a mixture of shock and fury.

"You finally know it's me?" His face never lost its smile. "It's about time you recognized your old play-mate, but then you never did pay much attention to me even when we were kids. The police told you, didn't they?"

"How could you do this?" she asked. "I trusted you!"

He grimaced. "You were wrong. Get out of the car now!"

Cat, Angie, and Daniel scrambled out of the half-listing car.

"That's Rocco?" Father Daniel rubbed his head, his legs rubbery. "I'm worse than I thought. That man looks like Marcello Piccoletti."

"It's a long story, Father," Angie whispered, gripping his arm tight in support.

"Why are you doing this?" Cat snapped, eyes blazing.

"Give me the chain!" he said.

"We don't have it," Angie said tersely.

"I want it. Now!" Rocco roared.

Daniel looked at Angie, his eyes questioning. She could see he was ready to give up. She wasn't, and neither was Cat.

"Why?" Cat asked boldly. "What are you going to do with it?"

"I've got plans. I've got a buyer."

"Then what?"

"Then I'm out of here. Two-point-three million euros isn't going to allow me to live like a king, but living like a prince is good enough."

"We put the chain in a safe deposit box," Angie announced abruptly. Father Daniel winced. "Only us or the police can get it."

"I don't believe you," Rocco said. "Stefano, go through their bags. Find the chain."

"Stefano," Angie said to the young man as he pulled their tote bags from the car and dumped everything onto the ground, "how could you be involved in this? Are you doing it to help your father?"

"My father?" He looked at her with a wry grin. "I'm the one with habits I can't afford. When my father found out, he did all he could to keep the authorities and the Vatican from knowing." Stefano's ruthless gaze slanted toward Father Daniel. "Or so we thought."

"Don't worry about him," Rocco said. "Father has been working with me to buy the chain for the Vatican, haven't you, Father? But then they chintzed out. They didn't want to pay what it's worth, cheap bastards, they wanted to steal it." He noticed Angie's and Cat's expressions. "Oh my, am I giving away a secret?"

"They really don't have the chain," Daniel pleaded as Stefano searched through the car. "Let them go."

Angie let go of the priest's arm.

He faced her. "It's not what you think, Angie."

"It's not here," Stefano said.

"Where the hell is it?" Rocco demanded.

"Bank of Italy, I told you," Angie said, trying not to think of Father Daniel's deception, and to come up with a spot with high security and a lot of people. "The branch next door to the St. Regis Hotel."

"Very smart." Rocco gave Cat a toothy smile. "I knew I could trust you two to keep the chain safe. To-morrow's Monday. They should open by ten o'clock in the morning." He addressed Angie. "We'll pay them a little visit, you and I. You'll have thirty minutes to get the chain, and then to get back to your sister and the priest. I get the chains," Rocco said with a malevolent grin, "or Rome will truly be, for all of you, the eternal city."

At midnight Rocco and Stefano drove their captives to the Forum. It was empty and eerie with moonlight and shadows. Angie realized where the old expression "Great Caesar's ghost" must have come from: this place, on a night like this.

The Mamertine Prison was up ahead. It was basically a cistern, cold, dank, and moldy. As much as Angie dreaded the idea of being put down there, the good part was that tourists often walked all around that area. Surely someone would hear their cries.

Rocco turned before reaching the prison and entered an area surrounded by a temporary chain-link fence with Keep Out signs all around. Stefano flipped a switch on a generator, then unlocked the door to a large temporary building. It covered and protected a deep pit, an excavation down to the old prison and most likely to where St. Peter's chain had been found.

The few excavation sites Angie had seen covered vast areas, with shelflike layers progressing downward, almost like a gigantic staircase, to the deepest point of the pit. Along each of those layers were smaller holes where archeologists had dug. Lots of machinery to move dirt was at those sites as well.

This site, however, was smaller than most. Although deep, it wasn't terribly broad. The layers were narrow, each ten or twelve feet down from the prior one. Angie tried to see to the bottom of the pit. It appeared to be about forty or fifty feet below the surface.

Small holes pockmarked the area, but the heavy machinery that was usually found wasn't in the area, and Angie wondered if the site had been abandoned for some reason.

Ropes and pulleys and a couple of ladders dropped down inside the pit, while wooden scaffolding and walls prevented any potential cave-ins.

"Wait," Angie said, her head whirling with thoughts of how she could distract Rocco from leaving them there. Time was what she needed—time to come up with a way to escape. "I know, Rocco, how you expect to get out of this mess, but have you ever figured out how you got into it?"

Hard eyes stared at her. "What are you talking about?"

"Who set you up, Rocco? Do you know? Or don't you care? Somebody wants the chain enough to kill for it. Whoever it is killed your own mother."

"I know, dammit!" he swore. "I think about it constantly, day and night. My mother died because of Marcello and that goddamned chain! That's why I have to get it. I have to make sure she didn't die in vain."

"How big of you," Cat muttered.

As they spoke, Stefano climbed down to the first layer of the pit. He lifted out some ropes and a long aluminum ladder. Angie forced her attention back to Rocco. "What you have to do, Rocco, is make sure her killers don't get away with it."

"I wouldn't if I knew who they were. I keep replaying everything in my mind, but none of it makes sense."

Angie watched Stefano climb out of the pit, look at Rocco and nod. She got a very bad feeling. "My fiancé is looking into it," she said hurriedly. "He's a homicide inspector. I'm sure he has information that will help you."

"Your fiancé's a cop?" Rocco's eyes narrowed.

"He is, and he's coming very close to solving this case."

"Including who killed Marcello and my mother?"

Angie had to think fast. She was quite sure Marcello's murderer was the person talking to her at that very moment. "He thinks the same person who killed your mother also killed Marcello. Probably something went wrong—maybe the two argued—and he ended up dead."

"Is that what he thinks?" Rocco's mouth twisted.

"That makes sense, doesn't it? When Cat arrived, Marcello had been murdered and you were running away from the killer."

Rocco stared coldly. "That's it exactly, but no cop would believe it."

Angie was sure he was lying, but it didn't matter. He was distracted, and that was the whole point. She was looking around, trying to come up with something to use as a weapon. Cat was doing the same. Loose material lay around the site, but the tools, like the heavy machinery, had all been removed.

"Enough of this," he snarled. "Get down into the pit."

"What?" Cat, Angie, and Daniel looked at each other and then the dark hole in the earth.

Stefano had left one ladder. It led from ground level to the first layer, a ledge about six feet wide, dotted with one- to two-foot-deep holes.

Brandishing his gun, Rocco forced them down the ladder. As soon as they reached the ledge, he and Stefano pulled the ladder up to the surface.

Angie immediately looked for a ladder leading down to the next level, knowing the three of them could lift it and use it to climb out. It was gone, and she understood what Stefano had been doing earlier.

"I'll see you in the morning," Rocco said, "when we go to the bank to get the chain. I just hope—for your sakes—you aren't lying to me again. *Buona notte.*"

The two left, shutting the door behind them. Almost immediately the lights went out.

The area was pitch-black.

Just as it must have been at the time of Peter.

Chapter 40

The three sat, stunned, in the unnerving darkness.

"We've got to find a way out of here." Angie dropped to her hands and knees. The edge wasn't far from where she stood, and equally treacherous were the smaller holes. A misstep into one of them might lead to an injury that could prevent them from climbing out when and if they came up with a way.

"There's got to be something," Cat agreed. Shuffling in the darkness toward Angie's voice, her arms waving in front of her, her toe hit an object, and she kicked at it.

"Ouch!" Angie poked Cat's leg, stopping her. "That's me!"

"Get down, Cat," Father Daniel said from behind her. "It's safest."

"Do you know what this place is, Father?" Angie held Cat's hand as she sat.

"I do," he said, finding the sisters. The three huddled in a circle like campfire girls. "They've been finding some artifacts here, but they've dug down as deeply as they dare with machinery. From this point they have to use their hands and brushes. It's slow, delicate work. They don't want the site to be destroyed by weather, or worse, by the public climbing down into it, so they put up a cover. This site, however, isn't being worked at the moment. The Vatican has temporarily suspend-ed it. We heard of several old, valuable finds that the Church was interested in but were never reported to us. The chain of St. Peter was the latest of those, and by far the most potentially valuable."

"You know a lot about this for someone in Rome just to study, Father," Cat said. Even in the dark, they could hear the frown in her voice. "What did Rocco mean about you trying to buy or steal the chain from him? Is that what you'd planned? To steal it?"

"I actually work for the Curia of Antiquities," he said. "When we discovered there was something amiss with the dig here, I was sent 'undercover,' so to speak. I hung out at Da Vinci's to watch the archeologists. The son, Stefano, was stealing from the digs and selling valuable pieces to Marcello, or I should say to Rocco, who'd send them to the U.S. in crates along with inex-pensive pieces for his furniture store. We were build-ing a case against them when the chain of St. Peter dis-appeared to the U.S. It was too valuable to allow it to become lost, so I approached Piccoletti with an offer. He wanted millions, and apparently thought he'd get more in the U.S. than from the Vatican. He wouldn't deal at first. I guess something went wrong because he came back with the chain.

"I tried to negotiate with him again, but he was still hoping to find a higher bidder. Then I saw the two of you, and soon realized you were after the chain as well. I hoped you'd lead me to it. I never wanted to deceive you."

"So the Vatican is sure the chain really once held St. Peter?" Angie asked, intrigued.

"Not at all. In fact, there's great doubt. It'll be stud-ied. If it can be confirmed, then it'll be displayed."

"Right now," Cat said, bringing them back to the pres-ent, "we need to find a way out of here, because when

they come back, whether they get the chain or not"
—her voice turned tearful—"they're going to kill us!"

The three had hoped that as their eyes adjusted to the
dark, they'd be able to make out at least a little of their
surroundings and find a way out. The darkness remained complete, however, and hope diminished with
each passing minute.

They needed somehow to find a rope, or a forgotten
ladder, or another means to climb out of there. Once
they reached ground level, they were sure that between
the three of them, they could break their way out of the
temporary shelter built over the excavation.

Reaching ground level was the problem.

Angie stood on Daniel's shoulders to see if that
helped, but she didn't have the reach or arm strength
to pull herself up. Maneuvering on his shoulders in
complete darkness was one of the scariest things she
had ever attempted.

Finally, they resorted to holding onto each other and
crawling around. Father Daniel was in the lead, Angie
held the hem of his pants' leg, and Cat held the hem of
hers. The ground sloped, and those strange holes were
all over it. Daniel stayed close to the side wall, but it
had rough wood on it, and when he felt around, hoping to find a way to climb up, all he got for his troubles
were splinters.

Cat's breathing was fast, and Angie knew she was
scared. "In case we don't make it, Cat," she said softly,
"I want you to know you've been a good sister. One I
could look up to always. You were an inspiration."

"Don't say that, Angie. It's not true. I've made many
mistakes—"

"It's true! No need to be modest. I just wanted you
to know."

"I expect Paavo has found out about my mistakes,"

Cat said, crawling after Angie. "It's going to be embarrassing seeing him again . . . if we make it."

"You've done nothing to worry about." Angie glanced back over her shoulder, but she couldn't even see Cat's outline.

"I wonder if my clients will think that." Cat's voice dropped to a whisper.

"I suspect your clients have nothing but praise for you."

"I don't think so," Cat said.

"Father Dan." Angie turned toward him, hoping to get him to stop a moment. They were going fairly slowly, but holding onto him meant she could only use one arm to crawl, and it was tiring. "Can you stop?"

"Sorry," Daniel said. He rested a moment, as did Angie.

"Over the years," Cat whispered, not wanting Father Dan to hear, "I've had several clients who really, really wanted some special piece of furniture or art object for their house. Something unique and expensive—something they'd seen in a catalogue or some architectural magazine."

"I can imagine you get that a lot," Angie said.

"I do." Cat sat back on her heels, her knees aching from crawling. The time had come, she told herself, to make her confession, to tell Angie exactly what terrible, probably illegal thing she'd allowed herself to get involved in with Marcello.

She kept her voice a soft whisper, hoping Father Daniel wouldn't overhear. "If I'd try and try and couldn't find that special something any other way—" She had to wait a moment as her breathing was coming hard and a buzzing sound was in her head at the trauma of admitting, out loud, what she'd done. "—I'd go to Marcello, I mean Rocco, and have him use his foreign contacts to make a copy."

She hurried on, not wanting to hear Angie's chastisement. "Before you say anything, I didn't sell them as originals. I never told my clients they were the real things. I'd simply say I got exactly what they wanted, the price was low, and they shouldn't question me. They'd nod knowingly, and were happy. So was Marcello—or should I call him Rocco?—who made a hefty profit." Angie remained quiet. "Okay, I'll admit it, so did I. But with all that happiness around me, how could I not do it? Charles doesn't know. No one knows but Rocco and me. Maybe I'm overreacting. If I don't say it's real, it's not exactly piracy or selling knockoffs, right ...? Right, Angie?" She felt all around her, then shouted, "Angie where are you?"

"Calm down, Cat," Angie called from what seemed to be a great distance. "I thought you stayed back because you were tired. There's nothing over this way. We're turning around."

Cat shook her head, stunned. "Did you hear what I said?"

"No. I thought you must be praying."

Cat thought a moment, then said, "How did you ever guess?"

Time crept by slowly.

The three had checked out the ledge as best they could. Stefano had left nothing they could use to help themselves. They were stuck. Plus tired. Scared. And irritable.

Cat stood to stretch and shake out her legs. "I can't take much more of this."

"Sit down." Angie yanked her pant legs. "You're making me nervous."

"You have a complaint?" Cat grumbled. "I'm the one with the right to complain! How the hell did I ever let you talk me into this mess?"

"Excuse me?" Angie enunciated sharply. "Are you talking to me?"

"Of course I'm talking to you! Who the hell else would I mean?"

"Ladies," Father Daniel soothed, "I think we should join together in prayer."

"I didn't get you into anything!" Angie exclaimed, also getting to her feet. She had just about had it with Her Royal Prissiness. "All I ever did was try to help."

"You call this help?" Cat screeched.

"You're the one who wanted to take matters into your own hands. Before I ever suggested a thing, you got into your car all by yourself and started to follow Rocco. Don't blame me for that!"

"Of course I wanted to take matters into my own hands," Cat said indignantly. "That's when things turn out right. Unfortunately, I got involved with a crazy woman!"

"Nobody forced you. And it wasn't so crazy. It was logical. You saw the logic in it, as I recall." Angie jutted her chin out belligerently.

"I was in shock!"

Father Daniel also stood and tried to get between the two. He would have had better luck if he could see what was going on. "Please, you two—"

"If I'd simply gone home after finding that body," Cat continued woefully, "called my husband, and gotten a lawyer to explain everything to the police, none of this would have happened. I'd be in my own house, my own bed. *Safe!* Not here, and definitely not waiting for some madman to kill me!"

Father Daniel tried again. "How about me hearing your confessions? This is a time to be sure your soul is free of sin—"

Disgust dripped from Angie's voice. "Too bad you didn't know he was a madman when you thought he was trustworthy and hot for your body!"

"Why, you—"

"What about the chain? The corpse? The witness? The handkerchief? All of them convinced you to run to that madman who you swore would help you prove your innocence." Angie hissed like an angry feline. "You think I like spending a week with you running from strangers, wearing grubby clothes, and listening to you bitch? You think I don't miss Paavo and wish I could be anywhere but here?"

"Let's join hands." Father Daniel groped and found each of their hands in the dark. As he drew the two together, Cat reached out, found Angie in the dark and grabbed her arm, her bony fingers squeezing just the way she had when they were young.

"You don't wish it any more than I!" Cat shouted.

Angie jerked free with such force, Father Daniel barely stopped her from falling backward. She slapped Cat's hand away. "You called me, remember?"

Father Daniel kept his voice calm. "Cat, Angie—"

"For all the good that did!" She got right in Angie's face. "I was hoping your worthless fiancé would help me. Was I ever wrong!"

"Ladies!" Father Daniel called haplessly.

"Don't you dare call Paavo worthless!" Angie shoved Cat. Hard. To her surprise and semidelight, it sounded as if Cat fell over and landed on her butt. "You didn't do one thing to make this any easier. You just wanted to make sure no one mentioned your sacrosanct name in connection with murderers and thieves! You cared more about your precious reputation than anything else, and you know it."

Angie heard Cat sputtering and fuming, and slapping at her clothes as if brushing dirt from them. "You little worm!" Suddenly, she barreled into Angie, knocking her down.

"It's better than being a big bitch!" Angie snarled as she dragged Cat to the ground with her. She gave Cat's hair a solid yank.

Cat screamed, pulling free and flailing at Angie. "This is all your fault! I've never been so miserable in my entire life!"

"How can you say that when you've been married to Charles for twelve years?"

"You snot!" Cat swung a right hook.

In the dark, Angie felt the breeze as Cat's arm sailed by. Outraged, she managed to get hold of the arm.

Cat clamped onto Angie's wrist and the two proceeded to pull and tug at each other, rolling and tussling around on the ground.

"No, no, no! Angie! Cat! Cut it out! Knock this off!" Father Daniel leaped into the melee, trying to pull them apart.

Seconds later he scurried backward holding a bloody nose.

Neither listened. Days of frustration, resentment, and every imagined childhood wrong burst out. With flailing arms and kicking legs, the two sisters continued the wrestling match, oblivious to the now increasingly angry priest.

"Angelina, Caterina!" Father Daniel blared. "Come to your senses! Stop it! Stop it now!" One hand protectively covering his nose, he moved forward cautiously in the dark to try again to separate them. He couldn't actually see the two women, but their grunts and yelps gave away their location.

Without warning, there was a terrified scream.

Father Daniel nearly jumped out of his skin. He squinted in the dark, petrified. Where were the women? One moment they were right in front of him, the next ...

Realization hit him. He forgot all about his bloody

nose. "The pit!" he shrieked. "For God's sake!"

To his horror, there was only silence.

Heart pounding in his throat, he dropped to his knees and inched forward cautiously. "Angie! Caterina! Where are you?" he shouted even as he frantically prayed to every saint that they hadn't fallen off the ledge. He reached forward with a shaky hand and touched bare sloping ground. "Cat? Angie?"

What was he going to do if they fell in? He had no light. He couldn't go get help. Then something nudged him.

A shrill howl escaped his lips.

"It's me," came Cat's strangled voice. "I can't let go! Thank God you found us."

"You can't let go?" He gulped. *If only he could see!* "What are you talking about? Where's Angie?"

"I'm holding her foot."

"Foot? Her foot? What do you mean her foot?" Father Daniel shouted. He could hear the hysteria rising in his voice, and gave himself a mental smack.

A disembodied voice floated up from the darkness. "I'm upside down! Hurry! Get me out of here!"

With visions of Angie sliding head first into the pit swirling in his head, Daniel wrapped both arms around Cat's waist and pulled while she somehow managed to keep her grip on Angie's foot.

In a bizarre human chain, the three pulled and dragged themselves off the slope. It felt like hours. Then they sprawled, panting and moaning, on the ground. Sweating, nose bleeding, breathless, and absolutely furious, Daniel was about to deliver a homily of the fire and brimstone kind when Angie rolled over and sat up.

In an incredibly chirpy voice, she said, "You'll never guess what I found!"

Chapter 41

Vice Questore Paolo Napolitano of the Commissariato di Polizia had smoked too many cigarettes and drunk too much coffee. All he wanted was to get home to his wife and children and the dinner he knew had turned cold hours earlier. It had been a long day, but he had to finish up a little more paperwork before leaving the office. That was the problem with a police system as unwieldy as Italy's. Everyone needed reports to protect their turf, to look important. And busy.

Napolitano was part of the Polizia di Stato, the civil state police, which operated out of stations in cities throughout Italy. The Polizia di Stato were under the Director General of Public Security, who was under the Public Order and Security Committee, which was under the Ministry of the Interior. The Carabinieri, of the fancy uniforms with white sashes across their chests, under the Minister of Defense, were also in cities, but were the primary force keeping order in the countryside. There was also a Guardia di Finanza, or financial police, a special antimafia patrol, an antiterrorist unit, and other branches of the police system. And they all stepped on each other's toes or danced away from problems, leaving a gaping hole for the problems to fall through.

In the quiet of the office tucked in the back of the

Questura Centrale, Rome's main police station, Napolitano heard footsteps and voices approaching. He didn't want to deal with any problems tonight. He was ready to leave.

There was a knock, and the door opened. Two unhappy officers entered with two men. The first was tall and fit, mid-thirties, with dark brown hair. Napolitano could hardly pull his gaze from the blue-eyed intensity of the man to scrutinize his companion. Portly. Thinning hair. Somewhere in his forties or fifties. American. Definitely American.

Napolitano stood. "What's going on?"

"I'm Inspector Paavo Smith of the San Francisco Police Department." He held out his badge.

Immediately, the *vice questore's* phone began to ring.

A breathless aide came in wide-eyed. "Excuse me, sir, the call is from the minister himself."

The blue-eyed foreigner glanced at his companion, and then to Napolitano. "I believe that call will save us both a lot of time."

"It's working," Paavo said to Charles as they sat waiting for the call to end.

Charles nodded, but looked confused and wary.

They'd been greeted at the airport by a police escort and whisked through town to a large imposing gray building. It didn't look like a police station, which was what they'd both been expecting, but more like a fortress.

The escort and the fortresslike *questura* was impressive. Paavo was sure that Charles now understood why he'd refused to allow him to bring the Luger to Rome. To avoid delays and red tape, he hadn't even brought his own weapon. Instead, after tossing some clothes into his duffel, putting out several days worth of food and water for his cat, and finding his passport, they said good-bye to the teary-eyed Amalfi women, then rushed to the airport where the private air charter company that Charles's company contracted with had a plane waiting.

Paavo had made a few phone calls to Rome from the private plane, but as soon as the full complexity of the Italian security force became clear to him, he contacted Serefina. The Amalfis were friends with San Francisco Police Commissioner Tom Barcelli.

Barcelli happened to personally know Italy's Minister of the Interior, who got Paavo and Charles into Napolitano's office.

As Napolitano hung up the phone, he regarded Paavo with all the friendliness of a pit bull. Although Barcelli might have been a friend of the Minister of the Interior, the day-to-day police work was Napolitano's. It was his decision to go along, or to cart them off to the American embassy.

"It sounds as if you've taken a big chance coming here, Inspector Smith," he said bluntly. "There are international laws and statutes to handle this sort of thing that don't necessitate this kind of American cowboy riding-into-town and handling everything yourself."

"I'm aware, sir," Paavo said sternly, "but I have all the information in my head, and time is of the essence."

Napolitano regarded him in silence, then said, "If this doesn't work, it could mean your career, Inspector."

Paavo's expression never varied. "It could mean much more to me than that."

"Is she worth it?"

Paavo knew exactly what Napolitano meant. His reply was simple, direct, and honest. "She's worth everything to me."

Napolitano smiled, but rather than warm, it was

world-weary, as if he could barely remember a time when love burned that way in his own soul. He picked up the phone. "I'm expecting an envelope," he told the person at the other end. "It's here already? Excellent. Bring it in."

He hung up, then began to explain the situation to Paavo and Charles. "A car registered to the Vatican was found abandoned near the airport at Fiumicino. It sustained a slight bit of damage to its fender. It looked as if it might have been driven off the road. We have been in contact with the Vatican to learn who had been given the car and for what purpose."

Napolitano paused as the same aide who had given him the information about the phone call returned with an envelope. "Tucked under the front seat," he went on as the aide departed, "as if purposefully hidden there, they found something that pertains to this case." He tore open the packet and shook out a small card.

A California driver's license. Name: Caterina Amalfi Swenson.

Rocco Piccoletti slammed down the phone. Bruno had just phoned in a panic. He'd been taken to the Questura Centrale and questioned by the police. They were looking for the two American women and heard they'd been working at Da Vinci's. Bruno denied knowing anything and was freed.

Rocco wondered how the *polizia* had gotten involved. He also wondered how much Bruno had told them, and if Bruno had told them where he lived.

He called Stefano. It was too early for the bank to open, so they could get into the safe deposit box, but he didn't want to wait at home any longer. An uneasiness had come over him. He reminded himself not to panic, not to rush. He must take it slowly, carefully.

Victory was near, and he didn't want to screw it up now.

A massive bulk of a man and a smaller one with a goatee peered from the shadows at the building where Rocco Piccoletti was now living.

They'd found it by following him two nights earlier.

They could no longer find the American women, which meant either that Piccoletti himself now had the St. Peter chain or that he could lead them to the women who had it.

They suspected the latter.

They weren't about to give up, not after all those American witches had put them through. Especially the young one. They could hardly wait to get their hands on her again. As much as they wanted the chain, it was secondary now.

They wanted revenge.

A yellow car drove up to the front of the apartment and stopped, the motor running.

Rocco Piccoletti bolted from the building into the car, and it drove off.

The goons followed.

It was early morning, but already tourists dotted the ancient Roman Forum like ants at a picnic.

Paavo rushed down a walkway to enter the area, Charles and a policeman following. Paavo could hardly believe how massive the Forum was, much larger than he'd ever imagined. Most of it was below street level. He realized it was essentially a gigantic archeological dig in the heart of Rome. The digging and restoration appeared to be still going on, as many marble and granite columns and pillars lay on their sides, and great portions of the area were cordoned off.

He could scarcely believe the scope of what he was

looking at. Much had been restored, and massive arch-
ways and pillars from temples reached high into the
sky. These were grounds where Roman senators and
orators gave some of the most famous speeches in history, and wrote laws that continued to form the basis
for many civilized societies to this day.

It was hard to believe that a civilization that could
build something so grand and powerful had eventually crumbled under the internal weight of unruly
mobs and attacks from those the Romans called "bar-
barians" from elsewhere in Europe and Asia. Evidence
that it had happened before gave sudden credence that
it could again.

Paavo watched as Rocco went down into the Forum.
He followed, careful that Rocco didn't notice him.

The plan he and Vice Questore Napolitano concocted
had worked.

Arrest Bruno, get him to tell them where Rocco was
living, then make him phone Rocco and let the man
know the police were on to him. They hoped it would
spur Rocco into action, and it had.

They had watched as Rocco got into a car driven by
a younger man. Before they pulled out of their parking space, however, another car started after Piccoletti.
They followed both.

The second auto stayed a safe distance behind Piccoletti all the way to the Forum. There, Piccoletti got out.

The entire episode was quite peculiar.

At the Forum, Paavo, Charles, and one of the officers
with them sprang from the police car to follow Rocco,
who went directly to a fenced area with signs for the
public to keep out. He had a key to unlock the gate,
and walked inside.

The only sound was Father Daniel quietly reciting
prayers, psalms, and the litany of the saints of the

Church, asking them for help on this long night. In the Catholic tradition, each sister had gone to a corner and made a confession to him in whispers, away from the prying ears of the other "just in case" things didn't work out well the next morning.

His duty done, Father Daniel now sat alone at his station.

"Do you think Rocco forgot about us?" Cat whispered from her corner.

"I don't know," Angie whispered from hers. "It's like watching water boil."

In her almost slide into the pit, Angie had managed to find some rope left behind. A great idea had occurred to her as she was being dragged backward by Cat. Well, she considered it a great idea. Cat and Father Daniel greeted it with a noticeable lack of enthusiasm. Nevertheless, since they were working in total darkness, it took them most of the night to set it up.

First, they felt along the wood supports until they found two spots at some distance from each other with loose boards. They pulled the boards free, making enough space for Angie to hide alongside one and Cat in the other. Even when the lights were on, they were fairly sure the area would be cast in shadow and they'd be obscured.

Angie took one end of the rope, Cat the other, and they stretched it between them, lightly covering it with dirt.

Their plan was that when Rocco showed up, Father Daniel would tell him Cat and Angie had fallen into the pit. They were hurt, maybe dead, he'd say.

Hearing this, their hope was that Rocco would get a ladder and climb down to the layer they were on. As he hurried to the edge, the women would lift the rope and trip him. Father Daniel would rush up from behind and give Rocco a shove.

They had to hope that while Stefano was a junkie or gambler—or whatever his "expensive habits," as he'd put it, were—he wasn't a killer, and he'd either run off or simply let them go.

And so they waited, each coming up with myriad ways the plan could fail.

"Father," Angie said after a while, "you told us earlier what will happen to the chain of St. Peter if it's authenticated. But if it isn't, what happens then?"

"It'll be locked away as just another unknown item in the basement of the Vatican. The basement storage area goes on for miles and miles. So much is down there, not even the Vatican has a complete inventory. Lay and clerical archivists have worked for centuries to catalogue the items, but it takes a lot of knowledge and expertise to know enough about what you're looking at in order to catalogue it. What one man might see as a piece of sheet music, a musicologist might recognize as a previously unknown work by Monteverdi or Vivaldi."

"So, very likely, it'll be buried again," Angie murmured. "That doesn't seem right. The elderly priest I met at St. Monica's seemed to think it should be displayed. He said, 'to help them remember.' I'm not sure what he meant."

"He said that?" Father Daniel asked. At her confirmation, he was silent for a long moment. "It reminds me of a strange experience I had when I was in the seminary. In the churchyard one day, I met a visiting priest from Italy. The other seminarians said they didn't notice him with me. They thought I was just sleeping out there and didn't disturb me because I'd been staying up late studying for exams. Yet, that priest was as real to me as you are.

"We talked about helping the poor and having a parish. The priest believed that most people search

for something deeply meaningful beyond themselves.
Some find it in Catholicism. Others elsewhere—Bud-
dhism, Islam, a tree, spirits and faeries, or—as I've
heard some people in your hometown of San Francisco once did—a fire plug. Anyway, it's in the nature
of man to search, the priest said, but many people get
so caught up in the tedium of their lives that they stop
looking. They grow bored and disillusioned and hopeless. It's a priest's duty, he said, to help them renew
their search for the truth that opens their lives. Help
them remember God, and remember faith." When
Daniel stopped speaking, quiet and darkness settled
over them again.

"The priest at St. Monica's seemed to think the chain
could do that," Angie said, "and that it was real."

"It might be," Father Daniel conceded. "The more
I think about it, though, I doubt it matters. You said
it, Angie, when you first saw that harsh, rough, ugly
piece of iron. It reminded you of the very earliest days
of Christianity, and how a motley group of apostles,
despite persecution and martyrdom, spread their faith
against what—using logic alone—were impossible
odds. Yet they did it. Now, when many people look at
the Church, all they see are riches, scandals, and politics. They don't remember anymore what it all means:
faith and divine grace. Maybe that's why the chain has
shown up here, now. To help all of us remember."

Angie wasn't sure if she should ask something so
personal, but she knew Daniel had been struggling.
"Has it helped you?"

His lengthy silence made her think she'd gone too
far, but then he spoke. "I was a very scholarly sort,
even in the seminary, and because of that, I was encouraged to come to the Vatican. It's a great honor. I
love the Vatican, I truly do, but that wasn't the reason
I joined the clergy. I did it to work with the people,

especially the poor. I'd forgotten that. I'd forgotten a lot, caught up in the majesty, the pomp, and the importance of my more intellectual pursuits. I need to go back to the beginning, back to the basis of my love of God. I don't know if I'd be any good at it...."

"I think you would, Father," Angie said. "Look at how you've tried to help me and my sister. You could have shut the door on us. Our own cousin did. But you're here with us, doing your best, no matter the danger."

"Thank you for saying that, Angie." Then, considering their circumstance, she heard the deprecating smile in his voice as he added, "I'm only sorry I didn't do a whole lot better."

"Did you ever meet the visiting priest again after you came to Rome?"

"No," he said. "I've concluded the others were right. It was only a dream. Although he didn't have a terribly uncommon name, there's no longer any living priest in or near Rome with it, and hasn't been for many, many years."

"What was his name?"

"Father Pio."

"Pio?" Angie shivered. That was the name of the priest she'd met.

And she, as well, had been told his visit was a dream.

She pondered what Daniel had just said, especially that there was no longer any Father Pio in the area. "When I think about yesterday morning," she began, "about the rain, the warmth of the little church, the comfort offered by the elderly priest, I can't say I know what happened. Maybe I did dream the entire thing. In my heart, I don't think so. As the nuns in school used to say, 'It's a mystery.' Or, 'You must have faith.' Maybe that's what this is all about. My faith, to a degree . . . but even more than that, it's about yours." She placed her hand on his arm. "It seems you have some decisions to make. Some very serious decisions."

As Paavo stood with Charles and the policeman watching Rocco, he saw two strange men, one big and hulking, the other slight, with a black goatee, creeping stealthily toward the gate Rocco had opened.

As Rocco entered the building inside the fence, the two men began to run.

Paavo began to run as well.

Chapter 42

The creaking sound of the heavy door opening was the first thing Angie heard. A thin
patina of sunlight fell over the excavation
area.

She pressed herself flat against the wall, the rope
tight in her hands, praying Rocco wouldn't be able to
see her. "It's time!" Rocco shouted. Angie heard him
grunt with effort, and soon realized why. The ladder.
He was carrying it toward them, to the edge of the pit.
He must be alone. She tensed. Soon she'd learn if her
plan was going to work.

"Where is it?" The voice was a familiar one, although
not Rocco's or the archeologist's.

"Who are you?" Rocco demanded, angry, surprised,
and with a hint of fear.

"That's none of your business." Angie recognized
the taunting voice: Goatee. "All you need to know is
that we're sick and tired of you stupid Americans making us look bad. We want that chain. Now."

Rocco dropped the ladder to the ground. One end
of it extended about three feet out over the edge of the
pit. "I don't have it!" he shouted.

"Where are the women?" The Hulk's heavy footsteps trod closer. "Down there?"

"I don't know what you're talking about," Rocco
fumed. "Get out!"

"You're lying!" Goatee's words were shrill and frantic. "You've got the chain here. You're going to give it
to us now!"

"I'll give it to you, all right," Rocco said.

A gunshot exploded, echoing through the excavation
pit. Father Daniel dropped to the ground. Cat curled
into a ball. Angie huddled, covering her ears against
the painful reverberation even as there was another
gunshot, then a third.

Suddenly the building was filled with shouts and
footsteps. The police!

They were yelling for the men to drop their guns,
calling for medics, ordering the gunmen outside.

Cat started forward, and Angie frantically gestured
her back. She looked surprised for just a moment, then
backed into the shadows. She understood. If the police
learned about them, they'd be gathered up and ques-
tioned for heaven only knew how long.

Father Daniel went to Angie's side. "What are you
doing?" he whispered. "We need their help to get out
of here!"

She pointed to the end of the ladder sticking out over
the pit. "As soon as they've gone, we'll toss the rope
over a rung and pull it down here. We'll use a ladder
to climb out of the pit."

Daniel looked dubious. "If it doesn't work ... ?"

"We'll yell our heads off. Don't worry, it'll work,"
she said firmly.

The police continued to shout orders. From what she
heard, Rocco, Goatee, and the Hulk had been shot, but
not seriously. All were able to walk.

The police hurried them out of the excavation site for
medical attention and to be arrested.

As soon as everything quieted down, Father Daniel
tossed a long length of rope over a rung, then worked
it so he held both ends. He tugged, and the lightweight

ladder tipped down, then slid like a shot off the edge toward them. Angie and Cat grasped and steadied it.

Father Daniel held it as Angie climbed up. Near the top she stopped and peeked. When she spotted a policeman in the doorway, she cowered again. "Wait," she whispered to the others. She hoped the police would clear the place soon and leave.

Anxious, she peered over the top again. The policeman was gone, but she saw the silhouette of a different man fill the open doorway. He was tall, trim, and broad-shouldered, and looked so much like Paavo her heart skipped a beat. But that, she knew, was impossible. Knowing how much she missed him, her mind was playing tricks on her.

"I thought for sure they'd be in here," he said.

Angie was so stunned, a moment passed before she could react. "Paavo!" She scrambled up the ladder, grateful to be on ground level once again. "We're here!"

She flew into Paavo's arms while Charles ran to the pit.

"Charles?" Cat looked at him with wonder as she climbed out. "I don't believe it. You came to Italy? To find me?"

"Of course I came to find you!" He stood near, not touching her, waiting. Then he said, "How could I not come? I love you, you silly woman! Don't you know that?"

She simply stared at him, then said, "You do, don't you?"

"Of course!"

"Oh, Charles!" Tears filled her eyes as they hugged and kissed. She drew back and gazed steadily at him. "You're what's important to me. You and Kenny—more than anything else in the world. I love you, Charles. How did I forget that? Can you ever forgive me?"

"There's nothing to forgive," he said, holding her close.

"Let's get out of here," Paavo said as he held Angie, a dopey grin on his face now that he was with her again. "We've got to talk. It's not over yet."

"It's not?" Just then, in the dimly lit excavation area, Angie saw Father Daniel toss the rope out of the pit and start to climb out himself. Suddenly, he stopped. Very quickly, he eased himself back down again.

She spun around to see what had frightened him.

"What a happy scene," a man's voice called out.

His silhouette was in the doorway.

"Jerome Ranker," Paavo said. His arm tightened around Angie as he noticed Ranker's gun. "Part owner of Moldwell-Ranker Realtors. I wondered if you'd show up."

"Put that gun down, Mr. Ranker!" Cat ordered, letting go of Charles and marching forward. Charles tried to stop her, but she shook his hand away. "You don't know what you're doing. You can't do this! You're a wealthy man. And an important one."

"I was. But you know what they say about housing bubbles—bubbles float higher and higher when the winds are good and strong, but then they burst and come crashing down to earth. When a person is leveraged, the slightest downturn hits hard. And maybe I did get a bit carried away with my investments.... In any event, I know a collector who'll spend a fortune for that chain. The money will come in handy."

"But murder? Oh, Jerome!" Cat looked at him with complete disdain.

Angie pulled free of Paavo and slowly eased herself toward the rope. He saw, and a puzzled, worried frown lined his brow.

"I didn't want anyone dead," Ranker countered. "I really don't know how it all became so complicated.

The young fool, Ferguson, knew how to enter the house. He knew how to get into the safe. All he had to do was walk in and take the chain. Then I'd sell it. That's all. No one was supposed to get hurt."

"Not get hurt?" Cat yelled. "Why did you involve me, then? Why did Meredith say Marcello called and accused me of stealing the chain? That doesn't make sense!"

The area was dark enough that by moving very slowly, Angie wasn't noticed as she bent to pick up one end of the rope and hold it tight against her side.

"I agree." Ranker glanced at Cat while keeping the gun fixed on Paavo. "Poor little Cat. You were only involved because I'm surrounded by incompetents. You see, it really was a simple plan. I'd been told by Ferguson that Marcello Piccoletti had gone to Italy. I wanted you off the sale—away from Piccoletti's house. I told Meredith to do something to get you away so you wouldn't meddle in this."

Angie stepped to Cat's side. "You had no business firing my sister!" she yelled. Standing shoulder-to-shoulder, she slipped the end of the rope into Cat's hand. Cat's eyes widened with confusion, but she kept the rope, shifting so her hand was behind her back.

"I didn't fire her!" Ranker shouted.

"Oh. Sorry." Angie apologetically held her empty hands up and moved back, near the rope again.

"That stupid cow Meredith," Ranker said to Cat, "decided that accusing you of theft was the best way to get rid of you. Ferguson must have heard and got the monogrammed handkerchief to pin the blame for the theft on you. Unfortunately, when he went to get the relic, he walked in on the two brothers. Guns were pulled. One brother shot the other; Ferguson dropped the handkerchief and ran."

"A nice story," Paavo said. "Too bad it's not true."

"Of course it is!" Ranker declared.

"Except that the bullet that killed Marcello Piccoletti is from the same gun as the one used to kill Meredith Woring."

"Meredith is dead?" Cat was stunned. She gripped the end of the rope tight.

Angie was very slowly easing herself farther away from Cat.

"You, Ranker, were the one in the Piccoletti house that day," Paavo said. "You decided to get the chain and plant the evidence yourself, but instead of an empty house, you walked in on the two brothers. You killed Marcello."

"No!" Ranker snapped, then lifted his chin. "It was Ferguson. He killed Meredith as well."

"Have you forgotten," Paavo said, "that Ferguson was at work until twelve-thirty that day? He didn't have time to travel all the way to Tiburon to break into Cat's house, steal the handkerchief, and be at the Piccoletti home one hour later to kill anyone. Besides, people saw him outside, dressed as a priest at the time of the murders. The whole thing was a ruse by you. A ruse to throw the police off your trail."

Cat noticed Angie was even farther from her. Angie, too, held an end of rope. Suddenly, Cat understood. Seeing that Ranker's attention was on Paavo, she began to glide slowly in the opposite direction.

"You had to instruct Ferguson to get the C.A.S. handkerchief sometime *before* the day of the murder," Paavo said. "The entire thing was premeditated. Steal the chain, kill the owner, run. Cat would be one suspect—and Ferguson, hanging around for all to see in a priest's outfit, and who happened to be the security system installer, would be the second. Ferguson could try to accuse you, but he'd have no proof.

"But you ran into problems right away, didn't you?

First"—Paavo held out one finger, purposefully trying to draw Ranker's attention his way—"there were two owners in the house, not one. You killed one brother, but the other escaped with the chain.

"Second"—two fingers pointed toward Ranker—"Cat Swenson showed up, and she saw what happened."

Then three fingers. "When word got out about Flora Piccoletti's death, Meredith Woring became very, very nervous—so hysterical, in fact, you decided to calm her nerves permanently. Also, Flora must have told Ferguson about Da Vinci's restaurant before he killed her because you hired two Italian mobsters to go there and follow Piccoletti, Cat, and Angie, or whoever else they thought might lead them to the chain.

"Your fourth problem"—four fingers extended—"was Rocco Piccoletti. After two deaths, you needed to get the chain from him in order to have the money to escape the law. That brought you here.

"And five"—he held out his hand, all fingers outstretched, at Ranker—"was Cat herself. She would be able to figure out who was behind it. You decided to get rid of her, too." He crushed his hand into a fist. "That's a lot of killing, Ranker, for one iron chain that nobody's even verified is what some archeologists who wanted to make a little extra money said it was."

"Shut up!" Ranker's shrill shriek reverberated through the enclosure. "All I want is the chain! Let me have it and I'll go. You'll be free." He looked at the two women and realized how far from him they'd moved. "What are you doing there? Get back here!"

"You want the chain," Angie said calmly. "I'll tell you where it is!"

He stepped toward her.

"Daniel!" she called, hoping he'd been peeking

enough to understand what she had in mind. "You have to give it up!"

"No!" he yelled. She nearly cried with relief that he'd given the right answer.

"It's over Daniel," she said. "Come up here and give it up!"

"Never!" his disembodied voice called. "Threaten me, and I'll throw it to the farthest reaches of the pit, where it'll take days to find!"

"You son of a bitch!" Ranker yelled. "You toss it and I'll shoot every last one of you bastar— Oops!"

As he rushed toward the edge to threaten Daniel, Angie and Cat lifted the rope. Seeing Ranker stumble, without even thinking about what he was doing, Charles gave him a shove.

Ranker toppled headfirst into the pit.

Angie beamed at Cat. "I told you my rope idea would work."

Chapter 43

Angie, Paavo, Cat, and Charles sat in the bar of the St. Regis Grand Hotel in Rome. They had finally finished many long, grueling hours at the Ministry of the Interior, giving their statements and explaining all they could about the situation with Jerome Ranker, the two goons he'd hired, Piccoletti, the archeologists, and the three employees of Da Vinci's restaurant.

Everyone agreed that the employees never took part in Rocco's schemes, and never understood the full extent of his criminality.

After Jerome Ranker fell into the pit, Paavo called in the Italian police, who retrieved and rescued the murderer. Ranker, along with Rocco Piccoletti, would be extradited back to the U.S. to stand trial. The Italian police would handle the goons.

And Father Daniel was going to ask his superiors at the Vatican to allow him to reopen St. Monica's and become its priest. With a little help from "on high," plus a generous donation from the Amalfi family in America, he didn't see how he'd be refused. Also, St. Monica's now had a newly found religious relic to display to the public. Whether it was authentic or not, no one could ever say for sure. But Father Daniel believed, and that was enough for him.

Angie looked at the time. It was Monday night.

"Well," she said, "so much for my great job with Chef Poulon-Leliellul. I missed my appointment. At least Paavo and I can stay in Rome a couple of days until all the paperwork is finished and the U.S. marshal arrives to take Ranker and Rocco back to San Francisco." Her hand squeezed Paavo's. The two had scarcely let each other go for a moment since they'd been reunited.

"*Pooh-long lay-you* who?" Charles asked, confused.

"Call him *Pooh-long-ee-ai-ee-ai-oh*," Cat sang good-naturedly. Then, even more surprising, she reached over and ruffled what little was left of Charles's hair. "My hero!" she gushed.

He turned twenty shades of red.

"You people are all being so childish about that poor chef's name," Angie said indignantly, "I can hardly stand it!"

"When was your appointment?" Paavo asked.

"Noon, Monday," she replied, chin in hand. "Oh, well. It was a great job while it lasted. Or would have been."

"With the time difference," Paavo said, checking his wristwatch, "you have ten minutes until your interview. Why not telephone? I should think he'd understand the reason you aren't there in person—especially when you explain all the publicity catching some 'international criminals' will give you."

"You're right!" she exclaimed, eyes bright. "I can try it."

"Call him now. Your brand-new GSM cell phone will work here."

She took out the phone and looked around. "I can't conduct an interview here with all of you watching. I'll either laugh, or feel self-conscious, or not be able to concentrate enough to answer his questions properly."

"We've got rooms here," Cat said, "thankfully not together! Go upstairs and call from your room."

"There's not time for all that," Angie said. "The elevator might be slow, and I don't want to be late. I know—I'll go into the women's room. It's got a beautiful sitting area. No one will bother me, I'm sure. I'll do it! I'll be right back."

"Good luck, Angie!" Charles and Cat called, while Paavo gave her a quick kiss. She gave all a thumbs-up and headed off.

Charles bought everyone another round of drinks, expecting such an important interview to take twenty to thirty minutes, at least.

Instead, before the drinks even got there, Angie came walking back, dejection cloaking her like the Shroud of Turin.

"What is it?" Cat asked.

Paavo took her hand and helped her sit.

"I blew it," she murmured.

"How?"

"I guess it was because no one I know can pronounce his name properly...."

"But you can," Paavo said.

"Yes, but the mistakes were on my mind." She sighed. "Heavily on my mind."

"Go on," Cat urged.

"I got through to the secretary on time, and explained all the reasons I was in Rome—the chain of St. Peter, the murder in the Sea Cliff, the entire thing. She understood perfectly, then had me wait as she explained it all to the chef. She came back on the line and said he was willing—for me—to bend his hard and fast rule. He'd allow me to do the interview by phone, and then we'd do a brief follow-up, in person, as soon as I returned to San Francisco. Of course, I agreed."

"Yes?" the others asked in chorus.

"I held the phone tight against my ear, anticipation high, waiting for him...."

"And ...?"

"He came on the line, and in a wonderful French accent, he said, 'Mademoiselle Amalfi, *c'est merveilleux* to speak to you!' And I was completely overwhelmed and wanted to be effusive in my praise of him, so I said, 'I've admired your cooking for more years than I can count, Monsieur Pooh-pooh.'"

The others looked completely stricken.

Angie reached for Cat's drink and downed it in one gulp. "And that's when he hung up on me."

From the Kitchen of Angelina Amalfi

ANGIE'S ORANGE-CINNAMON BISCOTTI

4 eggs
1 ¼ cups plus 2 tablespoons sugar
¾ cup canola oil
¼ cup orange juice
1 tablespoon grated orange peel
1 teaspoon vanilla extract
4 cups all-purpose flour
2 teaspoons baking powder
½ teaspoon salt
1 cup cinnamon chips (Hershey's or similar)
2 teaspoons ground cinnamon

Heat oven to 350° F. Line baking sheet with parchment or use nonstick spray on it.

In large bowl, add eggs, 1 cup *only* of the sugar, oil, orange juice, orange peel, and vanilla. Beat at medium, about 2 minutes until blended. In medium bowl, stir together flour, ¼ cup *only* of the sugar, baking powder, and salt. Then, at low speed, beat flour mixture into egg mixture, a bit at a time, until just blended. Stir in cinnamon chips. (Dough will be sticky.) Refrigerate 30 minutes.

With floured hands, shape dough into four logs, each about 2 inches wide. Place on baking sheet. Bake 25 to

30 minutes until light brown. Remove from oven and let cool slightly.

On small plate, stir together 2 tablespoons of sugar and ground cinnamon. Cut logs into ½-inch pieces, dip both sides into cinnamon mixture. Return to baking sheet. Bake 6 minutes or until light golden brown. Cool completely. Makes about 40 cookies.

PASTA WITH PANCETTA

6 ounces pancetta, diced
2 tablespoons olive oil
1 onion, chopped
4 garlic cloves, coarsely chopped
Dried crushed red pepper flakes to taste
½ teaspoon salt
½ teaspoon fennel seeds
½ teaspoon oregano (dried)
1 (28-ounce) can tomato puree
1 pound linguine
½ cup grated Pecorino Romano

Heat olive oil in heavy skillet. Add the pancetta and onion and sauté until pancetta is golden brown, about 8 minutes. Add the garlic and red pepper flakes. Sauté another minute, then stir in the tomato puree, salt, fennel, and oregano. Simmer uncovered over medium-low heat until the sauce thickens slightly and the flavors blend, about 15 minutes.

Meanwhile, boil the linguine in a large pot of boiling salted water until tender but still firm to the bite, stirring occasionally, about 8 minutes. Drain, reserving 1 cup of the cooking liquid.

Toss the linguine into the sauce in the skillet. Mix thoroughly. Add the cheese, mix while the cheese melts. Serve.

ITALIAN-STYLE BREAD PUDDING WITH CHOCOLATE AND AMARETTO SAUCE

Sauce:
½ cup whipping cream
½ cup whole milk
3 tablespoons sugar
¼ cup amaretto liqueur
2 teaspoons cornstarch

Bread Pudding:
1½ pound loaf panettone bread (if none available, use a
    good white bread or challah) trim crust and cut into
    1-inch cubes
1 cup chocolate chips
8 large eggs
1½ cups whipping cream
2½ cups whole milk
1 cup sugar
2 tablespoons amaretto liqueur

Sauce: Add cream, milk, and sugar to a heavy small saucepan. Over medium heat, bring to boil, stirring frequently. Mix amaretto and cornstarch in small bowl, stir to mix and to break cornstarch lumps. Stir into the cream mixture. Simmer over medium-low heat until the sauce thickens, stirring constantly, about 2 minutes. Set aside and keep warm. (If made ahead, store in refrigerator, and warm in microwave before serving.)

Bread pudding: Lightly butter a 13-by-9-by-2-inch baking dish. Put bread cubes evenly in pan, then sprinkle chocolate chips over them, spreading evenly. In a large bowl, add eggs, cream, milk, sugar, and amaretto, then whisk until blended. Pour the custard over the bread cubes and chocolate. Press the bread cubes gently to be sure they're all submerged. Let stand for at least 30 minutes, occasionally pressing the bread again into the custard mixture. (Can let stand up to 2 hours; but if much over 30 minutes, cover and refrigerate.)

Preheat the oven to 350° F.

Bake until the pudding is set in the center, about 1 hour. Cool slightly. (Best served warm—can be rewarmed in microwave.) Spoon the bread pudding into bowls, drizzle with the warm amaretto sauce, and serve.

Enter the Delicious World of
Joanne Pence's Angie Amalfi Series

From the kitchen to the deck of a cruise ship, Joanne Pence's mysteries are always a delight. Starring career-challenged Angie Amalfi and her handsome homicide-detective boyfriend Paavo Smith, Joanne Pence serves up a mystery feast complete with humor, a dead body or two, and delicious recipes.

Enjoy the pages that follow, which give a glimpse into Angie and Paavo's world.

For sassy and single food writer Angie Amalfi, life's a banquet—until the man who's been contributing unusual recipes for her food column is found dead. But in SOMETHING'S COOKING, *Angie is hardly one to simper in fear—so instead she simmers over the delectable homicide detective assigned to the case.*

A while passed before she looked up again. When she did, she saw a dark-haired man standing in the doorway to her apartment, surveying the scene. Tall and broad-shouldered, his stance was aloof and forceful as he made a cold assessment of all that he saw.

If you're going to gawk, she thought, come in with the rest of the busybodies.

He looked directly at her, and her grip tightened on the chair. His expression was hard, his pale blue eyes icy. He was a stranger, of that she was certain. His wasn't the type of face or demeanor she'd easily forget. And someone, it seemed, had just sent her a bomb. Who? Why? What if this stranger ...

In TOO MANY COOKS, *Angie's talked her way into a job on a pompous, third-rate chef's radio call-in show. But when a successful and much envied restaurateur is poisoned, Angie finds the case far more interesting than trying to make her pretentious boss sound good.*

Angie glanced up from the monitor. She'd been debating whether or not to try to take the next call, if and when one came in, when her attention was caught by the caller's strange voice. It was oddly muffled. Angie couldn't tell if the caller was a man or a woman.

"I didn't catch your name," Henry said.

"Pat."

Angie's eyebrows rose. A neuter-sounding Pat? What was this, a *Saturday Night Live* routine?

"Well, Pat, what can I do for you?"

"I was concerned about the restaurant killer in your city."

Henry's eye caught Angie's. "Thank you. I'm sure the police will capture the person responsible in no time."

"I'm glad you think so, because—you're next."

Henry jumped up and slapped the disconnect button. "And now," he said, his voice quivering, "a word from our sponsor."

Angie Amalfi's latest job, developing the menu for a new inn, sounds enticing—especially since it means spending a week in scenic Northern California with her homicide-detective boyfriend. But once she arrives at the soon-to-be-opened Hill Haven Inn, she's not so sure anymore. In COOKING UP TROUBLE, *the added ingredients of an ominous threat, a missing person, and a woman making eyes at her man leave Angie convinced that the only recipe in this inn's kitchen is one for disaster.*

She placed her hand over his large strong one, scarcely able to believe that they were here, in this strange yet lovely room, alone. "But I am real, Paavo."

"Are you?" He bent to kiss her lightly, his eyes intent, his hand moving from her chin to the back of her head to intertwine with the curls of her hair. The mystical aura of the room, the patter of the rain, the solitude of the setting, stole over him and made him think of things he didn't want to ponder—things like being together with Angie forever, like never being alone again. He tried to mentally break the spell. He needed time—cold, logical time. "There's no way a woman like you should be in my life," he said finally. "Sometimes I think you can't be any more real than the Sempler ghosts. That I'll close my eyes and you'll disappear. Or that I'm just imagining you."

Food columnist Angie Amalfi has it all. But in COOKING MOST DEADLY, *while she's wondering if it's time to cut the wedding cake with her boyfriend, Paavo, he becomes obsessed with a grisly homicide that has claimed two female victims.*

"You've got to keep City Hall out of this case. As far as the press knows, she was a typist. Nothing more. Mumble when you say where she worked." Lieutenant Hollins got up from behind his desk, walked around to the front of it, and leaned against the edge. Paavo and Yosh sat facing him. They'd just completed briefing him on the Tiffany Rogers investigation. Hollins made it a point not to get involved in his men's investigations unless political heat was turned on. In this case, the heat was on high.

"Her friends and coworkers are at City Hall, and there's a good chance the guy she's been seeing is there as well," Paavo said.

"It's our only lead, Chief," Yosh added. "So far, the CSI unit can't even find a suspicious fingerprint to lift. The crime scene is clean as a whistle. She always met her boyfriend away from her apartment. We aren't sure where yet. We've got a few leads we're still checking."

"So you've got nothing except for a dead woman lying in her own blood on the floor of her own living room!" Hollins added.

In COOK'S NIGHT OUT, *Angie has decided to make her culinary name by creating the perfect chocolate confection: angelinas. Donating her delicious rejects to a local mission, Angie soon finds that the mission harbors more than the needy, and to save not only her life, but Paavo's as well, she's going to have to discover the truth faster than you can beat egg whites to a peak.*

Angelina Amalfi flung open the window over the kitchen sink. After two days of cooking with chocolate, the mouthwatering, luscious, inviting smell of it made her sick.

That was the price one must pay, she supposed, to become a famous chocolatier.

She found an old fan in the closet, put it on the kitchen table, and turned the dial to high. The comforting aroma of home cooking wafting out from a kitchen was one thing, but the smell of Willy Wonka's chocolate factory was quite another.

She'd been trying out intricate, elegant recipes for chocolate candies, searching for the perfect confection on which to build a business to call her own. Her kitchen was filled with truffles, nut bouchées, exotic fudges, and butter creams.

So far, she'd divulged her business plans only to Paavo, the man for whom she had plans of a very different nature. She was going to have to let someone else know soon, though, or she wouldn't have any room left in the kitchen to cook. She didn't want to start eating the calorie-oozing, waistline-expanding chocolates out of sheer enjoyment—her taste tests were another thing altogether and totally justifiable, she reasoned—and throwing the chocolates away had to be sinful.

Angie Amalfi's long-awaited vacation with her detective boyfriend has all the ingredients of a romantic getaway—a sail to Acapulco aboard a freighter, no crowds, no Homicide Department worries, and a red bikini. But in COOKS OVERBOARD, *it isn't long before Angie's* Love Boat *fantasies are headed for stormy seas—the cook tries to jump off the ship, Paavo is acting mighty strange, and someone's added murder to the menu ...*

Paavo became aware, in a semi-asleep state, that the storm was much worse than anyone had expected it would be. The best thing to do was to try to sleep through it, to ignore the roar of the sea, the banging of rain against the windows, the almost human cry of the wind through the ship.

He reached out to Angie. She wasn't there. She must have gotten up to use the bathroom. Maybe her getting up was what had awakened him. He rolled over to go back to sleep.

When he awoke again, the sun was peeking over the horizon. He turned over to check on Angie, but she still wasn't beside him. Was she up already? That wasn't like her. He remembered a terrible storm last night. He sat up, suddenly wide-awake. Where was Angie?

Angie Amalfi has a way with food and people, but her newest business idea is turning out to be shakier than a fruit-filled gelatin mold. In A COOK IN TIME, *her first—and only—clients for "Fantasy Dinners" are none other than a group of UFO chasers and government conspiracy fanatics. But when it seems that the group has a hidden agenda greater than anything on the* X-Files, *Angie's determined to find out the truth before it takes her out of this world—for good.*

The nude body was that of a male Caucasian, early forties or so, about five-ten, 160 pounds. The skin was an opaque white. Lips, nose, and ears had been removed, and the entire area from approximately the pubis to the sigmoid colon had been cored out, leaving a clean, bloodless cavity. No postmortem lividity appeared on the part of the body pressed against the ground. The whole thing had a tidy, almost surreal appearance. No blood spattered the area. No blood was anywhere; apparently, not even in the victim. A gutted, empty shell.

The man's hair was neatly razor-cut; his hands were free of calluses or stains, the skin soft, the nails manicured; his toenails were short and square-cut, and his feet without bunions or other effects of ill-fitting shoes. In short, all signs of a comfortable life. Until now.

Between her latest "sure-fire" foray into the food industry—video restaurant reviews—and her concern over Paavo's depressed state, Angie's plate is full to overflowing. Paavo has never come to terms with the fact that his mother abandoned him when he was four, leaving behind only a mysterious present. But when the token disappears in TO CATCH A COOK, Angie discovers a lethal goulash of intrigue, betrayal, and mayhem that may spell disaster for her and Paavo.

The bedroom had also been torn apart and the mattress slashed. This was far, far more frightening than what had happened to her own apartment. There was anger here, perhaps hatred.

"What is going on?" she cried. "Why would anyone destroy your things?"

"It looks like a search, followed by frustration."

As she wandered through the little house, she realized he was right. It wasn't random destruction as she had first thought, but where the search of her apartment had appeared slow and meticulous, here it was hurried and frenzied.

"Hercules!" he called. "Herc? Come on, boy, are you all right?"

For once Angie's newest culinary venture, "Comical Cakes," seems to be a roaring success! But in BELL, COOK, AND CANDLE, *there's nothing funny about her boyfriend Paavo's latest case—a series of baffling murders that may be rooted in satanic ritual. And it gets harder to focus on pastry alone when strange "accidents" and desecrations to her baked creations begin occurring with frightening regularity—leaving Angie to wonder whether she may end up as devil's food of a different kind.*

Angie was beside herself. She'd been called to go to a house to discuss baking cakes for a party of twenty, and yet no one was there when she arrived. This was the second time that had happened to her. Was someone playing tricks, or were people really so careless as to make appointments and then not keep them?

She really didn't have time for this. But at least she was getting smart. She'd brought a cake with her that had to be delivered to a horse's birthday party not far from her appointment. She never thought she'd be baking cakes for a horse, but Heidi was being boarded some forty miles outside the city, and the owner visited her on weekends only. That was why the owner wanted a Comical Cake of the mare.

Angie couldn't imagine eating something that looked like a beloved pet or animal. She was meeting real ding-a-lings in this line of work.

Still muttering to herself about the thoughtlessness of the public, she got into her new car. A vaguely familiar yet disquieting smell hit her. A stain smeared the bottom of the cake box. She peered closer. The smell was stronger, and the bottom of the box was wet.

She opened the driver's side door, ready to jump out

of the car as her hand slowly reached for the box top. Thoughts of flies and toads pounded her. What now?

She flipped back the lid and shrank away from it.

Nothing moved. Nothing jumped out.

Poor Heidi was now a bright-red color, but it wasn't frosting. The familiar smell was blood, and it had been poured on her cake. Shifting the box, she saw that it had seeped through onto the leather seat and was dripping to the floor mat.

In IF COOKS COULD KILL, Angie Amalfi's culinary adventures always seem to fall flat, so now she's decided to cook up something different: love. But her earnest attempts at matchmaking don't go so well— her friend Connie is stood up by a no-show jock. Now Connie's fallen for a tarnished loner, and soon finds herself in the middle of a murder investigation. Angie's determined to find the real killer, but when the trail leads to the kitchen of her favorite restaurant, she fears she's about to discover a family recipe that dishes out disaster ... and murder!

"Here's some salad and bread, Miss Connie," Earl said. "I don't t'ink you need to starve just 'cause some jerkoff is late showin' up for your date."

"Thanks, Earl," she murmured. "But right now, I'm not even hungry." Okay, it was a lie, but she was too humiliated to eat.

"It's on da house." He left a green salad with Roquefort dressing, Connie's favorite, and walked away. The aroma of the French bread wafted up to her. She touched it. Warm. Firm crust. Soft center. Perfect for spreading butter, which, unfortunately, was loaded with empty, straight-to-the-hips calories ...

She checked her watch again: seven-thirty. Why bother with a guy who couldn't tell time? She kicked off her shoes and took a big bite of buttered, crusty bread. Heaven!

Just then, like magic, the restaurant's front door opened and a man entered, alone. Connie's breath caught, causing her to nearly choke on the bread. She swallowed it in a scarcely chewed lump.

It quickly became obvious that the man who walked in was no football player.

Angie hates to leave the side of her hunky fiancé, Paavo, but in TWO COOKS A-KILLING, she gets an offer she can't refuse. She'll be preparing the banquet for her favorite soap opera's reunion special, on the estate where the show was originally filmed! But when a corpse turns up in the mansion's cellar, and Angie starts snooping around to investigate a past on-set death, she discovers that real-life events may be even more theatrical than the soap's on-screen drama.

Now the cast was being reassembled for a ten-year reunion show, a Christmas reunion, and she, Angelina Rosaria Maria Amalfi, had been asked to be a part of it.

A major part, if she said so herself. She was so anxious to get to Eagle Crest, it was all she could do to stick to the speed limit.

Her father had phoned the day before. He'd gotten a call from his old friend Dr. Waterfield: the woman who was to prepare the important centerpiece meal of the show had broken her leg. Dr. Waterfield wanted to know if Angie could handle it.

Could she ever!

Against her instinct, Angie agrees to let her control-freak mother plan her engagement party—she's just too busy to do it herself. And in COURTING DISASTER, *Angie's even more swamped when murder enters the picture. Now she must follow the trail of a mysterious pregnant kitchen helper at a nearby Greek eatery—a woman who her friendly neighbor Stan is infatuated with. And when Angie gets a little too close to the action, it looks like her fiancé Paavo may end up celebrating solo, after the untimely d.o.a. of his hapless fiancée!*

Stan headed for the water, enjoying the dark, chilled air that so well matched his mood. A number of boats were moored, all rocking slightly from the tide. His peaceful solitude was broken, however, by the sound of raised but muffled voices.

His waiter berated a woman who sat on a rough-hewn, backless wooden bench at the water's edge. His face was hard, his expression intense, and she was shaking her head, not looking at him, but staring out at the water as if it hurt to hear his words. Her feet were propped up on a railroad tie. A hooded rain parka, the cheap kind that was basically a sheet of heavy green plastic worn by slipping it over the head, covered her hair. The way she sat scrunched on the bench, the parka draped her body like a tent.

The waiter bent close, grabbed her shoulder, and said something straight into her face. She turned her head away from him and the hood slipped down. The waiter then straightened and strode away. She reached out her hand toward him, but he didn't turn back. She raised her chin, apparently struggling to hold her emotions in check.

Angie and Paavo have had enough familial input regarding their upcoming wedding to last a lifetime. So, in RED HOT MURDER, Angie leaps at the chance to spend some time with her fiancé in a sun-drenched Arizona town. But when a wealthy local is murdered, uncovering a hotbed of deadly town secrets, Angie's getaway with her lover is starting to look more and more like her final meal.

Angie glanced toward the door, but Paavo was already down the walk near the SUV. "What other stories?"

Rheumy eyes met hers. "This place is called Ghost Hollow, you know."

A chill rippled along her spine. "And I'll bet you're going to tell me why."

"It's because of the stagecoach." Lionel folded skinny arms as he watched her, then continued without prompting. "Years back, a stagecoach and its passengers all disappeared. The coach was carrying a shit-load—I mean—a lot of money. Cash. Local folks said their ghosts could be seen out here at night, near the caves, still searching for the lost stage and their money."

"I see." A slight quiver sounded in her voice. Not that she believed in ghosts, of course.

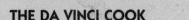

Scrumptious Angie Amalfi
mysteries from

JOANNE PENCE

THE DA VINCI COOK

978-0-06-075806-6/$6.99 US/$9.99 Can
Angie must hightail it to Rome, where her sister has been
accused of murdering a stranger she found already dead.

RED HOT MURDER

978-0-06-075805-9/$6.99 US/$9.99 Can
Suddenly Angie's tasty getaway to Arizona with her fiance is
starting to look more and more like her last meal.

COURTING DISASTER

978-0-06-050291-1/$6.99 US/$9.99 Can
There's already too much on the bride-to-be's plate . . .
and much of it is murderous.

TWO COOKS A-KILLING

978-0-06-009216-0/$6.99 US/$9.⁰⁰
Nothing could drag Angie away from San Francisco—except
for a job preparing the banquet for her all-time favorite soap
opera characters during a Christmas Reunion Special.

IF COOKS COULD KILL

978-0-06-054821-6/$7.99 US/$10.99 Can
When Angie's friend Connie Rogers' would-be boyfriend
is sought by the police in connection with a brutal
robbery/homicide, the two friends set out to find the real killer

BELL, COOK, AND CANDLE

978-0-06-103084-0/$6.99 US/$9.99 Can
When Angie is called upon to deliver a humorous confection
to an after-hours goth club, she finds herself
up to her neck in the demonic business.